THE THIEF TAKER

Visit us at www.boldstrokesbooks.com

Praise for *Secret Societies*

"*Secret Societies* is a sumptuous, riveting, erotic work of historical fiction by William Holden."—*Insightoutbooks.com*

"I don't usually like 'period' novels like this, but I found this one very engaging and well-written."—Bob Lind, *Echo* Magazine

"William Holden has a masterful voice and a stunning imagination."—Lee Thomas, Lambda Literary Award–winning author of *The German*

By the Author

Words to Die By

Clothed in Flesh

Secret Societies

The Thief Taker

THE THIEF TAKER

by

William Holden

A Division of Bold Strokes Books

2014

THE THIEF TAKER

ISBN 13: 978-1-62639-054-6

This Trade Paperback Original Is Published By
Bold Strokes Books, Inc.
P.O. Box 249
Valley Falls, NY 12185

First Edition: April 2014

Credits

Editors: Greg Herren and Stacia Seaman
Production Design: Stacia Seaman
Cover Design by Sheri (graphicartist2020@hotmail.com)

To Mark for your continued love and support,
and to Dale Chase and our amazing friendship.

CHAPTER ONE

"Will you please state your name for the record?"

"My name is Thomas Newton," I answered. The questioning gaze of the commissaire led me to think that he did not believe me. His head dropped as he wrote in his blotter. I could see his eyes move upward toward me, then down again as the pen scratched the surface of the paper.

"What is your age?"

"I am twenty-one." I studied his face as he looked upon me. I trembled with the fear of not knowing the purpose of my presence in front of the Paris police. Mother Clap's comforting voice rose through my mind. *Appearances are everything, my boy. If they see a weak, scared man, they will use that to their advantage. Stay strong and believe in yourself.* Despite my current uncertain situation, I could not help but to smile at her memory. While moments like this gave me joy of our time together, I still wept every night from the grief of her death. The pain of missing her had settled into my heart and would not leave. I took a deep breath to calm myself so I would not give this man the satisfaction of knowing his effect upon me.

"Do you find levity in being here, Mr. Newton?"

"No, sir. I do not."

"Would you like to share with me what you find amusing?"

"No, sir, I would not. It is a very private matter."

"I see, so you are going to withhold information from me."

"I do not understand how something that happened before my arrival in Paris could be of any interest to you." I looked around his office. "May I inquire as to why I am here?"

"How long have you been in Paris?" He ignored my question.

"I arrived a month ago." I met his gaze, trying to hold my own. He waited with growing impatience as if expecting more of an answer from me. I gave him nothing else. I learned that valuable lesson during my time in Newgate. I decided to ask my question again. "Perhaps if you could enlighten me as to why I am being interrogated, I would be better able to assist you."

"Pleading ignorance will not assist either of us, Mr. Newton." He cleared his throat. "May I have the names of your parents?"

"I do not know them, sir." I could see the disbelief in his eyes. "I was found abandoned and taken to a local parish church where I was raised." I hesitated to control my anger at his wordless accusations of lying to him. "Request my birth documents if you do not believe me!" I stood up. The chair screeched as it slid across the floor. "I am answering your questions with complete honesty. Yet you refuse to believe a word I have spoken!"

"Sit down, Mr. Newton, before I have your ass arrested for any number of infractions."

"Arrested? I have done nothing wrong!" I took my seat and tried to push my growing anger aside.

"Thank you. Now, if you could tell me where are you from?" He continued his questioning without an answer.

"I am from London."

"Do you care to elaborate?"

"London, it is a city in England." I spoke a bit too sarcastically.

"Do not fuck with me, Mr. Newton." He slammed his fist against the desk that separated us. "It is apparent that you do not understand the serious consequences of your being here." He adjusted himself in his chair. "How did you come to Paris, and for what purpose?"

"How did I come?" I could not help but repeat his words. "I swam. How do you think I came to Paris?" I held my tongue before it could pose a bigger problem. "I came by ship, sir. I boarded a ship at the port of Dover in England."

"Did you steal aboard the ship?" He wrote something in his blotter.

"No, sir, I did not." I became annoyed with his assumptions about me. "I paid for the trip myself." I sat up in my chair with false pride before leaning forward. I placed my elbows upon his desk. I smiled at him, hoping for a better way of communicating with him. I peered downward to get a glance at his notes. "Mr. Ladue, is it?" I leaned back in my chair. "Now at least we can have a civilized conversation, from one gentleman to another."

"I doubt that, Mr. Newton." He lit his pipe and blew the smoke over his head. "For me to have a conversation with another gentleman, there would have to be one present." He laughed and smoke flew from his mouth and nostrils. "May I continue?"

"Please."

"If you paid for your fare, then you must have a trade that pays quite well. What is it that you do?"

"I have worked several jobs over the years. I like to think of myself as versatile. I worked as a night soil man when I first became of age to work. Most recently I helped run a tavern."

"You expect me to believe that the wages of a bar keep allowed you to travel to Paris and live here without further trade for the past month?"

"The woman who owned the tavern died suddenly." Tears welled in my eyes before falling down my cheeks. "I am sorry for my display." I wiped the tears from my face. "She left me some money to live on."

"Is her death the reason you left London and came to Paris?"

"Yes, I needed to get away. On the invitation of a friend, I purchased a ticket and made the journey."

"And what is this friend's name?"

"Pierre Baptiste," I replied. Hearing his name brought me back to that cold winter night when he first entered Mother Clap's establishment—and me. The smell of his body's musk returned as if he stood beside me in this office. His strong, masculine chest covered in the blanket of black hair rushed into my mind. I remembered running my tongue through the curls searching for the erect nubs of his tits, his moans as I nibbled upon them, his chest heaving against my face, and the ever-quickening beat of his heart as his desire and lust for me grew in those first few moments.

"Mr. Newton?" the commissaire questioned, but my mind was lost in the memories.

I shifted in my seat, trying to give room to my growing prick, as the night with Pierre repeated itself in my mind. I remembered the gentleness with which he fucked me, a need for emotional connection rather than a vile and reprehensible need for release. My ass tightened as the memory of his initial thrust of insertion stung me. I could not help but lick my lips as the memory of his seed landed across them, still hot from his spouting prick. His salty flavor lingered on my tongue as the commissaire's voice brought me back to the present.

"I am sorry, I could not possibly have heard you correctly, for a moment I thought you said Pierre Baptiste was the man you came to see."

"That is correct. It was his invitation that brought me to Paris." Upon hearing the identity confirmed, Mr. Ladue's pen stopped. It fell from his grasp. He looked upon me with disdain. "Is there something the matter, sir?"

"You are delusional beyond belief, Mr. Newton." He intertwined his fingers and rested them on the desk. "You come to my city, flaunting your filthy, English ways, and if that is not enough, you have the audacity to sit here in front of me and lie about why you have come here?"

"I am sorry, Mr. Ladue. I do not understand why you think I am lying to you?"

"You expect me to believe that Mr. Baptiste invited you to come to Paris?"

"You know Mr. Baptiste?" I wondered why the commissaire of the Paris police would know Pierre, but at that moment it did not matter. "Send for him, he will confirm my story."

"You cannot be serious." Mr. Ladue laughed. "That statement alone tells me all I need to know about your dishonesty here today." He nodded. "But please, finish telling me how you came to know Mr. Baptiste."

"Mr. Baptiste and I met in London."

"When was this?"

"November past." I watched as Mr. Ladue went back to taking notes. "It was a cold evening. Mr. Baptiste came into the inn to warm himself before his journey back to Paris."

"What was your business there, Mr. Newton?"

"I lived with the owners, Mr. and Mrs. John Clap." I hesitated to keep my thoughts in line so I would not divulge more than necessary. "They gave me a room in exchange for tending to their customers and cleaning the tavern after close," I lied. "Mr. Baptiste kept me company while I cleaned up for the night. It was late, so he purchased a room for the night. The next morning, Mrs. Clap invited him to breakfast. He told me if I ever wanted to come to Paris for a visit that I should look him up and that he would give me a place to stay."

"That is an extraordinary tale, Mr. Newton. I commend you on getting your facts straight. Mr. Baptiste did in fact travel through London during the time you say the two of you met, but nothing you say can convince me that he would have anything to do with someone like you."

"What do you mean, like me?"

"You are a rogue, Mr. Newton. I have known Mr. Baptiste for many years. He is not the type of man who would lower himself to a conversation with someone so, shall we say, common. Mr. Baptiste would not have invited you to his home as you are claiming. He does have a reputation to uphold."

"I may be many things, but common is not one of them. The finest tutors in England have taught me. I attended Cheam Classical School, and while living in London, I was surrounded by some of the most respected members of society. Mine was not what one would call an easy life, and I may be a bit rough around the edges, but I will not sit here and be called a rogue." I lit my pipe and blew the smoke in Mr. Ladue's direction. "I came to Paris on the invitation of Mr. Baptiste, as I have already explained. When I arrived at his home, he did not answer. I spoke to an older woman who said he had gone away on business and that she did not know when he would return. She would not allow me entrance."

"Mrs. Bergone is a wise woman."

"How is it, Mr. Ladue, that you know everyone whom I have come into contact with since arriving? I demand that you tell me why I am here, or you will see just how roguish I can be!" I stood up. The chair groaned across the wooden floor. I looked down upon him as he sat unmoving in his chair.

"Mr. Newton." He looked up from his blotter. "At the charge of the King's prosecutor I was ordered to bring you before me to be questioned, and if deemed appropriate held at the hospital until such time as we feel you are fit to be released back into society."

"Hospital? I am not ill."

"The Bicêtre, Mr. Newton," he stood and walked around his desk, "is where we place the people arrested for crimes of such magnitude that they cannot be housed in our prison." He stood no more than a foot away from me.

"Have I been arrested?"

"Not as of yet."

"You cannot arrest me. I have not committed a crime." His words and accusations took me back to the trials in London and the uncertainty of life that came along with being of a certain persuasion.

Guilt followed the growing fear as I knew my innocence, and yet how many of the men that I sent to their deaths held the same knowledge of their own innocence? "What crimes are you charging me with?" I asked without wanting to hear Mr. Ladue's response.

"Do you know one Mr. Nicholas Bergenoir?"

"The name means nothing to me, Mr. Ladue."

"The old woman you spoke with sent word that a stranger was asking questions about Mr. Baptiste's whereabouts."

"Are you telling me that making inquiries about someone is against the law in Paris?"

"Of course not, except that Mr. Baptiste is someone who demands a certain level of privacy. Several of our men tracked you down to an inn where you have been living. On several occasions these men followed you to Jardin des Tuileries. Since these are royal gardens, the police are not allowed to patrol and therefore have no authority. We use our flies to report to us on the uncivilized activities that men like you involve yourselves with."

"You cannot be serious."

"When did you first meet Mr. Bergenoir?"

"I have already told you that I do not know anyone by that name."

"Perhaps he did not tell you his name for fear of public knowledge, but you did meet, did you not?"

"I am speaking the truth. I have never met this Mr. Bergenoir, nor have I ever been involved with anyone in the way you are describing."

"Perhaps a night in Bicêtre will do you some good. Once you see just how horrible life within our dungeons can be, you will have a better understanding of your situation and be willing to cooperate with our questioning."

"How do you see my answering every question of yours as being uncooperative?" My voice trembled. I began to wonder if God decided to play a cruel trick on me, turning my life around in this strange city so that I might have a taste of what others back in London felt from my blasphemous tongue. "Please, contact Mr. Baptiste. He will attest to my good nature. You cannot do this to me." I charged Mr. Ladue, who stood facing me with arrogance. "You son of a bitch!" I shoved him with the full force of my weight. He stumbled backward and fell against his desk.

"Guards," Mr. Ladue shouted. He tried to move to his left to escape my attack. I was too quick. My fist connected with his jaw. Blood flew from his lower lip. He tried to right himself as I struck him in the back of the head. He fell to the floor. Before I could release more anger upon his body, two guards charged into the room and held me back. I pulled and struggled against their hold, wanting nothing more than to beat the life out of this man who stood before me.

"You have made a very grave mistake, Mr. Newton." He wiped the blood from his mouth. "And you call yourself a gentleman, though I suppose I should not be surprised by your violent attacks. Londoners are nothing but barbarians."

"You fucking naff." I struggled against the guards. "All I have asked is that you contact Mr. Baptiste so he can clear this up, but you refuse to listen to reason."

"Get this fucking abomination out of my office." He spat blood. "Send him to the Bicêtre. One night in there and he should be more than willing to cooperate with us." He stood with his hands clasped behind his back as the guards turned me away and led me from the office down the hallway and to a waiting carriage.

The guards sat on either side of me as the coach made its way through the narrow streets of Paris. The drawn curtains covered the windows, keeping the carriage dark and the view hidden. I reached into my coat pocket, a difficult gesture with the shackles about my wrists. One of the guards grabbed my arm to stop me.

"I am reaching for my pipe, nothing more." The guard released me. I pulled out my pipe, packed it with tobacco, and lit it. The smoke drifted around us in the stale air. "This Bicêtre, the commissaire called it a hospital."

"An asylum is a more appropriate term for it, for men who are sick in the mind." The guard on my right looked at me and smiled. "You shall fit in rather well there." They both laughed.

"I am not insane. I do not belong in a place such as that."

"If a man practices or participates in the carnal knowledge of other men, he is deemed disturbed, Mr. Newton, and therefore does not belong in our society. He must be placed where he can be controlled and managed."

"Wait, you cannot do this. What about a trial, or a hearing to prove my innocence? I am not guilty of any of these crimes."

The guard on my left turned toward me. "This may come as a surprise to you, Mr. Newton, but the people of Paris live a well-mannered and civilized life. We do things a little different here in Paris.

Trials are for the uncivilized societies. They are used in vulgar ways to control the citizens through fear. No one who lives a proper life should have to endure the publicity, outrage, and scorn that trials bring about." He lifted the curtain to peer outside. The brightness of the midday sun stung my eyes. "The fine citizens of Paris deserve a better life than that. We do not worry them about the vagrants and criminals of this city. We find them as we did you and we interrogate them. If the commissaire determines that redemption is not possible, we dispose of them."

"Dispose?" A chill crawled over my skin despite the heat.

"You would be surprised at the numerous ways one can rid a city of the unwanted." The coach came to an abrupt stop. "I would like to say that it was a pleasure speaking with you, but lying is not part of my nature. Shall we?" He opened the door to the outside world.

I stepped out of the coach, raising my shackled hands to shield my eyes from the sun. I looked out over the vast rolling hills of barren land toward the hospital. Its pale-stone buildings connected end to end with one another, stretched out across the land, and disappeared into nothingness. Its immense size made Newgate Prison look like a young girl's dollhouse. As we approached, I could hear the hollow, desperate screams of the men from within, their torturous songs weeping out through the iron-gated windows.

"Please, I do not belong here. Just turn your backs and let me go. I'll leave Paris and…"

"Our lives are not worth risking in order to save yours." One of the guards opened the door while the other pushed me inside. My forced footing slipped on the smooth marbled floor of the foyer. The guards caught me before I could fall. The foyer opened up into a spacious and what could be described as a magnificent room if it had not been stripped bare of décor and housed within the walls of the asylum. "Doctor," the younger of the two guards shouted. A man in stark white clothing came from around the corner. "We need to place Mr. Newton in a cell for the evening. We will collect him in the morning."

"Your full name, sir?" The doctor glared at me but came no closer.

"Thomas Newton."

"Follow me."

"Come on." The guards shoved me forward as we followed the doctor around the corner and into a long corridor.

"I do not understand why I must be treated this way, I have done nothing wrong." I continued to plead my innocence though I knew it would fall upon deaf ears. The farther we walked into the bowels of the asylum, the darker and more desolate my surroundings became. The marble walls of the main entrance gave way to damp, cold stone, the chill of which permeated the halls. Wooden doors barred with metal locks lined both sides of the hallway. While I did not like the thought of spending one night in this place, I prayed to God that I would at least be placed in a private room.

I came to a sudden and terrifying halt as the piercing scream of a man shot out from behind us. I turned around, breaking the grip of the guards. I peered into the darkness from which we had come. The man's scream faded away as another one replaced it. A chill took hold of me and would not ease its grip. Though I could not see anything within the darkness where we stood, I could not help but feel a malevolent presence of unthinkable magnitude lurking within the shadows of the asylum, as if the hospital itself could open up and devour me at any time.

A large wooden door halted our progress. The doctor fumbled with the set of keys, found the one he needed, and unlocked the door. Even with his formidable and brutish size it took considerable effort for him to pull upon the door in order for it to open. It groaned against its own weight. The doctor disappeared into the darkened void. I peered around the corner of the door, hesitating to take a step inside.

"Move along." The younger guard pushed me through the doorway. I stumbled over the uneven edges of the rotting wood that made up the floor. I looked into the near darkness and witnessed a large cell several hundred feet in front of me. As my eyes adjusted to the faint light of the oil lamps, I could observe the shadows of a dozen or more men caged like animals from within the cell. Memories of being sent to Newgate rushed back to me as if no time had passed.

"Undress, Mr. Newton." The voice of the doctor came to me instead.

"Undress?" I approached him. He seemed nervous at our closeness. "The air is cold and damp within these walls. Why can I not remain clothed? Surely I am allowed at least that?" I watched as the doctor looked over my shoulder.

"Mr. Newton." The older guard approached. "We have this rule for your own safety as well as theirs. If you go into the cell clothed, they will have them torn off you within a few moments. Your belt, your shoes, or any other piece of your clothing may be used as weapons against you, not to mention the fact that if you haven't any clothes to wear tomorrow, you would have to appear before the commissaire naked, and I'm afraid that would not sit well with him." He unlocked the shackles.

I rubbed my arms as I looked into the cell. The men began to move closer to the door. Their chains scraped across the wooden floor. I could feel their eyes upon me. The thought of being cast within their sick and depraved minds terrified me. It was then that I heard Mother Clap's voice in my mind. *Remember to stand strong, my boy. Never show your fear. Appearances are everything.* Her words gave me the strength I needed. I was no longer going to beg for fair treatment. If they insisted that I was a filthy sodomite, I would show them all just how nasty I could get. "If the three of you wish to see me naked, so be it." I removed my waistcoat and handed it to the doctor with a wink of my eye. I smiled and began to unbutton my blouse. I glanced down at the dark curls of moss that sprouted out between the clasps of my undergarment. I released a few of the top eyelets to run my fingers through it. I looked back up at the doctor and met his gaze. My flirtatious behavior brought a twitch to his eye, the first emotion I had seen from him. I leaned against his body. "Do you like what you see?" I whispered in his ear as I let the shirt slide off my shoulders.

"I…" His lips trembled. He glanced across the dim room to the guards who stood behind us. He looked back at me and grimaced. "Fucking scum." He pushed me away.

I released my breeches and pulled them off my legs. I laughed as I handed them to the flustered doctor. I winked at him and smiled. I stood in the cold, damp corridor with only my thin undergarment to cover my nakedness. I did not need to see to know that their eyes were upon me. The delirious cheers of the men behind the bars penetrated the air. The chains from their shackles rattled against each other as they made their way toward the front of the cell as if waiting to be the first to get their filthy hands upon me.

"I know what you secretly long for. I can feel your eyes upon my body." I walked up to the doctor, unfastened the eyelets of my undergarment, and let my hefty prick fall between my legs. I fondled it. It stiffened with need. Their eyes could not help but fall to where the action lay.

"Get this filth locked up," The older guard spat. "I shall inform the commissaire of your behavior here."

"I am sure that he will be sorry to have missed this." I shook my prick as if finishing a piss, then slipped it back inside the linen. "Perhaps

I shall tell him of the fact that his two guards are stiff with their own secrets." I nodded toward the bulge growing in each of their breeches. They glanced at each other.

"We shall be back in the morning." The older guard turned and left the room. "Move." The second guard pushed me forward before turning and leaving. I stumbled into the doctor, who pulled out his keys. Our impact caused him to drop them on the floor. He bent over to pick them up. My stiffness had risen to such a degree that it stroked his buttocks. "Keep your distance." The doctor pushed me away. His fingers grazed the trunk of my prick. I could not help but moan from the sudden touch of another man. "Filthy wanker." The doctor unlocked the door. It swung outward. He pushed me into the cell.

I stumbled over one of the men who slept on the floor. He woke cussing. He reached out, grabbed my ankle, and bit it. "Bitch!" I kicked him in the face as I heard the cell door locking into place. I leapt over the man and fell against the door. My hands wrapped around the iron bars in a tight grip. "Please, wait!" The doctor shut the larger door, ignoring my plea. I closed my eyes and rested my head against the iron bars as I tried to think of a way out of this hell they had thrown me into.

The sound of whistling brought me out of my thoughts. I turned around to witness five men standing about me. Shit, piss, and blood stained what remained of their innermost garments. The old, tattered material hid nothing of their aroused state of affairs. One of the men unbuttoned the front flap and pulled his prick out into his hand. He stroked himself in a feverish motion, grunting and laughing in the same breath.

The whistler stopped as he looked upon his cellmate bringing himself off. He grinned, showing a mouth barren of teeth, and turned to me. He licked his lips and swollen gums. The others stood without a sound, grinning with excitement. Everyone was shackled to the floor, yet I could not tell how much distance they had remaining. I took a few steps back to give additional space between us. The damp, heavy air of the cell, combined with the rotting scent of the men's bodies, took my breath. I went to scream as they advanced upon me. Nothing but a strangled sound fell from my trembling lips.

CHAPTER TWO

P retty beau you are." His gruff, dry voice cracked. He laughed as he reached toward me. His fingers stretched. The chains that bound his ankles held him in place. "You to me, and me to you, a painful fuck will certainly do." His laughter resembled a fit of coughs. Foul-smelling spit flew from his gaping mouth. He rubbed his swollen affairs that pressed against his linen in a contorted and twisted fashion.

"Fuck you," I yelled with the deepest and most forceful tone I could manage, hoping that it would be enough to ward off any further advance. I pressed myself against the cold, clammy bars of the cell, trying to create even an inch of extra space between us.

"Not me my pretty beau, but you." His laughing coughs turned into a squeal of excitement that pierced the stale, heavy air. He leapt off the floor. He stretched the full length of his body toward me. His strange and determined action closed the small space that I had forced between us. He grabbed my hair, pulling me down to the floor with him. His haggard body fell upon me. His action stole my breath, not from his weight but from the fetid odors of his body. I gagged and spat as his drool fell across my mouth.

"Me fuck. Me fuck," he yelled as he tried to hold his position upon my back long enough to enter me. I bucked him like a wild horse trying to throw him off. He dug his nails into my shoulders and crawled his way on top of me despite my valiant efforts. The other men in his group stood cheering him on. The cell soon became full of their demented laughter and joy at witnessing two men nearing a fuck.

"Get the fuck off me, you naff!" I pulled my arm back and shoved my elbow into his face. He let out a howl that nearly deafened me. He pounded his fists against my back in retaliation. His strength astounded me.

"Bad beau. Bad beau. I must hurt you." He wailed as he pounded his fists harder against me.

"Son of a bitch." I grunted against his attack. I curled my fist and slammed it against the side of his head. "Get the fuck off me," I screamed. I raised my hips into the air. He had not expected it and went tumbling over my head. I heard him land on the wooden floor with a dull thud. He kicked out toward me. His calloused and diseased feet scraped against the side of my face. The other men flocked around us to protect their leader. Their hands clawed, stretched, and grasped for anything of mine that they could reach. I looked out past the five men and witnessed at least a dozen more sitting motionless as if afraid to speak out against the pack of wild beasts. Their vicious manners grew more violent by the minute.

"My fuck," the leader of the pack began to yell as he righted himself. He pushed one of the other men away from me and slapped him across the face. "My fuck, my fuck," he bellowed as if he were a bawdy child.

"Mr. Newton, quick, over here." A soft voice of feminine qualities spoke out of the shadows. "You must hurry while their attention has momentarily turned away from you."

I looked across the cell and noticed for the first time a small crook in the back wall that made for a makeshift corner. From within that darkened space I could see the silhouette of a man stand up. I did not hesitate. I pulled myself off the floor and scurried across the cell jumping over a few of the men who lay in my path. The others who stood about did nothing to impede my escape. A hand reached out of the darkness and grabbed my arm to guide my final steps.

"Thank you for your kindness," I said as our hands lingered together. "I do not know what would have become of me if you had not spoken up."

"You are most welcome. I could not sit by and watch another man suffer at the hands of that gang of men." He nodded toward the group. "They have stopped their bickering and have noticed your absence." He chuckled. "Mr. Caen is not going to be amused."

"No, no, no." Mr. Caen stomped his feet in protest as he looked across the cell and noticed me. "My fuck, my fuck." He pounded his fists against the side of his head as he glared at me.

I cowered against my new friend as Mr. Caen charged toward me. His shrill screams echoing against the damp walls chilled my blood. I jumped as I heard his shackles tighten against his approach. He stumbled and fell, letting out a howl of painful anger as he lay more than fifteen feet away from me. I relaxed with the new knowledge of my safety.

"You can see why I am where I am. No one can make it this far while restrained." His arm that had wrapped itself about me as I anticipated Mr. Caen's attack fell from my body.

"Thank you again for sharing your space with a perfect stranger." With reluctance, I pulled away from his warmth so as not to overextend my welcome and so that my prick would not become aroused by our proximity. "I am Thomas Newton." I extended my hand.

"I am Francois Regnault." He looked at my hand, smiled, then raised it to his lips and kissed it. "I am pleased to meet your acquaintance, Mr. Newton."

"Please, given the circumstances of our meeting, I think we can forgo the formalities. Call me Thomas." The caress of his lips against my hand woke my prick from its slumber. A faint glimmer of light squeezed through a crack in the wall, giving us a few moments in which we could see one another with some clarity.

Francois, who looked to be no more than nineteen years of age, stood a few inches above me—six feet at most. Even in the dim light I saw the black spheres of his eyes, set deep within his face. His nose appeared a bit small for his otherwise round face. His long, matted black hair fell below his shoulders. I wondered if his slender frame was the result of the poor conditions of his current imprisonment or of his own doing. Tattered rags, which appeared to have once been his undergarment, hung from his near-hairless body. I glanced farther downward and noticed his prick stir restlessly between his legs.

"It appears we are both in the same state." He looked down at my near nakedness with a slanted smile as my own needy prick responded. He glanced off to the side, then turned his head to look out across the cell. "Mr. Caen is still watching you." He nodded in the direction.

"I would rather not have anything more to do with that man." The light had begun to fade, casting dull shadows across Francois's body. I ran my finger down his smooth chest. A scattering of fuzz covered his navel. I followed the narrow rug of hair as it trailed farther downward and spread out into a deep, tangled bush that blanketed his affairs. The touch of his skin, the scent of his body brought about a desperate act to feel connected with someone, if even for a moment with this stranger. When Francois turned his attention back to me, I laid a kiss upon his lips. He did not pull away. We lingered in the darkness without moving. Our pricks rose to greet one another.

"Let us wait until the others are asleep," he whispered as he brought his lips to my neck. "Come sit with me and let us talk. Tell me stories about your life. Being alone in here for an uncountable time has taken its toll on me. I am desperate for conversation and company." He sat down upon the wooden floor. The boards creaked against the movement. He pulled me down with him. We faced one another, our legs intertwined around each other's bodies. Francois's prick lay gently against the linen of my undergarment. My prick responded. A gentle thud of anticipation beat within it.

"First, why are we not in shackles, like the others?"

"I cannot say with fact, but my guess would be that the men we are sharing this cell with are dangerous due to the sickness in their mind. While we are considered sick in our own way, I do not believe they feel we pose significant trouble."

"Is this not a hospital? If these men are indeed sick, what about their treatment, or rehabilitation?"

"The stories I have heard since my arrival here would make me believe that this is their treatment. It's a brutal place of unspeakable torment and hellish conditions. The man you called a doctor upon your arrival is no more a physician than I."

"How can that be?"

"Who is to question what is done within these walls? It is a place of disposal and one the citizens of Paris have no real knowledge of. They are told that it is a hospital for the insane, and that is what they believe, without questioning anyone's authority."

"You mentioned witnessing another man." I closed the space between us to comfort my growing discontent. I wanted nothing more than to hold Francois in my arms so that I would not have to think of this place or know of its past, yet something within me could not let go of it. "What happened to him?"

"I do not know how long ago these events happened, a month perhaps, but time and days do not belong in a place such as the Bicêtre. He came in much as you did, stripped of his clothing and tossed into the crowd of Mr. Caen's men." He brought his arms about my waist and pulled me closer to him. He released the clasps of my undergarment. My prick fell out between us and met with his. He wrapped his arms about my body. I reciprocated. He kissed me, then continued with his story. "The memory of that event haunts me to this day. I called out to him such as I did to you, but he had not the ability to fight. He tried to get away, but Mr. Caen came upon him almost at once, fucking him with such anger and brutality…" He closed his eyes and took a deep breath.

"You do not have to continue."

"I am fine. It will do me good to talk about it." He hesitated for a moment before continuing. "I sat in this exact spot, terrified that if I rushed in to help this poor man that I too would be overcome by their vicious hands. I did nothing except watch as at least fifteen men fucked him. I am convinced that they fucked him to his very death. I remember the sound of his jaw snapping as three men fucked his mouth at the same time. I do not know what the final cause of death was, suffocation perhaps, or loss of blood. The men were covered in it. The dead body lay in its own fluids and filth for what seemed like days before the guards noticed the growing stench and came to remove the body."

"I am sorry you had to see that. A man's death is not an easy thing to witness. I cannot imagine what you thought when you saw me thrown into the cell."

"I must admit that in those first moments, I thought you were done for. It did not take long for me to realize that my first impression of you was incorrect. I soon knew you to be different. You impressed me with how you handled yourself with the guards, using your body to seduce them. I knew then that you would not suffer the same fate." He gave me a quick kiss and dropped his gaze to the floor as if embarrassed by his action. "Judging by the way you handled yourself, I would guess that this type of situation is not new to you." His gaze reconnected with mine. "Am I correct in that?"

"I do not think that I conducted myself well at all."

"You did what you had to in order to survive. It is apparent from your actions that you know how to take care of yourself."

"I found myself in some trouble back in London and ended up spending time in Newgate Prison."

"If you do not mind discussing such a personal matter with me, what happened?"

"I was living with a woman and her husband. They took me in and made me a member of their family so I would not have to live on the streets. Margaret Clap became the mother I never had, and I her son. One night several constables raided her home. She was taken in and arrested for keeping a brothel. I tried to free her and ended up inside the prison with her. It was then that the constables learned of our love for one another and used that love to force me to testify against all of the men who paid me for my companionship."

"You are a catamite?"

"I was, and one of the best, at least that is what the men told me."

"I do not doubt that." He lifted my prick and coddled it in his hand. "Please, go on."

"After I realized that the constables had no intention of keeping their agreement with me, I took matters into my own hands. Unfortunately, my will to survive came too late. The officials took Margaret to the pillory, where she was stoned and beaten by the vicious people of London. She died of her injuries. In the end I could not protect her. So I left London and came to Paris to look for a gentleman I met November last." Tears fell freely from my eyes. My voice quivered from the memories of losing Mother. "I—"

"Shh." He held a finger to my lips. "I can see the pain that loss has caused you." His hand squeezed my prick. "Please do not think of this as pity, for I have wanted you from the moment my eyes feasted upon your body. Let me fuck you, for while you may still have a chance of leaving this place, I feel I shall never see the light of day again."

"You should not talk that way."

"Please, no more words." His hands gripped my waist and guided me upward.

I leaned in to kiss him as I rose off the floor. I opened my mouth and let his meaty tongue slip inside. I could taste a salty residue lingering there and realized he had tasted of himself earlier in the day. The thought of his stale seed within my mouth sent me near the edge of reason. I gripped the tattered fragments of his linen and pulled it from him. He grunted deep within my mouth.

My prick rose against his body. I moved my hips back and forth rubbing myself off on his smooth skin. My excitement dripped down the center of his chest, which I made good use of as the act came upon us with an urge that could not be stifled. As I rose upon him, his mouth found the nubs of my tits. His thin, moist lips sucked me while his teeth bit the sensitive skin. My body took to trembling as the flames of desire erupted within me.

"I cannot hold out any longer." I moaned. "I must have you. Take my ass and fuck me." I rose farther up his body until I felt the swollen tip of his prick pressing against my needy ass. I reached behind me and tore a hole in my undergarment before grabbing Francois's thick trunk and rubbing his early release between my buttocks.

"Oh do not tease me in such a fashion. Throw yourself down

upon my prick and swallow it whole." Francois begged between heavy breaths.

I lowered myself until the slightest edge of his prick pressed against the tight, wrinkled skin of my ass. He whimpered. I released the grip on his prick and wiggled my hips, causing great shudders within his body. He moaned against me as he made light bites into the skin of my stomach. I lowered myself farther, allowing only the head of his prick to slip inside me. The substantial width of his affair consumed my body as the initial sting of his pleasure stoked the fire that smoldered within my belly.

"Please, I cannot take the torturous wait. I must be allowed entrance." Francois's deep-throated groan vibrated against my belly. He looked up at me. "Enough is enough, my new friend. I forbid you to tease me in this way any longer." His hands came about my waist and pushed me down, impaling me upon his mighty prick.

"Mother of mercy." My voice echoed through the cell. Francois placed his hand upon my mouth.

"You must not speak with such volume. We dare not rouse the others."

"You fuck your way, and I shall fuck mine. Unless you have a way to silence me, I shall…" He covered my mouth with his. I raised my hips. His prick slipped out of me, sending sparks of pleasure through my body. I wiggled my hips, allowing the tip to settle between my buttocks, then pushed myself down upon him, shoving his massive trunk deeper into me. We grunted in unison, our voices vibrating against each other's in a near-silent harmony.

"Oh, fuck," Francois whispered as he broke our kiss. "You have such a divine body and the seduction of the devil himself. Oh, yes that is it, Thomas, tighten your ass about my prick. Oh glory to the heavens, I cannot hold out a moment longer." His voice rose. I placed my hand over his mouth as his prick swelled with the release of his seed.

"Oh fuck," I moaned between clenched teeth as the heat and full quantity of his release filled me to completion. I bounced on his still-swelling prick. His spent seed slipped from my ass and coated our bodies in the most glorious river of pleasure. Before I could utter a word, my prick opened its barrier and covered Francois's chest with thick white ropes of my seed. I continued to move up and down on his softening prick as we both took in the sight of my release dripping down his silken skin. I fell against him as his prick slipped from me.

"You are a gift from heaven," Francois whispered as he pulled me down to the soiled floor and held me tight. We spoke not a word as our bodies recovered from our secret activities. It was not long before my eyes became heavy with sleep. Without additional talk, we drifted away still wrapped in each other's arms.

We awoke to the sounds of rattling chains and Mr. Caen's frightful voice shouting obscenities. I looked out across the cell and witnessed Mr. Caen's disgruntled expression as he looked upon the two of us in our intimate embrace.

"You took my fuck! You took my fuck." Mr. Caen's sobs followed his words. He beat the side of his head with his fists. "No, no, no. He is mine, all mine!"

We scurried to our feet and faced our adversary, Francois naked and covered in the residue of our night of uncontrolled desire, and I dressed in only my torn and soiled linen. Mr. Caen's voice rose to new heights. His anger turned to rage as he looked upon the guilt written over our bodies and face. The commotion he caused led the others around him to stir. It was not long before the five members of his group began to pull upon the chains that bound his shackles to the floor.

"Surely those shackles will not give," I said to Francois without taking my eyes from the activities surrounding Mr. Caen.

"I would hate to think of our fate if they did. I do not know which of us his anger is focused on, but one of us, I'm afraid, would not survive his attack."

"Perhaps the guards will hear the commotion." It was at that moment that Francois and I looked at each other with fright upon our faces as we heard the moans of the old rotten wood as it began to give against the demands of the prisoners. "Mother of God, they are really going to do this." My voice trembled as I listened to the wood splintering. The men laughed and cheered, yet the poor light of the cell and the growing crowd of men made it difficult for us to see with any clarity what was happening. In a sudden and surprising turn of events, Mr. Caen came out of the darkness free from his shackles, his face contorted with rage.

"He was mine! Die, die, die!" He leapt through the air and aimed himself not at me, but at Francois. They collided and knocked me off my feet as well. I heard Francois scream as the iron bars of the cell rattled with the force of the impact. "Not yours, not yours," Mr. Caen repeated as he slammed Francois's face against the wooden floor. "He was mine, all mine. Not yours. You soiled him!"

I got up off the floor and stumbled over to where Mr. Caen was beating Francois, in hopes of dislodging the fight. Mr. Caen noticed my approach and raised his arm, striking me in the face. I tripped over their entangled bodies and fell against the iron bars. I touched my face and winced from the pain, then pulled myself up using the iron bars. Pain shot through my head as I rose, bringing with it moments of dizziness. I steadied myself, feeling the warmth of my blood trickle down my face. It pooled in the corner of my mouth and I wiped it with my arm and readied myself for the fight.

"Thomas, please help me." Francois's voice faded in and out as Mr. Caen beat him with unbelievable force. Over the shouts of the other inmates, I could hear the large wooden door opened from the other end of the hallway. The voices of the guards and doctor soon followed.

"What in the fuck is going on?" one of them shouted.

I looked about our area for anything I could use as a weapon. Hope rushed through me as I caught sight of the length of chain that was still fitted about the shackles of Mr. Caen's feet. I bent down and grabbed the chain with both hands.

"Mr. Caen," I screamed to get his full attention. He looked around as I swung the heavy chain through the air, striking him across his face. He howled in pain, released Francois, and turned his anger upon me. "Motherfucker." I charged him before he had time to react. The iron chains swung above my head. With all of the force I could manage, I brought the chain down and struck him again across the side of his head. Blood sprayed the wooden floor as his head shook from the impact.

"Francois, move." I raised the chain and swung it down upon Mr. Caen's back, ripping into his linens. "Fuck you, you piece of shit." The anger in me grew to a feverish pitch as I struck the man repeatedly until the skin of his back had broken open and blood pooled around his near-lifeless body. In the distance, I heard the voice of someone yelling at the crowd of men. I dropped the bloody chains as the doctor made his way to me.

"What have you done?" The doctor looked up at me as he knelt beside Mr. Caen's body.

"He attacked us," Francois responded even though the question was directed at me. "His cellmates helped him break free from his restraints. If it had not been for Thomas, he would have killed me."

"You murdered this man, Mr. Newton."

"I did so out of self-defense." I turned to look at the dozen or so men who stood around the cell. "Tell the doctor what you saw," I shouted at them. They stood silent as if still protecting the man who lay dead at my feet.

"Mr. Ladue is not going to be pleased." The doctor stood up. "Come on, the two of you have some explaining to do, though I doubt it will do you any good." He grabbed our arms in an iron grip and turned us around. We stopped in front of the crowd of men. "If anyone has anything to say, I beg you to speak now." He paused, waiting for a response that never came. "I did not think there would be."

He pulled us through the cell. Two guards stood outside the cell waiting for us. Once we reached the main door, they took Francois and me in opposite directions.

"Wait, where are you taking Francois?" I fought against his hold struggling to free myself.

"That is not your concern, Mr. Newton." He tightened his grip upon my arm and pulled me closer to him. I gave up the fight.

"I believe it does concern me. I want us to speak to Mr. Ladue together."

"That is not how we do things here, Mr. Newton. Let us go before you squander any more of my patience."

"Francois, do not worry. I shall come for you." My voice rose as the guard ushered me down the hallway.

"Get dressed." The guard pointed to my clothes. "Mr. Ladue has arrived and has been briefed on your barbarous behavior. He's waiting for you in my office."

"May I get something to clean the blood and wound?" I pleaded. "Or is medical treatment too much to ask for in this place?"

"Mr. Ladue will need to inspect you first." The guard turned and left the office, shutting the door behind him.

My body ached from the attack. It pulled against my movement as I slipped my legs into my breeches. I was lacing them up when Mr. Ladue came in. He went directly to the desk without even acknowledging my presence.

"Have you spoken with Mr. Baptiste?" I questioned as I slipped on my blouse and walked toward the desk.

"Why would I do such a thing?" he responded as he kept his eyes on the blotter and his notes from yesterday.

"Mr. Baptiste can vouch for me, that is why." I leaned against his desk and bent my head down to force him to look at me. Our eyes made contact.

"Mr. Newton, I am not going to waste my time or for that matter the valuable time of Mr. Baptiste on your whimsical fancies of whom you know."

"I am tired of your—"

"And I am tiring of you, Mr. Newton. I do not like coming to this place, but you make it impossible for me to stay away." He rose from his chair. "I have never met anyone as exhausting as you. You have more problems at the moment than whether or not I believe your illusions. I hear that you killed a man this morning, is that true?"

"I was defending myself and Francois." I took my seat. "Mr. Caen and his group of merry men attacked me last night the moment I arrived. He was insistent upon fucking me." I did not see the need to disguise my harsh language. Mr. Ladue winced at my words. "If it had not been for Francois calling out to me I would have been overcome by their sinful needs."

"Yes, Mr. Regnault."

"What about him?"

"How long have the two of you known each other?"

"We met last night, as I have just told you." I bit my tongue to keep from speaking out. I knew I was in quite a bit of trouble and could not allow myself to lose any ground due to my wagging tongue.

"You did not know each other prior to your arrival last night?"

"That would be quite impossible, would you not agree?"

"How do you figure that?"

"Mr. Regnault has been in this God-forsaken place longer than I have been in Paris." I paused and looked at his blank stare. "You must be joking. You do not see the impossibility of your claim?"

"So am I to assume that you just let a perfect stranger, how did you put it, fuck you up the ass?" He looked up and waited for a response that I could not give. "Why is it, Mr. Newton, that a fuck from Mr. Regnault is welcome where a fuck from Mr. Caen was so distasteful that you had to murder him with your own hands?"

"I did not kill Mr. Caen for that reason."

"So you admit to murdering him?"

"His death was an accident, and that is all. Neither Francois nor I asked to be brutalized at his hands. If I had not stepped in to help Francois, he would be dead right now, and perhaps I as well."

"If only that were the case, then my troubles would be over. I still do not understand. If Mr. Regnault is, as you say, a stranger to you, why would you kill another man and risk your own freedom to protect him?"

"I was assisting someone in need, Mr. Ladue. Is that so difficult for you to understand?"

"You speak in circles, Mr. Newton, a clear sign of your lack of mental stability."

"I am not sick," I shouted.

"Let me continue, Mr. Newton. First, you tell me that you know Mr. Baptiste well enough for him to invite you to stay with him, and yet your statements indicate that you do not know anything about Mr. Baptiste. I find this quite troubling. And now you inform me that you let a complete stranger have use of your ass, yet you killed another man for wanting the same thing. In my professional opinion, Mr. Newton, you are delusional and therefore sick in the mind. I have no choice but to detain you indefinitely. You are a menace to the fine citizens of Paris."

"You cannot do this!" I stood and leaned over his desk. "I have done nothing wrong, you fucking naff!" I grabbed him by the edge of his coat and looked into his eyes. For the first time, I saw fear held within them. "You are afraid of me, or at least of something about me." I released him from my grasp.

"You know nothing." He rose from his chair and came around to face me.

"If not of me, then of Mr. Baptiste." I shouted back. His eyes twitched when I mentioned Pierre. "That is why you do not want to contact him. You know he would not be pleased with the way you are treating me." I could tell I was unnerving him with my new knowledge. I pushed further. "I demand that you release me!"

"Or what, Mr. Newton? Huh? What in the hell can you possibly do about it?" He threw me against the wall. "You perverts are all alike. Acting as if you are better than everyone else, or that you are special because of the vile and perverse pleasures you take of the body." He grabbed the edge of my blouse and threw me across the room. I fell against a chair and tumbled backward to the floor. I tried to right myself, but before I had my footing he picked me up. He held me close. Our noses touched. His breath was sour. "Guards," he shouted.

"Fuck you." I kissed him on the lips. "That is what you wanted all along, is it not, Mr. Ladue?" I laughed at him. His disgust was apparent. He pulled a sword out from under his coat and held it to my throat.

"That is right, Mr. Newton. Go on give me another reason to slit your fucking throat. Would you like another kiss? Trust me, it would be your last."

"Sir." The guard rushed in. "Sir, you do not want to do that. Please, sir, think about what you are doing." With great care, he took the sword from Mr. Ladue's hand. He tossed it across the room. It rattled against the floor. The guard pulled me from Mr. Ladue's death grip. "I shall take care of this, sir. I shall put him away in his own cell. He will not be able to disrupt the others again."

"This is not over, Mr. Ladue." I cleared my throat and spat. It landed on his cheek. "If I have to sell my soul to Satan again, I shall do it for the sheer pleasure of seeing you in my shoes."

"Get this pervert out of here, Delacroix. Lock him up and forget about him."

"You will not be able to forget about me, Mr. Ladue," I called as the guard pulled me from the room. "I promise you that. This is not over," I shouted down the hallway.

CHAPTER THREE

S top here." Mr. Delacroix tightened his grip about my shoulder. "Undress down to your undergarment."

"Must those be used?" I looked at the shackles that hung from the wall. "I promise to behave myself," I added as I removed my blouse and breeches.

"And I am to believe the words that fall from your tongue? Turn around." He swung me around without waiting for me to respond to his request. "I saw how you were yesterday, flaunting your body with me and the two guards. And what about the vicious attack against the commissaire?"

"I did not attack him," I spat. "He was the one holding the blade. You witnessed it with your own eyes."

"Perhaps it is how you say, but that is not how I will remember it if asked." He laughed. He then leaned into me. His breath was sour, and hot. "That is, unless you and I can come to some type of understanding." He pulled away. "It does not matter who you were on the outside. You are in the Bicêtre now. You will do well to remember that."

Taking what he had said to heart, I reached between his legs and cupped his royal affairs with my bound hands. They felt quite substantial resting in my palm. I stroked his growing prick to let him know of my eagerness to make those understandings of which he spoke sooner rather than later, if for no other reason than to ease the hellish conditions I was sure to face within these walls. I was not expecting such a brutal response.

He grabbed my shackled wrists and threw me against the wall. My head struck the edge of a door. Darkness clouded my vision as the pain ripped through my head. I felt the wound on my face reopen against the rough stone. I slid down the wall and found myself kneeling on the floor.

"Fucking prat!" He kicked me in the belly. I coughed deep, heavy breaths. I felt my body convulse. I vomited, losing nothing but a bitter liquid. "Do not touch me in that way. Do you understand?" He crouched down and lifted my chin to force my eyes upon him.

"But I thought that is what you wanted," I responded as I took in his rather rugged features. His lips were thick with a slight blush to them. A heavy coat of whiskers flecked with gray covered his square jawline, chin, and upper lip. I licked my own dry lips wondering what it would feel like to have those sharp blades of hair pressing into my skin. His nose, a bit larger than it should be for his face, appeared to have been broken at some point, healing with a slight bend at the tip. I pulled my eyes away from his face to keep from staring. It was then that I noticed the long strands of dark blond hair spilling out of the collar of his opened blouse. His voice pulled me back from my fantasies.

"Do you understand me or not?"

I glared up at him without responding. He shook his head as if tiring of me. It was then that I noticed a rise in his breeches. It was with this new knowledge of him and his secret desires that I allowed myself to be manhandled knowing that it would eventually lead to the two of us fucking, and I knew I could use that to my advantage.

"You have a lot to learn, Mr. Newton, about how I like things here on my wing." He bent down and pulled me up. "Let us go." He grasped my elbow with a tight grip and pushed me forward. We continued down the ever-darkening halls of the Bicêtre.

The inner workings of the hospital were a dark, confusing maze of passageways. It took me little time to become aware that I was not being sent back to the large cell where I had hoped to be reunited with Francois. I occupied my silent walk by holding fast to the memories of Francois's body—the taste of his skin, his tongue, and his warm seed, which still lingered upon my tongue.

The sound of a whip cracking through the air pulled me out of my thoughts. A chill crawled down my back as I peered into a small room as we passed. A young man stood naked and shackled. His arms stretched over his head as he hung from the ceiling. Behind him, a guard held a whip. He brought it over his head and with the strength of four men sliced it through the air. The frayed ends landed against the young man's bare back and buttocks. The guard hesitated as the young man's body shook from the attack and his agonizing screams echoed through the room. The wounds on his back had already opened up. Blood seeped in long, narrow rivers down his back, dripping from his buttocks and pooling on the stone floor. Mr. Delacroix pushed me forward without a word.

"What did that young man do to deserve such punishment?" I questioned, resuming my slow pace down the hallway.

"He is not your concern, Mr. Newton."

"But he cannot be more than sixteen years of age. Surely his crime cannot be so bad as to warrant the whip."

"Age does not matter when a man is taken by debauchery," Mr. Delacroix replied. "Be thankful that I have other plans for you, otherwise you would be next in that room." Mr. Delacroix held me back as he opened a large wooden door at the end of the corridor.

I peered into the blackness that lay in front of me. Dread unlike anything I had ever known took hold of me. The fear that this unknown place instilled in me made Newgate look like a holiday resort for the wealthy. Even though I could not see past the tip of my nose, I felt its existence was separate from that of the hospital. I peered into the mouth of this endless blackness and readied myself to be devoured by it. I took an uneasy step forward, hesitating as I heard the soft, painful whimpers of numerous voices drifting out of the asylum's throat.

"Keep moving, Mr. Newton." Mr. Delacroix pushed me into the dark. I stumbled over the uneven stones in the floor and felt the slime and dampness ooze between my toes as I regained my footing. "You are almost home." He laughed and nudged me farther into the tunnel.

I blinked several times to try to adjust my vision to the lack of light. As my eyelids fluttered, my fate began to appear out of the dim light. The narrow tunnel was lined with individual cells, each no more than six feet in either direction. The side walls of each cell were made of stone, which sealed off one cell from another except for a small iron-barred opening—no more than three feet square—through which prisoners could peer at each other.

Some of the men who still had strength to move stumbled to the edge of their cells. They reached out to me with their near-skeletal hands. Others lay on small piles of straw. They were asleep, dying, or already dead. All were naked or covered in tattered rags. The murmurs and coughing came at me from all directions. I did not know which might kill me first, the deplorable conditions or the obvious disease that littered the cells. Mr. Delacroix pulled on my shackled wrists, holding me from progressing farther. I stopped and watched as he unlocked an empty cell to my left. The pressure against my wrists faded as he removed the shackles.

"Welcome to your new home." He laughed as he pushed me into the cell. I stumbled and fell to my knees. The stone was wet and covered in a slick substance I could not see. The dampness was quick to absorb into my thin undergarment.

"Please, wait." I pulled myself off the floor and went to the gate as Mr. Delacroix locked it. "If I must be locked up in this place, can I at least ask to be given my pipe and tobacco? It was taken from me…" My words faded as I watched Mr. Delacroix pull my smoking implements from his pocket.

"I do believe you are speaking of these?" He pulled them away from me and smiled. "If I were to give these to you, I would be breaking the rules."

"From what I have witnessed, there do not seem to be any rules." I could tell by the expression on his face that my comment did not sit well with him. "I am sorry for my sudden tongue."

"What could you offer me in return?" He smiled as his hand slipped between his legs and cupped his satchel. He looked over his shoulder, then back toward me. "Get down on your knees." He lowered his voice. "I have heard men like you are good at this." He unlaced his breeches. His fingers slipped inside and pulled his prick out. It fell heavily between his legs and swayed as it stiffened in anticipation. "I am not easy to please. Do you think you have what it takes to be my whore?"

"You shall never find a better mouth in all of Paris than mine." I reached my hand between the iron bars.

"No touching." He slapped my hand away. He dropped my pipe and tobacco on the floor out of my reach. "Bring your face close to the bars." He took the base of his prick and stroked it, bringing it to its full length and width. "Open up, bitch."

I moved closer to him, gripped the iron, and opened my mouth. I looked up at him. I could smell the musky oils of his body as he moved in closer and slipped the thick head of his prick between the bars. The slit in his prick was already damp with excitement. I took my tongue to it and licked it off. He shuddered as he let out a soft moan. I slipped my tongue under the folds of skin and took whatever moisture was there as my lips gently encircled the head of his prick. I milked him with gentle caresses of my lips and felt his body fall against the iron bars of my cell as he gave in to my attention.

"You are a fine trencher," he moaned. "Now how about you show me what you are made of." He grabbed the back of my head and pushed the entire length of his prick into my mouth and with a final abrupt shove, lodged the head of his prick in the back of my throat. "Yeah, that's what I call a fine hole." He groaned as he began to fuck my face with such force that I thought he would pull my head through the iron bars to get farther into me.

His bountiful early release soon filled my mouth with its savory flavors. I milked his prick to quench my scandalous hunger. What gifts he gave me that I could not swallow soon formed in the crevices of my mouth and dribbled down my chin.

My own prick, thick and swollen from the excitement, begged to be released. I lowered my hand between my legs. I fumbled with the eyelets of my linen, then pulled my prick out. The familiarity of it felt good in my hand. I fondled myself. Mr. Delacroix must have witnessed my own pleasuring and, not liking my activities, slipped his foot through the bar and pushed my hand away. His heavy shoe fell against my throbbing member and pushed against it. I moaned from the unexpected attention. His prick responded to the vibrations of my voice and spat a large quantity of seed down my throat.

"Does my whore like to be fondled?" Mr. Delacroix whispered as he slipped his shoe off and took to working my prick with his stocking foot. "Damn, you are a well-appointed young bitch," he grunted as he fucked my mouth with force.

I spread my knees and scooted closer to the gate so that more of Mr. Delacroix's foot could get to me. I moaned as the fire in my belly ignited. My own excitement dripped into the curly moss of my privates and saturated the thin fabric of my inner garment. My vocal demands grew as I felt the rush of my seed expelled through my engorged prick. Rocking upon my bent knees, I gripped the iron bars to maintain my balance as my prick released great quantities of my seed.

"You are quite the man." Mr. Delacroix grabbed my head and with one final thrust held me firm against his body. I took in the fragrant odors of his private area as his prick throbbed and pulsed deep within my throat. He soon filled me with his hot and plentiful seed. I drank it all down, not wanting a spill a drop. The actions of my throat on his softening prick expelled another quantity of his seed as he unexpectedly pulled his prick from me. I licked my lips and looked up at him. He shivered from the perspiration that covered his body. His prick dangled in front of me, teasing me with a final drop of its pearl clinging to the folds of skin. I reached out and took it upon the tip of my finger, slipped the finger into my mouth, and savored its bitterness, knowing it would not be the last time Mr. Delacroix would take me.

"May I have my smoking supplies?" I questioned nervously, not wanting to offend him with my query.

"I am nothing if not a man of my word, Mr. Newton." He slipped his prick back inside his breeches. He handed me the pipe and tobacco.

"Thank you." I filled my pipe, lit the tobacco, and took a long draw, savoring the first smoke in nearly two days.

"It is I who should thank you. That was a fine fuck, Mr. Newton." Mr. Delacroix bent down to my left and slipped his hand between the bars. He slapped me with a firm yet gentle motion. "Your reputation precedes you."

"I am afraid I do not understand. What reputation are you referring to?" I looked upon the sudden stern features of his face.

"I should go." He straightened his outfit and gave me a wicked smile before turning and walking into the darkness.

"Wait," I shouted. "Mr. Delacroix, please tell me what you meant." An answer was not forthcoming. My only knowledge that he had left was the loud hollow sound of the door closing from the far end of the hallway. I stood up, my knees aching from the cold stones, and used the iron bars to steady myself as I shook the numbness from my legs.

I took a long draw from my pipe as a sudden thought came to me. *Could they possibly know about my life in London? Is that what all of this is about?* My mind went wild with the possibility. I took another draw from my pipe to relax my mind, trying to not let my current situation exaggerate my overworked mind. I looked through the shadows of my cell. It was then that I noticed a tiny beam of dull gray light illuminating a corner in the back. I walked toward it. The late-afternoon sun broke through a crack in the wall. I lowered my face to let the light brush against my skin. Even in the gloom, the light gave off a faint hint of the warmth that was afforded to people on the outside. I closed my eyes and enjoyed the momentary comfort it provided.

It was not until my tired mind reflected on how light would be coming in through the wall that I opened my eyes and looked more closely at the crack. I pushed on the stone. It gave against my touch. I pushed harder. Dust and sand crumbled about the edge of the stone. I continued my work until the stone became dislodged from the rest of the wall. Dust and dirt billowed out from the hole as the stone fell to my feet. As the air cleared, I saw an exterior wall some seven or eight inches away. Set within that wall was a gated window. Through the small opening, I witnessed human bones lying against the exterior wall. Tattered rotting cloth hung from the dull gray bones. I tilted my head to see it from a different view and saw the dead face of the unfortunate former inmate staring back at me as if foretelling my future. A chill crept through my body. Whether it was from the damp cell or the former owner of the bones passing through me, I could not tell. I placed the stone back into the wall and sat down on the pile of straw that was to be my bed. I pulled my knees up to my chest and rocked back and forth to warm myself as I waited for sleep to take me. When it did, the dreams came with it.

Mother Clap stood by the stone fireplace as she hung bright red-and-green holiday bows across the mantel. The room soon filled with her soft voice as she began to sing "God Rest Ye Merry Gentlemen." George Kedear and I looked around the room at the scattering of men who had put their lives at risk to come out and be among other like-minded individuals. We glanced at each other and smiled. George and I soon found the contagion of Mother Clap's voice too much to stave off. We broke into song with her, and for a moment I forgot about the Society for the Reformation of Manners and their fervent hatred of anything they deemed unnatural.

"*Bonsoir,*" a man shouted as he entered the tavern, shattering our few moments of peace. He smiled as he removed his hat and beat the snow off it. He looked around at the decorations. "I hope I have not stumbled upon a private affair?"

"Heavens no, sir." Mother Clap looked at me and the other six men who had gathered during the evening. She approached him. "It is a bitter night outside, please come warm yourself by the fire. May I offer you something to drink?"

"You must be Margaret Clap." He came to her, his face beaming with joy. He hugged her without notice or warning. He looked at me behind the embrace. "A vision of such beauty has just stolen my heart." He pulled away from Mother and walked toward me. "Words pale beside what I see before me. You must be Thomas Newton." He took my hand in his and brought it to his lips as he bowed. I looked around the room and noticed George and Edward slipping out the back door; the others soon followed.

"Pardon my abruptness." Mother Clap interrupted. "How do you come by so much information, as we know nothing of you?"

"My apologies, Mrs. Clap." He bowed and kissed her hand. "I am Pierre Baptiste. We have a mutual acquaintance, Gabriel Laurence. I am passing through London on my way to Paris. I stopped in the city to see my old friend. He insisted that I leave his company so that I may visit your establishment and meet the two of you. I hope his invitation was not made in error?"

"Any friend of Gabriel's is always welcome here." She walked behind the bar. "Will a gin do?"

"A gin would be most appreciated. Thank you, madam." Pierre's gaze never left mine. "Is my presence here causing problems? I seem to have frightened off the other guests."

"It is not you, sir. We are all a bit on edge." Mother handed us both a drink. "I do not suppose you have heard about the Society for the Reformation of Manners."

"Gabriel told me of the dreadful things they are doing. I suppose my unfamiliar presence unnerved the others."

"As I said, we have all been unnerved by their actions. Please do not worry. Make yourself at home."

"I was hoping that perhaps I could hire Thomas for a few hours. I have been on the road for such a long time and have missed the pleasures of another man's company."

"That, Mr. Baptiste, is between you and Thomas. I shall go and lock up, and turn in for the night." She kissed my cheek. "Good night, Thomas." She winked at me and smiled. "It was a pleasure meeting you, Mr. Baptiste. Enjoy your evening."

"That will depend upon Thomas, my dear lady."

❖

I awoke to a rustling sound near my head. I struck my tinderbox and peered into the eyes of a large and ferocious rat. It screeched and bared its teeth at me. I pulled back, widening the few inches between us. It lunged toward me in an almost intelligent plot of attack. I yelled and threw my hand up to block my face. The back of my hand hit the rat and sent it through the air. It hit the wall with a dull thud. Moments later I heard it scurry away. I shook away the nerves and shifted up on the bed of straw until my back was against the wall. Through the silence of the wing, I could hear the trickle of water as it dripped down the wall. The foul-smelling water soaked the back of my undergarment and clung to the back of my head. I closed my eyes and tried to picture Pierre back in Mother Clap's tavern on that cold holiday evening. The comforting memories of the past allowed sleep to return—the dreams followed with it.

❖

"I am all yours." The excitement and anticipation of being intimate once again brought a heat to the edge of my skin and an ache to my lonely prick. "Would you be agreeable to joining me in my private quarters?" I took his hand in mine and led him upstairs and into my room.

"Now that we are alone, I do not believe I can wait a moment longer before having you in my arms." He leaned into me and pressed his lips to mine. His mouth opened. Our tongues met between parted lips. He broke the kiss with a smile and held a finger to my lips, stepped back from me, and unbuttoned his waistcoat, letting it fall to the floor. He kicked off his shoes and unbuttoned his blouse.

His body was lean with a darker complexion than what I was used to from the men of London. A heavy pelt of dark hair covered his chest and stomach. I walked toward him. He shook his head. I stopped. He unlaced his breeches and pulled them off his legs. His prick was long and lean, with thick folds of skin hiding its rather bulbous head. He came to me. We embraced as our tongues met in a fury of passion.

He opened my blouse one eyelet at a time and laid kisses upon my exposed skin. The fire in my belly grew with each and every touch. He knelt in front of me and released my breeches. He kissed my swollen prick, which lay covered beneath my undergarment.

I was not used to this type of handling—soft, gentle, unhurried. It was more passionate than anything I had ever experienced. He pulled my undergarment down and let it fall to my ankles. My prick brushed against his cheek, leaving a streak of its clear nectar in its path. He moved his head toward the downward motion of my prick and opened his mouth. My prick entered. He sucked and coddled me, bringing tears to my prick that ran over his tongue and down his throat.

The heat of the fire soon soaked our bodies in perspiration. He pulled me down on top of him and slid his cock between my thighs. Its length filled me at once, sending such pleasures through my body that a sudden outburst of seed sprayed across his chest. I leaned over him to lick my own warm release from his skin. I nibbled his tits where my seed had moistened the heavy layer of chest hair, relishing the taste and feel of his thick moss running through my tongue. I recaptured my seed in my mouth, then kissed him, feeding him the seed he had fucked from me. He took my spunk with eager abandon and fucked me harder, the force of which caused another wave of pleasure to expel more of my delight between our bodies. It was not long before I felt the familiar surge of impending release within my ass. I pushed myself down, impaling myself upon his prick. With several tremendous shudders, he released himself into me four if not five times, filling me beyond capacity. The final release exploded from my ass, showering our bodies with his spent seed.

Once he released himself inside me he begged for me to do the same to him—a role I was not usually asked to play. I was delighted by the change of position. By the time I had spent myself three times inside him and him once more inside me, it was nearing three in the morning.

"Thomas, you are an extraordinary lover." He pulled me close and kissed me. "As it is late, I wonder if I could impose upon your generosity and sleep here before continuing my journey in the morning."

"Stay as long as you wish, Pierre," I responded as my mind played with his use of the word *lover*. "You can have your choice of any of the rooms here."

"No, you do not understand." He sat up with his softening prick still inside me. "I wish to sleep in your bed, with you by my side."

"I have never been with someone under those conditions, though I must admit doing so with you would be most satisfying."

As I lay nestled in his armpit, the smell of his sex-laced body caused a new fever to burn inside me. After a few moments, he turned his back toward me and wrapped my arm around his chest. I lay there listening to the soft tones of his sleep as the warmth of our naked bodies melted together. It was the first time in weeks that I felt as if things were taking a turn for the better. As sleep began to take me, I wondered if there could be lasting love between two men, and if so whether it would feel like this.

We awoke the next morning with our bodies intertwined. My prick was stiff with desire as I lay against his back. He reached between us and guided me into him for another fuck. I dressed after emptying my morning seed inside him.

"You are welcome to join us for breakfast before departing," I said as I leaned across the bed and kissed his dry, chapped lips.

"Merci, mon amour." He smiled as he rubbed the sleep from his eyes. The scent of his night sweat drifted off his naked body. It followed me out of my bedroom and down the hallway.

Mother Clap was in the kitchen preparing breakfast. I went to her with a lightened heart as Pierre drifted through my mind.

"Good morning." I walked up behind her and kissed the back of her neck. She jumped from my immediate closeness.

"Good grief, Thomas, you gave me a start." She turned her drawn face toward me. Her eyes were dull and lifeless. "Has Pierre left?"

"No, he spent the night with me. I have invited him to stay for breakfast." I studied her face. It remained emotionless. "Why do you look so disheartened? Are you not feeling well?"

"I received the most disturbing news this morning." She placed the bread and tea on the table. "Good morning, Pierre. I am quite relieved that you are still here. I may need to ask for your help, and I hope it will not be too much of a burden on you."

"Mother, please tell me what has happened and what this has to do with Pierre."

"I will be happy to assist in any way I can."

"Please, let us sit and eat breakfast like well-mannered folk." Mother took her usual seat at the head of the table. Pierre sat next to me on Mother's right.

"Pierre, I want you to take Thomas with you when you leave this morning." She looked at me. Her eyes were bloodshot from earlier tears.

"I would like nothing more than to have Thomas by my side for my journey back to Paris. It is his choice, not yours or mine."

"Mother, I do not understand what this is all about. Please, tell me what has happened."

"It is not over, Thomas, and I fear it will get worse. The Society raided Thomas Wright's home last night," she said through fresh tears.

"I do not understand. How can they just do that without any warning or evidence?" I felt the burn of worry ignite in the pit of my stomach. I looked at Pierre. He wrapped his arm around me.

"The Society has grown in members and power in the past year.

Their members are a part of every government office in the city. Their strength is terrifying. They are the ones who interpret and enforce the laws. It appears that someone was present at Mr. Turner's hearing who heard of the liaisons and intimacies at Mr. Wright's home."

"That son of a bitch!"

"Thomas, do not use that language at the table."

"My apologies, Mother, but I know who the treacherous bastard was who did this."

"Who?" Mother asked.

"Mark Partridge. He warned everyone at Mr. Wright's home the night of my beating that he would take his revenge on everyone there. No other man there could have such a cold or twisted heart."

"Was anyone arrested?" Pierre rubbed my shoulder to ease my anger.

"Yes. They found two men in one of the rooms. They were naked and in the height of pleasure." She wiped her tears with the hem of her dress. "Seven men were taken in all. I am sorry to report, Mr. Baptiste, that Gabriel Laurence was one of them."

"My dear friend." Pierre shook his head. "Though I am not surprised, he was always the rambunctious one, never thinking before acting."

"What can we do?"

"Nothing, Thomas. We must distance ourselves from our friends and the men you have entertained."

"Perhaps they will find a way to clear themselves during the hearings so that they will not have to stand trial."

"I am afraid there will be no hearings, Thomas."

"How can that be?"

"The Society is demanding that hearings for sexual offenses be eliminated for fear of giving scandal. Those arrested are in Newgate as we speak in unthinkable conditions with nothing to look forward to except their own deaths. That is why I want Pierre to take you away from here. I cannot bear to think of them taking you in."

"I am not going anywhere, Mother."

"Thomas, do not be so stubborn. If you stay, you risk arrest. I cannot have that weight upon me as well."

"Thomas, listen to her. It is no longer safe for you here. You should come with me, at least until things quiet down."

"I cannot abandon my family. I will not let anything happen to you, Mother."

"It is not myself that I worry about, Thomas. I cannot be tried for sodomy. It is your safety that worries me. I do not want to imagine what would come of me if I were to lose you to the evil servants of the Society."

"Thomas, please reconsider and come with me."

"I am sorry, Pierre, my place is here."

"Then promise me that if things get any worse, the both of you will flee London and come to Paris." He pulled a piece of paper and pen from his coat. "Here is my address. Come anytime, I will be waiting for you to send word." He kissed me. "Take care of yourself, Thomas."

"Thomas." The voice drifted through my dreams.

"Pierre, please do not leave me," I muttered into the darkness that had become my sleeping mind. "Please, Pierre, wait."

"Thomas, wake up."

"Pierre?" I called out as my eyes fluttered open. My body had slumped down against the cold, hard floor as I slept. As I straightened, my body ached and pulled against my movement. It was then that I heard the familiar voice from my dream again.

"Thomas, it is I, Francois. I am in the next cell."

"Francois?"

CHAPTER FOUR

Yes, it is I," he whispered.

"Where are you?" I pulled myself into my waking mind as it wrestled between my dreams and the reality of my situation. I crawled over to the gated window that separated us. Our fingers immediately intertwined through the iron bars. "Where are your clothes?"

"It has been a most harrowing experience." He rested his forehead against the wall and peered at me wearily through the window. "They stripped me of my clothes and inspected my body. They whipped me to such a degree, and all for not giving them information about you."

"About me? What could you possibly tell them when we have just met?" I ran my finger down his tear-streaked face.

"They wanted to know everything I knew of you, which I confessed was nothing, but they did not believe a word of it." He grimaced. "They determined I was withholding information and tried to beat it out of me with the whip." He angled his body to give me a view of his back.

"Mother of mercy." My voice echoed through the wing, stirring the restless inmates in other cells. "Why did you not tell a lie in order to protect yourself?"

"It would not have mattered what I told them, they still would have abused me." He looked down and pulled a spider from the moss of his private area. He pinched it between his thumb and finger. "May I ask you a question of a personal nature?"

"I cannot imagine anything more personal than the act of fucking that we have already enjoyed." I smiled and kissed the tips of his fingers, still intertwined with mine. I looked into his youthful eyes and wondered if the warmth I felt for him was genuine or if it was forced due to our unfortunate circumstance.

"As you woke, you called out the name of Pierre." He hesitated. "Who is he?"

"He is a man I was introduced to November last. He invited me to come visit him in Paris if things in London became too difficult. It did, so I came. Unfortunately, he is away on business. Thanks to the lack of cooperation from the Paris police, he does not know that I have been locked away."

"I am not sure I want to know, but what is this man's name?"

"Pierre Baptiste."

"Son of a bitch," he said with a heavy sigh.

"Why is everyone so interested in my acquaintance with Pierre? Please, Francois, if you know anything, you must tell me. Do you know Pierre?"

"No, *mon ami*, not personally. I know him by name only."

"Do you suspect that the police believe otherwise?"

"No more questions, *mon ami*. Kiss me." I leaned forward and brought my lips to his. The softness and warmth calmed my nerves. We broke our kiss and smiled at each other. "Please, do not move yourself from this spot. I must be close to you while I still can."

"I shall stay right here. Please, you never answered my question."

"Let me tell you how I came to be here. Perhaps it will help."

"Help?"

"Yes, and if nothing else, it will assist in passing the time. Have you heard of the Marquis Chaveau?"

"The name means nothing to me. Should it?"

"The Marquis Chaveau was a very wealthy and high-ranking official of France. He was also a scandalous man of many sins, the least of which included the desire for intimate liaisons with young men."

"I take it you knew him intimately."

"*Oui.*"

"Is he the reason you are here?"

"In a matter of speaking, yes. You see, I was a kept man. I knew of his reckless ways. He could not contain his lust for the male body. Night after night, he would leave after dinner and sometimes he would be gone for two or three days. He never spoke of his activities with any specificity, but I knew he was fucking other young men."

"And you tolerated that?"

"Why would I not? For my silence and acceptance of his wandering ways, he lavished me with a lifestyle I would never have been able to obtain otherwise. The finest home in which to live, clothes that only the wealthy could afford, and the most exquisite parties, they were all mine." He looked away from me. "I hope you will not judge me for my ways."

"I should think not, for I have done similar things in my past to afford me a comfortable life. How did you end up in here and not the Marquis Chaveau?"

"It started about eight months ago when the marquis became utterly infatuated with a young man by the name of Paul-Henri Bucher. At first I thought not much of it, as he had these moments of indiscretions with other young men, but as the weeks went by this young man became an obsession of his. He could not find a way of quenching his hunger for him. He would come home in the early-morning hours raving mad about the tone of the young man's voice. When I inquired as to why that had upset him so, he replied that Paul-Henri's voice was becoming too deep and that it was not pleasing to him. I tried to explain to him that there was nothing he could do, that a young man's voice does change with age. He would either have to accept it or find a way to end the liaison with him. Something in my words sent the marquis to the edge of reason. He panicked and became more agitated. He began to yell at me and curse me for not helping him find a solution. I tried to bring reason to his delirious state, but that only made him more furious. It was the only time that the marquis abused me, and a time in my life that I shall never forget. I was laid up in bed for over a week with injuries."

"You remained?"

"What could I do? I have no education or trade other than being the private whore of the marquis. You must understand that I had no other choice. I could not give up that lifestyle."

"One always has a choice." I heard the words fall from my lips before I could stop them. I shook my head with feelings of remorse. "I am sorry for my comment."

"You have no need."

"But you see, I do. I have said or thought those same words more times than I care to remember."

"Apology accepted. After the abuse upon my body, he stormed out of the house. A few hours later he returned with another young man. He kissed and petted this one in front of me as I lay in my bed. The two of them were soon taken by alcohol. They undressed each other, getting more worked up in their desires and with the knowledge that I was unable to leave—forced by my injuries to stay and witness them fucking. The marquis was the most vicious and spiteful of any man I had ever met, and the cruelty to me did not stop there. Day and night for weeks the marquis would try to quench his ravenous desires with other men, but instead of doing it out of sight, he would bring them home and fuck them in any hole he could find, making sure I was there to watch. There were times he would try to force me to participate, which of course I was obliged to do."

"The marquis should be in this hospital, not you."

"He was. You see, it soon became obvious that he could not live without Paul-Henri. That is when he threw me out of the house. I had no clothes or money. Night after night, I begged him to let me come home, but he insisted that he had tired of me. I knew it was over one evening when I saw the marquis bring Paul-Henri home with him with a carriage full of new clothes and expensive jewelry. It was not more than a fortnight when I witnessed the marquis walking in Jardin des Tuileries. He saw me forthright and came running up to me. He begged my forgiveness and pleaded with me to come home."

"Did you go with him?"

"*Oui.* It was either that or spend another night under a tree."

"What about Paul-Henri?"

"When I asked about Paul-Henri, the marquis would get agitated. I did not want to be abused again, so I vowed to myself to never mention Paul-Henri's name again. To this day I do not believe anyone has heard from him."

"Do you think the marquis did something to him?"

"The marquis was many things, but a murderer he was not. No, there were rumors for a while about Paul-Henri and the marquis, but nothing ever came of it. What started the marquis's fall was the mother of one of the young men. She had reported that her son had acted differently ever since the day he was hired to do some work for the marquis. No one of course would believe her, or if they did, they did nothing about it. The woman was so distraught over her son's behavior that she hired some man who is known to find criminals and match them to their crimes. Once the detective was hired, it was not long before the Marquis Chaveau was taken in by the Paris police and charged with assault with sodomitical attempt upon this young boy, but also that of forty-three other young men."

"This still does not explain how you came to be in this place."

"The evening the police came to take the Marquis Chaveau in for sodomy, I had heard the commotion in the parlor. The marquis was furious that someone had suggested that he would be guilty of such crimes. I was fearful that if the police found me there, I would be taken in as well. I took some of my clothes and some money the marquis had at my ready disposal and left the building through the servants' quarters. I dared not rent a room, fearing someone would recognize me, so I spent that first evening in the Tuileries. The next morning I awoke under a tree with two policemen standing over me."

"How did they know of you, let alone find you?"

"They would never tell me of their ways or source, but I have guessed that the detective the woman hired had heard of my living arrangements with the marquis and somehow was able to find me."

"Perhaps he was watching the house the night you escaped, followed you into the park, and instead of taking you in himself, he fetched the commissaire."

"I have thought that the only logical explanation. That morning, I was taken in and questioned for days about my carnal knowledge of the marquis. After nights of living in these conditions, I finally relented and told them my tale as I have spoken it to you, with the promise that I would be released for cooperating. As you can see, they did not uphold their end of the agreement."

"They never do." My mind fluttered back to the constables of London and their broken promises that led to Mother's death. "What became of the Marquis Chaveau?"

"The police and the detective were determined to make the marquis's crimes visible to all of Paris."

"I was under the impression they wish to keep these topics out of the public view."

"That is how they have always operated, but for some reason they wanted to set an example by exploiting the crimes and his punishments. Perhaps they were hoping to scare the people of Paris into submission. Whatever their reason, after a few months inside the Bicêtre, the marquis was still proclaiming his innocence. In order to silence him and to avoid public embarrassment, they ordered him to the breaking wheel."

"I do not know what that is."

"It is a wooden wheel much like you would see on any carriage, but much larger. It is suspended on its side so that it spins in a circle.

The prisoner is tied to the wheel and is beaten with a club to break their bones until they confess to their crimes, or die—whichever is to come first."

"I cannot imagine such punishment. What crimes could a man commit that would require such treatment?"

"In the case of the Marquis Chaveau, it required very little."

"I cannot imagine the pain that you suffered knowing this was going on to someone you loved. Is this when he confessed to the crimes?"

"I suppose love played some role in my arrangement with the marquis, though I could not see that at the time. I can say that he stood against unbearable pain on the wheel and still proclaimed his innocence."

"You witnessed this?"

"*Oui.* The commissaire wanted me to see what my confession brought upon the good people of Paris. They shackled me and placed me in the same carriage as the marquis. I could not bear to look at him knowing that it was my tongue that led him to this place. We sat in silence as they took us to the Place Saint Louis where the breaking was to take place. The entire area was full of Parisians looking on with curious eyes. They pulled me out of the carriage and stood a guard on each side of me as I was forced to watch them place the marquis on the wheel. His arms and legs were stretched taut. The executioner took an iron bar from the carriage and stood near the wheel as it was rotated. The first application of the iron was to the marquis's left ankle. I had never heard a man scream in such agony as he did at that moment. I was close enough to hear the bones snap. By the second revolution of the wheel, his foot hung from his leg, attached only by the broken and torn skin."

"Please, do not torture yourself with more of this story."

"They brought him back to his cell that evening and left him, expecting that he would not survive the evening with the injuries he sustained. The marquis was a stubborn man. In the morning when they came to remove his body, he was still in the same position as when they left him, and very much alive. He stared in their direction and spat vulgarities at them for their treatment of him, the Marquis Chaveau."

"What happened to him?"

"The detective was so infuriated that he had survived, he became more determined than ever to bring an end to him. The detective went to the higher courts and got a declaration ordering that the Marquis Chaveau should be burned alive on the stake."

"Good Lord!"

"Indeed. Rumors started spreading about the detective and his sudden interest in murdering men arrested for sodomy. It is not a minor offense in Paris, but it has never warranted the punishments that the Marquis Chaveau received." His fingers stretched between the bars and stroked my face. "That is why seeing you in this cell next to me startled me so. It was the same cell that the marquis was thrown into after the wheel."

I do not know whether it was my own delirious mind or the story that Francois told, but I soon felt as if someone or something was in the cell with me. I turned and looked behind me only to find myself surrounded in darkness. My tired and troubled mind began to play tricks with me, insisting that every noise I heard was the dead Marquis Chaveau.

"Has my story troubled you?"

"I have to confess that it has." I lit my pipe and took a long draw against it. The tobacco eased my mind.

"I am quite tired." Francois ran his fingers over my lips. "I do not wish to fall asleep alone for fear of what might come for me while I sleep. Would you stay here and watch over me?"

"Yes, of course." I took another draw from the pipe, hoping Francois would not hear in my voice the uneasiness that had settled into me. "I shall not move until you wake. Sleep well, my friend." I smiled at him though I was not sure he could see the gesture, hidden within the shadows of the cell.

I sat in the darkness, alone and fearful of what would become of me as Francois slept. I could not imagine that the Lord had allowed me to survive the trials in London and the death of Mother Clap only to suffer a similar fate in Paris. The sounds of the night began to play tricks with my mind once more. Footsteps appeared and disappeared in all directions. The sound of water trickling down the walls soon took on the quality and rhythm of voices. A cold chill settled into my body and would not ease its grip. I shivered without control as I closed my eyes to the darkness and the damning fate it brought with it. I willed myself to remain strong and to fight instead of giving in. It was during those moments of doubt when I heard what sounded like a male voice, followed by a soft groan. I looked down at Francois in the next cell.

He shook from the cold, yet his breathing seemed steady as he slept. I released his hand, then stood up. I walked toward the voice, not knowing if it was real or an illusion of my weakening mind. As I approached the cell door, I saw the silhouette of a man standing in the hallway. "Mr. Delacroix, is that you? Please you must come here," I whispered. The dark figure turned and walked toward me. Mr. Delacroix came into view. "Please, you must do something. I cannot accept that this is my fate. All I have asked is that the commissaire contact Mr. Baptiste to collaborate my story. Surely that is not too much to ask?"

"What do you wish me to do about it?" He pulled a bottle to his lips and drank from it. "Would you like some gin?" He held the bottle toward me. I reached out, then hesitated. "Go on, I shall only make this offer once."

"What will this cost me?"

"I shall put it on your account." He laughed.

"Thank you." I took the bottle and drank heavily from it, letting the stout liquor warm my body. I handed it back to him.

"Keep it. I have plenty more." He unlaced his breeches and pulled his prick out. He shifted his stance as a heavy stream of piss fell to my feet. I moved to the side. His hot stream of piss followed me. I gave in and used its heat it to help ease the cold in my feet. "Now what is it you wish me to do about your situation? I have no influence over the commissaire." He shook his prick before releasing it. It swung freely between his legs.

"Please, if you can only get word to Mr. Baptiste, I know he shall come."

"The commissaire says that Mr. Baptiste cannot be found."

"I do not believe the commissaire has even tried."

"What makes you think you can trust me?"

"I believe that you know I am telling the truth. You know that I have never been with Nicholas Bergenoir, nor have I sold my body to earn any wages since arriving in Paris. I believe you also know that I am in fact a friend of Mr. Baptiste." I took another swig of the gin. "Please, I beg of you. If you do not want to contact Mr. Baptiste directly, that is understood. If I could be afforded a pen and some paper so that I may write him a note, perhaps you could pass it on to him. I know he will come and correct this misunderstanding without haste."

"That is a lot to ask, Mr. Newton. What would I gain in doing such a favor for you?" He stroked his growing prick until it protruded from his body, stiff with need.

"I shall give you whatever it is that you ask for. It matters not to me as long as I have your promise that a message will be delivered without delay to Mr. Baptiste." I held back the hope that began to rise within me for fear of being disappointed once again.

"This agreement will remain between us?" He took a writing tablet and pen from his inside coat pocket.

"Of course. Contrary to your views, I do not wish to make known what I am willing to do to save my own life."

"You write your note to Mr. Baptiste, and if you give me what I want in return I promise he will receive it." He handed me the writing implements. I sat down on the floor and wrote in great haste, fearing he would not give me the time to do it justice.

My dearest friend,

I write this in hopes that it is not done in vain. I have never forgotten your generous offer to come to Paris if things in London became too difficult. I arrived just over a month ago and have yet to find you. I find myself in terrible trouble here in Paris with hope diminishing every day. Your kindness of the past has done more for me than all of the malice and darkness of my enemies.

Mr. Ladue, whom I believe you are acquainted with, has taken upon himself to lock me away in the Bicêtre. He does not believe that I came here to Paris at your invitation and has refused to contact you for confirmation. It is inside this hell where I sit and write this letter.

I must ask you a favor. If you are still a part of my life as I hope you are, can you oblige me with a visit to the commissaire to convince him of my story so that he will release me from this hell?

I anxiously await your arrival. Until then, my dear friend, I commend myself to you.

Thomas Newton

I folded the letter and handed it back to Mr. Delacroix. "Please…"

"Remove your undergarment."

I did not question, nor did I beg. I knew what he wanted, and I was willing to give it to him for my freedom. I unclasped my torn and dirty linen. As I stepped out of them, Mr. Delacroix began to remove his own clothes. I could not help but be drawn to his handsome and dark features. My prick came to life of its own accord as we exposed our bodies to one another.

His chest, which was covered in a thick mat of blond curly hair, rose and fell against his heavy, excited breaths. I could see even in the dim light of oil lamps that his tits were erect with excitement. The tiny hard nubs poked through the thick moss across his chest. I knew in part that I was not supposed to be enjoying this interplay, but I could not stop myself from being swept away by the anticipation of a fuck.

"Walk to the back wall and turn away from me." He paused. "No, the other side." He righted my direction. "Near where your friend sleeps in the next cell."

I walked over and faced the wall as directed. I heard the lock disengage, then the gate opened and closed. The cold, sharp sound of iron striking iron echoed through the chilled air. I closed my eyes listening to the sounds of his footsteps as he approached me. With each step that brought him closer to me, my anticipation and need grew. An unexpected moan of pleasure escaped my lips when I felt his prick brush against my buttocks as he took his position behind me. He leaned into me and raised my arm high above my head and clasped my wrist into a metal band, securing me to the wall. He repeated the process with my other hand.

"Now let me see what you have to offer." He spread my buttocks. The chill of the air touched my tight, wrinkled hole, causing it to quiver. Mr. Delacroix inhaled, causing his breath to whistle. He blew against my ass as his fingers poked and prodded me. "You like having your ass played with?" I nodded. "Speak to me, you piece of shit!"

"Yes, yes, I like it," I whispered, not wanting to wake Francois to my having sold myself in such trade for the purpose of saving myself. I heard Mr. Delacroix spit. His fingers dampened my ass. I waited for his insertion as he pulled on his own prick. I braced myself, gripping the metal chains of my bindings, knowing that his insertion would be quick and forceful. I was not prepared to handle the full length and girth of his trunk at once. A scream escaped from my throat. I choked on my own breath as he plunged himself into me.

"That is a mighty fine hole in which to lay oneself." He moaned. He wiggled his hips and settled into me. "You are a much better fuck than my poor ragged wife." He chortled as he leaned against me, pressing me against the cold, damp, moss-covered walls. With short, sharp thrusts of his hips, he burrowed himself farther into me until I felt as if the tip of his prick would spill out of my mouth. "Are you ready to be fucked like the whore you are?"

"Yes, fuck me. Use me like the ravaged cunt you want me to be." I groaned as I felt the thick trunk of his prick retreat from the depths of my ass. My words seemed to be the invitation he was looking for, for within a few moments, he had me in such a delirious state of pain and desire that I thought I might faint. "Oh, yes, that it is. Fuck me harder." I knew from the moment I met Mr. Delacroix what type of man he was. He was no different from the men of London who desired a man's body but were fearful to let it be known. I felt his prick softening and worried that if I did not keep him going, my only chance to be free from this place would be lost. I gave him what he and other men of his nature wanted—a verbal compliment. "Oh you are such an abusive man," I cried. "Yes, give me that handsome prick. Use me like the fucking whore that I am." My calls of affirmation of his manliness worked as it always had. His need, desire, and prick swelled with pride. He gripped my shoulders and fucked the hell out of me.

"Tell me how good I am, bitch!"

"Oh, you are such a beast with that mighty prick." I shoved my ass toward him, offering a better view. "You are a master at using a whore's body. Yes, yes. Fuck me harder." I groaned and panted and soon realized that my words of affirmation had stirred my own need. Without warning or any coaxing on my part, I felt the familiar burn within my belly. I looked down as my prick, swollen with untouched need, began to spout thick ropes of white pearls from its gaping slit. It bobbed up and down as Mr. Delacroix's substantial prick abused me, milking me from the inside out. Another spasm raced through my body. I sprayed my seed over the walls, my legs, and my feet.

"Do not think just because you have released yourself that we are near complete." He groaned in my ear. He reached in front of me and pulled on my softening prick, bringing it back to full stiffness. "It is time for some real fucking."

He leaned back off me and gripped my waist as his pace grew to unbelievable strides. I began to shiver as the heat of our activities brought perspiration to the surface, covering our bodies in a thin, cold sheen. I began to feel sick as the abuse of my body grew to even more painful motions. Unable to withstand the weight of my own body, my legs quivered and buckled. They gave out. I screamed in pain as I fell, forcing my arms and shoulders to support the weight of my body that hung from the wall. I bit my lip to offset the pain in my arms.

"Yes, yes, that is it." He groaned as he thrust himself inside me one final time. He held our bodies together as he unloaded himself into me. His seed raised such a fever in me that I could not help but expel another quantity of my own.

"Oh yes, that was a good fuck." He slapped my ass and let go of my hips, sending me falling against the wall as his prick dislodged itself from me with a wet, hollow sound. I hung against the wall, fading in and out as my head swam with dizziness.

"Not bad for a man," Mr. Delacroix spat as he unlocked my wrists and let me fall to the floor.

"Please, what about Mr. Baptiste?"

"I shall deliver your note as promised," he said as he began to dress. Without additional conversation he bent down and tossed me my linen. I heard the cell door open, then close. His footsteps faded away in the darkness.

"Thomas, what have you done?"

"Leave me alone, Francois. I did what I had to do."

"No, not the fuck. Did I hear that you requested the presence of Mr. Baptiste?"

"Yes, what about it?" I turned to look at him.

"Did you not learn anything from my story? How could you bring that man here?"

"I do not understand what you are going on about."

"Pierre Baptiste. He was the man the woman hired. He was the one who stopped at nothing until the Marquis Chaveau was burned alive."

CHAPTER FIVE

F rancois?"

"I do not wish to speak to you, Thomas." Francois's frail voice drifted through the darkness. "We have said what needs to be said, let us leave it at that."

"I cannot accept that. We have not spoken in forty-three days." I tried to stand, using the wall to support my ever-weakening legs. The strength of a man of my age should not have failed me. It did due to the illness that had settled into my body. I slid down the wall falling into a puddle of my own piss. I looked through the dim light toward Francois's cell for any signs of movement, crawled toward the opening, and peered into his cell. I took in a breath and choked on the contaminated air, which burned my throat and chest. I packed my pipe with tobacco and lit it, hoping it would conceal the foul taste that came with every breath. As I took a draw on my pipe, I noticed Francois crawling in my direction. Despite his haggard appearance, I could not help but smile as he came into my view. "I have missed that handsome face."

"Given our circumstances, I know that to be a lie. I feel as if I have lost twenty years of my life in the last few months." He looked up at me, his face void of emotion. "Why are you counting days? Have you not realized that being ignorant of such things is more of a blessing than the knowledge it brings?"

"It helps me pass the time and gives me a sense of purpose to my otherwise pointless existence in here. But I did not beckon you to discuss my keeping watch on the days. I want to apologize for the way I acted toward you."

"Then you believe me?"

"It is not about believing. You must understand that the Pierre I know would not do those things. He was a magnificent lover, warm, passionate."

"The two of you fucked?" His voice raised in shock.

"Yes, numerous times during that one night together. That is why I cannot accept the fact that he condemned a man to death for the same activities that he engaged in with me."

"Men do things for a variety of reasons, especially when they feel challenged. You should know that as well as I." He touched my fingers, which curled around the iron bar. "My apologies I should not assume such things."

"You have no reason to apologize. You are correct. I have bedded hundreds of men in the short time I lived in London. Some of them turned upon me the moment it suited them to do so." Images of John Darwin and Thomas Wright came together in my mind. They haunted my memories, as if my own past was not enough to do the job. I shook my head and laughed with disbelief.

"What is so funny?"

"Fate, my friend, is what I am laughing at. Here I sit sounding righteous and talking shit about the men who have hurt me, while many of the hundreds of men that I fucked, if still alive, would talk the same shit about me."

"I cannot imagine such lies."

"If only they were fables. The men who hired me for sexual pleasure went to their deaths because of me."

"Surely you are speaking figuratively."

"No, I am sad to say that I am not. In order to save my own life and that of the women who opened her arms and home to me, I testified against every man who ever bedded me. I was the witness for the trials that the Society for the Reformation of Manners initiated. It was the words that spilt from my tongue that sealed their conviction of guilt and sentenced them to die, and while I stood in testament at the Old Bailey Courthouse, Mother Clap lay in a cell in Newgate Prison unaware that I was sending her lifelong friends to their death." I looked around at my surroundings. "And here I have been wondering what I have done to deserve this." I laughed. "All I had to do was to look in a mirror for the answer."

"Self-pity does not suit you, Thomas." He looked upon me with scrutinizing eyes. "I guess I should thank you for your honesty, for I have learned the kind of man you are behind the mask of victim you play with expertise." His tone was cold and uncaring. "And to think I was thinking you a good man. It appears I am not well equipped to choose among men of respectable character—first the Marquis Chaveau and now you."

"Francois, please, you are speaking much too early about things you do not understand. I spoke those words to you as an act of faith in our friendship so that you would know why I am hesitant to think of Pierre in those terms." I reached through the gate and touched his cheek. He recoiled as if disgusted by my touch.

"You reacted that way because you are just like him. You take what you want and do as you please without regard for others."

"You have no right to sit there and condemn me for things you do not understand. It is true that I chose a path that would have been best left untouched, but all men make mistakes, and if you do not believe that, then you are a childish fool with no understanding of the society in which we live." My voice trembled with anger, an emotion my weakened body did not need, but I could no longer control the emotions Francois always ignited in me. "You sit there preaching to me about being a good and trustworthy man, but you sit in the same condemned condition for no less an indiscretion as I. If what you say is true, then you would not be here at this moment to speak to me as if I am common street trash."

"Now the truth—"

"You have done nothing with your life." I cut him off, not wanting to hear him spew false accusations at me. "You have lived off the royal wealth of the marquis, and that is all you have to show for your miserable existence. Does it make you feel better about your own pathetic life to condemn others?" He opened his mouth as if to speak, but I did not give him the chance. I continued my verbal attack. "At least I set out on my own and made my own way, and even though I find myself in these uncertain times, I am still fighting for myself." I coughed up thick, heavy mucus, spat to clear my mouth of the foul taste that came with it. "And will continue to do so until I take my last breath, for I do not lie still for anyone, and I feel sorry for anyone who chooses to stand in my way. So yes, I have tried to send word to Mr. Baptiste and even if he is the man you say he is, I shall still take his assistance in gaining my freedom. That is the sign of a true man." Through the dim light, I saw tears filling his eyes. I doubted at that moment if anyone had spoken to him with such brutal honesty. I wanted to weaken, to say that I was sorry for my hurtful words. I wanted to hold him, to rock him, and to comfort him. I turned my back toward him instead, and crawled over to my pile of damp and rotting straw.

As I lay there with my eyes closed, trying to ease the various aches that had set up home within my body, I heard the soft whimpers of Francois drifting out of the darkness.

"Stop your infernal crying," a gruff voice shouted from a location that I could not determine. "Listen, boys, we have a cunny in our midst." Laughter erupted among the other inmates.

"Pretty boy, pretty boy, do you wish to play?" Another voice broke through the chuckles. "I have a large basket of goodies with which you can lay." The laughter grew as others took turns tormenting Francois for his youthful innocence.

Even with my anger toward Francois, I knew he did not deserve the attacks from the other inmates. I pushed myself up on my arms, trying to gain the strength I needed to shout over the increasing commotion in order to quiet their abuse. As I took a breath, my stomach knotted. I fell over from the pain. My body broke out in perspiration and a chill. The pain increased as if someone had stuck a blade into my belly. I felt my ass spasm. My stomach groaned. I tried to right myself to remove what little remained of my undergarment, but I did not make it in time. I collapsed on the cold, damp floor as a foul-smelling liquid shot from my ass. I lay shivering, weak, and covered in my own shit.

"Mr. Newton." A voice faded in and out of my delirious mind. "Mr. Newton?" The voice, now closer than before, was recognized somewhere within my mind. "Fucking hell, you stink."

"Leave me alone, Mr. Delacroix. I am sure you can agree that I am not fit to fuck any longer." I raised my head off the floor and looked upon the man who had taken so much from me and offered me nothing in return.

"I thought you would like to be informed that I just received word that your note was hand-delivered to Mr. Baptiste." He knelt down beside me. "I am telling you this so that you will know that I am, among many things, a man of my word."

"He is coming?" The thought of Pierre knowing of my plight gave me a moment of reprieve from the discomfort that invaded my body. I raised myself on my elbow and fought against the swimming in my head.

"My messenger did not wait for a response."

"No, of course not. Thank you for what you have done. I know your actions went against the commands of Mr. Ladue, and for that I am most appreciative."

"I am glad you feel so grateful. I was expecting a fuck for my strenuous efforts, but I can see that you are not in any condition to give me your ass."

"I am not."

"I guess I'll have to find another place in which to lay my prick." He smiled at me as he grabbed his hefty satchel that I had gotten to know all too well. "Lean up against the wall." He unlaced his breeches. I pulled myself along the floor, knowing there was no use in asking for a reprieve. I was obliged to satisfy him any time he wished regardless of my condition.

I turned and placed my back against the sludge-covered wall. The motion and effort it took to assume his preferred position was too much for my weakened state. The dizziness in my head grew to such a degree that my vision faded in and out. I tried to focus my attention on Mr. Delacroix, who had pulled his breeches down to his ankles. His prick, heavy with its own unstiffened and calmed weight, swayed and slapped against his thighs as he shuffled toward me.

"Get it stiff," he demanded as he tried to straddle me with his breeches about his ankles. "Fuck," he groaned as he regained his footing.

"Let me." I brought my hands to his raised foot and slipped his shoe off. The damp leather scent of his foot nearly brought a rise from my own uninterested prick. I pulled the leg of his breeches down over his foot so that he could get at me. There were no words of thanks. He stood silent with his hands against the wall to lean his body over mine. I took his prick, which he had yet to let me touch. It felt warm and alive against my cold fingers.

"Yeah, that is the way. Get that big prick ready to fuck." He groaned, then spat into my palm.

I pushed back the thick folds of skin and rubbed the swelling tip of his prick into my palm. His body shivered. His voice cracked with another gasp of pleasure. His prick spat a good quantity of early release onto my lips. I licked it off. It took both my hands to work his prick hard. Within a few moments his prick and my hands were wet with his early release. I closed my eyes to his body and listened to the wet sounds of working him off.

"You are as expert with your hands as you are with your mouth and ass, Mr. Newton." He looked down at me as I pulled the skin over the tip and let my tongue explore the cracks and crevices that filled with his excitement. "Oh, you are a devilish man!" He slipped his hand under his blouse and pulled on his nipples. His body shivered. His prick spat more of its moisture onto my tongue. "Yes, that is it. Pull on my satchel. Harder, yes, that is it. Oh, yes, make them hurt."

I milked his prick with my left hand and squeezed his furry satchel with the other, pulling, tugging, and twisting it until it was red from my abuse. He squirmed and shook in a fit of convulsions that I thought would surely be his undoing and yet he continued to beg for more.

Over Mr. Delacroix's moans, I began to hear the faint murmurs and wet smacking of something off to my left. I took my attention away from Mr. Delacroix's prick and realized Francois was getting himself off on my intimate activities with Mr. Delacroix. Mr. Delacroix must have noticed my attention or heard the moans himself, for it sent him ever closer to his final release.

"Oh, yes, Mr. Newton, that is the way I like my prick satisfied. Yes, open your mouth and tongue that slit." He whispered to keep his sexual activities unknown to the other inmates. His body tensed as he emptied a full satchel of his pearl-white seed onto my tongue. Even in my sickened state, I could no longer control my own urge. As the second expulsion of seed left his prick, I swallowed its full length and let him release a final time deep within my throat.

I raised my hands to his buttocks and pulled him farther into me. My nose was soon lost in a tight moss of damp blond hair. I inhaled his odor, taking in the scent of our sex. I squeezed the muscles in my throat and milked the last of his release from the folds of skin, which dangled in my throat. He quivered against me as he let out a final sigh of relief before pulling his prick from my mouth.

"You, Mr. Newton, are quite the seducer. I cannot seem to get enough of you." He stepped to the side and slipped his legs back into his breeches. He bounced a few times, pulling them up, knelt down beside me, and slipped his hand into his coat pocket. "I should not be doing this, but I took this from the supplies." He handed me a small bottle. "You should take some immediately before your condition worsens."

"What is it?"

"I do not know the ingredients, but it should help with your illness," he whispered. "I must go." He stood and scuffled down the hallway. I sat and listened for the far door to close before crawling over to the wall. A small trickle of water ran over the surface of the stone and moss. I had not dared drink from it before for fear of it being contaminated, but I placed the medicine on my tongue, then held my mouth to the stones sucking as much moisture from them as I could. The cool water soothed my sore, rough throat. I no longer worried about the condition of the water; if it was indeed soiled, then my death would come sooner and relieve me of my pain. I laid my head on the floor, closed my eyes, and fell into a deep sleep.

I awoke to a commotion coming out of the darkness. The main door slammed shut, shaking the dreams from my waking mind. I curled into a tight ball to help ease the damp chill that had taken over my body. The voices grew louder, but in my sickened state I could not determine the topic, nor place names to the voices.

"Thomas, Thomas are you in here?" a voice shouted.

"Sir, you cannot just make your way into this hospital," another voice responded.

"Unhand me, you fucking bastard! Thomas, it is Pierre. Where are you?"

"Pierre?" I called out, though I feared my weak voice would not be heard over the growing discontent of the other inmates. I wanted to believe Pierre had found me, that this nightmare would soon be over, but I feared my hopes were fantastical illusions brought about by my ever-weakening mind.

"Thomas, my God, is that you?" the familiar voice questioned. I heard the cell door rattle against its own locks. "Get this fucking door open at once!"

"But, sir, I cannot let you in without the direct order of Mr. Ladue."

"If you do not open this door at once, you will not live long enough to get Mr. Ladue's approval."

"Pierre, is that really you?" I tried to raise my head and look toward the sound of his voice. "Pierre? Please do not let this be a dream."

"It is not a dream, Thomas. I am here." I heard the cell door open, and before my mind could think a clear thought I was wrapped up in Pierre's arms. "Oh, my beloved. What have they done to you?" he whispered in my ear.

"Pierre…I do not…" The emotions swelled inside me, cutting off any ability to speak. My body shook as I tried to hold back the tears. The emotions won out. I gave into the uncontrollable sobs of grief and joy, frantically grabbed hold of his waistcoat, and pulled myself closer to him. He rocked me as I wept against his shoulder.

"It is going to be all right, Thomas. I am here now." He kissed the top of my head as his voice and gentle sway of our bodies soothed my mind and body. "Hang on to my neck. I am going to get you out of here. Are you ready?"

"Pierre." My voice was barely audible. He leaned in closer to me. "I am ashamed to admit this, but I am covered in my own filth. Perhaps I could walk so you will not have to soil yourself."

"I do not care about that, Thomas. You are too weak at the moment to walk. Spending what little strength you have will worsen your health." He shifted me in his arms. "Are you ready?"

"Yes." I sobbed into his neck as he lifted me up.

"My God, you weigh nothing at all. Why this treatment of you?"

I shook my head in response. He tightened his arms about me. I never thought I would feel such security again. "Thank you for coming, Pierre."

"You do not have to thank me. Why did you not send word sooner?" As we walked toward the cell door, I looked into the darkness and saw Francois staring back at me.

"Mr. Ladue promised to do so, but he never did."

We stopped just outside the cell. He leaned his head back to look at me.

"Mr. Ladue knew of our acquaintance, and this is how he treated you?" He pulled me back into a tight embrace. "Mr. Delacroix, I want you to accompany us to police headquarters."

"That will not be necessary sir, Mr. Ladue has some unfinished business at the hospital."

"Even better. Take me to him. He has to answer to me now."

"Yes, sir." Mr. Delacroix led us through the endless labyrinth of corridors. "I did everything I could to ensure that Mr. Newton had at least some comforts. I let him keep his undergarment and gave him some medicine for his ailment."

"Stop your pathetic reasoning, Mr. Delacroix. By the look of Thomas's condition, you failed miserably at your intentions."

"Pierre, no." I spoke so that Mr. Delacroix could hear my defense. "He was the one who had my note delivered to you. Without him…" The motion of being carried churned my stomach. I closed my mouth, hoping to keep what little was in my stomach from coming up. I swallowed the bitter liquid that had seeped into my mouth.

"My apologies, Mr. Delacroix, I did not know."

"You could not have known, Mr. Baptiste." He paused. "Mr. Ladue is down the hall, last room on your left." As he turned to leave he looked at me. I caught his eyes and the fear they held. "I shall retrieve Mr. Newton's clothing so that he may get out of that tattered undergarment and into something more suitable."

"Thank you, Mr. Delacroix. It might be easier on you if you were to remain in the hallway while I speak to Mr. Ladue." I could feel Pierre's heart pounding in his chest. His breaths became heavier as we stood outside the office. He knocked on the door.

"I am not to be disturbed," Mr. Ladue shouted from the enclosed office.

"Hold on, Thomas," Pierre whispered as he held me tighter. He raised his leg and, with a force much greater than I anticipated, kicked at the door. The wooden frame splintered at the latch and smashed against the inside wall. The vibrations of Pierre's kick sent waves of pain rushing through my body.

"Son of a bitch!" Mr. Ladue jumped out of his chair with a look of shock and anger on his face.

"You shall make time for me, Mr. Ladue." Pierre walked in without waiting and laid me down on the couch. "I want answers!" He moved toward Mr. Ladue's desk.

"How did you…What in the hell is this all about?" Mr. Ladue took several steps backward.

"How I came to know of this is not the question at hand. I want to know why you did not contact me about Thomas Newton, when he made it painfully clear to you that he was here on my personal invitation."

"Mr. Baptiste, I am sorry. Mr. Newton…I thought he was like all the others." Mr. Ladue pulled on the edges of his waistcoat and came around the desk. "How was I to know that he spoke the truth?"

"Mr. Newton begged you to contact me. Instead, you locked him up and forgot about him as if he were one of your filthy inmates."

"But I have witnesses that…"

"I do not care whom you have in your employ for your questionable tactics. Do you have any idea…?" Pierre looked at me, then back toward Mr. Ladue. "Mr. Delacroix!"

"Yes, Mr. Baptiste, I do," Mr. Ladue responded as Mr. Delacroix came into the room.

"Stay with Mr. Newton for a few moments and attend to his needs. Mr. Ladue and I are going to have a conversation in the other room." Pierre took hold of Mr. Ladue's arm and pulled him into the adjoining room. He looked like a father getting ready to scold or punish a son.

"I have brought your clothes." Mr. Delacroix broke the silence of the room. His entire body shook with nerves. Perspiration broke out across his brow. His glances at me were quick and uneasy. "Here, let me assist you." Mr. Delacroix helped me dress in the dirty rags that were my sole wardrobe. Even the worn material warmed my chilled body. "Is there anything else I can get for you?"

"I noticed that Mr. Ladue has a bottle of gin on his desk. If it is not too much trouble, I would love a small drink." I smiled at him hoping to ease the tension between us.

"Of course," he replied without looking at me. His eyes were affixed to the door leading to the other room.

"You look troubled. I hope you are not worried that I might talk of our activities." I took the glass that he handed me. "Under other circumstances, it would have been quite enjoyable." I took a sip of the stout liquor.

"No." He shook his head as he turned toward me. "I am sorry. I appreciate your discretion, of course. My immediate concern comes from what is being discussed behind those doors." He nodded in the direction of Mr. Ladue and Pierre. "Nothing good can come of it."

"I am sure they are addressing the issues of my release." I tilted the glass and finished off the last of the gin.

"I would wager that they are discussing more than that, Mr. Newton." He knelt down beside me. "How well do you know Mr. Baptiste?"

"Why is everyone so interested in my involvement with him?" Mr. Delacroix looked at the floor between our feet. "What is it that everyone thinks I should know? Please, Mr. Delacroix."

"I do not—" Mr. Delacroix began, but before he could continue, the door to the adjoining room opened. Mr. Delacroix stood with a shy, stunted smile. He took the empty glass from me as Mr. Ladue and Pierre came toward us.

"Mr. Newton, how are you feeling?" Mr. Ladue stood over me, his hands clasped behind his back. He smiled, though anyone with a smidge of intelligence could see the insincerity in his expression.

"I am surprised you care enough to inquire," I responded with as much vigor as I could manage.

"I suppose I deserve your bitter tongue." He walked toward his desk, picked up the bottle of gin, added more to the glass that Mr. Delacroix held, and offered it to me. "It is from my private stock."

"Thank you." I pulled myself up to a sitting position. I looked at

Mr. Ladue, then at Pierre, who stood motionless with a stern expression etched into his face.

"I would like to offer you my sincere apology, Mr. Newton, for what you have suffered here at the Bicêtre." Mr. Ladue glanced at Pierre as if making sure his words were satisfying some secret agreement. He turned his attention back to me as he continued. "You must understand where I was coming from. In my position, one does not find many trustworthy men. Most are vicious criminals who would turn in their brother or sister to save their own ass. That is why I did not take your claim of knowing Mr. Baptiste seriously. One does not come across such an unusual pairing that often."

"What about your witness, Mr. Bergenoir?" I questioned.

"After discussing the situation with Mr. Baptiste, I have determined that his story was fabricated. I will be questioning him about it in the coming days to determine how far his lies reach. Please understand, Mr. Newton, that I am only trying to protect the fine men and women of Paris."

"I am grateful for this new outlook toward me, but I have to question why the sudden change? Pierre, what did you say to him?"

"Does it really matter, Thomas? I thought you would be delighted to get out of here."

"Then I am being released?"

"Of course. Mr. Ladue is releasing you of all charges. He is also placing you in my care. Once you have recovered and are able to do so, I have promised Mr. Ladue to see you safely back to London."

"I am being exiled?"

"Unfortunately, I do not have a choice in the matter." Mr. Ladue interrupted. "The record of your time here has been recorded, and I must vouch for each and every entry. I cannot set the precedent of releasing an inmate without sending him back to his homeland. It is just not possible."

"But I cannot go back to London." I looked at Pierre.

"Thomas, please, you must trust me." Pierre sat down next to me. "Nothing is going to happen to you as long as you are in my custody."

"Custody?"

"Thomas, please. It is just a figure of speech. You trust me, do you not?"

"Yes." I spoke without hesitation, though the words of Francois and Mr. Delacroix still spooked my mind.

"Again, Mr. Newton, you have my sincere apologies for your treatment here. Before Mr. Baptiste takes you home, is there anything else I can do for you?"

I looked up at Mr. Ladue with a cautious eye, wondering why the sudden change in his attitude toward me. It was then that Francois entered my mind. I wondered if he knew I was going to be released—perhaps he did not care after the way I had spoken to him. Both of our tongues were coated with venom, and while I believed we both spoke the truth as far as we knew it, I could not do to him what my tongue and actions had done to so many other men back in London. I had to try to save Francois, even if he did not want to be indebted to Pierre's obvious influence over Mr. Ladue.

"Thomas?"

"Yes, as a matter of fact." I looked at the three men who gathered about me. I tried to stand. Pierre stood and wrapped his arm about me to support my weak legs. I looked at Mr. Ladue with conviction and determination.

"Please, anything you want. It is the least I can do."

"Francois's freedom."

"I beg your pardon?" He scoffed. I watched as Mr. Ladue and Pierre glanced at one another. "You cannot be serious?" he asked with a chuckle as he turned his attention toward me.

"Oh, but I am most serious about this. You are to release Mr. Regnault into Pierre's custody immediately." If Pierre had as much power as I thought he had, I was going to use it to my full advantage.

CHAPTER SIX

This request is out of the question. It is preposterous to even contemplate such a thing, let alone carry it out."

"Pierre, please, I know it is a lot to ask, but there is good in him. He saved my life."

"He what?" Pierre and Mr. Ladue questioned in unison.

"It is true. He saved my life. It was my first night here. You should remember that night, Mr. Ladue, or has your mind suddenly become soft?" I coughed as my labored breath hitched in my throat. "I was thrown into the cell with a group of men. They came upon me, shackled to the floor, trying to get at my body. They meant to fuck the life out of me, and I mean that quite literally. If it were not for Francois's actions, my life would have ended that very night." I wanted to speak of Francois's involvement with the Marquis Chaveau, to test Pierre's commitment to me or his own agenda, but feared that my knowledge of those events might bring about unwanted repercussions. I held my tongue, knowing that it was neither the time nor the place to begin searching for answers to the questions that continued to weigh upon my weary and troubled mind.

"Mr. Ladue." Pierre's tone was emotionless. "With this new knowledge, I am requesting that you do as Thomas has instructed and release Mr. Regnault." Pierre looked at me and smiled. I stood speechless with the knowledge that Pierre was once again taking my side. The feeling of triumph did not last long as I felt the eyes of Mr. Ladue burn me with his anger.

"Fuck." Mr. Ladue spat. "Mr. Delacroix, fetch Mr. Regnault. I shall get the release papers." Mr. Ladue stopped at the door and turned around. "Mr. Baptiste, I hope you know what you are getting yourself into. I would hate to think of things going astray at this point."

"I appreciate your concern, but it is unnecessary. I know exactly what I am doing." He turned to me. "Thomas, please sit down. It shall be a little longer while they process the necessary papers." He hesitated. "Are you sure this is what you want?"

"If you are asking me if I want Francois over you, I do not." I took his hand. "I have done a lot of things since we last met that I am not proud of, Pierre…"

"We do not need to have these conversations now. Let us get you home and back to good health. We can talk once you're back on your feet."

"As for Francois," I continued against his wishes, "leaving an innocent young man in the Bicêtre is not a regret I wish to have. No one deserves the treatment and deplorable living conditions of this place. I do not care what he has done—no one should suffer this way." My emotions were rattled. Tears filled my eyes and trickled down my face.

"Mon amour," he whispered. "I hope never to see you in this condition again. You are safe with me, I promise you that."

"Thank you, Pierre, for all of this. I do not wish to contemplate my fate if you had not answered my note." I looked down at the floor and wiggled my toes to help them regain their feeling. They were dirty and covered in sludge. "I would like to know how you managed to get me released, but I suppose that information can wait for another time as well."

"It can. Your safety and love are all that matter to me."

"I suppose I should tell you about Mother."

"I know, Thomas. I wanted to wait until you were feeling better to tell you how sorry I was to hear the news of her death." He wiped a tear from my cheek.

"But how could you have known?"

"It does not matter, *mon amour.*" He smiled. "She loved you very much. Even in the short time that I knew her, I could see the love when she spoke your name or looked at you. You were her pride and joy."

"I miss her." I choked on another wave of tears. "I cannot begin to count the times that I have wondered if life is worth living without her. I've been lost ever since she took her last breath. I cannot find my own way without her guidance." I looked up at him through tear-filled eyes. "Please, Pierre, given what transpired in London, I need to know how you heard about her death. Did word of my actions in London travel this far? Is that why Mr. Ladue treated me as he did?"

"My dear, Thomas, I know nothing of the actions that you refer to. After my return from visiting you and Margaret, I received word that I had perhaps left London too early, as trouble with a business arrangement came up within days of my departure. I was called back to London, and while there I went back to the Claps' coffeehouse hoping to see you again. I was told by Mr. Clap of Margaret's death. I inquired about you, but he said he did not know your whereabouts."

"Mr. Clap returned home?"

"I had not realized that he had left."

"He abandoned Mother during her time of need. He chose to save his own reputation over the needs of his wife. I shall never forgive him for that."

"Thomas, Margaret would not want you to hold a grudge against him. People do things for all sorts of reasons. These reasons are sometimes never realized even by the person involved."

"I understand that more than you realize."

"I have just completed the necessary paperwork on both releases." Mr. Ladue came into the room. He looked at our closeness with contempt. "I do hope this is the end of these outrageous requests, Mr. Baptiste."

"It is." Pierre stood.

"In there." Mr. Delacroix's voice carried in from the hallway.

"What is this?" Francois looked at me. "I want nothing to do with that man!" He pointed in Pierre's direction and turned to leave. Mr. Delacroix held him back. "Thomas, I told you he could not be trusted. Are we to face the same torture and death as the Marquis Chaveau?"

"Francois, hold your tongue." I felt Pierre's eyes upon me and looked up at him, hoping to disguise the fact that I knew the marquis's story. I failed. He saw the truth of my knowledge almost at once.

"Mr. Regnault, you should be more respectful to people, especially when they are saving your life." Pierre spoke with authority.

"Save my life?" Francois laughed. "You expect me to believe that?"

"Your knowledge of the events you are referring to are one-sided and jaded because of your intimate relationship with that man. Do not attempt to disgrace my name, or I shall find myself leaving your sorry ass to rot in this hospital."

"Please, Francois. Pierre is here to help us. He has agreed to have us released into his custody. We shall be free from this place."

"And why would this man do me such a favor?"

"He is doing this because I asked him to." I stood up with the agility of a ninety-year-old man. Pierre saw my efforts and reached out his hand to steady me. "Why must you always look for the bad in others? Can you not just accept that there are people who do not wish you any harm?"

"No, I cannot, I am sorry to say. I have spent my entire life trusting those around me, and not one of them has earned that trust or respect. I am this way because of my treatment by others. Can you look me in the eye and tell me you are doing this out of friendship or honest concern for my well-being and not some twisted act of self-worth to right the wrongs that you have created?"

"You are fucking impossible." My voice cracked. I choked and coughed on my own anger. Pierre held me until the fit passed.

"This is quite touching." Mr. Ladue grabbed Francois's arm. "Am I to assume this piece of shit is going back to his cell?"

"No." I looked at Mr. Ladue.

"Yes. Take me back. I'd rather die alone in my cell than live one moment in this man's custody."

"Francois, please. I beg of you, do not make this mistake. I want to help you."

"I have managed so far without your assistance, Thomas. Go and leave me alone. I wish never to hear from your treacherous heart again." He turned toward Mr. Delacroix. "Take me back. The air in here is more dangerous to my health than the wretched conditions of my cell." He walked into the hallway without turning back.

"Get me out of here," I demanded of Pierre. "I am tired and need to rest."

"Of course." He looked up at Mr. Ladue. "Are we finished here?"

"Yes, go and please do not come back." Mr. Ladue returned to his desk and took up his pen.

"Shall I carry you?"

"I would like to walk if I can."

"Here, at least let me support you." He placed his arm around me, cupping his hand just under my arm. We took slow, easy steps out of Mr. Ladue's office and down the hallway. As we walked out of the building, the brightness of the sun blinded my vision and sent a sharp dagger of pain through my head. I closed my eyes and turned my head, burying my face against Pierre's chest.

"Is the sun too bright?" He placed his hand over my face, further protecting me from the painful light. "My carriage is right over there. We shall be home soon."

The silence that fell between us was heavy with unspoken questions as Pierre's coachman drove us through the city streets. I stared out the window, watching the streets of Paris and the life of its citizens, and wondered what life would be like if it were not so rutted with trouble and unhappiness. I smiled as the memories of my time with Mother danced around in my head, and closed my eyes to keep the memories alive. A tear rolled down my cheek.

"What is wrong, Thomas?" Pierre placed his hand on my shoulder.

"Nothing, I was remembering a better time...Mother Clap." I said no more. I returned to my solitary thoughts as the city passed us by.

"I cannot imagine what you have been through since arriving in Paris. The Bicêtre is a place no sane man should ever be allowed to witness." He placed his hand on my leg and squeezed it. "Those days are over, Thomas." He paused. "Look at me." He placed his finger under my chin and turned my head. "I want you to know that the promise I made to Margaret on that cold November night is one I intend to keep."

"Why?" I took his hand and kissed the finger that had held my chin. "Do not mistake my question for a lack of gratitude. On the contrary, I owe you my life. Mother Clap," the words stuck in my throat, "is gone. As far as she is concerned, you have fulfilled your promise to her by taking me from the Bicêtre."

"On the surface it might appear that I have fulfilled her wishes, but not everything is always as it appears, *mon amour.*" He paused. "I have a more personal reason for making sure you are safe."

"Pierre, I do wish you would not speak in such riddles. If you have details that I should know, please tell me."

"I am sorry if the words I speak make you uneasy. I do not mean to speak, as you say, in riddles. It is one of the unfortunate results of my trade. I must say, however, that I am surprised that you do not know the reason for my actions."

"Why should that surprise you? I know very little of you." The words escaped my tongue before I could halt them. "Your trade, for example. What is it that you do?"

"My trade requires me to travel a great deal, and while I am sure my response brings more questions than it answers, I do not believe that the details are what you need at this moment. We shall indeed talk, but I do not want to tire you in doing so."

"There are so many questions—" The carriage came to an abrupt stop. The words and my breath caught in my throat. I coughed with a deep raspy breath. I groaned.

"Are you all right?"

"Every cough feels like it is tearing at my chest." The coughing returned as I finished my words. Perspiration broke out upon my brow as every breath brought about more fits and discomfort.

"Oh, *mon amour*." He kissed my forehead. He used the ruffles of his sleeve to blot the perspiration from my skin. "We are home now. Let me come around and carry you into the house." He eased me back against the seat. I took slow, shallow breaths, hoping to avoid further fits. As I stared out the window, I noticed an elderly woman peering out of the window in the flat next to Pierre's. It was the same woman to whom I spoke on my first visit to Pierre's home. She pulled the curtain shut as she caught my gaze. Her shadow against the thin fabric told me that she was still watching.

"Pierre, that woman, your neighbor, she is watching." I nodded toward the window as Pierre opened the carriage door.

"As she should." He slipped one arm behind my back and the other under my legs. "Do not worry, Thomas, she is harmless." He lifted me from the seat and adjusted my weight in his arms as he called to his driver. "Mr. Sheppard, please shut the doors and take the carriage away. We shall not be needing it for the remainder of the day."

"*Oui, monsieur.*" Mr. Sheppard stepped down and moved about the carriage.

"Let us get you inside and into bed, and while you rest I'll have Eleanor prepare dinner."

"Eleanor?"

"Yes, the woman in the window. She is my maidservant. She has been with me for more years than I care to say, and before that she was my father's. She's been with the family for about thirty-five years. She was with my family before I was born."

To hear Pierre speak of his family struck me with an odd sense of comfort. I began to think that perhaps my apprehension over his privacy and my lack of knowledge of him were no more warranted than my time in the Bicêtre. The door opened up as we approached. Eleanor stood cautiously on the other side. She smiled and nodded at Pierre; I, on the other hand, received quite a different welcome.

"You." She hissed and pointed a crooked finger in my direction. "What is he doing here, sir?"

"Eleanor!" Pierre scolded. "I shall ask that you watch your manners."

"I beg your pardon, sir. I mean you no disrespect, but this young ruffian—"

"His name is Thomas Newton, and that is what you shall call him."

"But he was here many months ago, nosing around and asking questions. I sent him away with good cause. He is back, and in your arms."

"That is quite enough, Eleanor." Pierre adjusted his arm under my legs. "I will not have you speaking this way about Thomas. He is my guest, and as long as he remains here you will treat him with the same respect and urgency as you have served me. Is that understood?"

"Yes, sir." She bowed her head. "My apologies, Mr. Newton." She glanced up at me. "I am sorry for my ill temper and sharp tongue. It is just that I have served Mr. Baptiste and his father before that for many years. I was only trying to protect—"

"That is enough, Eleanor. Thomas is ill and needs his rest. Prepare dinner for two tonight, and all nights hereafter." Pierre walked away, leaving Eleanor standing alone in the parlor.

"What did she mean by protect?" I questioned as Pierre carried me up a staircase set against the wall in the back of the house.

"She gets a bit anxious when a stranger is around. She is just overcautious and tends to see her role as a protector of my house instead of my maidservant. I shall have another talk with her if you wish."

"No, please do not make more of it than it is."

"I want you to tell me if she says or does anything to make you uneasy. She may act like family, but she is still just a servant." He pushed a door with the toe of his shoe and walked into one of the largest bedchambers I had ever seen.

Dark wooden tables were placed on either side of a bed that was large enough to hold five men. Tapestries in vibrant colors draped the walls. A bowed window with a sitting bench overlooked the street below. Even with all the other furniture and decorations, it was possible to entertain a dozen or more men.

"I take it by the look on your face that you approve?"

"I cannot imagine anyone who would not approve of these living conditions. Even my father's home cannot compare to this."

"I have never heard you speak of your father, or for that matter, anyone in your family." He laid me down upon the bed.

"Oh, Lord, this bed feels good. It has been so long since I have slept on anything but stone and straw, I had forgotten what comfort is." I looked up at him as he sat on the edge of the bed. He had a most curious look upon his face. "The story of my upbringing is not a pleasant one, and therefore, I do not speak of it." I paused. "Mother Clap was the only one I ever spoke to about it."

"I hope one day soon that you will feel as comfortable with me as you did with her. I would be most interested in your story." Pierre slipped my shoes off my feet.

"What in my background could interest you?"

"A man's character is formed by his upbringing. Knowing yours would fill in the gaps, so to speak."

"If that is the case, then I am doomed." I forced a smile.

"As long as you are with me, you shall be fine. Do not worry about a thing, your time here is for rest."

"What about the exile order?"

"You are not going anywhere until you are well enough to travel." He rolled my torn stockings down my legs, bundled them up, then slipped them inside my shoes. "I would imagine that the sea air would aggravate your current ailment." He unlaced my knee breeches and pulled them down.

"What if Mr. Ladue finds out?" His touch brought gooseflesh to my overheated skin. My lazy prick stirred.

"Thomas, you are not to worry about a thing. I shall take care of Mr. Ladue." He paused and placed his hands upon his hips. A smile grew on his face. "I have missed that hearty prick of yours." He chuckled as he swept a light touch over it.

"Oh, your touch is such sweet delight," I moaned as my prick bobbed against his finger.

"We should not let ourselves get carried away. There will be plenty of time for intimate activities when you are well enough to sustain your energy." He winked at me. "Now, let us get the rest of these rags off you. As soon as you are well enough, we will need to purchase you a new wardrobe for our trip to London."

"Our trip? But I thought…"

"I am not about to send you back to London by yourself. You will need company, and someone to help you through the difficult days there."

"Difficult. What are you not telling me?"

"All I am saying is that being back in London, after…Margaret's death is sure to have its effects on you. I do not want you to face that alone. Let us put our conversation off for another time and get you undressed so that you can rest."

I pulled myself up to a sitting position with Pierre's assistance and allowed him to untie my blouse and pull my arms through. He tossed the soiled silk blouse on top of the other garments. Pierre, with a playful slap, knocked my hands away as I went to unlace his breeches. He smiled and winked, bringing to his cheeks the deepest, most handsome indentions. I had forgotten that aspect of his features until that moment when the memory of our first fuck brought it to the forefront of my mind. I blushed from the vivid thoughts. I reached up and ran my fingers down his face as his fingers slid through the moss of hair that spread out across my chest. His finger grazed my erect tit and brought a glimmer of life into my sick and weary body. I lay back against the mattress as he gathered my clothes in his arms. He looked at me, not just my face, but all of me.

"You are such a beautiful man, *mon amour.*" He came to the edge of the bed. "I want nothing more than to climb upon you and ravish your body." He leaned down and kissed me. "Know that my hesitation in being with you is only temporary, and not for a lack of want; for once you are well I shall take you immediately wherever it is you lie." He stood and walked to the door. "Try to sleep. I shall wake you for supper." He walked out and shut the door.

I glanced around the silent room. The fact that I was inside Pierre's home and within his bedchamber gave me reason to fight the sleep my body was so desperate for. It felt as if I were spying into what I was beginning to believe was a very private life. I wanted to pull myself from the bed and peek in his bureau drawers with the hope of seeing a glimpse of his life. What I wanted to look for I could not have said, perhaps answers to questions he was not ready to reveal. If it were not for the ailment affecting me and a feeling of guilt as my thoughts wandered, I would have pulled the place apart. Instead, I gave into what my body needed. I closed my eyes and fell into a deep sleep.

❖

"Thomas?" A voice called to me from a distant place. "*Mon amour*, wake up."

"Pierre?" My eyes were slow in responding. I blinked as Pierre came into focus. He sat on the other side of the bed, a tray of food at his side. I shifted to lean against the headboard.

"How do you feel?" He leaned down and kissed my forehead.

"Better, I suppose, if for nothing more than a good sleep. My chest feels as if it is weighted down with stones. I'm chilled and yet perspire, and it hurts to breathe." A fit of coughs shook me, and I groaned as the pain broke through my chest. I looked toward the drawn curtain of the window. The sunlight that had drifted in through the window was gone, replaced by the silvery glow of the moon. "How long did I sleep?"

"About nine hours, I believe. Dinner has long since passed. I have brought you some food. Take it easy and do not eat too much. Your stomach needs to adjust to solid food again." He sat down next to me and cut a small piece of meat, picked it up, and brought it to my lips.

The warm, juicy meat filled my mouth with pleasures I had forgotten. Pierre licked his fingers as I chewed, swallowed, and took another piece. My belly grumbled and I felt it knot as it took the food. I swallowed and held my hand to my mouth to warn off any revolt.

"Are you to be ill?"

I shook my head in response. "No, but I think that is all I can do for the moment," I said as the sickness passed.

"We will try some more later." He stood, picked up the tray, then headed for the door.

"Do not leave. Please, lie with me for a while."

"I thought perhaps you might sleep some more." He sat the tray on the bureau and came back to the edge of the bed. He stretched out next to me, wrapped his arm about me, and pulled me to him. I rested my head on his chest. It was while I played with the clasps of his blouse that I realized he was not wearing any undergarments. The gentle movement of his silk blouse billowed the air about me and I could smell his odor. I slipped a finger into the opening between the clasps and ran it through the tangle of hair that lay beneath the material. When I grazed his tit, it rose with my touch.

"How I have missed your touch, *mon amour.*" He kissed the top of my head and pulled me even closer to him.

"And I you." I wanted to thank him, to give him something in return for what he had done for me. I proceeded with what I knew best. I released the other ties of his blouse and pulled it open, exposing the thick moss of hair that covered his body.

I kissed his chest and traced the darker, fuller line of hair that ran down the center of his belly until the band of his breeches blocked my path. Then I brought my head back to his chest so I could suck upon his tit as my fingers made easy work of the laces of his breeches. I slipped my hand beneath his breeches and found his sex stiffening as I drew light circles against the deepest part of his belly. His prick bobbed, spilling its clear nectar in a thick, sticky stream that clung to the thick folds of skin that clothed its bulbous head.

I wrapped my anxious fingers around his prick. Its warmth felt good against my chilled skin. I squeezed his thick trunk, bringing my hand forward to extract more of his excitement onto his belly, then rubbed his prick through the puddle on his belly using his own need to slicken my grip.

Pierre moaned as I fondled and stroked him, trembling against my head as I licked and nibbled his tit. He bent his legs and reached past my hand toward his large, furry satchel. Watching him assist me in his own pleasure brought about a new sensation I had not before experienced. I quickened the motion of my hand, pulling and tugging upon his prick, watching with growing fascination as the head of his prick played an odd game of peek-a-boo with me.

Perspiration broke out against Pierre's body. He moaned and trembled as I pleasured him with my hand. His toes curled as his breathing changed to short, heavy breaths. I pumped him harder and faster, knowing he would not be able to refrain from his release much longer.

His arm tightened about me, and his body took to trembling. In a fit of convulsions he reached his moment. I witnessed the beautiful sight of the first heavy spurt of his seed shooting from his prick. It landed across my face, warming me with its heat. Pierre thrust his hips into the air, pumping his prick within my hand. He continued to release himself, drowning us in his godly bliss. His prick began to soften. His seed lay drying across my face, lips, and the fur of his belly. I licked his still-warm pearls off my lips and ran my tongue through the damp hair, not wanting to waste a drop.

We lay together with only the sounds of our breath to break the silence of the bedchamber. Words were not necessary, for our intimacy, no matter how tame, was all that either of us needed to convey our desire for one another.

I tried to concentrate on the rhythm of Pierre's heart beating, and yet as much as Pierre's embrace comforted me, I could not dispel the uneasy feelings that continued to weigh upon my mind. I had willingly placed my life into the hands of this man, a man who had obvious influence over others and wealth I knew nothing about. The only comfort that I could offer myself was the fact that Mother Clap had seen something genuine in him that cold night long ago, enough so that she had felt comfortable in asking him to protect me. I held on to her strength and wisdom as a sign that my insecurities were just that, mine. It was not long before I heard Pierre's gentle snoring. I closed my eyes and joined him in sleep.

❖

The morning sun woke me with the warm, soft touch of its rays. I stretched and groaned as the muscles of my body responded. I sat up in bed and looked around the room. The discomfort in my chest had eased after the first three weeks under Pierre's care, but Pierre had insisted that I take another week to ensure that I was well enough to travel.

I tossed the covers off, giving up the warmth that they held, and walked toward the window. Pierre came into the bedchamber.

"Good morning, *mon amour*, and Merry Christmas." He came up and wrapped his arms about me. He kissed my neck. "What was so interesting outside my window that you forgot to dress?" He laughed and rubbed my buttocks.

"I was just looking out over the city. I had hoped that Paris would be my new home, but I must leave with only the knowledge of how unwelcome I felt here. Ever since that night you visited Mother Clap's, I dreamt of what life would be like in Paris. It is nothing like what I imagined it to be."

"Few things in life ever are, Thomas. I must say, however, that having your health returned is the best Christmas gift I could have received." He kissed me. "What is wrong?"

"It seems strange to me to think that I am here, free and ready to go back to London, when Francois sits beyond the horizon in the most deplorable conditions."

"You may pay him another visit if you like. We could stop by on our way out of town if you wish. With the time that has passed perhaps you could talk to him, convince him to come with us. I am quite sure I could still get him released." He turned me around to face him.

"I would not ask that of you."

"You did not ask. I offered." He smiled and kissed me. "Now

get dressed. The coachman has packed my belongings and is ready for yours. We shall make one final stop at Bicêtre before leaving for Calais." Pierre pulled various articles of clothing from the bureau as I began to dress.

"How did you do it?" I pulled on my linen undergarment and laced it up.

"Do what, *mon amour*?" He looked up from folding several of my blouses. His smile faltered.

"Convince Mr. Ladue to release me from the hospital." I pulled my silk blouse over my shoulders.

"I know you have many questions." He came to me and placed his hands upon my shoulders. "Is that what is bothering you?" I nodded, as I could not find the words. "I was afraid of that. Unfortunately, my trade requires a certain level of privacy. I am sorry that my lack of explanation has brought trouble upon your mind. I promise we will talk soon, and I shall tell you as much as I can." He walked back to the edge of the bed and continued to fold my clothes. He stopped and looked at me. "Mr. Ladue owes me a great deal for some work I did for him. Your release was part of that debt being repaid."

"Shall we go?" I smiled at him, hoping to reassure him that his brief explanation satisfied me, but the truth was that it left more questions yet unanswered. I tied the last lace of my breeches and walked toward the door.

"Eleanor," Pierre shouted as we walked out of the bedroom.

"Yes, sir." She met us at the foot of the stairs.

"Eleanor, Thomas and I are leaving."

"Very well, sir." She looked at me with a questioning gaze.

"Thank you for your hospitality." I bowed.

"No need for that, Mr. Newton. I was only doing as I was instructed." She looked at Pierre and shook her head. "I shall await word from you." She glanced one last time in my direction and left the room.

The morning sun had warmed the interior of the carriage. I settled into my seat as the carriage took off down the rough, dusty streets. Pierre and I spoke little during our ride through the city, which disheartened me. I wanted nothing more to curl up next to him, to love on him, to hold him, but the secrecy and questions had built a wall between us. I worried that if the walls were not torn down soon, that there would be no hope for us.

The Bicêtre stretched out in front of us, looming over the landscape like some predator from the bowels of hell. Pierre reached over and squeezed my hand.

"I shall come inside with you to make sure there are no problems."

"Thank you, Pierre, for everything. Facing this place alone is not something I wish to do. I realize if you had not come for me I would be dead by now, rotting away in that cell…"

"Remove those thoughts from your mind, *mon amour*." He leaned over and kissed me. "Shall we?" He stepped out of the carriage. I opened my door. He stood with an outstretched hand to assist me and kept his hand upon my shoulder as we made our way into the Bicêtre.

"Fuck." Mr. Ladue looked up at us as we entered the office area without an invitation. "What is it this time?"

"As always, it is a pleasure to see you again." Pierre spoke with a tone of sarcasm. "We shall not be long. I am taking Thomas to Calais for his exile orders, but he wishes to say good-bye to Mr. Regnault before he leaves. Surely you will not object to that?"

"Mr. Delacroix!"

"Yes, sir." He stopped abruptly as he saw me standing in the office. "What…"

"Take Mr. Newton here to see Mr. Regnault."

"Mr. Newton?" He signaled with his arm for me to pass him. "I trust you remember the way?"

"I shall never forget it." We walked down the labyrinth of hallways until we stood once again in front of the large door that led into the cells. Without warning, I broke out into a sweat. My breathing became labored as Mr. Delacroix opened the door and led me into the rancid air of the cells. "I shall only be a moment." I walked down the pathway between cells. The men were too weak to speak, though I could feel their eyes upon me.

"Francois?" I called out to him. "Francois?"

"Thomas?" His weak voice drifted through the heavy air.

"I came to see…" My words failed me as I looked upon the once-healthy man who had saved my life. He was pale in color and had lost most of his weight. His head, dampened with a fever, rested against the cool iron bars. I knelt down in front of him. "Francois, I cannot believe…"

"How awful I must look to you now." He coughed. Blood bubbled in the corners of his mouth. "Freedom appears to agree with you." A crooked smile creased his dry and cracked lips.

"Please, let me take you out of here."

"With Pierre?"

"Yes, he is with Mr. Ladue."

"You should not have come back, Thomas. Perhaps you can put your trust in a murderer, but I cannot."

"Francois, you are being…"

"I am being honest." He grasped the bars and pulled himself to a sitting position. The stench that drifted off his body stole my breath. "I will take nothing from the man who has taken so much from me."

"You are impossible, Francois. I knew I had to try one last time to bring you to reason before I left. I can see that it was a waste of my time." I stood up.

"Last time?"

"Yes, Pierre and I are leaving for London today."

"You are more of a fool than I thought," he spat. "Go, take your leave of this place and never look back."

"For your sake I hope your death is a quick one." I looked down at him. "Good-bye, Francois." I turned and walked down the hallway for the last time.

"Was that it?" Mr. Delacroix asked as I approached him.

"Thomas, please come back." Francois called out to me from the darkness.

"Well?" Mr. Delacroix stood with his hand on the door.

"Let us go. I am done here." As the door closed I could hear Francois's painful pleas.

CHAPTER SEVEN

Thomas?" Pierre looked upon me as I walked into the office. He and Mr. Ladue were laughing and sharing a glass of gin as if no disagreement had ever transpired between them. Pierre came to me.

"We should go. We have a long journey in front of us." My voice sounded distant to my own ears as I tried to console myself with the fact that I had walked out on Francois. His pleas for help would join the choir of other men whose misery I partook in. Their voices would haunt me until my dying day.

"You are noticeably shaken. Take a drink of my gin, it will help settle you." He handed me the cup.

"Thank you." I took what remained in the glass and choked it down. The liquid had an immediate effect upon me. "Mr. Ladue, I know that we have had our differences, but I must ask you a favor, one that you must promise to uphold."

"I will do my best." Mr. Ladue's tone was less than convincing.

"Mr. Ladue, please. Francois is dying. One can see it in his eyes, hear it in his voice, and see it in the blood that he spits when speaking. I beg of you, do not let Francois's body rot in that cell upon his death. When he has taken his last breath, please, if you have any decency in you, bury him in the yard. It need not be a proper funeral, but he deserves better than to have his remains decay like some common vagabond. There once was an innocent boy inside him, a good boy, who through no fault of his own was tainted and made into the man inside that cell."

"Of course." Mr. Ladue stood. "Mr. Delacroix, attend to Mr. Regnault, whatever he needs to ease his suffering."

"We can hold off our journey until after…"

"No, that is not necessary. I have spoken to him and have said my good-byes whether he wished to hear them or not. I want nothing more to do with this city, except to see it sinking into the horizon." I turned toward Mr. Ladue for a final time. "I would appreciate anything you can do for him."

"I shall send word to you."

"That will not be necessary, Mr. Ladue. Good day." I turned and left the office, letting Pierre and Mr. Ladue finish any business that they had.

"Are you ready, *mon amour?*" Pierre wrapped his arm about my shoulder and escorted me to the carriage. "Calais shall be our final stop, Mr. Sheppard."

"Yes, sir." Mr. Sheppard prepared the horses and coach before pulling away. I watched the Bicêtre disappear from my eyes until the only thing that was left of it was what was branded into my memory.

The trip to the port of Calais was not an easy one. I attempted sleep on several occasions, but the rutted paths made for a rough ride, one that allowed for only a few minutes of rest. If it had not been for Pierre's lap, which I used as a pillow, the long journey would have been intolerable. On a few occasions when sleep would not come, I stared out the window, admiring the countryside that only a few months ago I had walked through on my way to what was to be my new life in Paris. I resolved to myself in those quiet moments to find a way to make a life for myself in London. It was that thought that reminded me of the trouble I would be facing if the Society for the Reformation of Manners got wind of my return. The hope of a new life was snuffed out and died like the flame of a candle against a violent wind.

"Thomas, we are here." Pierre brushed the hair off my forehead.

"I do believe that my journey to Paris by foot was easier than by coach." I rubbed my sore buttocks, stepped out of the coach, and raised my arms to stretch. My body resisted. The cool ocean air felt good as I took a deep breath and let the moisture of the air fill my chest. I assisted Mr. Sheppard with the luggage while Pierre checked with the vessel's captain.

"It looks as if we have a wait ahead of us, Thomas."

"How long?"

"They could not give me a time. The winter winds have unfortunately, turned against us. We shall have to wait here until it corrects itself."

"Shall I wait, sir?" Mr. Sheppard questioned.

"That will not be necessary. Thomas and I shall get something to eat, and if the wait is longer then we shall settle in with a bottle of gin."

"Very well, sir."

"Mr. Sheppard."

"Yes, sir."

"The length of my time away is uncertain at this point."

"I understand, sir. I shall await word from you."

"And…"

"Yes, sir. I shall take care of any urgent matters that come up in your absence."

"Thank you, Mr. Sheppard."

"My pleasure, sir." He bowed to Pierre. "Good day, Mr. Newton." He bowed, then without waiting for a response climbed upon the coach and rode away.

"This village has several taverns where we can get something to eat and drink to help pass the time." He paused. "Is something troubling you?"

"Perhaps we should talk over drinks. I want to tell you about what happened after you left London. You may decide to have nothing to do with me once you hear my story."

"I cannot imagine anything so terrible that I would turn my back on you." He picked up our travel bags. "Let us find a comfortable table and order some food. You can tell me what transpired if you feel it is necessary while we wait."

The tavern was near empty. The few men who were scattered about the room looked in our direction as we entered. Their conversations never stopped. We found a table in the back corner. I settled in with our bags as Pierre fetched our drinks and ordered us something to eat. I trembled at having to recount my days leading up to Mother's death.

"You seem deep in thought, *mon amour*." Pierre sat the two drinks on the table and took his seat.

"You remember the morning you left, Mother Clap was worried about my safety with the Society for the Reformation of Manners involved in the riots and arrests of men?"

"I do. She was quite concerned."

"Mother's house was raided not long after that." I took a sip of the gin. "She saw through the charade of two of the men in her house and demanded that I leave through the back door. I wanted to stay, but she insisted that they would not take her. I ran as I always have. I did not stay to protect her."

"There was nothing you could have done."

"Perhaps not, but that does not ease the burden of running out on Mother Clap. I hid in an alley across the street and listened to the beatings and wails of my friends and intimates. I was so terrified that when I saw Mother coming out of the house in shackles and having been manhandled by those men, I could not move. Instead, I watched them take her away from the only home she had ever had." Tears fell from my eyes as I recounted the events of that night. "She opened her home and her love to me. She gave me everything I had always wanted, and when she needed me I was not there for her."

"You are being too hard on yourself."

"After everyone was sent away I saw Mr. Partridge coming out of her house. He was smoking and whistling a song as if sending everyone to their deaths meant nothing to him." I took another sip of my gin. The glass shook in my hand. "Something in me changed in that moment. I became someone I did not recognize or like. I followed Mr. Partridge into the churchyard and watched him fuck another man. My rage was so great that I could not contain it." I paused, not wanting to admit my actions. "I murdered him with his own sword so that he would not be able to testify against Mother, and I dumped his body into the Thames. That was when I knew that I had to do whatever it took to save her."

Pierre sat without words, without expression as I began my story. I spoke of the rape and beating I took at the hands of Mr. Turner, of Christopher turning his back upon me when I needed him. I ended with the confession of selling of my soul to the devil himself, testifying against everyone who had fucked me, the same men who were a part of Mother's extended family. When my story was told, I looked at Pierre, waiting for something, anything that would give me knowledge of his thoughts. He gave no indication.

"Please, Pierre, say something. Am I so tarnished in your eyes that you cannot speak to me?"

"Mon amour." He took a bite of the roasted meat that had so far gone untouched. "I am unsure what to say." He swallowed. "I fear no words of mine can take away the pain that you have experienced. Know that your tale does not change anything between us. If anything, I am in awe of your strength and courage."

"How can you call my actions courageous?"

"Thomas, I had received word of the horrific circumstances that were afflicting the city, but your having put yourself in that situation without regard for your own safety out of sheer love for Margaret is one of the most remarkable displays of loyalty and bravery. Do not look down upon yourself in self-loathing for your actions."

"But I betrayed all those men who trusted me, who Mother loved as her own family. I murdered a man in cold blood." I forced myself to lower my voice.

"You did what needed to be done. You stood up for what you believed in. I would think much less of you if you had run away from the trouble."

"Excuse me. If you are waiting for the ship, it is ready to set sail."

"Thank you, sir." Pierre replied without taking his eyes off me. "We should go. We can continue this conversation once aboard the ship." Pierre stood up and gathered our bags.

"What more is there to say?" I questioned as we left the tavern.

"It is my turn to confess," he replied without pausing or looking back at me.

"Welcome, Mr. Baptiste." A rugged and handsome man spoke as we boarded the ship. I looked at Pierre, surprised to find yet another individual who knew him, but held my tongue.

"It sometimes seems as if this ship is my home." Pierre laughed.

"I take it that you will want a private room to conduct your business in."

"If you have one, we would be most appreciative."

"I will always make room for you. Let me take you below." He patted Pierre on the shoulder as he walked away. "If the winds remain as they are, we should arrive in Dover within a few hours, but as you know things can change without warning on the open water." He stopped at the first door we came to. "I hope this will be suitable."

"I am sure it will be fine. Thank you, my friend."

"I shall notify you when land is in sight." He bowed to us both before leaving.

"It does not have the amenities of home, but it shall do." Pierre opened the door for me. The humble room was barren of furniture except for a small mattress on the floor and a single table and chair. "We can make ourselves comfortable on the mattress." Pierre placed our bags on the floor, taking up what little space remained.

"How is it that you seem acquainted with so many people?" I lowered myself to the mattress and leaned against the wall. Pierre joined me and kicked off his shoes.

"My trade affords me the opportunity to meet many people, though some of them are not the type of people I would associate with in my personal life."

"How do you mean?"

"First, let me start by asking you something, if I may."

"Of course."

"When Mr. Regnault was brought from his cell, he spoke of a gentleman, the Marquis Chaveau. How much did he tell you of this man?" He looked upon me with unsettled eyes.

"That he was kept by the marquis." I paused, not knowing how much of the marquis's story I should admit to knowing.

"And that is all?"

"No." I looked down at my hands and gave in to my hesitation. "He told me how the marquis was tortured and burned alive for nothing more than loving men. He said that you were the man behind the witch hunt, stopping at nothing short of his own death." I looked at him. "That is why he wanted nothing to do with you. Is it true?"

"The details of the marquis's death are true, but the circumstances surrounding his death are fabricated for protection."

"Protection from whom?"

"The citizens of Paris. The police and especially Mr. Ladue did not want to release the true story of the marquis to the public for fear of panic within the city. I became their scapegoat. I took the blame for the marquis's death, and the police were able to maintain order within the city as well as help keep public displays of sex out of the parks and streets, without having to make arrests."

"That is why you said that Mr. Ladue owes you?"

"Yes, but what you do not understand is that the marquis's death was not due to his love of other men. He was a brutal man, and became obsessed with a young man by the name of Paul-Henri."

"Francois mentioned the young man's name and that he did not know what happened to him."

"I do. The marquis loved young men, and especially Paul-Henri. His obsession took hold of him when Paul-Henri's voice began to deepen. The marquis could not tolerate his boy to have such a masculine voice."

"That is when the marquis threw him out of the house."

"That is where Francois's story fails to speak the truth. The marquis could never have just thrown him out for fear that Paul-Henri would report him to the authorities for the abuse that he suffered."

"Abuse?"

"The marquis use to burn him with his pipe. Paul-Henri's body was marred with burn scars, especially on his prick and buttocks."

"But how do you know all of this?"

"His body was found in the cellar of the marquis's home. The smell had gotten so bad that neighbors reported it to the police. When they went to investigate, they found Paul-Henri's body. His prick was cut off and shoved into his throat. He had bled out and died."

"Son of a bitch, I trusted Francois."

"Please do not blame him. As I said, none of these details were made public. Francois could not have known. He was only telling the story as it had been told to him and everyone else in the city. I would have told Francois the truth, regardless of the consequences with the police, if I had thought it would make a difference. You must believe me in that."

"I do, and you are right, Francois had so much mistrust and hatred that he would not have been able to hear the truth. But tell me, how did you become involved in this?"

"Paul-Henri's mother hired me to find him."

"Hired you?"

"Yes. Paul-Henri moved in with the marquis without word to anyone. After a few days had passed, his mother became quite worried. He had a way of getting himself into trouble. So she asked Mr. Ladue whom she could contact to find her son."

"I still do not understand."

"That is what I do, Thomas. I am a thief taker. I track down criminals and bring them to justice."

"Thief takers are criminals, are they not?"

"In a sense, yes."

"Then you are…"

"Some would say I am a criminal, but my work in that area is overlooked because the constables need my services to control the crime brought upon the city by men who are doing the same thing I am, but for more evil purposes."

"How did you get involved in this?"

"I was a rambunctious youth. I was born in Paris. My mother was a whore whom my father had become involved with. After my birth she left, leaving him to raise me. I ran away when I was ten, stealing my father's money to journey to England. Once I arrived in London, I did whatever was necessary to survive. I was good at thieving, so I began to break the laws for no other reason than to see if I could get away with the crimes. Then about ten years ago, I got arrested for highway robbery. It was to be my initiation into a gang of men who would hide out along the major roads leading in and out of London for the sole purpose of robbing the wealthy during their journeys."

"What happened?"

"As I said, I was arrested. The constable for some reason took pity on me, as he could tell I was utterly terrified at being sentenced to death. I had become so good at thieving that I thought I was beyond being caught. It was ill-placed arrogance is what it was. He offered me a deal. If I would go back into the gang and bring them in, one member at a time, he would relieve me of any prosecution. I would also receive one hundred pounds for each conviction. I, of course, accepted his arrangement, and within a month's time, I had brought in all but one of the members of that gang."

"What happened to the last member?"

"Jonathan Wilcox."

"The magistrate?"

"The very one. He not only has complete authority within the city of London to arrest, try, and convict criminals, he controls the crime. He has created an entire underground criminal network. His wealth and power have come from his abuse of the laws and courts."

"Why does someone not stop him?"

"Who? No one with a correct mind would go against him. He would have them executed before they could prove any of their allegations."

"How did you get away with turning in his men?"

"He did not know my real name, that and the fact that I used my criminal connections to have his men taken in by others."

"How did you convince others to get involved?"

"Most of the men I used were desperate for money. They had wives and children that needed to be taken care of. They gave their lives for a good cause and in return their families were cared for."

"So are you employed by the city?"

"I am not employed by anyone other than myself. Because of my skills and experience in the underground with the criminals, I have special knowledge, as do all the thief takers. I use the system to my advantage, earning the money that the city pays me and at times receiving a reward for the return of stolen property."

"What happened once the men were taken in?"

"A few days later I was contacted by the same constable. He needed my services again, but this time he said that the victim was willing to pay a reward for the arrest of her husband and the return of her child whom he had kidnapped, the problem being she did not know where he had gone. I found out that he had left for Paris, so the woman paid for my travels there. It was not long before I returned her child to her. Her husband is in Newgate for his crimes."

"The night you came to Mother Clap's house, were you in London looking for someone?"

"I was in London on business, yes. As I said that morning that I left you and Margaret, I was heading back to Paris, but before I could return, I had been sent word that my presence in London was urgently needed."

"What or who are you looking for?" I questioned. His story had piqued my curiosity.

"Thomas, I cannot say. It is not that I do not trust you, but if word of my actions or those of my clients reached the person whom I am investigating, I would fear for not only my client's life, but also yours. I cannot risk your safety."

"Perhaps I could help."

"No!" His eyes widened and face reddened. He took a deep breath as he closed his eyes. When he opened them, his tone had quieted. "No, I must work alone. You can have no part in this."

"But why?"

"Mon amour." He came to me. I could feel his breath against my face as he placed an arm to either side of me. "We are alone for the time being. You are well now." He kissed me. "What I want cannot be given in words." He unbuttoned my waistcoat as a smile drew across his face.

I watched with hungry eyes as his hands made quick work of my coat. I raised myself off the wall and let him pull the coat from my shoulders. His fingers made way to my blouse and began the same rapid release of the ties. He bent down and kissed my neck, moving his lips farther down my body as each tie was undone. He licked my chest, wetting the dark hair that lay across it. I held his head and trembled when he took my tit into his mouth and sucked on the hard nub.

"Oh, *mon amour*. How I have waited for this moment." He raised himself on his knees and pulled his coat off. As he untied the top two laces of his blouse, the dense tapestry of chest hair came into view.

"Do not bother with the lace." I knelt in front of him and pulled his blouse over his head. His scent engulfed me. I kissed his chest, wanting to savor the warmth of his body, moved my mouth up and kissed the damp cavity of his armpit. His odor was powerful, intoxicating. I licked the perspiration that clung to the coarse hair under his arm, nibbled the tender skin that lay beneath it.

"Your mouth is a tool from the heavens above." He moaned. Our bodies swayed as he leaned back, bringing me down on top of him.

"Then my mouth is what you shall have." I nibbled his chin as I lowered myself down his body, licking and biting his chest as I went. My lips came to the edge of his breeches. I unlaced the ties with my teeth and felt his prick stiffen against my face and lips. "Once again, I find you without undergarments." I chuckled, pulling his breeches down his thick, hairy legs. I removed his stockings, enjoying the edges of the silk against the hair of his legs. His nakedness lay before me in all of its splendor. I rose to remove my own clothing.

"I find undergarments confining and unnecessary." His eyes widened as he watched me undress.

"I shall have to remember that." I kicked off my shoes then pulled my breeches and undergarment off at one time. My prick fell heavily between my legs. Its early release trailed off the head of my prick. Pierre raised his foot and fondled my affairs. My clear nectar clung to the tufts of hair that grew on each of his toes. I took his foot and brought it to my mouth to kiss and nibble the rough, calloused skin, drawing each of his toes into my mouth. I savored the taste of him infused with my own extract.

I worked my way up his leg, kissing his foot, his ankle, his calf, and the crease behind his knee. I gazed upon his ridged prick. It bounced against his furry belly, spitting its own joy as I caressed his body.

I knelt down between his legs and continued to taste of him. The black hair of his lower legs rose past his knees and became more dense the farther up I moved. The scent of his private area stole my breath and made my satchel ache. I spread his legs wider and lay down between them.

I drew light circles with my tongue over the tender, hairy flesh, feeling the solid spheres roll against my lips. I took one into my mouth and rolled it over my tongue.

"Thomas, you are the devil himself." Pierre arched his back and groaned, throwing his arms over his head. "Take them both, yes, that is it. Oh, the pleasure you bestow upon me."

I let his satchel pop out of my mouth. I licked my lips and a few drops of my spit that dangled from his satchel, then cupped it in my hand and pulled it out of my way. Pierre sensed my direction and raised his legs. Even in the dim light, I could spy his puckered hole, hiding within the dense moss. I touched it with my tongue. It quivered. I spread his buttocks and buried my face against his most secret place. I sucked the entrance to his body, giving the tender, wrinkled skin gentle bites of affection. Once it was coaxed open, I slipped my tongue inside. He tensed upon my insertion, and I paused to give him time to adjust his breathing. I felt him relax and his puckered hole loosened, giving me greater access.

"Oh, the blessings of your tongue are more than I can handle." Pierre groaned. "Please, do not make me wait a moment longer. I must have that most handsome prick shoved up my ass."

I pulled my tongue out of his ass, gasping for air as I did, then knelt between his legs and fondled myself so that the trunk of my prick was well saturated with my balsam. Pierre grabbed his legs and pulled them farther over his own body, exposing his opening to me. I brushed the tip of my prick over the soft oval door that opened to receive me.

"Do not linger, my man," Pierre begged. "Please, fuck my ass this instant." His voice echoed around us.

"I shall give it to you when I am ready." I laughed at his neediness of my prick and gripped my swollen trunk to give it proper aim before slipping it inside him. The heat of his ass took to me at once.

"Oh Lord above, I have forgotten how blessed you are." Sweat had already covered his body. Its scent drifted off him and hung in the air between us. I took a deep breath of his masculine odors and plunged the full length of my prick into him with one single thrust. "Motherfucker," he screamed as the initial pain of my insertion ripped through him.

"Oh, you have the most welcoming ass," I whispered as I let myself linger inside him without moving. I felt the muscles of his ass constrict around my prick. I pulled out of him, watching with growing lust as the hair of his ass glided over my wet prick. The sight of our union drove me to the edge of madness. I shoved against him, sending myself over on top of him. I fucked him like a wild beast as I bit his erect tits. He clutched my hair and forced me down his body as I continued to pound his ass with such vigor I thought I might tear him in two.

"Yes, yes. Fuck me, my love. Oh, you are an untamed animal." He pulled his legs until his feet were beside his head. I bent my head downward and saw his large prick lying in a puddle of its own clear balsam.

I licked the puddle, moving my tongue around the thick fold of skin that housed his sex. I shoved my prick back and forth, rocking against him as I took his bulbous head in my mouth. I fucked and sucked him simultaneously without relenting as I felt the familiar burn within my belly.

"Oh, my love, you are going to give me the finest moment of my life," Pierre panted. "Yes, do not stop. Oh, my love, take my seed upon your tongue." His voice trailed off into short pants and groans as he filled my mouth with the warm, thick pearls of his release. He expelled twice more before his prick began to soften. I released him from my mouth in anticipation of my own delivery.

"Oh, your ass…" My words caught in my throat as the urge to expel rushed through my prick. I fucked him hard in the final moments before holding myself deep inside him as my prick quivered and spat wave after glorious wave of my seed. His ass milked my stiffened prick and brought me to a second and third release. Out of breath and out of mind, I collapsed on top of him. My prick slipped out of his ass with a wet, heavy sound.

Our bodies, covered in perspiration, were unable to catch a gentle breath. We lay upon one another. The ship, which rocked us with a gentle, yet steady sway, allowed us to drift off to sleep.

Chapter Eight

"Sir?" A knock came to our door. "Mr. Baptiste?" The whispered voice stirred me from my sleep.

"One moment, please." I hurried to pull on my breeches and blouse, leaving my undergarment in the corner where I had discarded it. I went to the door and opened it only an inch or two, mindful that Pierre lay naked across the room. "Is there something I can do for you?"

"I wish to convey that we shall be arriving in Dover within the hour."

"Thank you. We shall be ready." I closed the door. Pierre stirred behind me.

"Was that the captain?"

"Yes, we should get ourselves ready." I removed my breeches. Spying Pierre's naked body dampened with the warm air of the room woke my prick. The familiar feeling of desire swept through me as I stared at Pierre's prick wrapped in the thick folds of skin. Mindful of my eyes, it bobbed and rolled to the left. Heavy splatters of dried seed were matted to the fur of his belly. Unable to resist the urge, I crawled between his legs.

"Thomas, we do not have time for this." He chuckled.

"I shall only be a minute." I gathered spit within my mouth then ran my tongue over his belly, wetting his dried seed. I licked the remnants from his body, savoring the stale, yet pungent flavors. I looked up at him as I licked my lips.

"You shall be my downfall, *mon amour*." He rose and kissed me, taking what remained of his old release from my tongue. I gave him my hand and pulled him up. He embraced me with the warmth of his body.

We dressed without words and tidied up our bed, hoping no one would notice the evidence of our activities that remained on the linens.

Pierre took our bags over his shoulder. He looked at me and winked. I smiled back as we left the room and headed to the upper deck of the ship.

The pre-dawn air was filled with moisture, chilling me with its near-icy embrace. We stood as close as we could without being too obvious about our intimate nature as we looked out over the horizon for any sign of land. I was about to suggest that we go below to warm ourselves, when Pierre spoke.

"There she is. England is quite a beautiful thing. How does it feel to be going home?"

"I wish I could say that it feels good, but I am unsure how I will be received by old acquaintances, and the constables." A knot soured in my stomach at the thought of walking through the city of London with the spirits of those last few months haunting my every turn. "Where shall we stay?" I questioned as I tried to focus on the future instead of the past.

"I have a place I rent for when I am here on business. It is rather small, but it should do until we can make other arrangements."

"How long are you going to stay?" I was not sure if I wanted to hear the answer.

"As long as you shall have me."

His words silenced my mind. I had not anticipated such a direct response, and remained quiet and let the beauty of the coast come upon us with her slow and majestic grace. As the ship made port, we gathered our bags and made our way onto dry ground.

"I have a carriage waiting for us." Pierre nudged me and nodded to the right. The coachman met us at the back of the carriage.

"Good morning, Mr. Baptiste, welcome back."

"Good day, Mr. Sutton. I would like to introduce you to Mr. Newton. He will be staying with us. I would hope that you will afford him the same courtesy and assistance as you do me."

"Of course." Mr. Sutton turned to me and bowed. "It is a pleasure to meet you, Mr. Newton. Anything I can do for you, please do not hesitate to ask."

"Thank you, Mr. Sutton." Our eyes lingered upon each other for a moment longer than customary. He smiled and blushed as he took our bags and loaded them upon the carriage. He was a few inches shorter than my five foot nine inches with a stout middle, though the extra pounds complemented his other features. A short coat of whiskers dusted his jaw. While he was probably many years my senior, he wore a youthful look.

"Do you wish to stay in Dover to rest from your journey, or are you both anxious to get back to London? Barring any highwaymen or problems with the horses, I can have the two of you in the city before the sun sets."

"Thomas, how are you feeling? Do you need to rest for a day?"

"I am tired, but would prefer to press on and get settled in the city."

"Very well." Mr. Sutton scooted around us and opened the carriage door, helping each of us inside. "We will need to stop along the way every few hours. These horses are fresh, so we should get another twenty miles before having to switch them for new ones." He shut the door, and within a few moments, the carriage jolted forward.

"We have a long journey ahead of us." Pierre patted his lap. "Come lay your head down and try to rest."

"What if Mr. Sutton were to see our closeness?"

"Mr. Sutton and I have known each other for many years. He knows of my predilections." He blushed.

"Have you been intimate with Mr. Sutton?"

"We have enjoyed each other's company on many occasions. I hope that does not sit ill with you?"

"It does not. He has quite a look about him that would attract many men." I laid my head on his lap.

"Do you fancy him as well?" He ran his fingers through the tangles of my hair.

"If we were to have met under different circumstances, I would have been happy to bed him." I looked up at Pierre and smiled. He leaned down and kissed me.

We stopped at regular intervals to switch out the horses and to revive ourselves with gin and fresh meat pies. Pierre and I did not take up lengthy conversations during our journey. Instead, I took our comfortable silence and let the sights of the countryside occupy my mind. On occasions when my thoughts turned to Pierre, I would look at him as he stared out the window and wonder what thoughts had captured his attention. He would sense my eyes upon him, turn and smile at me. We held each other's gaze for mere seconds, long enough to have our unspoken moment before we turned our eyes back to the rolling countryside.

It was late in the afternoon when we came upon London. Even though many months had passed, I felt as if I had never left. The memories of my years here flashed in my mind as we drove by familiar places. The same street vendors hawking their wares yelled from every street corner. The smell of freshly baked breads and pies drifted through the stench of the city's waste and rot. Men, women, and children hustled through the narrow streets, leaping over dead animals and puddles of unknown origins. Despite the troubles of daily life, I felt a renewed sense of belonging to the city.

"What part of the city do you live in?" I broke the long silence.

"Near Bethnal Green Road and Shoreditch," he replied without looking at me.

"You live in Spitalfields?" I held my tongue from saying too much. "I am sorry, I did not mean for my tone to be so abrupt. I am just surprised that you choose to live in the slums, as it is apparent that you have the ability to live in a more suitable neighborhood."

"No need to apologize. I realize that with my good fortune, I could live in better accommodations, but I fear it might distance me from the people who could most benefit from my trade. I do not wish to be looked upon by people as upper class. I want people to feel comfortable coming to me for assistance. I wish to be seen as their equal. I also have business reasons that keep me in Spitalfields."

"May I ask what those reasons are?"

"I find it helps to sustain my relationships with the thieves and beggars. If I were to live elsewhere, the thieves and beggars whom I use as informants might not trust me as they do. Trust is what keeps my services viable. The place I rent is not much, but up until this point, living alone as I have, I have not needed more. That, of course, will need to change with you here."

"I did not mean to imply that I am above living in Spitalfields."

"It is more out of necessity, Thomas. My living quarters are where I meet with both the victims and thieves. My work, as I have indicated, requires some discretion, and your presence might make some feel a bit uneasy." He paused. "As soon as we can, we should find other living arrangements. I can keep the place in Spitalfields strictly for conducting my business." The carriage came to an abrupt stop. Pierre patted my hand as I peered out the window into the old, dilapidated buildings of the area. The carriage door opened.

"It has started to rain," Mr. Sutton commented as he looked toward the sky. "I shall fetch your bags and bring them up." He held out his hand for mine and helped me out of the carriage. I turned and assisted Pierre.

"I believe my coachman has become quite taken by you, Thomas. I hope that you will take full advantage of his accommodating nature. It would do me well to know that the two of you are as close to one another as I have been with the both of you." He winked as he raised the umbrella over our heads. We trotted through the crowded street, dodging children playing in the rain. I took the umbrella as Pierre fumbled with the lock and key. Mr. Sutton had joined us by the time Pierre managed to open the door. "I must remember to bring a locksmith around," he muttered as he escorted me inside.

Pierre's rented flat was modest, to say the least. Even from the front door I could tell that it was no larger than two small rooms. The main room immediately off the front door held a few pieces of furniture, a desk, and a small stove perhaps providing necessary warmth to the whole of his flat. I walked across the room to another entry and peered inside to find two tiny beds on opposite sides of his bedchamber. I looked at Pierre, then at Mr. Sutton.

"As I said, my living arrangements are quite simple. I hope this will suffice for a few nights." Pierre wrapped his arms about me, rubbing the chill that had settled in around me.

"Shall I light the stove?" Mr. Sutton placed our bags on the floor.

"Thank you, Mr. Sutton. Thomas was very ill in Paris, and while he has recovered, it is best to keep the place warm." Pierre kissed me. "Unfortunately, I must leave to make some inquiries before it gets much later. I shall be back within the hour. Perhaps we can have some dinner at that point." He kissed me again. Our mouths opened to receive each other's tongues. He broke our embrace and headed to the door. "I trust that the two of you shall enjoy each other's company while I am away."

"It will be my pleasure, sir." Mr. Sutton busied himself with lighting the stove as Pierre closed the door. "Come, sit with me and we can keep each other warm while the stove heats up." He sat down on the couch and patted the space next to him. The thought that Pierre had willingly invited our intimacy stirred something inside me that I had not been familiar with. I unbuttoned my waistcoat and sat down next to him.

"How long have you been Pierre's coachman?" I questioned as our eyes met. I felt the blush of attraction rise against my neck and face.

"We have had our arrangement for eight years."

"Arrangement?"

"I am not simply his coachman." He placed his arm about my shoulder and drew me closer to him. "I am his confidant, his informant, and his manager when he is called away." He ran his fingers down my chest, hesitated, then proceeded farther down my body until his hand covered my affairs. "You, my new friend, are quite the man." He fondled my stiffening prick. A soft moan escaped my lips. "Let us talk later. At this time, I want to strip you naked and see your body in all of its magnificence."

He straddled my body and released the buttons of my blouse. Desire ignited in his eyes as he looked upon the dampened hair that covered my chest. His hands made quick work of my blouse. He pulled the tails out of my breeches and ran his hands over my chest. His touch sent shivers of delight through me. He leaned down and took my left tit in his mouth. I arched my back and moaned at his caress. I felt his hands move farther down my body. He unlaced my breeches, stood, and pulled them down to my ankles. His eyes widened as my prick, stiff with need, thumped against my body, spraying an early release through the soft thatch that covered my belly.

"I have never seen such an exquisite prick. You must please Mr. Baptiste well. I only hope you will offer me the same delights." He did not bother unlacing his blouse; instead, he pulled it up over his head, exposing his smooth, hairless body to me. I reached up and ran my fingers down his belly. The muscles quivered against my touch. I pulled on the lace of his breeches with growing interest in what lay beneath. He pulled them down and stepped out of them. His prick, shorter in length to my own but with an impressive girth, fell between his stout, hairless legs. I moved forward and took his clear nectar upon my tongue. He pushed me off his prick and climbed on top of me. He kissed me, using his tongue to gather his own fluids from my mouth.

"You do not believe in wasting time." I moaned as he nibbled the hard nubs of my tits.

"I see no reason to be shy about what I want, and what I want is a hard and fast fuck." He raised himself above me, spat in his hand, and rubbed it over the length of my trunk. He gripped my prick and settled himself over the swollen head. "Oh yes, this shall be quite the fuck." He groaned as he lowered himself upon me.

I wanted to close my eyes so as to be drawn into the feel of his ass as it swallowed my prick, but I could not take my eyes from the youthful man who rose above me. I watched a grimace of pleasure form on his face as he impaled himself upon me with short, slow movements. The warmth and moisture of his ass caused gooseflesh to cover my body as a chill raced through me. He settled down upon the full length of me. A smile crossed his face. Perspiration beaded across his brow. He raised his arms above his head and leaned back. His ass squeezed my prick, milking me of my early dew. The pits of his arms were as barren of hair as the rest of his body. The damp odor radiating off him intoxicated me. I rose, wrapped my arms about him, and buried my face in one of his pits. I licked the pungent oils from his skin. His body shook. We fell against one another. He raised himself, then plunged downward in long, repeated thrusts.

"Your prick and my ass make a beautiful pair, my new friend." His hot, bitter breath battered my face. "Mother of mercy, I could die a happy man." He moved up and down on my throbbing prick without relenting. Perspiration soon covered his body and ran in small rivers down his chest, gathering in the stubble of his affairs.

I reached between us and fondled his prick. It spat its excitement into my hand. I rubbed the moisture over his satchel, rolling the small rocks within between my fingers. I pushed farther between us and found the feel of my prick entering his hot, wet ass more than I could take. The fire erupted inside me. My prick stiffened with its impending release.

"Oh, Mr. Sutton, I am getting close."

"Yes, do it, my dear man. Fill me with your blissful seed," he shouted. The news of my event seemed to drive him mad with desire. He frantically bounced upon my prick as he squeezed his ass tighter around me. "Oh, Mr. Newton you are such a man. Please, you must finish off inside me this instant."

"Oh yes, that is it." I thrust against his downward motion, shooting a thick rope of my seed into his ass. He raised himself upon his knees and let me fuck him as I emptied three more times inside him. As my prick began to soften, I felt my seed drip from his ass.

I pulled out of him and threw him to my side to where I could get between his legs. I slipped three fingers into his gaping hole and fucked him with my hand as I slid my tongue over his prick. He grabbed my head and fucked my mouth, unleashing a river of his own white spunk into my mouth. I gagged on the quantity, swallowing some and letting the rest spill from my lips. He pulled me off him and kissed me. I opened my mouth, sharing his own release with him.

"You have no shame, Mr. Newton." Mr. Sutton laughed as he raised his arm over his head.

"Please, you may call me Thomas." I snuggled down in the crook of his arm. I took a deep breath to steady my overexerted body and took in the deep aroma of our sex that lingered between us. A spurt of seed spilled from my prick, landing on Mr. Sutton's leg. We both looked down and smiled.

"Thank you, but Pierre prefers that I maintain some formality. I suppose it is to keep up appearances of our business arrangement while we are in public."

"May I ask what your given name is?"

"It is Dominic."

"I like that. It fits you." I ran my finger down the damp skin of his chest, enjoying the feel of his body responding to my touch. "As you are Pierre's informant, you must be privy to the various cases he is working on."

"As much as he feels is necessary for me to assist him. I never ask him more than he offers. I hope you do not think that I would betray Mr. Baptiste's trust by giving you information. If he wishes you to know, he will tell you."

"I would never ask you to do such a thing. Trust has always been a bit elusive in my circle of friends. I hope that my relationship with Pierre, and now with you, can change that. I only ask because I have no purpose as of yet in London."

"You have just come back. Give it time, Mr. Newton. I am sure you will find your place."

Silence fell between us as I lowered my hand down his belly. His prick responded. I ran my hand down its short trunk, readying myself for another fuck, when Pierre entered the room. I sat upright, still a bit unsure of his true feelings of me having an affair with his coachman.

"Please, *mon amour*. Do not get up on my account." He chuckled. "Though by the looks of things you have already been up, and knowing Mr. Sutton as I do, possibly two or three times by now." He came over to the couch and kissed us both. He licked his lips and smiled. "I do not wish to intrude on the two of you getting acquainted with each other, but I thought Thomas might like to get something to eat."

"If you would not mind," I stood, pulling my breeches up and tucking in the tails of my blouse, "I would like to go to the coffeehouse and see Mr. Clap."

"If that is what you wish. Mr. Sutton…"

"I shall prepare the carriage, sir." Mr. Sutton stood and began to dress. The cold winter rain had scattered the earlier crowds, leaving the city streets with an eerie calm. The horses and wheels of the carriage sank into the saturated ground, making the ride across the city slower than usual. The carriage slid to a stop in the rutted muck. I peered out the window at the sign rocking in the breeze announcing Clap's Coffeehouse. Mr. Sutton came and opened the door, holding an umbrella over our heads as we trudged across the road and stood in the entryway.

"Shall I wait?" Mr. Sutton questioned.

"Please." I replied. "I do not think this will take long." Pierre smiled at me as he opened the door. We walked through the main public room. It was as I remembered it. Several men sat around the tavern drinking and playing cards. Their eyes drifted toward us with curiosity.

"Mr. Clap has not changed a thing." I lowered my voice so as to not draw attention to myself. We continued our visual tour as we made our way to the back of the room, then stole through the back door and into the area of the house that Mother had run. I looked around the room at the empty tables and chairs. Dust and grime covered the surfaces; the air was stale and heavy. The room was but a haunted memory of its former glory. It was all I could do to hold back the tears. Perhaps it was my mind playing cruel tricks upon me, but as I walked around I thought I could smell Mother Clap's rose-scented perfume.

"Thomas?" A voice came from behind us. "My God, it is you." Mr. Clap threw open his arms and embraced me. I patted his back but could not return his warm gesture. "What happened to you?"

"I could ask you the same question." I broke from his embrace and walked around the deserted room, then turned to face him. Even though it had only been a year since he walked out on Mother, he had aged at least ten. He face was drawn and hollow, and the weight loss was substantial.

"I know you must be upset with me for running out on Margaret—"

"Upset does not begin to describe how I felt."

"Thomas, please." Pierre came to me and placed his arm on my shoulder.

"No, I deserve Thomas's sharp tongue. Please, let him get this off his chest." He walked toward me with cautious steps. "I loved Margaret. You of all people should know that."

"Then how could you run out on her? You did not have the decency to wait even a few days to see if she was going to get released from Newgate." My voice rose with months of frustration and anger. "You left her as she was still shackled to the wagon."

"Thomas, I understand that I hurt you."

"You do not understand a thing. This is not about me. It never was. It was about your wife. Mother trusted you, and you betrayed her when she needed you the most. Do you have any idea how much that hurt her?"

"And I shall have to live with that—"

"She died thinking you hated her! Live with that, you son of a bitch!" I pulled away from Pierre and ran up the back staircase. I passed Mother's old room, and then mine. The memories of the night of the raid shot through my mind. Fear and helplessness began to suffocate me as if I were reliving that awful night that changed all of our lives. I ran down the steps, through the dark cellar, then out the back door and into the pouring rain. I stopped dead in my place as my eyes fell upon Mother's grave. The cold rain pelted me and soaked my clothes. My breath escaped my mouth in puffs of white clouds. Tears fell down my already wet face. I walked to the edge of her grave that Alistair had made for her. The guilt and grief of that night hit me like a runaway horse. I collapsed on the ground and dug my fingers into the cold earth, desperate to get closer to her.

"Mother, I miss you." I wept, trembling from the grief and the cold rain that continued to assault my body. It was then that her dying words rang through my ears. *Thomas, my dear boy, live for the both of us.* "I do not know how to live in this world without you," I replied to her memory. I closed my eyes in hopes of seeing her beautiful face smiling at me, and to imagine her arms wrapped about me, comforting me.

"Thomas." A voice rose through the cold wet air.

"Mother?" I opened my eyes, hoping she would be standing next to me, yet knowing it was not possible. I looked up and saw Pierre and Mr. Clap standing at the foot of Mother's grave. Pierre came to me and wrapped a blanket about me.

"Thomas, you must come in. You will catch your death if you are not careful."

"Leave me alone." I turned away from him. "Perhaps my death is what is needed. At least then I can find peace and be with Mother once more." I ran my fingers over the small headstone at the top of her grave.

"I bought that for her." Mr. Clap came up to me. "It is not much, but it was the least I could do." He knelt down beside me. "She deserved far better than me. I was not man enough to be there for her, but you were, Thomas. She loved you with every ounce of herself. That is why she made the changes that she did."

"What changes?"

"Please, Thomas, let us take you inside where we can talk and get you warm." Pierre bent down and took hold of my arm. This time I did not fight.

"Come, I have much to tell you." Pierre and I followed Mr. Clap back into the house. Pierre sat me down on the couch as Mr. Clap stoked the fire. He joined us.

"You said something about changes," I said as Pierre handed me a gin. I took a sip to calm my anger toward Mr. Clap and to warm myself.

"This belongs to you now, Thomas." He reached into his waistcoat, pulled out an envelope, and handed it to me.

"What is this?" I opened it up and looked at the document.

"After you came into her life, she asked me to go to the solicitor's office to have this drafted. It is the deed to the coffeehouse. She left it to you."

"What?" I looked at Pierre and Mr. Clap.

"The coffeehouse, it is yours, Thomas. She wanted you to have it in case anything ever happened to her."

"*Mon amour.*" Pierre placed his arm about me. "This is what Mother wanted for you. She would not want you to grieve your entire life for her. She made this coffeehouse what it was, and she wanted you to carry on her tradition. You can do this, Thomas, as a way to honor her memory."

I looked at the document and saw her elegant penmanship signing over the property to her son, Thomas Newton.

CHAPTER NINE

Thomas, you should get out of these wet clothes. I worry about your health." Pierre broke the uneasy silence that had fallen over the three of us. He sat next to me as I stared at the deed.

"I am fine." My reply sounded distant to my own ears. I looked up as Mr. Clap handed me another gin.

"I have not removed anything from the house. Your clothes are still in your room where you left them." He sat across the table from us. "I know this is a lot to fall on you, but it is what she wanted."

"Thank you for the drink." I looked around the room. "I have wonderful memories thanks to you and Mother, though I must admit I worried that coming back would be too painful. It helps…to be here… to feel Mother's presence and to remember the good times. I am still having trouble with the fact that she gave all of this to me."

"She would want her place to live on, Thomas." Mr. Clap finished his drink.

"I am a bit concerned that people will not patronize it, as the name has such vivid and unpleasant memories for so many."

"If that would ease your mind, the name can be changed."

"But what would I call it?"

"I think it should be something that honors your relationship with Margaret." Pierre rubbed my back.

"That is a splendid idea, Mr. Baptiste." Mr. Clap slapped his hand on the table. "And I know the perfect name."

"What?" Pierre and I questioned at the same time.

"Clapton's. Clap for Margaret's name and the last three letters of your family name, Newton."

"I like that," I replied as a smile broke across my face. "Clapton's, yes, it is a perfect name." I looked around the room and nodded. For the first time in over a year, I felt a sense of calm and happiness warm my cold and bruised heart.

"Excellent. If you are agreeable, then I shall have my solicitor draft the necessary papers." He stood up and gathered our glasses.

"Thomas, you must be tired. Shall we go?"

"If it is all right with you and Mr. Clap, I would like to stay here tonight."

"As I mentioned, your room is untouched, but you do not need my permission, Thomas. This is your home, not mine." He took the glasses behind the bar.

"Then I shall let Mr. Sutton know that we will be staying the night."

"I would prefer to spend the night by myself." I could see the uncertainty in his face. "You have done so much for me, Pierre. I should like to do this one thing for myself. We can make more permanent arrangements tomorrow." I kissed him.

"As you wish." He smiled. "I have an early appointment tomorrow morning with a client, so I shall not need my coach. Mr. Sutton can come back in the morning to take you wherever you wish to go."

"Mr. Baptiste, if I may." Mr. Clap came upon us. "I shall drive you home, and on my way back, I shall stop and make inquiries as to the changing of the name. Tell your coachman to come inside where it is warm. He can spend the night in one of my…Thomas's guest rooms."

"Then I shall come by here tomorrow after my appointment." Pierre wrapped his arms about me. "It shall be a cold, lonely night without you by my side." He smiled and kissed me.

"We shall have many others."

"You can count on that, *mon amour*." He kissed my nose and winked. He turned to Mr. Clap. "Shall we?"

"Good-night, Pierre."

I headed up the back stairs, then paused and peered into Mother's room. Her scent still lingered in the heavy air. I closed the door to keep her memory safe.

As I entered my room, the weight of the past few months began to subside, leaving me spent. I pulled open drawers and shuffled through my clothes that I had left. The fabric still held Mother's rose-scented perfume as if she had just held them against her breasts before placing them in the drawer. A feeling of being someplace else crept over me. I turned to the door as if expecting Mother to come into my room singing one of her favorite songs. The memories seemed to ease rather than intensify my grief. I looked at the pocket watch, one of the many items I left behind. I closed the drawer to the memories and undressed before slipping naked under the linens of my bed. In the distance, I could hear the bells of St. Paul's Cathedral chiming. I closed my eyes and let the comforts of home send me off to sleep.

I awoke the next morning well before dawn to the smell of fresh-baked bread, bacon, and tea. My stomach rumbled. I stumbled out of bed and pulled on one of my dressing gowns that still hung from the bedpost. I was prepared to greet Mr. Clap as I entered the kitchen, but instead found Mr. Sutton preparing breakfast.

"Good morning, Mr. Newton." He smiled at me as he turned to place the meat and bread on the table. "I thought you could use some breakfast this morning."

"Do you always serve breakfast without any clothes on?" I accepted the cup of hot tea that he offered, taking in the sight of his hairless body. His prick, already stiff with his morning desire, brushed against my leg as he passed by.

"Mr. Baptiste prefers me in this fashion when we are alone. I thought you might as well." He winked.

"It is most appealing, I must admit." I sat down at the table and filled my plate with an assortment of delicacies that he had prepared. Mr. Sutton sat across from me sipping his tea as I began to eat in earnest. "Are you not concerned with Mr. Clap coming down and seeing you in your current state?"

"Oh, that reminds me." He reached behind him and took hold of a large envelope. "This was here this morning when I came down. It has your name on it."

"I wonder what it could be." I opened the envelope and pulled out a handwritten letter that was wrapped around a large sum of money. I unfolded the letter and read it.

My dear boy,

Now that the coffeehouse is yours I feel it is best for me to leave. I worry that if I were to stay, I would be a constant reminder to you of my failure as a husband to Margaret and a surrogate father to you. Know that my actions last year were not due to a lack of love for you or my beloved wife. My

*actions were out of my own cowardice. I hope someday you
can find it in your heart to forgive me. I am leaving you with
two thousand pounds to help get you on your feet and to start
your new life as the proprietor of Clapton's. A new deed shall
be forthcoming.*

*Take care of yourself and always remember Margaret's
love for you.*

John Clap

"He must have left before dawn. I wonder why he did not wait to
say good-bye to you."

"Mr. Clap was never good at that." I half smiled. "I wish I could
have told him thank you. I was quite harsh toward him last night."

"I am sure that he understands."

"I hope so."

"We have the morning free, is there something you would like to
do?" He finished his tea and bread.

"Yes, there is one place that I would like to visit, so I would
appreciate it if you would get the carriage ready to leave after
breakfast."

"By all means. Where is it that we are going?"

"Bishop's Stortford."

"Pardon me?" Mr. Sutton looked upon me with a questioning
gaze. The uneasy expression upon his face surprised me.

"Is there a problem, Mr. Sutton?"

"No, no problem. I just cannot imagine why you would want to go
there. I thought perhaps you would want to revisit parts of the city or
stay here and clean up the coffeehouse now that it is yours."

"How do you know about that?" I asked.

"Pierre told me last night that Margaret left the place to you. It was
very generous on her part. I am sure she would rather you stay here and
get the place ready to reopen than to go off to some small village for
no reason at all."

"I would appreciate it if you would not use Mother's memory as a
ploy to maneuver me."

"My apologies, Mr. Newton." He lowered his head. "It was in
poor taste."

"I have a reason for visiting Bishop's Stortford."

"May I ask what that is?"

"I will take Pierre's stance on this matter."

"How so?"

"My reasons for my visit are of a personal nature. Therefore, I do not feel it necessary to explain myself." I gulped the last of my cooling tea and stood up. "If you could ready the carriage, I would like to leave as soon as I change my clothes."

"I have a better idea." Mr. Sutton stood up and came around to my side of the table. He sat on the edge and ran his foot up the hem of my dressing gown until his toes found my affairs. His seductive manners did not seem as genuine as they had the previous day.

"We do not have time for this if we are to make the round-trip today." I replied as I pushed my seat back to distance his foot from my stiffening prick. I looked between his legs and saw a clear sheen of nectar pooling from the eye of his prick.

"Fuck me, Mr. Newton." He fell back on top of the dining table and raised his legs in the air. He wiggled his ass.

I knew then that he was trying to stall our departure. I wanted to stand strong against his advances, but when I laid eyes upon his tight puckered hole winking at me, I gave in to his wishes. I pulled off my gown and tossed it across the room, not caring where it landed, moved my chair between his legs, and sat down, pulling his ass to the edge of the table.

"Yes, do me now." He squealed in delight at my rough handling of him.

I ran my tongue up the crack of his ass. It, like the rest of his body, was barren of any hair. The stench of stale shit and perspiration caught in my throat as I nibbled his tender hole. I inhaled his odors. My prick stiffened. I fondled myself, bringing with it the most intense pleasure.

"Oh dear God," he bellowed as I slipped my tongue inside him. "Yes, feast upon my ass. Oh Lord, there is nothing finer." His voice carried through the empty room. He squirmed and trembled against my tongue's invasion. I began to pull my tongue from him when his hands grabbed my head and held me in place. "Please, fuck me with your tongue, you devilish man."

I buried my face deeper into his ass, wetting my face with spit and perspiration. My tongue dug farther into the secret depths of his body. He rocked against me as he pushed his prick farther between his legs. He stroked himself over my head as the muscles in his ass tightened about my tongue. His soft whimpers turned to heavy pants as I felt his pending release build deep inside him.

"Yes, yes, yes," he bellowed as the first of three heavy spurts shot from his swollen prick. His warm seed landed against my face and dripped down my cheeks as I continued to work my tongue farther into his ass. "Oh, you must stop this treatment before I expire."

I pulled my tongue from his ass. I licked my lips, tasting his remnants, leaned against the chair, and spread my legs, fondling myself as his eyes feasted upon my activity. My breathing became heavy. Sweat dripped down the side of my face. I released myself, sending rivers of pearly rope across my chest. It clung to the damp hair before dripping down my stomach. Mr. Sutton rose from the table and licked the seed from my chest. He kissed me, sharing with me my own release, then knelt between my legs and nestled his face against my wet, softening prick. He licked me dry, cleaning me of my semi-private activity.

"That was a fine fuck, Mr. Newton." He stood and stretched. "Perhaps we can retire to your bed for a while and rest."

"Do you think that I do not know what you are doing?"

"I beg your pardon."

"You are using sex as a way to avoid taking me where I have requested to go." I stood and picked up my dressing gown. He looked at me, his eyes narrowed as if unsure of how to answer my question. "Do not misunderstand me. I have enjoyed our diversion, but it has not deterred me from my intended destination. If you do not wish to take me, then I shall find someone who will."

"My apologies, Mr. Newton." He spoke with his back to me as he gathered our breakfast dishes. "I do not mean to defy your wishes, it is just that Bishop's Stortford is quite a distance. I think it would be best to wait for Mr. Baptiste's return before making that kind of a decision."

"Pierre left you here in my employ. What purpose would it serve to wait for him?" I was becoming annoyed with Mr. Sutton's questionable motives.

"I am merely making a suggestion, Mr. Newton. I have known Mr. Baptiste for many years. I also know that he worries for the safety of the people he cares about, but if you wish to go that is what we shall do. I am just trying to understand your urgency in making this trip." He wiped the table as he continued to avoid meeting my eyes.

"Perhaps you are right." I decided to give in to his persistence, thinking it might be wise to not involve either of them in any business where my father was concerned. "You seemed surprised at my sudden reversal."

"I think your change of heart is a wise one, Mr. Newton." He turned to look at me. "Now, let us retire to your bedroom." He took my hand and led me up the back stairs and into my room. As we slipped under the covers, Mr. Sutton moved his body against mine. I felt the softness of his prick nuzzle between my buttocks, spilling the last of his release between us. I kissed his hand as he brought it around me. His fingers combed through the hair of my chest. I gave in to the silence that fell over us and used that time to plot my next move.

It was not long before I heard the soft rhythmic breathing as he slept. I lifted his hand from my body and placed it on his leg. He stirred but did not wake. I slid from the bed, picked up my clothes, and eased out of the bedroom without a sound. Once downstairs I dressed and wrote a brief note to Pierre and Mr. Sutton, letting them know that they should not worry about me. I gave them no indication of my whereabouts, but knew Mr. Sutton would be able to figure out where I had gone. I stole away from my own home like a thief leaving his victim's home, and without much difficulty found a coach and driver for my journey.

The rain from the previous night had ended, leaving the city wrapped in a damp morning chill. As we passed through the outskirts of London and into the countryside, my mind returned to the day my father had sent me away. I was a lost young man that day, having no purpose or plan. "If only father could see me now," I said to myself and smiled. While the thought of confronting my father gave rise to temptation, I knew it was not the right time for such a meeting. The House of Lords would be in session, and therefore my father would be staying in London, leaving my childhood home empty of his venom and hatred. It was nearing noon when our carriage drove through the narrow streets of Bishop's Stortford.

The coachman nodded his response with each direction I gave him and continued on as instructed. The carriage came to an abrupt stop. I did not allow myself to peer out the window. Instead, I stepped out of the carriage and for the first time in several years came face-to-face with the monster that contained all of my childhood fears.

"If you would not mind waiting here, I will not be long."

"Not at all," he responded without care. I paused at the iron gate that surrounded my father's home. A sudden thought to turn and go home crept through me. I peered over my shoulder toward the safety of the carriage. The coachman stood by the horses, lighting his pipe. He looked at his pocket watch. He must have noticed my stare. He looked up and nodded at me.

I nodded back before opening the gate. The house loomed over me as I approached. I peered through the large windows to either side of the door. The house appeared empty. With a nervous twitch, I knocked on the door and waited. I stood a moment longer, then turned the latch. To my surprise, the door was not locked. I pushed it opened and stepped inside.

"Hello?" I called out. I stepped into the parlor, grateful that no one had responded. The room was unchanged. The smell of my father's tobacco lingered in the air. Memories of my childhood flooded my thoughts. My father's wingback chair sat near the fireplace as it always had. I could see myself as a little boy, sitting in front of my father, pleading with him to tell me a story before bedtime. It was as if I were watching a ghost of myself from fifteen years ago. I smiled at seeing myself that little, remembering the innocence of youth. The grin slipped away from my face as my father brushed me, or my ghost, away as if I were some burdensome fly instead of his son. The ghostly images faded, and as they did I noticed a book lying on the floor next to my father's chair. I walked over and picked it up: *Erotopolis, the Present State of Betty-land.* I dropped the book. "Fucking hypocrite," I spat to an empty room.

The wooden floor above my head creaked, bringing me out of my memories. I listened with more intent. A door opened on the second floor, followed by footsteps. By the location of the sounds I could tell someone was in my old bedroom.

I began my ascent to the second floor. Knowing the house as I did, I instinctively knew where to step so as not to make the wooden boards creak under my weight. The door to my room stood open. My heart pounded in my chest, its frantic drumming echoing in my ears. I approached the bedroom door and paused, gripping the wooden frame of the doorway. I held my breath and listened over the rapid beating of my heart, then peered around the corner. The room was empty, yet I felt as if I were being watched. I looked farther down the hallway, then behind me, before entering the room.

I stood and stared at my childhood room. The furniture was as I had left it, but unlike the parlor below, my room had been disturbed. The bureau drawers were open in an uneven pattern with the contents tossed about the room. The mattress itself was tossed halfway off the bedframe. Someone had taken a knife and cut down the center. In the shock of seeing my room in such disarray, I had forgotten about the sounds that brought me here. My first thought was that this had happened during the trials. That perhaps members of the Society for the Reformation of Manners had somehow found out my true identity and came here looking for me. *But why would father leave my room like this for so long?* I asked myself. As I waited for my mind to reply, I heard more footsteps moving down the hallway. *This did not happen some time ago,* my mind reasoned. *Someone is in my father's home looking for something in my room.* I moved through my bedroom and to the door. "Who is out there?" I called. The footsteps picked up speed and headed toward the back of the house and the servants' staircase.

I came from around the door. The footsteps were below me. I heard the back door to the house slam shut, then the house fell silent about me. I took a few deep breaths to relax and walked down the hallway, pausing in front of Christopher's old room. The memory of standing outside the door spying on Christopher as he undressed pained me. I reached up and clutched the silver pin he had given me on my eighteenth birthday. It was then that I noticed the door was ajar. I pushed it open with my fingers, stepped into the room, and stood frozen in fear. The body of Mr. Johnson, my father's coachman, lay on the floor in a pool of his own blood. I took a few uneasy steps toward the body. I knelt down beside him, touched his still-cooling hand, and leaned in closer to study his stomach to see if he was breathing. His belly lay still. Memories of the day he drove me to Cheam Classical School drifted through my mind. His warning to me that day came back as if he were speaking to me after death: *Money trumps all things in life. Without money, you will go nowhere. With it, you can control your future, and the future of those around you. There is no friendship, love, or family that money cannot destroy.*

I looked at his expressionless eyes staring up at me with the smell of death drifting through the air. I had been so focused on my own memories of him that I had not noticed anything else about the room. What I saw when I stood up almost took me to my own death. I shook as I backed away, staring at the bloody letters for several moments before I realized the implication of them. Mr. Johnson had written my old name, Addison, on the floor as he took his last breath.

I backed farther away from the body, unable to take my eyes off my bloody name. My heart stopped as I felt someone come up from behind me and grab my shoulders.

CHAPTER TEN

I held my breath, curling my fingers into a tight fist ready to fight. I turned around to face the murderous son of a bitch who took Mr. Johnson's life.

"Whoa, my love." Pierre grabbed my arm as I swung my body around. "It is only I."

"You scared the shit out of me." I said with a sigh of relief and relaxed. "What…how did you find me?"

"The more important question is what are you doing here?" His words faltered as he caught sight of the dead body behind me. "What happened? Are you all right?"

"Yes, I am fine. I came here—" I stopped myself before disclosing too much. I decided to change the subject of our conversation back to him. "You did not answer my question. How did you know where to find me?"

"Mr. Sutton," Pierre shouted down the hallway and turned back to me.

"Obviously I cannot trust Mr. Sutton with certain sensitive information. I guess I should not be surprised where his loyalties lie."

"Thomas, it is true that he and I share a long history, but he is not the traitor you make him out to be. He did not divulge anything to me. I came home needing him to bring me here to Bishop's Stortford. It was only then that he told me you slipped out while he was sleeping and were more than likely heading in the same direction."

"Sir?" Mr. Sutton called as he came upon us. "My Lord, is that…"

"Yes, it is he," Pierre replied.

"What business could you possibly have here?" I asked.

"Mr. Sutton," Pierre ignored my question, "we need to get Thomas out of here immediately. Take him back to London. I will take his coach for my return."

"Wait. What is going on?" I spoke to the both of them.

"Thomas, this is not a time for debate."

"I did not do this."

"Do you think that I am accusing you of murdering this man?"

"What else…"

"I know you did not do this, Thomas." He took a deep breath and shook his head. "This is not how I wanted you to find out."

"Find out what?" I became more agitated by the moment. "What in the fuck are you not telling me?"

"I know Thomas."

"Know? Know what?"

"The name, Thomas." He pointed to the bloody letters written on the floor. "You are Addison. I know what your father did to you at Cheam Classical School. How he faked your death to rid himself of you. Mr. Johnson wrote that as a warning."

"But how do you know my father's coachman?" I looked at Pierre, then at Mr. Sutton, who looked away the moment our eyes met. "What in the fuck is going on?"

"Please, Thomas, you have to go with Mr. Sutton."

"I am not leaving here until you tell me who you are and how you know so much about my family. No one knew about my father's murderous plan except—"

"Please, you are in danger if you stay."

"I am not leaving without you."

"But I cannot leave."

"Why?"

"Damn it, Thomas you can be so infuriating." His face blushed with frustration. "Mr. Sutton, please tell the other coach that he will not be needed. Pay him for his time and ask him to fetch the constable on his way through the village. Then ready our carriage. Thomas, I will go back to London with you and tell you what I can, but you have to promise me that you will stay out of this."

"I do not even know what this is."

"Thomas!"

"Very well, I will do as you ask."

"Good. Let us go before someone finds you here." He took my hand and we ran through the house and out into the street. "Fuck." He hesitated as we reached the carriage. "I shall be right back."

"Pierre, where are you going?"

"Thomas, get inside the carriage and do not leave. Is that understood?"

"Yes, but…" I let the words fade from my tongue as Pierre turned and headed back toward the house. I watched him disappear through the front door. An uneasy feeling crept through me as each minute passed without Pierre's return. As I waited, I ran through the names of the people in my life who knew about my past in hopes of finding an explanation as to how Pierre came upon such knowledge. The only two people from my childhood, Christopher and James, were not a part of my life in London during the time Pierre had visited the coffeehouse. The only other person who knew I was Addison was Mother Clap.

I thought back to the events leading up to Pierre's arrival at the coffeehouse. We were all on edge due to the unexpected police raids and impending trials. I remembered Mother's unsettled nerves as Pierre, a stranger to all of us at the time, had entered the coffeehouse. *Did Mother tell Pierre of my childhood?* I questioned myself. *There would have been no reason for her to do so. No, it's not possible. Mother and Pierre were never alone that night. I was with him the entire time.* The carriage door opened, startling me from my thoughts.

"Mr. Sutton, we need to be off," Pierre shouted as he climbed into the carriage without warning and nearly unseating me. "My apologies, Thomas."

"What is the rush?"

"Mr. Green." He looked at his pocket watch. "He should not be too far behind us if my calculations are accurate." The carriage leapt forward, tossing us both about.

"He should be in session. Why do you believe he is on his way here?"

"You are a day behind, Thomas. Sessions ended this morning. I can only guess that when Mr. Johnson did not show up, Mr. Green hired a driver to bring him back. If he left within thirty minutes of the sessions ending, it would put him back here within the hour."

"I am sorry that I have made you come back with me. It is just that I have spent most of my life living with secrets. I thought those days were past me then I find out…" I turned my head and looked out the window as we passed the shops of the village.

"Thomas, I am sorry for the secrets, but remember I am not the only one who suffers from closed lips." Pierre grasped my chin and turned my head toward him. He met my gaze. A saddened smile crossed his face. "I do need to talk with Mr. Green, but I am not sure I could have fabricated a believable story as to why he found me in his house with the body of his coachman. I certainly could not tell him the truth."

"What is the truth?"

"I suppose I owe you that much." He turned toward me and rested his leg between us. "Remember, Thomas, with this new knowledge that I am about to share with you comes a responsibility to manage it. I need your solemn promise that you will not do anything to endanger yourself or my investigation." He held my hand. "Can I have that?"

"You can."

"I have already disclosed my trade to you. I am a thief taker, but what I was protecting you from is the current task at hand and the person who originally hired me."

"You were hired to investigate me?"

"No, Thomas. I was hired to look into your father's private affairs." Pierre's eyes shifted back and forth as if looking for a sign from my expression. He lowered his head and took a deep breath.

"Go on."

"The night I came to the coffeehouse, it was not by accident. I came to meet Margaret Clap."

"What?" A lump grew in the pit of my stomach with his confession. "Why?"

"She was concerned for your safety."

"I do not understand."

"Margaret was concerned that your father had somehow found out you were in London." He paused and studied my face. I can only imagine what he saw written upon it. "Thomas, your father was and still is funding the Society for the Reformation of Manners. If it were not for his financial and governmental support, the Society could not have grown to such power and influence as they have. Margaret was worried that your father found out that you were in London and had ordered the raids in hopes of flushing you out."

"Mother hired you to protect me?"

"In a matter of speaking, yes. She asked Gabriel Laurence if he knew of someone that was beyond the Society's reach. Someone who could not be bought that she could trust with this information. He sent word for me…"

"And that is why you were there that night?"

"Yes, Margaret did not know when I would show up or who I was until I introduced myself."

"I was with you the entire night. Where did you and Mother find time to talk?"

"I waited for you to fall asleep, then went to meet Margaret in the tavern."

"That is why she asked a perfect stranger to take me away. She knew she could trust you."

"Yes. She loved you with all her heart. She worried what would happen if your father got his hands on you."

"But why would my father go to such lengths to, as you say, flush me out? I was nothing to him."

"That is where you are wrong, Thomas. You have the power to destroy him. You are the only one who knows the truth of what he did to you."

"But that is not true. There were others who knew." The words stuck to my tongue as I realized the implications of what Pierre was suggesting.

"That is precisely my point. Do you think it was by accident that your schoolmate, James Sanxay, came to London when he did?"

"You know about James?"

"I know a great deal about your life, Thomas. It is what I do. I track down information. Your father wanted to make sure that James would never reveal what he knew."

"How?" I paused as a rush of emotions flooded me. My head swam with unanswered questions, anger, and a renewed sense of grief over the loss of the people I loved.

"Your father led Christopher to Cheam Classic School. James, knowing how much Christopher meant to you, took it upon himself to bring the two of you together."

"But how did James know I was in London? Wait, my father?"

"Yes, at least that is what I have been able to piece together. Your father wanted to make sure that anyone who knew you as Addison and knew of his fraud and forgery was silenced. He had the Society do his dirty work, that way his hands would remain clean."

"Son of a bitch." I closed my eyes to block out the world. "Why not just kill me? No one would have suspected anything."

"That would have been too easy, Thomas. Your father is a wicked and vindictive man. He wanted you to suffer. It did not matter whether you knew who was responsible. His satisfaction came from murdering the people who tried to help you and whom you cared for."

"And all along I blamed myself." It was then that a thought entered my mind, a thought that raised such rage within me I thought it might kill me where I sat. "Mother Clap?" I looked at Pierre. He could not meet my gaze. "Please, Lord, no."

"I am sorry, my love. This is the news I wanted to spare you from. You were promised that no harm would come to Margaret as long as you testified against the others. Your father began to suspect that Margaret was the one who started the investigation against him. He placed the order for her to stand in the pillory, not Constable Willis."

"So many people were hurt for no other reason than their association with me." Tears welled in my eyes. I looked out the window in hopes of holding back the flood I felt rising inside me. I choked back the emotions as they reached the surface. The pressure of guilt was too great upon my head. I broke down and sobbed as I had never done before.

"Thomas, I am sorry." Pierre placed his hand upon my shoulder.

"It is not…your…fault…" The words came between the gasps of air. I wanted to fall into his lap, to let him comfort me and cradle me to make all the pain subside. I held fast against the urge. I took in several heavy breaths to control the shaking throughout my body. *Mother, I am so sorry for everything.* As if she could hear my thoughts, the memory of her voice echoed through my mind: *Do not mourn my death, my love, live life with grandeur. Be strong and live for the both of us.* I had heard these words haunting my dreams a thousand times over the past year, but there was something this time that was different. It was as if I could feel her sitting beside me, holding my hand and giving me the strength she always saw in me. I turned to look at Pierre. His face was streaked with tears. "I want my father's head."

"Thomas, please. I understand that…"

"No, Pierre, you do not understand any of it." I spat more venom than he deserved, but knew I could not apologize. "All my life, I was told by my father that I was broken, dirty, and beyond help. He even blamed me for my mother's death. I believed everything that son of a bitch said to me over the years because that is what a son is supposed to do. Believe in his father's love and wisdom, because why would any father say such cruel and hurtful words to his son if it were not true? I have blamed myself for everything that has gone wrong in my life, the deaths of all my friends and the death of the only woman who truly loved me. Today for the first time in my life, I know I am not to blame. I will not live my life in shame any longer. He needs to pay for what he has done, and if you will not help me, then I shall do this on my own. I will not rest until my father is destroyed."

"Mother was right about you. You have the strength and determination most men only dream of." He smiled. "Of course I will help. That is what I have been doing all along. I promised Margaret that I would protect you and see you through this if the day came—it has." He moved closer to me. "Thomas, you have to listen to me, really listen. If I am to help you, you have to do it my way. I have spent the better part of this last year following your father, talking with people. I cannot have you going off half-cocked on some personal vendetta against your father. I need you focused, and I need you to follow my orders. No more running off on your own. Do we have a deal?"

"If that is what it takes to get to my father, then yes, we have a deal." I extended my hand as a pledge of my word.

"I want something a little more from you than a handshake, *mon amour*." He smiled at me as he released the clasps of his waistcoat.

"Here?"

"Do you have a problem with that?" He released the first three buttons of his silk blouse.

"No." I smiled and wiped the tears away as I laid eyes upon the rich tapestry of dark hair across his chest. The anger and emotions I felt had stirred something inside me without my knowledge. As I gazed upon Pierre's exposed chest, I noticed that my prick was stiff with need. I needed to fuck, to find an outlet for my anger and pain. It was in Pierre's body that I found that release.

I pushed him down against the cushion and climbed on top of him. I finished with the buttons and pulled his blouse out of his breeches, lowered my face to his body, and inhaled his odor. As I licked his tit, he arched his back and moaned. I brought the nub of his tit into my mouth and sucked, biting and nipping at the tender, raised flesh, then released it and gazed upon the spit-soaked hair. An urge unlike anything I remembered exploded within my belly as I contemplated the delicious view of his hairy body immersed in water. I smiled with the anticipation of that vision. I released the laces of my blouse and pulled it off my shoulders.

Pierre reached out and caressed me. The carriage bounced up and down, tossing me to one side. We chuckled at the antics of undressing in a moving carriage as I took the opportunity to untie my breeches and pull them off. As I struggled within the confined space, Pierre took to his own breeches. His height made maneuvering inside the carriage difficult. He gave up the struggle, leaving his breeches gathered around his ankles.

I climbed back on top of him and felt the firmness of his trunk nestle between my buttocks. I rubbed myself against him, enjoying the warmth of his clear nectar as it seeped from his prick and dampened my hole. The rough roads of our journey aided in the motion of our desire. I rose, grabbed his prick, and settled myself over its large tip. Pierre moaned as I sat upon his prick, engaging us in the throes of a much-needed fuck. A sudden bump in the road forced his prick inside me. The thrust of his immediate insertion brought a moment of dizzying pain. I took a deep breath and shoved myself downward, fully engaging our bodies.

I raised my hands to the roof of the carriage to steady myself as Pierre thrust against me. The sounds of our sex, our moans, our sweat-dampened bodies slapping against one another rose between us as our desire to fuck grew with feverish abandon. Trails of perspiration dripped from the pits of my arms and trickled down my body. Pierre raised himself and took his tongue to me, licking the dampness that our bodies created. I closed my eyes to his advances, enjoying the feel of his lips, his tongue, his mouth, working their way through the hair of my armpits to nibble the tender flesh that lay beneath.

Pierre grabbed me and pulled me down on top of him. He kissed me, feeding me his thick tongue coated with the oils of my body. The taste of my own perspiration made my urge of release rise to the surface. I wanted to speak, to call out his name with the moment of release growing closer. He held me tight against his mouth and groaned against my heavy breaths, increasing my excitement until I gave into the urge. My prick erupted, spraying thick white ropes of my hot seed over his body.

We rocked against one another as he fucked me, smearing my release between us. His prick swelled within me as he reached the final moment of human bliss. I pulled myself from his arms and raised myself upon him as the first of several heavy rivers of his seed expelled from his overworked prick. He filled me with his gratification. I moved up and down on his trunk as another spasm raced through me. My prick spat another large quantity of seed over his stomach. I fell against him. His arms wrapped about my body. He kissed me and smiled, and we lay together in silence as the carriage jostled us against one another.

"I suppose we should make ourselves presentable." Pierre

chuckled breaking the long silence and bringing me fully out of my sleep. He kissed my forehead as I pulled myself from him. We dressed without words, our eyes lingering from time to time upon each other's bodies. "Is something wrong, my love?"

"Am I?" I glanced at him.

"Are you what?"

"You have done so much for me, I sometimes wonder whether you are doing this to fulfill a promise to Mother, or…"

"Or?" He laughed.

"You call me your love, but I do not know what the implications of what those words are."

"The night we first met, I must admit that my advances toward you were for personal reasons, simply to enjoy another man's company. That did not last long, for it was after our third or fourth fuck that night that I began to feel something for you. I must add that what I felt was foreign to me. I did not know a man could feel such love and devotion to another man. So when I call you my love, it is what it means. I love you, Thomas."

"But I have fucked Mr. Sutton. On several occasions," I added. "Does that not bother you?"

"I like to think of us as a couple, Thomas. You and I, but that does not mean that we cannot enjoy Mr. Sutton's company from time to time. He is a most agreeable fuck, as I am sure you have come to know."

"I have." I smiled as my face flushed from embarrassment. "I have only said this to one other person before, but I love you as well." The heat on my face rose.

"Then I shall take that as a compliment, as I am sure you are referring to Margaret." He leaned over and kissed me. We both chuckled at our awkward confessions of love as we turned to peer out of our respective windows. Moments later I felt Pierre's hand on top of mine. I smiled with the reassurance of his gesture.

"Pierre?"

"Yes."

"Why do you suppose Mr. Johnson was murdered?"

"I suspect for the same reason your father had James silenced. I would wager that Mr. Johnson knew details of your father's dealings. Why else would he write your birth name in his blood?"

"Then you believe my father is responsible for his death?"

"It is possible, is it not?"

"Mr. Johnson would never betray my father's trust."

"Apparently someone does not share that sentiment."

"What next?"

"We need to keep you safe. If your father or whoever is doing these things finds out that you are in town, they will come after you."

"At least I have the coffeehouse to occupy my time."

"Shit, the coffeehouse. I had forgotten about that."

"What is wrong?"

"Your name will be on record as the proprietor. If someone is searching for you, they would be looking for places where you might be staying. Margaret's old place would be on their list. They are bound to find you."

"These people have taken too much from me already. I will not let them keep me from living in Mother's home." I hesitated before adding, "I shall die before I let that happen."

"I would never ask you to give up something so important to you. I shall have Mr. Sutton move into the coffeehouse to keep watch over you."

"You really believe my life is at risk?"

"I am more convinced than ever, considering the events of today. The death of Mr. Johnson has complicated matters."

"How so?"

"I began by investigating claims that your father was secretly funding the Society, something that as a member of the House of Lords could be seen as treason. If convicted, he would stand for execution. Something has spooked your father, enough so that he was willing to have his coachman murdered."

"That is what does not make sense. Mr. Johnson, in fact, all of my father's servants were terrified of him. They went out of their way to avoid him at all costs."

"Mr. Johnson knew something. I just do not know what yet."

"How can you be sure?"

"After I left you and Margaret, I headed back to Paris. Upon my return, I received word that it was most urgent that I return to London. I assumed it was Margaret with more information, but when I arrived, I was greeted with the news of her death. So you can imagine my interest when I learned that someone else was also looking into your father's affairs."

"Did this man know of Margaret or your arrangement with her?"

"I asked him that same question. He said he knew of Margaret but had never met her. His inquiry was, as he put it, of a personal nature."

"Who was it?"

"For reasons of personal safety I need to keep his identity a secret. His request, not mine."

"Did he have information for you?"

"He did, but what concerns me is that I was talking with him this morning. He was the one who told me I needed to pay Mr. Johnson a visit. When I inquired as to the purpose of this meeting, he told me that Mr. Johnson was most eager to meet me. My client had not received word from Mr. Johnson in several days and was quite worried something had happened to him."

"So that is why you came to Bishop's Stortford?"

"An odd coincidence, would you not agree?"

"It is, especially given the likelihood that Mr. Johnson wanted to tell you something about me. Why else would he have written my name?"

"That is what troubles me, and why I need to figure out a way to talk to your father without him knowing I was there today. It would raise too many questions."

"Knowing my father the way I do, he will want to keep Mr. Johnson's death quiet, even if he is not responsible for it. He would not want the publicity."

"Yes, of course, publicity. That will get his attention."

"Pardon me?"

"Mr. Sutton!" Pierre knocked on the window. His excitement overshadowed my question.

"Sir?" Mr. Sutton replied as he slowed the carriage.

"Once in London, take us to *The Tatler*."

"Yes, sir. I shall have you there within a couple of hours."

"Thank you." Pierre leaned back against the seat with a curious look upon his face.

"What are you up to?"

"Thomas, you and I are going to place an advertisement."

"Can one just walk in and do such a thing?"

"Mr. De Vries owes me a favor."

"I am starting to think that everyone in this city owes you."

"Some days it feels like that."

"What did you do for him?"

"Mr. De Vries has never been very good with his money. He was late on paying his window taxes and was about to be arrested. In his desperation, he stole some priceless jewelry from his wife's mother. She hired me to locate her stolen items. My investigation led me straight to Mr. De Vries. When I confronted him with my knowledge, he confessed and turned over the stolen goods. I used part of his mother-in-law's reward money to pay his taxes for him. He promised to return a favor for keeping him from the debtor's prison. I believe it is time he repays that debt."

"How can placing an advertisement help us?"

"As you said, your father will not want to be implicated in Mr. Johnson's death, even by rumors. An advertisement announcing Mr. Johnson's death along with a plea to the God-fearing citizens of London for information about his death should be enough to make your father more than a little nervous. He shall be forced to contact me if for no other reason than to get me to stop my investigation."

"Your plan sounds too dangerous, if you ask me."

"Not knowing who is murdering these people, or for what purpose, is far worse than angering your father."

"Just be careful, Pierre. My father is unpredictable." I leaned down and rested my head on Pierre's lap. "I am not prepared to lose you as well." I looked up at him. He was staring out the window, with his attention focused elsewhere. I closed my eyes and prayed that we would make it out of this with our lives.

CHAPTER ELEVEN

The carriage came to a crude stop, rocking Pierre and me out of our sleep. I rose from Pierre's lap and stretched as much as the small space would allow. As the stiffness in my back eased, I peered through the window looking out across Fleet Street. It felt good to be back in London even with the looming dangers of my father's wrath upon me.

"May I accompany you?" I asked with a bit of apprehension. I was not sure where my place was in regard to his work and current investigation. "If you would prefer for me to stay behind—"

"I want you with me, Thomas. I thought that was clear." He leaned over and kissed me. "We are in this together, all of us, including Mr. Sutton."

"I like that sound of that." I smiled at him, feeling more at ease with our budding personal and professional relationship.

"Sir." Mr. Sutton opened the door. I thanked him as I stepped out onto the congested street. Pierre was right behind me. "I shall stay here and keep an eye on things."

"Thank you, Mr. Sutton." Pierre clapped him on his shoulder and smiled. As we walked down the street, Pierre grasped my elbow. "Come, this way." He pulled me down an alley between several old, derelict buildings. They hung over the street with their cheap construction and crumbling walls. I often wondered what would become of these buildings in a stout wind.

"Where are we going? *The Tatler* is on the other street, is it not?"

"It is, but we cannot go in through the front doors."

"Why?"

"With all of the newspapers and presses concentrated here, this area is known for its gossiping streetwalkers who sell information to the highest bidder." He stopped and looked behind us. "I do not want us to be seen going into *The Tatler*. Rumors and gossip as to our activities are the last things we need at the moment." He paused. The seductive, wicked smile that I had grown accustomed to during our moments of intimacy crossed his face. He leaned in and kissed me.

"What was that for?"

"Must there be a reason for me to want to kiss you?"

"Never. It was just unexpected."

"I have been known to be spontaneous." He winked as he took my shoulder and led me down the alley.

"I am beginning to see that." I chuckled. We came to a stop at the entrance to a smaller, less inviting alley. "You must be joking."

"I am not. The back entrance to *The Tatler* is down there."

"It is a good thing we are both lean. It would be too easy for someone with more weight on them to get stuck in there." I looked at him. "After you." I stretched my arm out in front of us and gave a mock bow.

"Remember, when we get inside just play along with anything that is said."

"I will play the quiet observer." I replied as I slipped down the narrow passage.

"A quiet observer is not your strong suit." He threw a quick smile over his shoulder to let me know he was joking.

"I cannot help that my tongue is quicker than my head." I gave him a gentle nudge with my hand. He stopped. I did not see his pause coming and stumbled into him. "Sorry." I patted his ass. He shot me another wicked smile before knocking on the door.

"Who is it?" a voice with a pronounced Dutch accent asked through the closed door.

"It is Mr. Baptiste." Pierre seemed agitated by the apparent rituals of gaining access through the back. The door swung open, giving us both a start.

"Mr. Baptiste." The man raised his arms and gripped Pierre's shoulders. "It is good…" He paused as his gaze met mine. "Who is this?" A strand of blond hair fell down over his eyes. He stared at me through the wisps of hair.

"No one you need to worry yourself about, Mr. De Vries. This is my associate, Mr. Newton. Thomas, I would like to introduce you to Johannes de heer De Vries."

"Since when have you taken up with an associate? I always thought of you as someone who preferred to work alone." He placed his hands on his hips and looked me over. "A bit rough around the edges, but I suppose in your line of business that can be useful. If Mr. Baptiste sees fit to work with you, then so do I. It is a pleasure to meet your acquaintance, Mr. Newton." He reached out his hand.

"Likewise, Mr. De Vries." I shook his hand. His grip was stronger than one would expect for such a tall, lean man.

"Please, come in." He stepped aside and pushed his spectacles back upon his nose. "I take it that this is not a social call." He chuckled as he looked down the alley in both directions before closing and latching the door.

"I need a favor, Mr. De Vries," Pierre stated without hesitation or other informal chatter. Pierre and I followed the old man through a storage room and into a smaller room that he used as his office. I knew Pierre and his body with the most intimate of connections, but to watch him conduct business, to see this yet unknown side of him made my feelings for him deepen.

"I was wondering when you were going to come and cash in that favor I owe you." He looked at me with a curious eye, as if worried to say too much in front of me.

"I..." Pierre cleared his throat. "I mean *we* need to place an advertisement." He glanced at me and smiled.

"Is that it? An advertisement?" He dipped his pen in the ink and grabbed a sheet of paper. He looked up at us with an eagerness about him.

"I would like the advertisement to read..." Pierre began. "'I am looking for information in the brutal murder of Mr. Clyde Johnson of Bishop's Stortford, coachman of Mr. Bartholomew Green, a long-standing member of the House of Lords.'"

"Good God, Mr. Baptiste. Have you lost your fucking mind? I cannot go to press with such an advertisement, not where Mr. Green is concerned." He let the pen fall from his grip. He pushed his spectacles back upon the bridge of his narrow, straight nose.

"Have you forgotten, Mr. De Vries, the lengths that I went to in order to clear your debt and withhold the knowledge from your beautiful wife and family?"

"I have not, but you did not risk your life in doing so. Mr. Green has the ability to ruin me."

"You are correct that my life was not at stake, but something more precious was, my reputation." Pierre spoke with a calm firmness that I had never seen in him, a trait I wished I had the skill for. I sat with a quiet concentration as I took in all that I needed to learn about conducting business. "You are a businessman, and this advertisement is a paying job. Mr. Green cannot fault you for that." Pierre paused as if waiting for a response. Mr. De Vries sat in his chair, motionless, and stared at the two of us. "I must insist that this run in the next issue. If it does not, I might be inclined to pay your wife a visit and let her know of some of the less-than-tasteful business deals you have made with her money. It was her money that afforded you this business to begin with, was it not?"

"Fuck." Mr. De Vries shook his head. "She told you?"

"She did indeed." Pierre smiled and nodded. "Now, shall we get back to the business at hand?"

"We shall." He picked up his pen and continued writing. When Pierre was done dictating his advertisement, Mr. De Vries said, "You realize that nothing good will come of this. Why do you insist on provoking that man? You of all people should understand how deep his money and power runs in this city."

"Mr. De Vries, I do appreciate your concern, but it is misdirected. I have a client who is looking for information pertaining to Mr. Johnson's death, and nothing more. I am not implicating Mr. Green. It is not my place to do so. I am searching for some answers that can be relayed to my client, and nothing more."

"I will leave my questions at that," Mr. De Vries replied. "The less I know of this inquiry, the better off I shall be." He pushed the chair away from the desk and stood. "I am to assume that once this advertisement runs, I am free of any debt owed to you?"

"You are for now." Pierre stood. I followed suit. "Knowing you as well as I do, Mr. De Vries, I would wager that our paths shall cross again." Pierre smiled and reached out his hand. Mr. De Vries came around the desk and shook it. He then held out his hand to me. I bowed and took it.

"Your associate here does not have much to say, does he?"

"Oh, you would be surprised." Pierre and I both laughed. Mr. De Vries appeared a bit confused at our private joke. "Thank you again for your time. We shall let ourselves out."

"Very well." Mr. De Vries nodded. "Good evening to the both of you." He returned to his desk. I felt his eyes upon us as we walked out of his office.

"Son of a bitch." I half laughed as we opened the back door and walked into the alley. I took a hold of Pierre's hips, letting him lead the way through the narrow path. "That was fucking amazing. You had so much control and power over him."

"I hope that you do not think…" He stopped as we reached the cross street at the end of the alley and turned to face me. "Please, do not ever think that I am anything like your father. It is true, that in my line of work, I have built a reputation that allows me some power over others. However, I use these skills to guide and direct the decisions of others. I use my influence to help, not destroy."

"I would never consider you like my father. I mentioned this because it brought about an urge to fuck you." I smiled with my confession. "This business side of you has sparked a flame within me that I must find a way to extinguish." I squeezed his round, ample buttocks.

"Then may I suggest we get back to the coffeehouse as soon as possible." He grabbed my hand as we took off running down the alley. As we approached Fleet Street, our hands separated. We slowed our pace and, with an air of gentlemen about us, we walked back to the carriage where Mr. Sutton stood smoking his pipe.

"Where to, sir?" Mr. Sutton snuffed out his pipe and opened the door.

"The coffeehouse." Pierre winked at me. "We have some urgent matters to take care of." He climbed into the carriage behind me.

"I hope it is nothing too serious," Mr. Sutton responded as he hung on to the door and peered into the carriage. He hesitated a moment longer before adding, "Oh, I see." A blush rose upon his neck at the realization of what was so urgent. He snickered and closed the door.

"One thing you shall realize about Mr. Sutton is that it is very difficult to keep matters from him. It is as if he can sense what I am thinking." He placed his hand between my legs and fondled my affairs. "I can only imagine what is running through his mind at the moment." He laughed, then leaned back against the seat cushion as the carriage bounced down the street. He did not take his hand from my stiffening prick until we stopped in front of the coffeehouse.

"Shall we invite Mr. Sutton?" Pierre leaned toward me with a kiss.

"Three at once?" I asked. "I would not know what to do with myself."

"Are you telling me you have never had two men in your bed at the same time? That is difficult for me to believe, considering how you earned a living." He smiled and rubbed his nose against mine. Our lips touched.

"I have not, but with the thought lingering in my mind, I must say I find it quite intriguing."

"Let us play a little joke on him, shall we?" He chuckled. "Follow my lead. We shall have him so worked up with frustration and desire that he will burst his breeches."

"You are a wicked man, Mr. Baptiste, and I love it." I scooted across the seat as Mr. Sutton opened the door. I followed Pierre out of the carriage. "Thank you, Mr. Sutton."

"You are welcome." He shut the door. "Is there anything else I can do for the two of you?"

"If you would not mind turning down Thomas's bed, Mr. Sutton, we would be most appreciative. I do not believe we have the patience for it at the moment." Pierre chuckled.

"Very well, sir." Mr. Sutton trotted ahead of us. He went straight to my room and had readied the bed before we had entered.

"I cannot wait for you to fuck me, Mr. Newton." Pierre groaned as he pulled his waistcoat off and tossed it to the floor. He kicked his shoes off as he made quick work of his blouse; before too long he stood in only his stockings and breeches.

I pulled my waistcoat off as I approached him. I licked beneath his chin, and his whiskers poked my tongue. I moved down his chest, licking the oils and sweat from the tight moss of curls that spread across his body. When I bit his erect tit, he moaned. He pulled me off him and tore at my blouse, not bothering with the lace. I pulled the ripped fabric from my body and threw it across the room. From the corner of my eye, I witnessed Mr. Sutton standing in the back of the room. He cleared his throat as if reminding us of his presence. We ignored him.

I fell to my knees and rolled Pierre's stockings down as he unlaced his breeches. I tugged on the tight-fitting material, pulling it down his hairy legs. His prick, full of unmet needs, bounced out of his breeches and slapped me in the face, leaving a trail of his clear nectar across my cheek. I looked up at him as I ran my tongue beneath the long, hard trunk of his prick. He winked at me, bent down, and lifted me up.

He kissed me as he unlaced my breeches. I pulled them off, bringing with them my stockings. I backed away from him, enjoying the full view of his masculine qualities. The air in the room became sodden with our heavy breath, naked bodies, and mounting desire. We turned to face Mr. Sutton. The lump in his breeches told of his need for our attention. He began to untie his blouse. I shook my head. "No. You are not to do a thing." I walked toward him and finished what he had started.

Pierre came up behind us and fell to his knees. He unlaced Mr. Sutton's breeches. I moved in closer, enjoying the subtle touches of Pierre as he undressed Mr. Sutton. I pulled off Mr. Sutton's blouse, leaned down, and brought his erect tit between my lips. I rolled my tongue over the hard nub. Mr. Sutton trembled against me.

I lowered myself down his body, licking the perspiration from his smooth skin. Pierre and I pulled his breeches down his legs and let them gather at his ankles. I slipped the shoes off his feet and removed his breeches as Pierre spread his buttocks and laid quick kisses through the crack of his ass.

Mr. Sutton moaned as he bent over me. I slipped one, then the other of his tender rocks into my mouth and rolled my tongue over them before letting them slip from my mouth with a gentle pop. His legs trembled against my face. I lowered myself and moved my tongue farther into his private region. My tongue met Pierre's as we reached the dark crevice at the same time. We licked his body together, sharing with each other the flavors of Mr. Sutton's private area. He groaned and I felt his legs quiver against my face. His knees bent as he fell over the top of me, landing face first upon the bed.

He rolled over on his back. Pierre and I stood and moved to the edge of the bed. Mr. Sutton's prick lay in a puddle of its own excitement. I ran a finger down Mr. Sutton's leg. My touch excited him. His prick bobbed up and down against his belly and smacked into the growing pool of his early release.

"Do not stand there and just look at me," he pleaded. "Touch me, fuck me. Do something other than make me wait a moment longer." He grabbed his legs and raised them into the air. He wiggled his hips, begging further with the use of his body.

"Shall we?" I asked Pierre as I grabbed Mr. Sutton's legs. I bent down and ran my tongue through the stale crack of his ass, inhaling his odor. My prick responded to his scent with a spit of clear nectar. I grabbed the trunk of my prick and rubbed the moisture over Mr. Sutton's quivering hole.

"Oh, yes fuck me, please fuck me," Mr. Sutton yelled in anticipation of my insertion. "Oh, do not delay, you wicked man." The whole of his body, covered in sweat, shook and rocked upon the bed while he demanded my prick to enter him.

"Give him what he wants, Thomas." Pierre watched over my shoulder as he rubbed his massive prick up and down the crack of my ass. He pushed his body against mine. My prick popped inside Mr. Sutton, who yelped with the sudden force. "All of it, Thomas. Give it to him good."

I took Pierre at his word and shoved the entire length of my prick into Mr. Sutton's waiting ass. He screamed in delight as I filled him with my needy prick. I pulled out, watching with growing urgency as my soiled prick glided out of Mr. Sutton's damp, hairless hole.

Pierre reached around me and pulled Mr. Sutton closer to the edge of the bed. He grabbed my waist and forced my insertion once more. Our bodies slapped against each other. The bed creaked. Mr. Sutton groaned.

"Get your knees on the bed, Thomas. Let us see if we can fuck him together."

"Oh yes," Mr. Sutton screamed in delight. "That is what I want, my two masters fucking me. Do it, yes, do it!"

I crawled upon the bed and bent over Mr. Sutton, my prick shoved deep inside him. We rocked upon each other as I gave him soft, gentle thrusts of my hips, sending blissful pleasure between the two of us.

The pressure against Mr. Sutton's ass grew as Pierre aimed the head of his prick beneath the trunk of mine. I watched Mr. Sutton grimace as he took the length and girth of Pierre's prick while still indulging in mine.

"Son of a bitch." I moaned as I felt Pierre's solid prick glide beneath mine in the tight, warm confines of Mr. Sutton's ass. Pierre grabbed my hips. We rocked with slow, steady thrusts against Mr. Sutton. Our pricks slid in and out in unison as we fucked.

"Mother of mercy, you are splitting me in two," Mr. Sutton cried. "Oh, God, I have never," he gasped for air, "been given over to such… please, fuck me and end this unbearable pleasure." He grabbed his own swollen prick and began to stroke himself with ferocious speed. "Oh, I cannot hold back a moment longer." Mr. Sutton groaned as the quick work of his prick brought with it three, then four thick ribbons of his white pearls. His chest was soon covered in his release. He let go of his red, swollen prick and threw his arms up over his head.

"Oh Lord." I groaned as the pleasure mounted within me at the sight of Mr. Sutton's sweat-dampened pits. His body's sex-drenched aroma drifted around us and made me drunk with desire. "Yes, Pierre, oh, your prick feels so good against mine." I placed my hands upon the bed as Pierre wrapped his arms around me. We sank into a quick, heavy rhythm as we continued to fuck Mr. Sutton. I felt myself reach the end of my moment. "Oh fuck," I screamed as my prick exploded a heavy spurt of seed into Mr. Sutton's ass. He groaned and begged for more as I shot another large quantity of myself inside him.

I wanted to stop and rest my weary body, but Pierre continued to fuck, forcing the continued action upon me. His prick shuddered against mine, filling Mr. Sutton's ass with more of our release. We continued to fuck him, spurting our seed in alternating waves of the most wonderful pleasure I had ever known.

"My Lord." I panted as Pierre and I pulled out of Mr. Sutton's ass and fell to either side of him. I shivered from the chill of our activities. No one spoke. The only sounds within the room were our heavy breaths as our bodies rested.

It was not long before I heard the gentle snoring of both Pierre and Mr. Sutton. I closed my eyes and let myself fall to sleep.

I awoke with the dull rays of sun shining across my face. I looked over at Pierre and Mr. Sutton. Their naked bodies were intertwined; their stomachs rose and fell with their breath. I smiled and looked around at my room. A twinge of sadness rippled through me as I thought of the many mornings I had woken from a restful sleep with the sounds of Mother singing. I hummed one of the songs as it floated through my memory. It was then that I spotted the issue of *The Tatler* that I had picked up the night before. I got up from the bed, being careful not to wake the others. I lit my pipe, picked up the paper, and settled into a small chair in the corner of the room. I glanced up at Pierre and Mr. Sutton. A feeling of comfort washed over me. I opened the paper. My heart stopped as I glanced upon a notice on the front-page.

"Son of a bitch," I shouted, waking up both Pierre and Mr. Sutton. I rose from my chair and took a drag of my pipe to ease the tension rushing through me.

"Thomas, what has come over you?" Pierre rubbed the sleep from his eyes as he came toward me.

"This," I shouted and pointed at the advertisement announcing the hanging of Alistair Phillips. "I cannot believe he is still alive. I must go visit him." I tossed the paper on the chair.

"Thomas, please, this is not a good idea." Pierre stopped me as I went for my clothes.

"Pierre, I must. Alistair was the one person I trusted back then. I would be dead if it were not for him. I have to try to help him."

"Help him?" Mr. Sutton interjected as he pulled his breeches up and reached for the discarded news. He looked at the advertisement. "He is due to hang tomorrow morning."

"That is why I must go. I do not have much time." I looked at the two of them standing in defiance of my plan.

"What about the promise you made to me, Thomas? You cannot go around stirring up trouble."

"Trouble has found us, has it not?" I waited for a response that never came. "Fine, then help me. I would rather not do this alone, but I will if I must." I took Pierre's hands in mind. "Please, it is the least I can do for him. I cannot let my father take the life of someone whose sole crime was to befriend me."

"What about Mrs. Fernsby?" Mr. Sutton questioned.

"Who?"

"Elizabeth Fernsby. She came to Pierre several months ago to ask for help."

"What does she have to do with Alistair?"

"Yes, she came to my mind as well." Pierre looked at Mr. Sutton. "She and her husband are desperate enough to agree to such a plan."

"Thomas, if you promise to stay low and out of trouble after this, then I think I know how to help Alistair." Pierre pulled on his blouse. "Mr. Sutton, you and I shall go to Moorfields and look for Mrs. Fernsby. We can drop Thomas off at Newgate on the way."

"Will someone please explain to me what we are doing?" I reached for my clothes on the floor and began to pull on my breeches.

"Thomas, my love, I shall explain everything to you on the way." Pierre buttoned his blouse and slipped on his shoes. "Will you be all right at Newgate on your own?"

"Yes, I can handle myself."

"That is what worries me." He leaned in and kissed me. "Time is not on our side, and we have much to do before the hanging. If one good thing is to come of this, it will be that we shall have pulled one over on Mr. Green."

"I like the sound of that." I slipped on my shoes, hopping on one foot, then the other as I followed Pierre and Mr. Sutton out of the house.

CHAPTER TWELVE

Newgate Prison loomed in front of us as our carriage made its way down Fleet Street and into Central London. Its foreboding presence seemed to call to me, welcoming me back to the hell, which lay waiting within. Memories of my time inside the prison rushed through me, striking me with unexpected blows. I took a deep breath to settle my nerves as Mr. Sutton guided the carriage to a stop. Even before I stepped out onto the street, the disease and death that permeated the old walls reached out and touched me, suffocating me with its grip. My mind returned to Mother Clap locked away in the rot and stench of the cell. It was as if no time had passed since the day I told her of my deal with the Society for the Reformation of Manners. She cried when I told her that I had agreed to testify against our friends in order to save our lives. It was the only time that I remembered her crying. She had begged me to reconsider, reminding me that our own execution would be more agreeable than living with the blood of our friends upon our hands.

"Are you all right, Thomas?" Pierre questioned as I stared up at the prison from the safety of the carriage. Pierre placed his hand on my leg and squeezed it, pulling me back from the memories that haunted me.

"I believe I am. I was just lost in my mind for a moment." I tried to bring a reassuring smile to my face. It quivered and fell away. "When I left London, I swore that I would never enter this place again."

"It is not too late to turn back."

"I am afraid I cannot do that. Alistair is in there because of me."

"Your father is to blame for Alistair's incarceration, not you, *mon amour*." He held my chin in his fingers and turned my head toward him. "You must stop blaming yourself for what happened. Everything that transpired last year did so because of your father's actions. You are as much a victim as anyone."

"Whether it is my father's fault or my own poor decisions, I have to try to right some of the wrongs that were inflicted upon people." I exited the carriage, turned back, and looked at Pierre sitting inside. Another brief smile creased my lips. I hesitated before shutting the door, then stood in the shivering cold and watched as the carriage pulled away from me. Snow began to fall as if the sky were crying frozen tears. I turned to face the prison. It towered over me, and I felt insecure and small in its presence. The nerves rippled through me, causing my belly to ache. I closed my eyes and inhaled, hoping to settle the sickness I felt coming upon me.

I walked into the central courtyard. My heart pounded in my chest and caused my head to ache. I hesitated, turned back toward the city at the people going about their daily lives, and wondered what it would be like to live a normal life free of fear and my father's wrath.

"Do you have a purpose here?" a gruff voice shouted at me from the entrance of the prison doors.

"Yes, I do." I walked toward the man. His eyes fell upon me with uncertainty. "I hear that the execution of Mr. Phillips is slated for tomorrow morning. I wish to see him."

"What business is it of yours?"

"The treacherous prat owes me money." The lie came to my tongue with ease. I had played these games too many times before to pretend otherwise. "I wish to find a way to settle his debt with me before he hangs."

"His allowance for visitors extends to his wife and son. I am sorry, you shall have to find another way."

"I trust this will gain me entrance?" I took five shillings from my waistcoat and held them in my hand.

"It will." He took the money and pocketed it. "And I trust this exchange will be kept a secret?" He turned and headed inside.

"Of course." I followed him into the prison without further conversation. The deplorable conditions of the prison attacked me from all sides as we entered. It was then that I realized how memory fades with time, even from within a year. What I remembered and dreamt of those days seemed childlike compared to the conditions that I observed with fresh eyes and nose.

As we passed the overcrowded cells, several men called out to me with vulgar propositions. I looked through the dim light, hoping I would not recognize them as former customers. They were all strangers to me. They lay or stood shoulder to shoulder, head to feet in the rot and stench of shit and piss. Their hollow eyes and sunless skin made them ghostlike, as if death had already claimed them. The farther we walked into the depths of the prison, the worse the conditions became. I coughed and choked on the foul stench that was the only air to breathe. *How did we survive?*

"His cell is down here on the right." The gaoler's voice startled me out of my thoughts as we walked into an area of the prison I had not seen before. Gone were the open cells crowded with dying men. Walls of stone lined both sides of the narrow corridor. Every few feet, a wooden door appeared with a small window in the center of it. "If you want to go into his cell, it will cost you an extra two shillings. Otherwise, you can stand outside and talk through the window."

I handed him the money without further comment and waited with growing nerves while he unlocked the cell door.

"Mr. Phillips, it is your lucky day. We have a visitor for you." He turned to me. "You have thirty minutes." He let me enter the cell, then shut and locked the door behind me. I watched him leave before turning toward Alistair, who sat chained to the floor. He was thin, and like the others, appeared pale and sick. The stained and tattered clothes hung from his frail body.

"Alistair?" I walked toward him with careful steps, as I was not sure how he would react to my presence. He looked up at me. Recognition did not come at once.

"Thomas?"

"Yes, it is I." I knelt down beside him.

"What are you doing here? Where have you been? I suspected you were dead." He reached his arms out as far as the chains would allow. I embraced him, feeling every bone in his body. He shook, though whether it was from an illness or shock at seeing me, I did not know for sure. It was in those few moments I knew I would do whatever it took to save the life of the man who had saved mine.

"I have come to help," I whispered in his ear before breaking the embrace. As much I knew he needed human touch, the foul odors from his body made my stomach sour.

"That is very noble of you, Thomas, but no one can help me."

"Please, you must listen to me."

"You are serious about this?" The sadness in his voice eased.

"Yes, I am. Plans are being made as we speak." I lowered my voice even more.

"How is that possible?"

"Shh." I held a finger to lips. "It is much too dangerous to discuss the details in here. I fear being overheard." I looked back at the door, but the light inside the cell was too dim to tell if the gaoler stood on the other side, listening to our conversation. "You shall have to put your trust in me."

"It is difficult for me to comprehend all of this. I have spent so much time in here thinking of my own death and reconciling myself to never seeing my son and wife again. Then here you come with this news." He began to weep. I held him despite his odor, rocking him as Mother had done for me when words were not enough to console the mind.

"Can you," he struggled to speak between the tears, "find my wife and tell her the good news?"

"Alistair, we cannot tell anyone at this point. The more people who know of our plan, the more dangerous it becomes for everyone involved. We cannot take the chance on anyone finding out. But I shall try to find her once you are out of this place."

"Please, do not take this as ingratitude, but why are you risking the freedom you worked so hard to obtain to help me?"

"You risked everything for me during those last few months, trying to warn Christopher as you did even though your disguise had been uncovered. I caused you and your family a lot of grief—"

"But you saved our son. I repaid your kindness to me, nothing more."

"Yes, but my freedom cost you yours. I cannot stand by and let them take another life."

"He is with you, is he not?"

"Christopher? No, I never saw him again."

"I am sorry."

"No need for that. You did everything possible to help him." I squeezed his shoulder to reassure him. "I am starting to believe that events in people's lives happen for a reason whether we know those reasons or not. I have met the most amazing man who accepts me for who I am. Something Christopher was never able to do."

"Is he the man who is helping us?"

"Yes."

"Then I look forward to meeting him."

"Your time is up," the gaoler bellowed through the window.

"It has not been the thirty minutes I paid for," I shouted.

"Perhaps not, but I have been ordered to bring you to the receiving room."

"Who?" I called out. "No one knows I am here."

"Oh, Thomas, be careful." Alistair took my hand. "If the plan to free me is too full of risk I shall understand."

"Do not worry yourself, Alistair. You shall see me again." I stood and walked toward the gate as the gaoler opened it.

"Follow me." His emotionless expression had not changed, but something in the tone of his voice had. I held my tongue and followed him through the prison halls. "In there," he said as we approached the closed door. He stood aside as I entered, then came up behind me. Pierre and Mr. Sutton sat at the table in conversation.

"Why the charade?" I looked around the room. "Why not tell me who had come to see me?"

"My apologies, Mr. Newton. We must keep our arrangement a secret. These prison walls have many ears. One rumor of this meeting in the wrong hands would be the end of all of us."

"Arrangements?"

"Yes, Thomas." Pierre remained seated. "This is Mr. Collins." Pierre waited as Mr. Collins reached out and shook my hand. Pierre continued, "I helped him out a few years back with some personal matters around his vicious wife."

"Wretched whore." He spat.

"He has agreed to help us."

"I believe these belong to you." He smiled, an obviously awkward expression for him, as he returned the shillings.

"Do not be offended by my remarks, but why Mr. Collins?" I slipped the money back into my pocket.

"Mr. Collins has worked at Newgate for fifteen years. We need someone on the inside if our plan is going to be successful. Please, sit. We have a lot to talk about and very little time to prepare."

❖

I woke the next morning before the sun had risen over the horizon. My sleep had been restless as the dreams and anxieties of the escape would not ease their grip on my mind even as I slept. I looked over at Mr. Sutton's naked body. His prick was stiff with night dreams. I licked my lips, wanting nothing more than to slide my tongue over the length of his trunk and wake him with a morning release. My own prick stiffened at the thought. I tugged on it and a soft moan escaped my lips. I gripped my satchel and pulled, bringing with it a stinging pleasure that lit a fire deep within my belly. I hesitated but soon realized it was too late to stop. I fondled myself with growing urgency as I gazed with hungry eyes upon my sleeping bedmate. The pleasure came too sudden to fully appreciate. I did not fight it but let the release take over and sprayed my seed across my body. I shook and trembled from the intense satisfaction that my release brought and licked my fingers clean, tasting of my own gratification.

I sat up, swinging my feet to the floor, and watched my prick recede as another spasm shot through me, spilling the last of my seed on the floor. I stood up and walked to the window, pulled the curtain back, and peered out into the night. I thought of Alistair alone in his cell, spending what might have been his last few hours alive hoping we would come for him but unaware of how or when—or if we would come at all.

"Is everything all right?" Mr. Sutton's sudden question caused me to jump.

"I suppose."

"What is troubling you?"

"The last time someone counted on me to get them out of Newgate, I failed."

"Mother Clap?"

"Yes." I held back a tear as it pooled in my eye. "It still hurts after all this time."

"Be thankful for the time you had with her, Thomas." He came to me. "Most people never get to experience that kind of unconditional love. Rejoice in the memories, and do not let it burden you. If you hold on to the grief too long, the memories become tainted. She would not have wanted that for you." He wrapped his arms about me and his stiffness settled into the crevice of my ass.

"Thank you for those words. I shall remember that, and I shall take you up on this offer when this is over." I wiggled my hips, turned, and kissed him. "We should dress and get down to the prison." I broke our embrace as anxiety and nerves riddled my body like a thousand sewing needles piercing my skin.

The cold morning air caught in my throat as we left the coffeehouse and made our way to the carriage. I sat up front with Mr. Sutton to finalize our plans. It was just before dawn as we rode through the still-slumbering streets of London.

"I hate this fucking place." I broke the cold silence as we pulled the carriage around to the back of Newgate. Pierre was standing in the shadows of an alley waiting for us. He approached us as we tied the horses down.

"Mr. Collins is waiting by the back service entrance for the two of you. I shall be here waiting." He looked around, and seeing that we were alone, he embraced us. "Be safe in there."

"We shall." Mr. Sutton replied for the two of us. "Wish us luck."

We walked down the street and into the narrow alley behind the prison. I knocked on the door. Mr. Collins was waiting on the other side with a look of apprehension on his face.

"You look worried, is everything all right?"

"I am a bit nervous. There are many things that could go wrong with this plan. So far everything is on schedule." He let us enter, then shut the door. He looked at his watch. "Here is the outfit, Mr. Newton. I hope you do not mind changing in the dark? I do not want to draw unnecessary attention back here."

"Not at all." I undressed down to my linens with great speed, handing the discarded clothing to Mr. Sutton, and slipped on the black breeches, shirt, and waistcoat. "Someone will have to help me with the collar." Mr. Collins came and placed it about my neck. "So will I pass for a member of the clergy?"

"I am sorry, Mr. Newton." Mr. Sutton chuckled. "Knowing your background, it is a bit comical." He held several fingers to his lips to keep his laughter quiet.

"It will have to do," Mr. Collins said. "I do not mean to be a killjoy, but we still need to get Mr. Fernsby out of his cell without raising suspicion."

"Yes, of course, my apologies." Mr. Sutton looked at me and winked. He stepped aside, and as I passed he whispered, "I have always wanted to fuck a priest." He snickered in my ear as we followed Mr. Collins through the dark, damp halls of the prison.

"The cells holding men for transportation are through these doors," Mr. Collins commented as we came to a stop. "I shall go in and bring Mr. Fernsby to you. You shall have five minutes to make your way to Mr. Phillips's cell before I release the rest of them." He took a key from his pocket. "This will unlock Mr. Phillips's cell. Good luck, men."

"Thank you, Mr. Collins," I whispered. Mr. Sutton nodded. We stood back as Mr. Collins opened the door and slipped inside. Through the darkness we heard the prisoners calling out to him; some begged for tobacco, others asked for their wife or a whore. I looked at Mr. Sutton, whose eyes were fixed upon me. He raised his eyebrows and puckered his lips. I shook my head at his insatiable appetite and returned my attention to the commotion coming from behind the door. The sound of the cell door unlocking echoed down the corridor. The prisoners in the holding cell cheered and shouted profanities as Mr. Collins called out for Mr. Fernsby. I heard the door shut and relock. The uproar grew more aggressive as Mr. Fernsby was led down the corridor.

"Go. Remember you have five minutes before the riot starts," Mr. Collins whispered.

"Are you ready, Mr. Fernsby?"

"You must be Mr. Newton," he said as we ran down the corridors. "Thank you for doing this."

"I should be the one thanking you," I replied as I escorted him down the corridors. The three of us stopped as we came upon the area of private cells. "Mr. Fernsby, please go ahead and undress while I go and fetch Mr. Phillips. You will need to exchange clothing as they have already dressed him for the execution." I turned and opened the door to yet another wing of the prison.

As I walked down the hallway with individual cells on both sides of me, men saw me in my cleric attire and came to the edge of their cells, asking me to pause so that they could confess their crimes before God. I raised my hand to them and shook my head as I passed.

"Are you ready, Mr. Phillips?" I called into the cell as I unlocked the door.

"Yes, Father, I am ready." He looked up. His expression of sorrow faded as he saw it was me who stood before him. He held his head low. "Thank you, Father, for coming."

"Have you confessed your crimes to God and asked for his forgiveness?" I hoped I sounded convincing enough for the other prisoners.

"Yes, Father, I have."

We walked out of the area and shut the door behind us.

"Mr. Phillips, please put these on." Mr. Sutton handed him Mr. Fernsby's clothing.

"I cannot thank you enough for what you are doing for my family." Alistair hugged Mr. Fernsby. I pulled them apart. "I am sorry, yes my clothing." Alistair began to undress, handing Mr. Fernsby his clothes one article at a time. Before Alistair had fully dressed, we heard the commotion coming from the other wing of the prison.

"Shit. We must hurry." We took off running through the prison as the men who were scheduled for transportation scattered about the hallways, yelling and screaming for their freedom. The other gaolers shouted for help as they tried to control the desperate men running wild through the prison. We managed to pull ourselves through the growing crowds and found ourselves at the back entrance of the prison. "Alistair, Mr. Sutton will see that you get back to the coffeehouse. Pierre has the coach waiting."

"What about you? I am not leaving you in here."

"You have no other choice. I still have work to do here. Now go, I promise to come to you when all this is over."

"Come on, Mr. Phillips." Mr. Sutton escorted him to the back door. They both turned around and looked at me. I nodded to them as they stepped outside and closed the prison door.

"Come on. They will be expecting us." I took Mr. Fernsby by the elbow and led him down the hallways. Several of the escaped prisoners rushed by us, knocking us out of their way as they passed. We remained where we stood as two gaolers gave chase. Our purpose for being there went unquestioned. "All right, we are almost there. Are you ready for this?"

"Yes, I am." Mr. Fernsby smiled at me, the last person he would ever see.

"I shall be there right to the end." I slipped the hood over his face and secured it with some twine.

"Be there for my wife and children is all that I ask." His voice was muffled. I tied his hands behind his back. He trembled as he readied himself to hang for someone else's crime.

"Here we go." I grabbed hold of his arm and led him down the final hallway and out into the courtyard, where the wagon waited to take him to Tyburn.

"Why is this man hooded?" A man came upon us as I was helping Mr. Fernsby into the wagon.

"It was his last request." I leapt up onto the wagon. "You will not begrudge a man's dying wish. Let us go," I shouted to the driver.

The wagon leapt forward. Mr. Fernsby, unprepared for such a sudden departure, staggered backward. I grabbed him before he tumbled into the street.

The crowds grew thicker as we came upon Tyburn Square. The streets were filled with people shouting obscenities and throwing fruits and stones toward the moving wagon. Many of them missed their target, but the few that struck Mr. Fernsby did so with great force. Mr. Fernsby screamed as a large stone struck him in the side of the head. I leaned toward him to ask if he was injured. Through the canvas sack, I heard Mr. Fernsby repeating the Lord's Prayer. I pulled back and let him spend his final moments in peace.

The wagon came to a rough stop. The crowds had tripled since we had left the prison, which made any movement between the wagon and the gallows difficult. The people cheered and applauded, drinking gin and other liquors. Street vendors sold fresh-baked meat pies and bread, all for celebrating another hanging.

"Bless you, my son." I spoke as the officials climbed aboard to prepare him.

I climbed off the wagon. The officials bowed their heads toward me. I smiled and stepped away, no one the wiser that the man being hanged was not the condemned criminal.

I pushed my way through the multitude of onlookers and found an open spot from which to watch. My heart went out to the man who stood before the city. Unlike the three other men upon their respective wagons, Mr. Fernsby had requested his hanging. The knowledge that this was what he and his wife wanted made little difference to the fact that Pierre, Mr. Sutton, and I were trading one life for another. I watched on. The knot in my belly grew as they slipped the noose over Mr. Fernsby's head and secured it about his neck. The screams of the crowd quieted while they waited with eagerness to witness another group hanging.

Gasps echoed through the streets as the executioner gave the signal. The horses were slapped. They lurched forward, causing the wagons to be pulled out from underneath the men. The four bodies swung in the air. A hush fell over the crowd. In those first few moments, the only sound that came through the air was the creaking of the ropes as the bodies swung and twitched with the last of their lives. When the bodies quieted, the people celebrated with a triumphant cheer. I shook my head and turned away from the vulgarities of life.

"You fucking wanker!" A high-pitched voice came from behind me. I turned around and was met with the most stinging of slaps against my face.

"Caroline, Henry." I rubbed my cheek.

"How dare you show your fucking face here today?" Caroline spat. "Alistair and I risked everything for you, and you just disappeared when Alistair was arrested. Where have you been?"

"Whoa, Mrs. Phillips, please you do not know what you are talking about."

"Do not patronize me." She raised her hand to me again.

"Stop this." I caught her hand in midair.

"Mr. Newton, let go of my mother's hand." Henry spoke.

"My apologies, Caroline." I released her hand.

"How could you show yourself today?" Caroline began to weep.

"Excuse me, are you Mr. Newton, Thomas Newton?" A young woman holding two small children approached me.

"Yes, I am. Are you…?"

"Yes, Elizabeth Fernsby." She wiped a tear from her cheek before taking my hand. "I am so glad I have found you here. I wanted to thank you for everything you have done for my husband and me."

"It is I who should be thanking you, my lady. In fact, Caroline and Henry owe you a great deal of gratitude as well." I glanced over at the two, who stood with confused looks upon their faces.

"Are you Mrs. Phillips?"

"I am. Who are you?"

"Oh, do they not know?"

"What is this woman talking about?"

"No, I am afraid they believe it to be Alistair upon the noose." I turned to Caroline and held her trembling hand. "Caroline, Alistair did not die up there this morning," I explained with as much tact as possible, knowing what the shock might do to her. She looked at her son, then at me. Her lips moved but no words formed. I continued. "It was Elizabeth's husband who hanged in Alistair's place. Alistair is alive and well. He is waiting for the two of you."

"What? I do not understand. What are you telling me?" Her voice trembled as the tears puddled in the corner of her eyes. She reached out for her son's shoulder as if holding steady against fainting.

"I am sorry," Mrs. Fernsby said. "I must go. The carriage is waiting to take us away to our new life. I just wanted to thank you, Mr. Newton, for giving my husband his final request and letting him die knowing we are taken care of." She stood on her toes and kissed me. "Thank you again." She turned and hurried away down the street.

"Mother, are you all right?" Henry asked.

"I am not sure." She looked at her son, then at me. "A few moments ago I watched a man who I thought was my beloved husband hang, and now I find out it was some stranger who gave his life so that Alistair's could be saved."

"I am sorry that we were not able to tell you of our plan in advance of the hanging. The last thing we wanted was for you to suffer with the false knowledge of Alistair's death. It was too dangerous for us to get word to you."

"My Lord." She sighed as new tears fell from her face. "The things I said to you, Thomas." She ran her fingers down my reddened cheek. "How can you ever forgive me?"

"Forgiveness is not necessary. You did not know." I handed her my handkerchief. "Here, dry your tears so that the cold air does not freeze them to your face."

"Thank you." She blotted her eyes.

"What is important is that we get out of here before someone notices us in conversation. Alistair is waiting for you at the coffeehouse."

"Yes, of course. Please, take us to him."

I took Mrs. Phillips by the arm and led her and Henry through some of the back alleys and less-traveled streets in hopes of avoiding any unwanted attention or worse yet, questions. Our faces were red from the cold by the time we reached the back of the coffeehouse.

"We shall go in through the back to avoid being seen." I opened the door to the cellar and escorted them up the flight of stairs. The house seemed too quiet. I looked at Mrs. Phillips. Her face was streaked with concern. As we continued down the hallway, a sudden burst of laughter drifted through the closed door leading to the private tavern. I opened the door. Pierre, Mr. Sutton, and Alistair were sitting at a table drinking. They looked up at us. Alistair stood using the table to support his weakened body. He looked at his wife and son and took a small step forward. Pierre held him up from falling.

"Alistair," Mrs. Phillips shouted.

"My love." Alistair's voice cracked. Tears trickled down his face. A feeble smile crossed his lips.

"Good Lord." She leapt down the stairs, followed by her son. "I cannot believe this." She fell into his arms. If it were not for the support of Pierre, they would have tumbled to the floor.

I stood at the top of the stairs and watched as the three of them were reunited. Pierre looked up at me. He nodded and smiled. I went to his outstretched arms and wrapped my arms about him. "Thank you."

"The joy on your face is the only thanks I need, my love. You did a wonderful thing today, and I am glad that you trusted me enough to let me help you."

"I would love to see the look on my father's face when he learns of the body switch."

"Yes, that is what worries me. We still have to get Alistair and his family out of town before anyone learns what we did."

CHAPTER THIRTEEN

I do hate to break up this celebration," Pierre interjected, "but we are running out of time. We need to get the three of you to safety before anyone realizes what has happened." He pulled himself from our embrace.

"Mrs. Phillips, it is a pleasure to meet you. I am Pierre Baptiste and this is my associate, Mr. Sutton."

"I have no words to show my gratitude for what the three of you have done for Alistair and my family."

"It was our pleasure, my lady, though I must admit that we have received something out of this as well." Pierre looked at me and nodded.

"What is that?" Mr. Phillips questioned.

"Saving your life means that we were able to get one up on Mr. Green and his vendetta against Thomas. I am hoping that once he realizes what has happened he will make the next move and perhaps give us something more concrete to use against him. The more nervous he becomes, the better our chances are that he will make a mistake. That is why we must get you out of London."

"Is that wise, considering Alistair's health?" I questioned. "Would it not be better to let him rest here?"

"It would, but we cannot risk it."

"I am sorry, but what does Bartholomew Green have to do with Thomas and my conviction?"

"May I tell them, Thomas?" Pierre questioned. I nodded for him to continue. "Mr. Green is Thomas's father."

"What?" Mr. Phillips spat.

"It is true." I continued, "My father is trying to keep our familial relationship a secret. With the knowledge that I have gained since my return, I am convinced that your arrest had nothing to do with your infiltrating the Society as one of their own, and everything to do with your association with me. I believe my father was afraid you knew my true identity and needed to silence you."

"My Lord." Mrs. Phillips sighed.

"I have been investigating Mr. Green for some time, and I would have to agree with Thomas's assessment. Mr. Green is eliminating anyone who knew the truth."

"Mother Clap?" Alistair asked.

"We believe she was getting too close for my father's comfort. Without the court's approval, he sent her to the pillory. I would wager he paid people quite a bit of money to make sure she did not survive her injuries."

"Nor would he have to dirty his own hands," Mr. Phillips added. "Make the townspeople do the work for him."

"Why not just kill Thomas?" Mrs. Phillips asked. "Sorry, Thomas, please do not take my question as anything but curiosity."

"I thought the same thing. Pierre believes he is looking to hurt me by murdering the people closest to me."

"We must be going." Mr. Sutton interrupted. "I am sure by now people know of the switch and are looking for Mr. Phillips."

"Should we not stay and help?" Mr. Phillips looked at Pierre.

"I cannot let you do that." I went to Mr. Phillips and his wife. "We have worked too hard to bring your family together after a year of separation. I will not let you risk it. I appreciate your willingness to help, but this is my fight now. Please, go with my blessing."

"Mr. Sutton has the carriage ready to depart," Pierre interjected. "I have some acquaintances in Leeds who have a place waiting for you. I have also secured you a position with a local locksmith. I am sure you will find it a comfortable place."

"I do not know what to say for your kindness." Mr. Phillips wrapped his arm about his wife's waist. "What you have done for us will not be forgotten. If you need anything at all during this difficult situation, I hope that you will call upon my service."

"Thank you." I hugged the three of them. "Take care of yourselves."

"You do the same, Thomas."

"I promise to get word to you when this is all over with." I stepped away. Pierre was there to put his arm about my shoulder. We stood and watched Mr. Sutton escort them out of the coffeehouse and on their way to a new life.

"What now?" I asked, lifting the heavy silence of the room.

"I need to go to my office and check in on a few items. With Mr. Sutton gone for several days, I think it best that we do not separate. We shall pick up some food on the way and eat at my place. I have some gin in a cabinet there. I think we both need a drink about now."

"I would like that." I looked around the empty room with a sigh. "What is troubling you?"

"I would like to reopen the coffeehouse, but with everything that is going on, I do not think it would be wise to bring attention here."

"It is probably best if we wait on the opening."

"I just hate to have it sit here empty. There was a time that this place was filled with laughter and promises of love."

"Love?" Pierre chuckled. "And here I thought it was filled with unanimous fucking."

"You know what I mean."

"Yes." He leaned in and kissed me. "There will be plenty of time to rebuild once we get your father out of the way, I promise."

"I know. I just keep thinking about Mother and how much she loved this place."

"Knowing her, she would want you to wait until it was safe." He patted me on the back. "Shall we take our leave?"

"Sure." I snuffed out the oil lamps on our way out. Before closing the door, I turned back to the spirits that seemed to haunt the room. "Soon, Mother," I whispered into the silent darkness. I closed the door and caught up with Pierre, who was already outside.

"With Mr. Sutton's absence, we do not have a carriage." Pierre pulled his coat tighter about himself to guard against the chill of the afternoon.

"I do not mind walking." I adjusted my cravat to bring it higher about my neck. We set off on Shoe Lane, heading toward Fleet Street and Central London. The streets were marred with cold sludge that seeped into our shoes as we walked. We passed men and women holding on to each other, bracing themselves from the cold. I looked up at Pierre on those occasions wishing that we too were free to walk along the street in an intimate embrace. He would give me a saddened smile, letting me know his thoughts were as mine.

As we crossed through Central London, the streets became dense with people. Men and women, against the cold, hawked their wares. Butchers covered in cold, icy blood slaughtered their merchandise in front of their shops. The discarded innards were tossed into the street without care. Steam rose from the still-warm parts as they sat in pools of icy waste and puddles.

It was well into the afternoon by the time Pierre and I reached Spitalfields. My nose burned from the cold. I slipped it under my cravat and breathed, hoping to warm it. We came upon Spitalfields Market just off Crispin Street and purchased an assortment of breads, meats, and cheese. With our meal ready and our stomachs grumbling, we made the last of the long journey to White Row, where Pierre kept his lodgings.

"Where do you eat?" I entered the cluttered room with no hope of finding a surface to eat upon.

"Most evenings I find myself at one of the local taverns, but if I do find myself eating while I work, I often find my bed the most comfortable place to dine." His wry smile let me know that there was more to his comment than the meal.

"Shall we?" I walked into the bedchamber and placed the food upon the bed. Kicking my shoes off with a swiftness that said *fuck me* more than *let us eat*, I crawled upon the bed, sitting cross-legged with my back against the wall. I patted the spot next to me, picked up a piece of beef, and slipped it into my mouth. My stomach responded with a rumble of delight.

Pierre settled down next to me and took a piece of meat. He rubbed it upon my lips and squeezed the meat, letting the juice run down my chin and neck. I parted my lips and took the meat into my mouth. He moved in closer and licked the juice from my chin, following the trail of flavors down my neck. He came to the first clasp of my blouse and removed it, then descended farther down my body. I moaned from his warm, soft lips upon my chilled skin. He released another clasp and nuzzled against the fur of my chest. A sudden pounding on the front door interrupted our moment.

"Mr. Baptiste," the all-too-familiar voice shouted.

"Shit, my father." I pushed Pierre off me and scrambled to get off the bed. My heart raced with fear and anger as his voice crowded my mind with childhood contempt. I looked at Pierre. "Fuck. The advertisement."

"It appears he has seen it." Pierre stood up from the bed. "Thomas, listen to me. You are to stay in this room. Do not even think about showing yourself to him. We cannot let him know you are back in London, let alone that we know each other. Is that understood?"

"Do not worry. I have no desire to see that son of a bitch." I put my blouse back together, trying to concentrate on the sensation of Pierre's lips that lingered across my chest. My father's voice came again, this time more agitated. Its violent tone chased away any pleasure from my mind. His fist rattled the door within its old, brittle frame.

"Pierre?" I called out as he left the bedchamber. He turned to look at me. "Please, be careful."

"If anything should happen to me, my love…"

"Do not rile my father. He is unpredictable. Know that my promise to stay put will not hold if he comes after you." I gave him a worried smile as he shut the door. I raced to the door and opened it an inch or two so that I could be ready to intervene if necessary.

"Mr. Baptiste. I need to speak with you." The pounding on the door grew louder.

"Mr. Green, what a pleasant surprise. Do come in." Pierre was a master at disguising his moods. His voice was innocent and congenial.

"Cut the crap, Mr. Baptiste. You know perfectly well why I am here." I heard my father move farther into the room.

"Ah, yes. You must be referring to the advertisement in *The Tatler*." Pierre's tone was almost playful. I worried that he was toying with my father's patience, something I'd learned early on was not a good idea. The pits of my arms became damp with perspiration as the nerves continued to ripple through me.

"Who do you think you are, placing an advertisement such as that to soil my reputation?"

"I assure you, Mr. Green, that your reputation, as you call it, is not my concern. What is my concern is that your coachman was murdered in your home, and you do not seem the least bit affected by it. Did you even report the crime to the authorities?"

"How I handle my affairs is none of your fucking business."

"I would have to disagree with you on that point." Pierre glanced in the direction of the bedchamber. His eye twitched when he noticed my curious eye looking out. He moved farther into the room to keep my father's back toward my direction. Pierre leaned against his desk and crossed his arms. "I have been hired to look into Mr. Johnson's death. Therefore, if your affairs, as you call them, become entangled in my investigation, then it is and will be my business."

"Who hired you?"

"My clients' identities are confidential, Mr. Green. I am sure you can understand that. Please, have a seat."

"What kind of games are you playing with me, Mr. Baptiste?"

"I assure you this is no game." Pierre's voice was unwavering.

"This is how it is going to work, Mr. Baptiste." My father's voice was full of conceit. I watched as my father approached Pierre, gripping the door handle and readying myself in case things turned brutal. "You are going to place a retraction in the next issue of that paper, you people call news. You will cancel your agreement with the client, tell them whatever you have to, but make it clear to them that the investigation is dry."

"Mr. Green, I understand your apprehension. After all, your reputation is on the line—"

"My reputation will remain as it is. I can guarantee you that."

"As a law-abiding citizen and businessman, you can understand the financial loss that your arrangement would have upon me."

"Whatever they are paying you, I shall triple it. Name your price, Mr. Baptiste."

"I am sorry, Mr. Green." I heard the old wood of the desk groan as Pierre stood. "My silence cannot be purchased."

"You fuck!" The rage in my father's voice was the same as the day he found me and Christopher together. The door handle rattled from my trembling grip as I heard a loud smack. I knew my father had struck Pierre but forced myself to remain hidden knowing I would make matters worse if I were to show myself.

"I will not be threatened by you, Mr. Green. I think it is time for you to leave."

"You have no understanding of what a threat I can be, Mr. Baptiste. This is your last chance."

"If I did not know any better, I would think you are worried about what I am going to uncover. What are you afraid of, Mr. Green?"

"You should be the one who is afraid, Mr. Baptiste. I am not finished with you." I heard my father's footsteps as he walked across the room and the door slammed shut. I opened the door and ran into the room. Pierre stood near his desk, rubbing the reddened handprint that my father had left upon his cheek.

"Pierre, are you all right?" I pulled his hand away from his face, replacing it with mine.

"Your father is an arrogant son of a bitch." He winced from my touch.

"That is not news to me." I gave him a concerned smile as I removed my fingers from his face. "You should not have pushed him so hard. I worry what he might do."

"I had no choice. I needed to see how he would react to being pressured. He was involved in Mr. Johnson's death. I am convinced of that. The question is how, and more importantly, why."

"But I thought we knew why, to silence everyone who knew my true identity?"

"Your father was terrified just now. I saw it in his eyes." Pierre paused and walked around to the other side of the desk. "No, something more is going on here than either of us is aware of. Mr. Johnson's death is just the beginning."

"But his death is not the first. What about Mother's death? If it were not for us, there would have been Alistair's death to add to the list, and what about James Sanxay?" I did not understand where Pierre was taking his thoughts.

"The others were easy, Thomas. Your father had no known connection to any of them. He would have been able to pay for their deaths without dirtying his hands, but Mr. Johnson's death changes things. He was too close to your father. No, your father had to be desperate in order to risk his position within the House of Lords. He would not risk everything just to keep you a secret. He has done something far worse. We need to find out what."

"I think we need to stop." I walked away from him.

"Why would you say such a thing?" Pierre placed his hands on my shoulders and turned me around to face him. "What is wrong, Thomas?"

"I cannot let anything happen to you." I felt the emotions begin to rise within me, growing until they suffocated me. I knew if I did not get control of them, that I would not be able to form a coherent word. I paused and inhaled, continuing once my emotions subsided. "My father has taken too many people from my life. This is not worth the risk. If he did murder his coachman, he will come after you."

"Thomas, my love, please, we cannot let his threats deter us. Your father must be stopped, otherwise we will never have a chance at a normal life. I do not want you to live in fear of this man any longer."

"But the risk is too great."

"If we do not find a way of stopping your father, those deaths will be for nothing. We will get through this—I promise." He leaned in and kissed my trembling lips. "Now, where were we when your father interrupted us?" The wry smile that I had come accustomed to creased his face.

"Pierre…" I stopped myself from arguing. I let his lips caress my neck as he untied my blouse. I closed my eyes and surrendered to his advances, letting his touch wipe away the fear that had settled into me. "These fucking eyelets," he growled. "Oh Lord." I gasped as Pierre clutched the trim of my blouse and ripped it from my body. He picked me up in his arms and buried his face into my chest, licking the sweat-dampened hair. His lips and tongue groped for the rising nub of my tit. He bit it with gentleness and sucked it into his mouth. My body trembled against his. He carried me back to his desk. With his free hand he swept the papers off the top and laid me upon it.

He unlaced my breeches. I looked upon the urgent desire in his gaze as he took in my body. He rolled the stockings down my legs, raised my feet, and slipped my toes into his mouth. His tongue slipped between each toe as he untied his blouse and shook it off his shoulders. He released my foot and stepped back as he kicked off his shoes and dropped his breeches, stepped out of them with haste, and came at me, fully extended.

He crawled on top of me. Our pricks rubbed against one another, wetting our bodies with early dew. I wrapped my legs about him as his tongue explored my neck, shoulder, and chest. He nibbled and sucked the tender skin that lay beneath the hair in the pit of my arm. He kissed me, sharing with me the flavors of my own body that he too enjoyed. He lowered himself down my body, running his tongue through the fine line of hair that ran down my belly. He stood up and gazed at my nakedness, his face wet with his spit and the early release that he took from my body on his way down.

"Fuck this nonsense," he groaned as he threw my legs over his shoulders with such force I thought I might slide right off the desk. He gripped his solid prick and without hesitation plunged it into my ass.

I screamed as the searing pain of his insertion tore through me. My prick stiffened and expelled a heavy quantity of early release. I wiggled my hips against the trunk of his prick, bring shooting pains of delight through my quivering body.

"Oh, the joy you bring me," I shouted as he pulled his prick from me, then shoved it back inside. "Oh fuck." I raised my arms over my head and gripped the edge of the desk to brace myself for what I knew was going to be a rough fuck.

"Oh, you are such a delight to fuck." He groaned and threw my legs up in the air. He fucked me without pause, without limits. His body slapped against mine, bringing with it the most enduring pleasure I had ever known. I looked at him. His eyes were closed. I did not need to see into those beautiful dark eyes to catch the expression of bliss upon his face.

"Oh, you are such the man." I groaned. "Yes, fuck me harder. Yes, yes, that is it." I coddled my prick, feeling it pulse with urgency and need, smearing my own gratification over the trunk and stroking myself, bringing with it further pleasures that sparked the fire deep within me.

I feasted on Pierre's body. The sweat from his exertion trailed off his face and neck and ran in tiny rivers through the dense hair that covered his chest. I reached out and ran my hand over his body, smearing the hair against his skin, then slipped my fingers into my mouth and savored his sweat upon my tongue. I grabbed my satchel and pulled as the flames burst inside me.

"Oh, yes. Fuck it out of me," I begged. "Oh, Lord of mercy." I arched my back against his thrusts as a thick rope of my pearls exploded from my prick. It splattered my face and neck. Pierre bent over and licked it off my cheek and lips as he fucked me with such force another heavy stream spurted out of me, covering both of our bodies.

"Oh, that is it. Tighten your hole against me." Pierre growled and righted his body, bringing my hips off the edge of the desk. He threw his head back and groaned as he filled me with his hot seed. His assault upon me did not let up as he continued to pound me, sending me into fits of desire. He released several more times until my ass was too full to contain his gifts. His used seed leaked from my ass and covered his affairs.

With his prick still lodged inside me, he lifted me up into his arms and kissed me. His tongue entered my mouth and tasted my own seed that he had fucked from me. He carried me into the bedchamber and laid me upon the bed before removing himself from me. He lay down next to me. Our uneaten meal lay at our feet. He held me. He kissed me. He allowed me for the time being to forget about my father. Our bodies, covered in each other's perspiration and spunk, fell into a state of deep satisfaction. I fell asleep wrapped in Pierre's arms.

❖

Pierre's coughing woke me up. I looked about the darkened room, took a deep breath, and choked on the hot, dirty air. My eyes began to tear. I sat up in the bed and realized the room was full of gray smoke and soot.

"Motherfucker." I jumped out of bed. "Pierre wake up." I shook him. "The building is on fire!"

"What in the hell?" He jumped from the bed and pulled me up with him. "Grab your clothes and get out of here."

"What about you?" I said with growing panic as I bundled my clothes in my arms.

"I shall be right behind you, but I must save all of my notes."

"Pierre, this is no time to worry about that." The air grew thicker with soot and smoldering fragments of the building. I coughed as I took in the hot, heavy air. I looked up as I heard the wood pop, splinter, and groan against the flames. The deafening sounds of the house readying itself for collapse added to my frantic mind.

"Go, God damn it!" He pushed me out of the bedchamber and into the main room. Flames licked the walls, biting and chewing on the old, brittle wood, feeding on it for more destruction to come. The oil lamps sizzled in the near darkness. I heard them crack then shatter, shooting fragments of glass and tiny balls of flames through the air. I felt the burning pain as several of the flaming fragments cut me. I looked behind me hoping to see Pierre. He was down on his hands and knees gathering the journals in his hands.

"Pierre," I screamed as the building gave and shifted upon its frame. I ran over to Pierre and pulled his arm. Pieces of wood, glowing red with burning embers, began to fall from above us. "God damn it, Pierre."

I gathered up a few of his journals that were out of his reach. He stood up and we ran toward the door. The entire room was an inferno from hell. The building was giving up the fight, releasing itself from its wooden frame. The floor became soft and hot, blistering the bottom of my feet. I ran out of the door and into the street and turned around, expecting to see Pierre behind me. He was not there. Through the burning windows I noticed the darkened outline of his body. He had gone back in. Frozen in a state of panic, I watched with growing horror as the building began to collapse.

CHAPTER FOURTEEN

"Pierre," I screamed. My throat hurt from the volume and strain of calling his name. My stomach was in knots. Tears fell down my cold cheeks as the crowds rushed into the winter streets with the heat of the fire burning against their bodies. "Pierre, where are you?" I screamed above the growing noise of screeching timbers and yelling neighbors. An elderly woman came up to me. Her dark eyes shimmered in the flames. She pulled the bed linen up over my shoulders and tried to cover my nakedness from the cold, damp winter air.

"I have to go back inside." I pulled away from her.

"Wait, look." She held my hand. "Mr. Baptiste, he has survived."

"Pierre?" I called as I saw him run from the front of the building. His face, marred with soot, took on an almost deathlike quality. A heavy coat draped over his otherwise naked body smoldered from falling fire and debris. I ran to him. He stumbled and fell into my arms as the back wall of the building gave in and crumbled to the ground, spraying the street with black smoke and balls of fire. The onlookers screamed and scattered in all directions. Burning wood and glowing embers fell around Pierre and me. I covered his body with mine to protect him as the blistering heat pricked our bodies. The horse-drawn fire wagons arrived moments later and began pumping water onto the adjoining buildings to dampen the fire's chances of progressing to other buildings and engulfing the entire area.

"Pierre, what were you thinking?"

"This." He coughed as he pulled the coat from his body. Slung across his back was a heavy satchel. I took it from him, pulling the leather strap from about his neck.

"The two of you will catch your deaths out here," the elderly woman who'd assisted me earlier called to us as she approached. She carried two blankets. Her tone made me think of a woman scolding a couple of naughty children, yet her gestures were from a place of concern.

"Thank you, Mrs. Reed." Pierre choked on his soot-laced breath.

"It is the least I can do, honey." She smiled as she draped the warm, dry blanket over my shoulders then proceeded to do the same for Pierre.

"Yes, thank you, for everything." I took her hand. I hesitated on my next words, not wanting to trouble this woman with more favors. "Do you..." I coughed. My chest ached. "Do you suppose you could locate someone to take us back to my home?"

"I have already done so, my dear." She pointed across the street. "You take care of Mr. Baptiste for us, dear."

"Mr. Newton, my lady, Thomas Newton."

"Take care of Mr. Baptiste, Mr. Newton. He is an important part of this neighborhood. Anything you need, you let me know, and I will make sure that it happens." She patted my face, then turned and hobbled away with the aid of her walking stick.

"Come, Pierre, we need to get you home." I took his elbow in a honorable way so as not to raise suspicion as to our true nature and escorted him to the carriage. I said to the coachman, "We are going to Clap's Coffeehouse on Shoe Lane."

"How is Mr. Clap? I heard that his wife died." There was genuine sadness in his voice.

"Yes, she did. He has moved on. He found it difficult to stay on without her."

"She was a fine woman, that Margaret." He nodded at me and smiled. For a moment, I thought I recognized him as one of Mother's customers. "I take it no one has reopened Margaret's side of the business?"

"No, but you are more than welcome to come in for a drink. I am living there while Mr. Clap is away. The bar is still full of liquor." I climbed up into the carriage and settled in next to Pierre as the carriage pulled away, following the wall to the north of Central London.

"What is in the bag that was so important that you had to risk your life?"

"There was one journal in particular that I could not lose in the fire. I went back inside to fetch it, but soon realized that there were too many to carry. I had to look for something to transport them in. I threw them into this satchel. The one I went back for contains the information I have gathered on your father. I know he started that fire as a warning to me. If we had lost the journal in the fire, our investigation would be finished. I will not let your father win."

"And if I had lost you in that fire, my father would have won anyway."

"Point taken." He coughed. "I am sorry to sound so cavalier with my own life. It is just that you tend to get used to living on the edge in my line of work." He patted my leg. "I suppose I shall have to set up my office at your coffeehouse for a while until I can find another place."

"Why must it be temporary?" I shot him an annoyed glance. "If we are in this together, as you say, then it would seem logical to set up your office in the coffeehouse as a more permanent location."

"I did not want to assume that you would be interested in continuing as my business associate after the investigation of your father was over. You have your business to run."

"As do you," I replied as I looked out the window and saw the coffeehouse come into view. "I see no reason why we cannot run our businesses concurrently. You need a place to meet with your clients, and I have a tavern that needs some activity, some life brought back into it. It is a perfect fit."

"But where—"

"We can discuss details later," I interrupted as the carriage came to a rocky stop. "We need to get you inside and cleaned up." I looked at him with the aid of the street lamp. "You look a mess." I chuckled despite my best efforts to restrain myself. His face was still covered in black soot and smoke. The whites of his eyes almost glowed against his stained skin. Rivers of dried perspiration caused clean lines of skin to appear amid that blackness.

"Sir." The door swung open. The coachman stood in the cold and nodded. We stepped out of the carriage. I reached in and grabbed the satchel of Pierre's journals.

"Have we made each other's acquaintance?" I asked, still feeling as if I knew him.

"Not officially, Mr. Newton. Perhaps a drink is in order?"

"Yes, of course. Come in out of the cold. I shall start a fire, and you can tell me how we have not formally met." I looked at Pierre and saw a cautionary expression set into his soot-covered face. I led the way into the coffeehouse, followed by Pierre, who was aided by our unknown coachman. I gathered some wood from the hearth, and after a few failed attempts to light the wood, the room came aglow with the warmth of the fire. I gathered a few buckets of water and hung them inside the fireplace to heat, knowing Pierre would need to bathe to rid himself of the soot. "Please make yourself comfortable while I pour us a drink."

Pierre was already behind the bar with a pan of cold water washing the soot from his face, neck, and hands.

"I told you, you were a fright." I smiled as I pulled out a bottle of gin and three glasses, then tossed Pierre a dry towel to wipe himself with as we walked across the room to where this stranger sat.

"Thank you for your hospitality."

"We should be thanking you for bringing us home." Pierre poured the drinks, handed one to the unintentional guest, then took a seat next to me as he gave me my drink. "Can I ask you your name, and how you know Thomas?" he asked with a casual yet curt tone. I was beginning to see that he gave very little concern for proper etiquette and manners. He was polite, a gentleman in every sense of the word, but he had little patience for formality.

"Yes, I am sorry. My name is Kendrick Crowe."

"That name means nothing to me." I looked at Pierre.

"It should not. As I said, we were never introduced as two men should be. I know of you through your reputation. I hope someday to experience your skills firsthand." His face reddened with the personal confession. "I was one of the men at Mr. Wright's home the night you were brutally raped in his cellar by Mr. Turner."

"Son of a bitch. That is why you looked familiar to me."

"I think you better leave, Mr. Crowe."

"No, Pierre, let him stay. I would like to hear what Mr. Crowe has to say."

"Very well." Pierre took a sip of his drink as he leaned back against the couch.

"We did not know what was transpiring down in the cellar. We heard the two of you shouting but were not able to make out what was being said. We assumed it was a part of the game to entertain Mr. Turner." He paused. His face reddened. "You know, to please the customer. When you came up the stairs covered in your own blood from the beating and violations against your body, we offered to help, but you refused. I felt terrible about what had happened. I did not think

I would have an opportunity to apologize to you, but when I saw you tonight it was as if God had given me a second chance. That is why I volunteered to bring you home. A small gesture, to be sure, one that I hope gives you some idea of how sorry I am for what Mr. Wright and Mr. Turner did to you." A nervous smile crossed his face as he took a sip of his gin.

"Thank you, but those days are behind us and I wish to keep them that way."

"Yes, unfortunately they are. Since the raids, men of our special nature have no place to go. I have not seen any of my friends or intimates in almost a year. We are afraid to gather, mingle, or be intimate. That is why I asked about Mother's place. I had hoped that you might be persuaded to open it up again."

"I would like nothing more, but I have no one to help run it. Mr. Baptiste and I are in the middle of some unfinished business that is taking most of my time—"

"I would like to offer my assistance."

"You?"

"Why not? I have worked in taverns before. I am sure I can handle the business side of things, at least until you and Mr. Baptiste finish with your business." He looked at our concerned faces. "Please, I do not mean to force myself upon you. I wish for a few close friends to gather once or twice a week."

"It would be nice to bring some life back into the old place. Mother would have wanted that."

"Then it is settled." Pierre raised his glass. "To the reopening of Clapton's." Our glasses clinked together as we drank to our new partnership and the new future of the coffeehouse. "Mr. Crowe, I have a more immediate proposition for you."

"Please, anything I can do to help." He finished off his drink and refilled his glass.

"Since my coachman is away for a few days, it would be most helpful if perhaps you would be so kind as to spend the night here in one of the spare rooms. That way you could drive Thomas and me back to Spitalfields in the morning. I would like to take a look at the remains of the fire with the aid of daylight."

"Of course, and with several glasses of gin in me, I think it would be best to call it a day." He stood on liquored legs. Pierre and I followed his lead and stood. "Would you like help with the water?"

"Thank you, but no. We shall manage." Pierre and I took two buckets each. "You may choose any of those rooms." I nodded toward the four doors that lined the back wall. "You should find everything you need to make yourself comfortable." I smiled. "Good night, Mr. Crowe."

"Enjoy your evening." He bowed, turned, and sauntered into one of the rooms. He closed the door, and by the time Pierre and I had put out the fire and reached the back stairwell we heard the deep sounds of snoring.

"That did not take long," Pierre whispered with a grin.

"Hush," I scolded playfully as we walked down the hallway and entered my bedchamber. As Pierre removed his soiled clothing, I poured the buckets of warm water into the iron tub set into the corner of my room. I stood aside as Pierre slipped into the water, then stood over the tub and watched as the hair on his chest floated back and forth in the ripples. The nubs of his tits were just below the surface. He splashed water onto his face and rubbed the soot and dirt from his skin.

"This feels so good. We should do this more often." He moaned as he leaned back in the tub with his arms hanging over the sides and closed his eyes.

The sight of his nakedness caused my tongue to fail. I did not want idle words to spoil the moment of blissful silence. I knelt down at the edge of the tub and ran my hand down Pierre's chest, marveling at how the hair felt wet against his skin. He moaned and opened his eyes.

"You are—"

I placed my wet finger upon his lips to silence him and shook my head, indicating that words were not necessary. I let my finger trail back down his body until it was nestled in the wet moss of his affairs. His prick stiffened at once with my touch. It grew long and firm as I cupped his satchel and rolled the round rocks between my fingers. He moaned and quivered, sending out ripples in the water. My eyes grew with lust and my prick leaked its desire as the bulbous head of his prick surrounded by the thick folds of skin broke through the surface of the water.

Pierre raised his arms and placed them behind his head as he settled farther into the tub. The dark tangles of hair that covered the pits of his arms dripped water as the hair stuck to his skin. The odor of his body drifted around me, pulling me further into the depths of desire. I lowered my face to the pit of his arm and licked him. He trembled as I tasted of him. I ran my fingers up the trunk of his prick. It rose and quivered, splashing the water with its heft.

I stood and kicked off my shoes. Pierre's eyes caressed my body as I removed my blouse and breeches, exposing the rise of my own prick beneath the thin layer of my undergarment. He reached out as if wanting to touch me, and I moved in closer. His wet fingers fondled my prick, wetting the fabric it hid behind. With the most wicked of smiles upon his face, Pierre reached out with both hands, grabbed me, and pulled me into the tub with him. The water splashed over the sides and pooled around the floor as I sank into the warm water. The thin material of my undergarment stuck to my body as if it were a new layer of skin. He laid his lips upon mine and forced his tongue inside me. The kiss was deep, hungry, and determined.

I wrapped my arms about his neck as the kiss continued. Our teeth clicked as the heat of our passion drove us into fits of frantic sex. I kissed his neck, nibbled his earlobe, and lowered my head to bite on the extended nib of his tit. His hands squeezed my buttocks. He gripped me and with a force of a desperate man tore into my undergarment, exposing my bare ass to his fingers.

He raised my hips in the air and shoved me down. I gasped from the sudden introduction of his prick. I settled myself upon him and let my ass surrender to his entire length, riding his prick hard as if I were riding a wild horse that was hell-bent on never stopping. The water splashed and tossed about in the tub as we rocked against one another. I felt his prick swell within me indicating his release was not far off. In desperation to keep him going, I slowed my pace. He groaned into my mouth. The vibration of his breath reached down into my belly. He held my hips in place and shoved his prick back and forth, not allowing me to slow his arrival. Rivers of bath water and perspiration rolled down his face and neck. His prick quivered before a sudden release of his seed exploded into me. He pushed me down on top of his prick and held me there, silent, and still as the spasms slapped me from the inside as it released three, then four more times.

I looked down between our bodies and noticed that I too had released my desires. He had fucked it out of me with such force of pleasure that I had not realized my own release. We both looked at the cooling seed seeping through the thin material of my undergarment and rising to the surface of the dirty water. We looked at each other and laughed at our situation. He pulled me to him and wrapped his arms about me as we settled into the water to rest our weary bodies.

❖

"What about the constable? Mr. Willis, was it?" Pierre broke the morning silence as Mr. Crowe guided the carriage through the city.

"What about him?"

"Can we trust him?" He took his eyes off the sights of the city to look in my direction.

"Then he survived?"

"Why would you assume he was dead?"

"That last night in London, he came after me bent on either taking me in or killing me. I hit him several times in the head with a fireplace iron. I started the fire in the house with the intention of burning him as well, but in the end, I could not do it. I went back inside the burning building and pulled him out. He was drifting in and out. I left before I knew if he survived."

"He did, for better or worse." He paused. "So we cannot trust him?"

"There was a time I thought I could trust him, but he turned upon me. It was as if someone had gotten to him." I paused. "My father."

"It is possible."

"Why are you bringing him up?"

"I wonder if I should question him. How involved was he with the Society?"

"He was a member, and a powerful one. The other constables were all fearful of him. He was responsible for my release from Newgate, which allowed him to use me to help the Society in gaining the convictions."

"Then we should arrange a meeting with him." He turned back toward the window. "I shall send word to him when we return from Spitalfields."

"How can we know if we can trust him?"

"We cannot. Perhaps the time has come to bring you out of hiding to see what type of response we get. Are you able to face Mr. Willis again?"

"It would be my pleasure to make that fuck squirm at seeing me stand before him."

"Then it is settled, I shall…What in the fuck?" Pierre spat as we came upon the rubble that was once his home.

"What?"

"Motherfucker! That son-of-a-bitch father of yours is out there with a group of men shuffling through the debris." Pierre knocked on the window that separated us from Mr. Crowe. "Pull over here." The carriage came to an abrupt stop. "Thomas, do not leave this carriage." Pierre opened the door. In his anger, he had forgotten to close it. I slipped across the seat but kept my head low in order to better hear their conversation. The smell of damp ash and smoldering wood drifted into the carriage. The tainted air felt rough in my throat as I breathed. I held in several coughs as my father called out to Pierre.

"Mr. Baptiste."

"What in the fuck do you think you are doing?" Pierre spat. "Get your men out of here."

"I can only imagine how upset you are with this tragic event." I heard the sarcasm in my father's voice. "Even so, I do not believe you should take that kind of tone with me. They are here on official business."

"On whose orders?"

"Mine, of course. I heard of the fire and felt it my duty to come by and see if I could assist with anything."

"You have done enough. Do not think for one moment that I believe you had nothing to do with this."

"You give me more credit than I deserve." My father laughed. "Though I did warn you something might happen. In my position I hear things, you understand."

"You mean you control things," Pierre interrupted. "I hear things as well, Mr. Green."

"My offer still stands if you wish to change your mind. I would hate to see any further misfortune come your way."

"I appreciate your understanding." I heard the anger building in Pierre's voice. I readjusted myself in the seat and peered through the window in time to see him strike my father in the face, the impact of which sent my father tumbling to the damp waste of the city street. "You come anywhere near me or my investigation again, Mr. Green, and you will be the one who is struck by tragedy."

"Fucking wanker!" my father spat as he rubbed the side of his face. I slipped back down in my seat so that he would not notice me as Pierre made his way back to the carriage. Pierre's face was red with anger as he climbed into the carriage and slammed the door shut. I stayed out of sight until we were at a safe distance.

"I have no patience where your father is concerned. Where can we find Mr. Willis? I do not want to wait for a message to get delivered to him." He looked at me as I sat back up.

"I am not sure. He used to go to the Queen's Arms on Fleet Street. I found him there on several occasions."

"Shit." Pierre looked at me with a worried expression. He knocked on the window. Mr. Crowe opened it.

"Yes, sir."

"We will be going to the Queen's Arms. If you would stop a block or so away and wait there for me. I shall not be long." The window closed without further words.

"What is wrong? You seem troubled by what I said."

"Your father is just impossible, though I suppose you knew that already." He tried to give me a reassuring smile. It did not work. I saw that there was something else going on in his mind, something he did not want me to know. For once I held my tongue. By the time we had reached the Queen's Arms, Pierre appeared even more unsettled than before. He peered through the window as if he were looking for something, or someone.

"Perhaps it is best if you stay here." He broke the silence that had fallen between us.

"I will not," I replied. "You said that we were going to do this together, and together we shall." I looked at him. A bead of perspiration dripped down the side of his face. "What has touched you?"

"Are you ready?" He ignored my question. I nodded and opened the door without further questions.

"Nice to see you again, Mr. Baptiste." The doorman bowed as he opened the door. Pierre did not return a comment. It was his lack of manners that made me realize that whatever troubled him it was getting worse as we entered. The doorman looked upon me with a hint of recognition. I nodded and thanked him, then hurried my step so as not to linger too long as he searched his memory.

The tavern was near capacity. Tobacco smoke filled the air with a dull gray hue. Laughter and drunken shouts rang through the air. Men with too much liquor in them fondled the barmaids as they made their way through the crowds delivering more drinks to the already intoxicated group.

"Mr. Baptiste!" A boisterous voice rose above the noise. A large-breasted woman squeezed her way through the men carrying two pints of ale. She slapped the pints on one of the tables as she approached. "What can I do for you, darling?" She leaned in and kissed him on the cheek. She looked at me but said nothing.

"We are looking for Mr. Willis. Is he here?"

"He is in the back, honey—his usual table. Shall I bring a couple of pints?" She squeezed her breasts that were already half-exposed from her tight bodice. "I do not suppose I can interest you in these babies."

"Ah, come now, Flora. You know how it is. I respect you too much to think of you that way."

"One can always dream." She winked at him. "Go on, I'll bring you your drinks."

"Thank you, Flora."

I half listened to the conversation as I tried to prepare myself for what this confrontation might bring. I let my gaze drift through the tobacco haze hoping that I would not see anyone who might recognize me. Of course, my mind imagined the worst. How would Mr. Willis react to seeing me? Would he leave without allowing Pierre to interrogate him? Would he strike me, or worse, shove a dagger into my gut for the pain and embarrassment that I had caused him? My mind seemed to stutter to a halt when I realized that I did not know how I would react to seeing this man who spent so much of his time finding ways to ruin my life and the lives of those I loved. As I pondered that last thought, Pierre touched my elbow. We walked or rather stumbled through the mass of bodies. A drunken man tried to make intimate friends with a barmaid. She slapped him. He staggered backward and dumped his ale over another man's lap. The man stood and threw the drunkard across the room, smashing a small wooden table. Pierre and I hurried into the back room before we got entangled in the brawl.

As we turned the corner, I caught sight of Mr. Willis, sitting alone drinking what I figured to be a gin—his drink of choice. The memory of confronting him at that same table struck me with force. I paused as apprehension and fear rippled through my body. I looked toward Pierre for support. He did not notice my hesitation. His attention was elsewhere as he looked to the stairs and the scattering of men in the back area of the tavern. It came to me that he was looking for someone other than Mr. Willis. We came out of our own thoughts and approached the table.

"Fuck me," Mr. Willis whispered as he looked up from his drink and noticed me standing there. He rose. "Newton." His tone was accusatory, yet not at all angry as I had anticipated.

"Mr. Willis," I replied as I tried to form a welcoming smile.

"Mr. Willis, I am Pierre Baptiste." He reached out and shook Mr. Willis's hand.

"Yes, I know who you are, Mr. Baptiste, and so do many others. You are well known to people on both sides of the law."

"May we have a moment of your time?"

"What is this about?" His question was directed toward me. When neither of us answered, he took his seat and motioned for us to join him. As we settled in, Flora sat our drinks down without comment. "I thought you were dead."

"I am sorry to disappoint you."

"Not disappointed, just surprised is all. What can I help you with?" His tone had changed. It was almost pleasant.

"We would like to talk to you about the Society and the activities of Mr. Green." Pierre interjected.

Mr. Willis looked at Pierre, then at me. He did not speak at first. Instead, his lips tightened into a thin tight line.

"Please, Mr. Willis, this is important," I pleaded.

"Nothing is that important to implicate myself in any of his business." He looked around the room, leaned forward, and whispered, "We cannot speak here about such things." He leaned back in his chair. "Have you seen your...friend, Mr. Newton?" He changed the direction of the conversation.

"My friend?"

"Yes, that young man that we trapped in Moorfields. What was his name?"

"James Sanxay?" I questioned with a sense of urgency.

"Yes, that is it. Mr. Sanxay." He nodded and smiled as if he had come to the answer on his own.

"What about James?"

"He is still in Newgate from what I understand." He leaned back into the table. "I heard that the Society has postponed his execution on three separate occasions. Those delays do not make sense to any of us. If I were a gambling man, I would wager money that someone is keeping him alive to get something from him, something valuable enough to anger many of the members of the Society who want nothing more than to put a noose around that young man's neck in Tyburn."

"My—" I caught myself. "Mr. Green."

"Yes," Pierre remarked. "And I think I know what he is after." He turned to Mr. Willis. "Please, will you come with us? We can find a more private place to talk. Our carriage is outside and around the corner."

"I cannot be seen leaving with the two of you." He looked around the room. "Go to your carriage and I shall meet you." He finished off his drink, then added, "I may be many things, but I am always a man who keeps my word."

"I have memories that prove otherwise," I remarked.

"I was not the one who sent Margaret Clap to the pillory."

"Yes, I know that now. We did have our moments, did we not?" I winked at him, remembering the night he released his pent-up aggravation and fucked the hell out of my ass.

"You are still a wicked young man," he chided.

"If my memory serves me well, you took full advantage of my wickedness."

"Go, before I change my mind." He tried to sound angry, but I knew his tone was a way to cover his true desires.

Pierre and I stood. I took a long drink from the gin before we made our way through the tavern and out into the street. "Can we trust him to come?" Pierre asked as we approached the carriage.

"He will come. But I will not. I must go to Newgate and see James."

"Thomas."

"I promise to be careful, but this is something I must do. I shall meet up with you back home." I did not wait for his response. I left him standing by the carriage as I traveled the short distance to Newgate.

As usual, I had to bribe my way into the prison. The gaoler was more than happy to accept the four shillings as an entry fee. I found myself once again being escorted through the dark, damp corridors of Newgate.

"Mr. Sanxay is up ahead, the last cell on your right." The deep seductive voice of the gaoler caused my prick to quiver. "You have five minutes." He turned and left without allowing me the opportunity to pay for admittance into James's private cell.

I walked toward the wooden door thinking of the men behind them waiting for their date of execution. I stood by the door that held my schoolmate and intimate friend James, not wanting to look inside. The day of his trial he cursed me for my testimony against him. I deserved his harsh words. I worried he would not want to see me, or that if he did, it would be to lash out at me. I peered through the window and saw his frail body curled up in the back corner of the cell. I held on to the small iron bars with both hands to steady my nerves.

"James," I whispered. He did not respond. "James," I raised my voice. "It is Addison." My birth name fell from my tongue, leaving a foul taste in my mouth. He stirred.

"Addison?" He looked up at me. "Addison, is that really you?" He rose and came toward me, his gait slow and uneven. "My Lord, it is good to see my old friend." He reached out between the iron bars and touched my cheek. A tired smile fell across his face.

"I am so sorry for what I put you through—"

"It was not your fault." He interrupted my apology. "I know that now."

"What do you mean?"

"Your," he curled his finger, indicating for me to lean in closer, "your father," he whispered in my ear. "He is the cause of my arrest and torture, not you. You were the pawn in his game of lies and deceit. You could not have known." His lips touched my ear. My heart sank from the memories of our time together. I pulled back and looked at him. Tears fell down his face, streaking the dirt with a clean river that ran down to his neck.

"I have to get you out of here," I whispered.

"You cannot risk it. No one escapes from this place. But I shall die a thousand deaths to keep you from your father's hands." He pressed his face against the iron bars and kissed me. My body ignited with childhood visions of our endless fucks.

"I shall get you out of here." I broke the kiss. "I must go, but I will return tonight. Be ready."

"Be careful, Addison, your father is out for your blood."

"He is the one who needs to worry, not me." I faked a smile. "I shall see you tonight." I left without another word.

As I walked through the streets of London, I happened to notice the carriage still sitting along the side street of the Queen's Arms. Anxious to see Pierre and to ask for his assistance in gaining James's freedom, I decided not to go home. I approached the carriage.

"He went back inside, Mr. Newton," Mr. Crowe announced. "Shall I go fetch him?"

"No, that will not be necessary. I shall go. Please, ready the horses. I may need your assistance this evening." I turned and walked back into the tavern. I ordered a gin at the front bar, paid the shilling, then moved between the ever-growing numbers of patrons toward the back of the bar. My eyes grew wide with anger, shock, and betrayal as I witnessed Pierre sitting at one of the tables deep in conversation. The heartache I felt weakened my legs until my knees buckled. Tears of joy, anger, and disbelief welled in my eyes. The grip on my gin gave way. The glass slipped from my hand and smashed against the floor. The noise startled the two of them. They both looked up at me in shock at being caught at their secret meeting. Sitting with Pierre, heavy in conversation, was Christopher.

CHAPTER FIFTEEN

Christopher stood. A smile replaced the unease that his face wore only moments ago. I looked upon my first love, unsure of how to react. I wanted to hate him, to turn my back on him and leave without speaking a word. A deeper part of me wanted to run to him, to have him wrap his arms about me, to kiss me, to stroke me. Hell, I wanted him to fuck me. I looked over my shoulder toward the front door, thinking the best plan would be to run from this tavern and never look back. As I turned to leave, Mother's voice rose in my mind. It was not words, but the melody she always sang around the house. It was in those few moments that I realized I would no longer run. It was time to stand up for myself so that no one else would be able to hurt me again. Christopher owed me an explanation—it was time he delivered one. As for Pierre, I would deal with his lying actions later. I turned back around and laid my full attention upon Christopher.

Christopher took a small step toward me. He hesitated as if unsure what to do. He gave in to his emotions. He ran to me with his arms extended. His eyes were wet with tears. As he came closer to me, I raised my hand and slapped his face. The connection was exact. The sound of my hand against his skin was loud enough to get the attention of others sitting near us.

"You son of a bitch!" My hand came away from his cheek stinging. I looked upon Christopher, his eyes full of hurt at my venomous reaction. "What is the meaning of this?" I looked past Christopher as Pierre stood. "And you." My vicious words were aimed at Pierre. "Why did you not tell me? I thought we promised each other that there would be no more secrets between us?"

"Addison, do not blame Mr. Baptiste for the deceit. It was my decision not to tell you."

"Why?" I looked at him. My anger dissipated. "I have spent the last year wondering what happened to you. I did not know whether you were alive or dead, and all along the two of you have been scheming." I hesitated as I looked at the two of them. "I do not even know what is going on anymore."

"Thomas, please." Pierre came toward me. "I did not want you to find out this way." He looked around the tavern.

"No? Then you should have fucking told me," I spat as I felt the heat rise across my face. "How long did you think this could go on without me finding out?" I waited for a response that never came. "Do not just stand there and look at me with those fucking blank stares. I demand an explanation."

"We are drawing unwanted attention to us, which cannot be good." Pierre spoke. "Please take the carriage back to the coffeehouse and let Christopher explain. I must go and meet Mr. Willis again. There were some documents he said might help. Remember, we did this to protect you."

"Yes, go," I spat. "I cannot deal with you at the moment." I turned my eyes away from the sadness written across Pierre's face. He touched my shoulder and walked away.

"Addison, I am sorry."

"My name is Thomas." The anger in my voice was back. "For once I wish you would remember that. Addison does not exist anymore." I turned and walked through the tavern without further comment. The curious men in the tavern leered at me. I ignored them, ready with my tongue for anyone who dared speak to me. We walked to the carriage in silence.

"The coffeehouse, Mr. Crowe," I ordered as I opened the door and climbed inside. The ride through the city was uncomfortable, not physically from the rutted streets, but emotionally from the bruises and gouges that lined my and Christopher's lives. With the brutal silence that covered us like a suffocating cloud of soot, I had to wonder if there was anything left for us to fight for. I wanted to look at him. To let my eyes feast, once more, upon the man I thought was lost to me. And yet I still longed to be with him, to feel his hot breath against my face as he invaded me with his prick. I glanced at him from the corner of my eyes. He looked out the window, his face streaked with tears and the impression of my hand upon his cheek. I rubbed my hands together wondering if that had been the last time that I would ever touch him.

❖

"So tell me, what was so important that you and Pierre felt the need to keep your presence hidden from me?" I released the hold upon my tongue as we entered the coffeehouse. I walked behind the bar, poured myself a drink, and emptied the contents in a few quick gulps, letting the burn of the liquor quell my anger. I refilled my glass, as well as one for Christopher.

"Addison." The name caught upon his tongue. "Sorry, but you shall always be Addison to me." He took the drink. "May we sit?" He waited for my nod, then took a seat on the couch nearest the fireplace. "I do not know where to begin. There is so much I have wanted to say to you since the night I received your letter, and I thought for months that I would never get the chance. But here I am with you, and I am lost for words."

"Then let me begin," I said. The anger I had expected was not to be found. "What happened to you that night? Alistair told me he delivered my letter to you."

"He did, but that was not the only letter I received that night." He took a sip of his gin and continued. "As I was packing to come to you, I received a letter from Mr. Johnson. I do not know how he found me, as we had not been in contact since that day, well, since the day I left your father's employ. Mr. Johnson had always had handsome penmanship, but this letter was almost impossible to decipher, as if it had been written in haste. He told me that you were in grave danger and that if I wanted to save your life, I had to meet him at the entrance to the Sodomites Walk in the Upper Moorfields." He took another sip of his gin. His hand trembled. "He went on to indicate that if he did not show up at the appointed time, then I was to consider this as an indication that something had gone wrong, and I was to locate Mr. Baptiste."

"So you are the one who contacted Pierre to come back to London?"

"Yes. It took me a while to know whom I could trust. I started asking people where I might find Mr. Baptiste. Then one night as I was having a drink in the Queen's Arms, a man approached me. He told me that my questions had raised the suspicion of some members of the Society and that I should be careful."

"Who was he?"

"Mr. Sutton. It was not until later that I discovered the relationship between Mr. Sutton and Mr. Baptiste. Neither of us at that time knew what had happened to you. It was not until Pierre received word that you were in the Bicêtre in Paris that we knew you had survived."

"Wait, I do not understand something. Mother hired Pierre to look into my father's affairs and possible financial agreement with the Society. What does Mr. Johnson have to do with it? As a coachman, he would not have any knowledge of my father's business."

"Mr. Johnson indicated that he had found proof."

"Proof of what?"

"I do not know, nor does Pierre, but we suspect it is much bigger than the financial support he was and still is giving the Society."

"Such as?"

"No one knows. All we know is that your father is willing to murder anyone to keep this information from getting out." He paused. "Let me get back to that night. I arrived at the Sodomites Walk well before the scheduled time. Mr. Johnson never showed. By the time I came looking for you, Alistair's house was engulfed in flames. I worried that you had been caught up in whatever this scandal is that your father is trying to cover up."

"I set that fire."

"You—but I assumed your father did."

"No, it was I. Mr. Willis came to the house hell-bent on arresting me. We fought, and I hit him over the head with an iron. I thought if I burnt the place down, the Society would think that I perished in the fire and would stop looking for me. I assumed that Mr. Willis was looking to reinstate his reputation with the Society, but I believe it was my father who was making the demands."

"Addison, damn it." He paused. "Thomas, you must understand that Pierre did not want to keep us apart. I insisted that you not know of our meetings."

"Why would you do such a thing?"

"For your own safety, that is why." He lit his pipe, then offered me his tobacco. I filled my pipe and struck the tinderbox, enjoying the rich flavors. "Honestly, Thomas. Do you for one moment believe that if this secrecy were not necessary, I would not have come to you before now? I know of at least three occasions where my day's activities were followed. I could not take the chance that I might lead your father to you." He took a deep draw from his pipe and exhaled the smoke. "May I ask you something?"

"Of course."

"Why did you feel that you could not confide in me about your life as a catamite and the agreement you made with the Society to save Margaret's life? May we?" He raised his empty glass.

"Yes." I stood and took his glass. "To answer your question," I continued as I walked behind the bar, "I thought you would stop loving me if you no longer saw the innocent young man that you knew in Bishop's Stortford." I looked down as I poured the gin. "I had struggled all of my life to find my way. It was not until I met Mother Clap that she gave me the courage, strength, and confidence to do so."

"I suppose I can understand that. All I ever wanted was to be a part of your life, whatever that life was. It did not matter to me that you sold your body to earn a living. All I wanted was your heart. If I could have had that, then I would have let others have your body. Looking back at all of this now, I even understand why you made the deal with the Society. If it had been your life at risk, I would have done the same thing to protect you." He stood and came to the edge of the bar. "There is just one more thing I need from you."

"What is that?" I handed him the glass. He took it from me and shoved it down the bar. It toppled and fell to the floor. As I looked at him, he reached behind me and grabbed my neck. He pulled me toward him and placed his lips upon mine. He opened himself to me in a rush of heat and passion that I had not expected, but was not going to refuse.

When I tried to break our kiss to catch my breath, he held me firm against his lips. His free hand wrapped about my body. He drew me to him, pulling me across the bar with his tongue deep inside my mouth. He had never taken me with such passion and determination. My anger melted away as if it had been placed in the hot summer sun. I grabbed his blouse and tore it open. He grunted from my immediate advance, filling my mouth with his hot breath. The odors of his body, ripe with need, billowed out and I became intoxicated from him. My mind and body begged to be used. I continued to tear at his blouse until it hung in rags.

He released me and I fell back against the bar. He shrugged off the tattered material. His eyes were dark ovals of lust and desire that pierced my body, pricking my skin and leaving me breathless. I gazed upon his chest as it rose and fell with his breaths. Beads of perspiration gathered in random places across his body and dripped down through the golden blond-hair that covered it.

He pulled himself upon the bar and straddled me. I inhaled his odor as he lowered himself to me. I braced his body with my hand and raised my head to bring the hardness of his tit into my mouth. I felt him tremble against my face as I rolled the tender nub between my lips and teeth. I bit it. He shivered with untold pleasure. The thick tangles of hair held within the pits of his arms were damp with the heat of his body. I released his tit and licked his perspiration as it trailed down his torso. His taste was bitter. I wanted more. I wiggled beneath him, making my way down his stout chest and the moss of hair that covered it. I used my tongue as a guide to follow the hair as it spread out across his belly before disappearing beneath his breeches.

I ran my tongue over his navel and felt his skin tremble as I unlaced his breeches. I unfastened his undergarment, exposing the hidden treasures that I had longed for. The heat and odor of his body washed over my face. I reached inside his most private area. The curly moss of hair was wet with his desire for me. I wrapped my fingers around the trunk of his prick and pulled it and his hefty satchel through the opening in his linen. His prick fell free and slapped me in the face. Its impact left a thin sheen of his clear nectar across my lips and cheek. I let his moisture linger where it landed.

"Oh, you devilish boy." Christopher moved his hips back and forth, running his prick over my outstretched tongue. "Oh yes, play with my satchel. Yes, that is it. Oh, Lord save me." He groaned as I pulled upon his furry bag of rocks. I fondled his prick with my tongue, taking in more of his sweet early release. He moved down my body and licked my face clean of his moisture. He kissed me, sharing with me what lingered upon his tongue.

Christopher pulled himself from my embrace and stood upon the floor. He swung me around so my legs hung off the edge of the bar. He pulled my shoes off and removed my stockings, then kissed my feet, bringing each of my toes into his mouth and running his tongue between them. My prick, in the highest state of need it had been in for months, spat great quantities of clear nectar that seeped through the heavy material of my breeches, staining the spot dark. Christopher's mouth was upon it at once, sucking the moisture from the fabric. I felt his lips and teeth against my quivering prick as he sucked and nibbled it through the layers of clothing.

"Fuck this," he growled. He released the swollen lump of my prick from his lips and with great urgency unlaced my breeches and pulled them off me with several forceful tugs. He threw my legs over his shoulders and buried his face in my affairs.

"Oh, Lord have mercy upon me." I groaned while Christopher's tongue ran up the long, stiff trunk of my prick. "Christopher, please take me at once. I cannot bear this pleasure-torture a moment longer."

"I shall not take you here on this bar." He lifted his head from my affairs and ripped open my blouse. He licked his lips. "You have indeed become a man." He ran his hand through the hair that covered my chest. "The last time I saw you, your body had just begun to sprout." He licked my chest, the deepest and thickest part of the moss.

I felt his hands slip between my back and the bar. He nibbled upon my right tit as he raised me from the bar and supported me in his arms. I wrapped my legs about his waist. He carried me to one of the extra rooms at the back of the tavern, never releasing my tit from his hungry mouth. He kicked the door closed. It rattled in its frame from the impact. By the time we had reached the bed, my body was alight with a fire I had not experienced since that day three years ago when I had first caught sight of Christopher's body as I peered with secret desire through his dressing room door. He tossed me on the bed with a playful grin upon his face.

He kicked his shoes off and rolled his stockings down his hairy legs, then tossed them to the side of the bed. He removed his breeches. His prick, which still hung through the opening of his linens, dripped with his desire and need. He tore the rest of the linen from his body and stood naked as he looked down upon me. I reached up to touch him. He slapped my hand away and shook his head.

"You are not doing a thing. It is my turn to ravish your body." His voice was deep, sensual and firm. He climbed upon the bed. His early release dripped upon my belly and gathered in my navel. He bent down and sucked his early release from my body before running his tongue up the center of my chest to the tip of my chin. He kissed me, spitting his warm nectar into my waiting mouth. I drank from him as I wrapped my arms about him and pulled him down on top of me. Our pricks touched and a fire ignited between us. He rubbed against me, stroking and coddling my prick with his.

As his tongue explored the deepest parts of my mouth, he raised my legs over his shoulders. He caressed my inner thighs until his fingers found my glory hole. He gripped his prick and guided it between my buttocks. His eyes never left mine. My heart raced with building anticipation as I felt the tip of his prick pressing against me.

"Do not be gentle. Do not tease," I begged, gasping for breath as our mouths parted. I wiggled my hips as a nonverbal plea to have his prick invade me. "Please, fuck me," I panted. "Oh Lord," I yelled as he indulged my cravings and shoved the entire length of his lean prick into me without hesitation, without pause, without sparing me a moment of the painful pleasure. "Yes, yes, my love. Fuck me hard." I grasped my ankles and pulled them up and over my head as Christopher's thrusts increased in speed and force.

"How I have missed that beautiful ass." Christopher leaned back and took in the view of his prick sliding in and out of me. He slowed his pace and adjusted himself, using his free hand to grip my needy prick. He fucked and fondled me with opposite rhythms, taking me further into the heights of bliss.

"Fuck me harder, my love," I shouted. "Yes, please, that is it." I threw my hands over my head and braced myself against the wall. The old frame of the bed creaked and groaned with the force of our fucking. Sweat dripped from Christopher's face. His blond chest hair had gone dark as it matted to his dampened skin. "Oh, you bring me to such pleasure." I screamed as the fireball within my belly exploded, unleashing the first of several thick streams of my white pearls across my chest. "Yes, fuck it out of me, you wild man!" He leaned into me and fucked me harder than I had ever been taken before. My body quivered as another burst of seed expelled from my prick with great distance.

Christopher leaned down and licked my cooling seed from my face and fed it to me as his prick swelled inside me. I felt his prick quiver as he released himself into me. He filled me with such delights that I thought I might lose my mind. Exhaustion at last took hold of Christopher. He groaned and fell on top of me. His sudden move pulled his prick from me in a wet, messy pop. Shit and seed leaked from my used hole, soiling the bed linens with the remnants of our sex.

I wrapped my arms about his sweat-soaked body. We panted and groaned without words. They were not necessary. We were reunited and for the first time free, for the most part, from the violence and the lies that had shattered our lives over a year ago. I vowed to myself to never let him go.

❖

The door to the room creaked against its own weight, waking me from a deep and restful sleep. Fright took hold of me as my foggy mind tried to produce a clear thought. I kept my eyes closed and pretended to shift in my sleep, and as I did, I peered through my half-opened eyes.

Pierre poked his head through the open door. The light of the moon drifting into the other room gave me a moment of illumination to see a smile across his face. He pulled his head back and shut the door without a sound. I heard his footsteps upon the stairs and then above me as he readied himself for bed.

As I lay there with the comfort of Christopher's warm body against mine, I remembered the promise I had made to James. I forced myself to stay awake with the hope that Pierre would fall asleep soon. After a while, I tossed the covers off and with slow deliberate moves slipped from the bed. Christopher did not move. I walked across the floor with as much care as possible to keep the wood from announcing my progress. I opened the door and stole up the stairs.

I stood and listened through the door of my room. In the silence of the night, I heard the soft, gentle breaths of Pierre as he slept. With quiet steps, I walked into Mother's room with hopes of finding something that would fit me and transform me into a woman. I opened her closet door and riffled through the clothes. Her rose perfume drifted up from the fabric and battered my nose with the memory of her scent. In the back of her closet, I found what I was looking for. I pulled out several old outfits that she must have worn in her youth, for the Margaret Clap that I knew would never have been able to pull herself and her large breasts into such a tiny outfit.

After a long struggle of dressing myself in Mother's clothes, I stood in front of the looking glass to get a glimpse of the fruits of my labor. It was not up to the standards that Alistair's wife had created, but it would have to do. I lifted the petticoat up off the floor so it would not drag as I moved about the house and crept along the dark hallway heading toward the tavern. A pen and paper were sitting on the top of the bar. I took the time to write a quick note to Pierre and Christopher to let them know my plan in case something was to happen to me.

I headed toward the door when I remembered that I needed to locate some tool to help in the escape. I sighed with the thought of having to walk through the hallway once again in this heavy outfit, but knew I had no other choice. I stole back through the house and down into the cellar. The damp, dark room glowed with an eerie light as I lit one of the oil lamps. I shuffled through the boxes until I found some tools that I thought might come in handy for the escape. I slipped the small, yet heavy objects into the bodice of my dress, snuffed out the oil lamp, and with the use of memory found my way in the dark to the cellar door. I slipped out into the cold winter night.

CHAPTER SIXTEEN

I had planned to take less visible streets to Newgate, in hopes of not being accosted by drunken men out for a quick fuck with one of the common street whores, but as the cold wind blew up my dress and bit my affairs, I realized the most direct path would be the best. I redirected my feet and soon found myself walking down Fleet Street.

I kept my head low, using a large hat I had taken from Mother's room to cover my face from prying eyes. The metal instruments that I had concealed in my wear had become cold from the wind, making my attire even more uncomfortable. The outskirts of the city were quiet. Such was not the case once I passed through the wall and entered Central London. Whores, drunks, housebreakers, and wool-pullers wandered the dark, cold streets looking for something to entertain themselves with. Fights erupted on every corner. I learned early on that a person should not look in the direction of an argument on the street unless they wished to become an unwilling participant. I hurried along, ignoring the whistles and vulgar insinuations of the men offering me money for indecent acts upon my body and soon found myself standing in front of Newgate Prison.

"I am here to see Mr. Sanxay," I stated in a soft, silky tone, hoping to disguise the underlying hints of my somewhat masculine voice.

"I would prefer you were here to see me," The gaoler said as he squeezed his affairs.

"Perhaps another time." I played to his emotions. "I am quite sure it will be the best fuck you have ever had, but I have been sent to give this poor incarcerated man the last fuck of his life, and I plan to make sure he goes to the gallows with a smile on his face." I took two pounds from my pocket, knowing from experience that it took four shillings for entrance. "I take it that this should be sufficient for the entire evening?"

"It will." He cupped my ass with his hand. "Promise me, my dear lady, that when you are done, you shall give me the thrill of a lifetime." He winked.

"You have no idea." I pushed his hand from my body. "Shall we?" I nodded toward the entrance. He sighed, turned, and led me into the bowels of the prison. I felt the tools shift within my bodice. I adjusted myself with care, not wanting the cold metal to clank together and give away the secrets that I held. We came to the familiar hallway lined with wooden doors. The gaoler unlocked the door and stood to the side to let me enter. "You are a gentleman," I whispered to him as I let my hand trail across the front of his breeches. He was stiff with need, and from the brief connection I knew he was well equipped. "You are quite the man."

"As I hope you will give me the chance to prove."

"If you can guarantee our privacy for this dying man's last wish, I will come looking for you when I am finished with him. I am sure in his weakened state that I will have much more to give, and at no cost to you." I smiled beneath the hat.

"As you wish." He waited for me to enter, then shut and locked the cell door. I stood without moving and listened to the sounds of his footsteps as he walked down the hallway. When they had disappeared, I turned to James, who lay sleeping in the corner. "James," I whispered as I knelt beside him and rocked his shoulder with a gentle movement.

"What?" He raised his head and looked at me with confusion. "What in the hell? Who let you into my cell?"

"James, it is I." I look off the hat. I saw recognition come to his face. I held back a laugh.

"Addison, what are you?"

"Shh." I placed a finger to his lips. "I promised to get you out of here, and here I am."

"I cannot believe you made it past the gaoler. You look ludicrous in that disguise." He chuckled as he sat up. "Are men in here that desperate for a fuck, that they would consider you an attractive whore?"

"I am glad I can be a source of entertainment for you," I said in a playful tone. "While I have promised the gaoler a fuck of his own for allowing us privacy, I cannot guarantee how much time we have before he makes his rounds."

"How do you expect to get us out of here?"

"I brought these from home." I pulled out the gouge, the billhook, and the crooked knife. I placed them on his bed of straw.

"You cannot be serious?" He picked up the crooked knife and ran his hand along the curved blade. "You expect us to dig through the walls? We are surrounded by other cells—what good would that do? It will just lead us into another cell."

"Not through, down. We are going to dig out one of the stones in the floor."

"Why?"

"When I was arrested, I remember hearing talk of tunnels beneath the city. The Fleet Street Ditch runs right under Newgate. If we can get to that, we can follow it out to where it dumps into the Thames River."

"That is the sewage ditch."

"And our way out." I took the knife from his grip and held his hand. "James, it is the only way. We can do this. Help me look for a loose stone in the floor. As old as this place is, it cannot be that solid."

We moved along the stone floor on our hands and knees, pushing and prodding each of the stones. Halfway through the inspection, I came across a large stone to the right of the door that rocked upon itself with my touch.

"James, over here," I whispered. I stood and peered through the small window of the door. The hallway appeared empty.

"I cannot believe you found one." James fell to his knees, grabbed the billhook, and began running it over the old, brittle mortar. "Stand and keep an eye out for the gaoler." He spoke without looking up.

"Shit. Quick, get over on your bed and drop your breeches." I pulled him up from his work.

"Why?"

"I cannot very well be fucking you with your breeches fastened, can I?" We scooted over to his bed. I watched with fear and excitement as he unlaced his breeches and pulled them down to his ankles. He dropped to the floor. I lifted my petticoat and straddled his body. His prick stiffened from our closeness. I smiled at his embarrassment. I held his prick in my hand. The length and firmness that I remembered from our days at school remained. I rose up and down upon him as if we were in the height of pleasure. He moaned and I groaned as we heard the footsteps stop on the other side of the door. The thought of the gaoler watching us gave rise to my own needs. My body, which was flush with desire, and my prick on the rise made my attire even more uncomfortable. It was not long before the footsteps retreated. We continued our farce for a while longer, making sure that the gaoler would not return. My hand pulled away wet with James's clear nectar.

I licked my fingers and tasted of him. In a moment of utter loss of control, I leaned down and slipped his prick into my mouth. He arched his back and his prick spat a large quantity of his seed into my mouth. I drank from him as I did all those years ago in school. I pulled myself up and licked my lips. "Another time."

"You always were a tease." He groaned as he stood and pulled up his breeches. We went back to our positions, he cutting out the mortar around the stone, and I as watchman of the cell. It felt as if hours had passed before James threw down the tools. "I think we have it. Come help me." I took the billhook and used it as leverage to lift the stone from its resting place. We strained to maneuver the stone out of its tight confines. It fell backward against the floor with a loud crash. We looked at each other, paused and waited, expecting to hear footsteps from the hallway. When I felt it was safe, I stood over the hole and stomped upon the earth that lay beneath. It began to give at once.

"Damn." James covered his nose against the stench that drifted through the gaping hole in the floor. "You expect us to go down there?"

"I do. I remember what it is like in here. You have been shitting and pissing in the corner of your cell. You think I cannot smell that? It is no different." I fell to my knees and used the gouge to break more of the solid soil away, widening our escape hole.

"Perhaps not for you, but the stuff in my cell is at least from my own body."

"A minor difference at best." I looked up at him, a bit annoyed at his lack of adventure.

"Yes, but God only knows what is down there besides the shit and waste of thousands of people." He continued to hold his nose.

"Grab two of the torches from the wall over there." I pointed behind him, ignoring his complaints. "We can use them to help light the way." I stood and took one more look through the window in the door. The hallway was quiet. "Come on, now is our chance."

"I cannot believe I am doing this."

"Would you rather waste away in here waiting to be sent to Tyburn? Stop your fucking whining." I leaned over and kissed him.

"When this is over, I expect more than a fucking kiss."

"I am saving your ass, is that not enough?"

"No."

"Here, hold my torch until I get down there." I sat down and slipped my legs into the hole that was not more than one foot by two. As I lowered myself, my feet dipped into the cold, slimy waters of the sewage. "Damn, I just lost my shoes. Fuck it." I pulled my legs out of the hole and pulled off the female costume, leaving me in nothing but my thin undergarment. James's gaze caught my prick, and even in our current situation, I felt it stir with restless aggression. I sat back down and repositioned my legs, sliding through the hole and into the rot, waste, and debris that floated in the bowels of the city.

I held my breath as the chill and filth surrounded me. I paused, wondering how deep the sewage was. My feet sank into several inches of slime and muck before coming to rest on the bottom of the ditch. The level of the water rose just above my tits. I released my breath, coughing and choking on the foul stench that hung in the damp, fetid air. I reached up and took my torch that James handed to me and saw the grimace upon his face as the conditions of the ditch became visible.

"Come on, James. Stop wasting time. We have to be gone before the gaoler makes his next round." I stepped out of the way. The thickness of the water made walking difficult. Heavy lumps of unidentifiable matter bumped into me beneath the surface. I tried not to think of what it might be, but my mind would not let go of its morbid curiosity, wondering if it was lumps of shit or parts of a rotting dog or cat. Another blend of ripe perfume billowed up from the water as I moved out of James's way, swallowing hard to keep the contents of my belly intact. I grabbed hold of James's legs as they dangled from the hole above me. "James, stop kicking your feet unless you want to splash this filth all over me."

"Son of a bitch," James gasped as he lost his grip and fell into the ditch. I managed to maintain my footing but could not do much for James. He went straight under the water. The water and sludge splashed around us. I closed my mouth and eyes. The coldness dripped down my face and neck. I turned my head and spat gritty water from my mouth. The taste lingered.

"Fuck." He gagged as I pulled him up, then spat a mouthful of blackish-green sludge. He began to heave, turned his head, and vomited. "If I were not so grateful for your assistance," he coughed and spat as he wiped the shit from his face, "I would beat the shit out of you." He cleared his throat and spat once more.

"Nice choice of words, my friend." I gave him a wry smile. "At least we have one torch left." I took hold of his hand and led him farther into the ditch.

"Do you have any idea where we are going, or how to get there?"
"No, but the Fleet Ditch only goes in one direction, toward the Thames."
"Yes, but which direction is that, behind us or ahead of us?"
"Wait." I held a finger between us. "Listen." Overhead we heard the gaoler call for others. The door to the cell groaned as he opened it. I took the torch and submerged it in the water to hide our whereabouts.
"Fucking wankers," the gaoler hissed through the hole in the floor. "You have two options, you fucks. Come back now, or die trying to escape."
"He is too large to fit through the hole. We should be safe for now," I whispered to James as we proceeded through the sewage.
We continued walking through the ditch with slow, careful steps. The waste and sludge became thicker, seeping between our toes. Every ten to fifteen feet a grate appeared above us. They afforded us a dim light from the oil lamps burning in the hallways in the prison above. We heard the rapid footsteps of the gaolers running through the prison above us as they continued their search for us. We kept to the edge of the cold, slimy walls to aid in our progression, but also to keep our movement hidden from the gaolers, who stopped and peered through the grates as they looked for any signs of us. We stopped on occasion to rest from the labors of each step we took.
"What happened to the grates?" James questioned during one of our periods of rest.
"We must have passed outside the walls of the prison," I replied as I looked at our surroundings. "We are under the city, which means the river cannot be too much farther. Come on, keep going."
The farther we walked, the thicker and more pungent the odors became. Dead animals floated around us, bumping into us as a sudden, slow but steady current in the water caused their lifeless corpses to stir.
"Look," James said after a long silence. The sewage rippled about our bodies as we stopped. "Up ahead. The darkness is fading. That must be the way out."
"We must have reached the river," I said with a glimmer of hope. "We have made it." I tried to run through the thickness, but the bottom was slick. I lost my footing and fell head first into the filth. James pulled me up. I spat a mouthful of the tainted water and wiped the shit and rotting flesh from my face. I nodded at James when I was ready to

proceed. We moved with caution as we came to a large iron grate that covered the opening.

"Listen," I said. We stood in silence as the air of the night drifted through the opening and chilled our wet bodies. "I do not hear anyone. I think it is safe." I grabbed the iron bars and pulled, then pushed. The grate would not budge.

"Now what?"

"Maybe if we both work it, we can loosen it." We gripped the bars and began to push and pull, trying to loosen the old, crumbling stone and mortar. The muscles in my back strained. I shook the grate with a rapid, angry motion. The grate remained intact. "Fuck." I released my grip and shook my hands to ease the cold ache that had settled into them. I turned back and looked at the direction from which we had come. "We shall have to go back and try one of the grates in the ceiling. Perhaps we can get through one of them."

"But what will that do?" James questioned. I heard the frustration in his voice. "You said yourself those grates just go back up into the prison. We would be caught for sure."

"I do not see that we have any choice. We cannot stay down here."

"Before we go, I just want to say thank you." James took my hand beneath the water.

"For what?"

"For trying to free me. What troubles me the most is that you will be arrested as well for your hand in my failed escape."

"We have not failed, James. We will get out of this. I promise you."

"Give up, Addison. We can do nothing else but surrender and face our deaths."

"What has happened to you? Where is the strong young man who once stood before me telling me that we do not follow the rules, that we were born to set them?" My voice rose to more than a whisper as desperation settled in. "I have struggled most of my life, and I vowed thanks to the strength you showed me, to never give up. It is the weak who do not succeed in this city, and I for one do not intend to be one of them." I looked at James. He did not reply to my comments, but even in the dim light of the room, I saw a familiar sparkle in his eyes.

"Thank you, Addison." He leaned in and kissed me. "I have been so beaten down during my time in Newgate, I have lost that part of me, or at least misplaced it." He smiled. "Let us go back, and we will find another way out of this." He stroked my cheek with tenderness, took my hand once more, and led us back in the direction of the prison.

As we came upon the first of the grates, we paused and looked above us in hopeful optimism. I reached up, straining my arm to grasp the iron bars. They were several inches out of reach. I tried to jump, but the thick sludge held my feet. The best I was able to manage was an awkward bounce. James snickered but did not offer any assistance.

"Instead of standing there laughing at me, how about you coming up with some suggestions." I raised my brow and waited for a response that never came. "Bend over."

"You want to fuck me here?"

"You are impossible, James Sanxay. I wish to climb upon your back so I can reach the grate. Now turn around and grab your knees." I waited as he positioned himself as directed, then I climbed upon his back. His clothes were wet and slimy. I gripped his shoulders and pulled my knees to the middle of his back. They slipped off. I held on to his shoulders, hoping he could hold us up. The feeble attempt failed. The weight of my body pulled us both under the foul water. We came up together, choking and spitting bits of matter.

"Here, try this." James cupped his hands together, interlacing his fingers. "Perhaps I can lift you up this way." He nodded his readiness. Using the wall as a support, I lifted my foot into his cupped hands. He lifted me up to the roof of the ditch. I gripped the iron bars and shook. They would not give.

"Fuck. We shall have to try the next one. Let me down." I bent down and held James's head as he lowered me back into the water. "Do not worry. We will find one." My smile waned as we moved farther into the ditch. In the distance, we saw the glimmer of light coming through the next grate. As we reached it, James turned around and cupped his hands together. I slipped my foot into his grasp and let him lift me up. When I gripped the iron bar, it shifted. "This is it," I whispered down to him. "Hold on." I grabbed hold of the grate with both hands and pushed. The mortar and stone began to crumble. I pushed harder. The grate broke free. I heard James grunting below me as my weight shifted in his hands. I pushed the grate off to the side. "Lift me up." I gripped the edge of the floor above me and pulled myself up through the hole. I heard James breathe relief as I left his grip. I looked around as I pulled my legs through. The hallway was empty. I leaned over the hole and reached back into the ditch. James grabbed hold of my arm and I pulled him up through the floor.

Our damp bodies shivered from the cold air that hung in the corridor. We replaced the grate. We stood and turned around. Without us realizing it, one of the gaolers had snuck up behind us.

"Mr. Newton, what in the hell?" Mr. Collins stood with his hands on his hips.

"Mr. Collins," I said with a sigh of relief. "Please, you must help us." I looked at James, who stood shivering. He was about to speak. "I shall explain later," I said to him before returning my attention to Mr. Collins.

"Fuck, I cannot believe this. Was the first time not enough for you?"

"Please, Mr. Collins. Just tell us how to get out of here."

"The gaolers are guarding every exit. They even sent a few men down to the river to claim your bodies, thinking you would not survive down there." He shut his mouth and looked behind us. Footsteps approached. "Quick, get in here." He opened a door and pushed us inside a small room that was appointed with a table and chair and nothing else.

"Now what?"

"The only way out is through the chimney. If you can break through the top, head toward the row of buildings on your left. You should be able to make it over the roofs of the buildings far enough away from the prison where you can get to the streets and make your final escape. Good luck." He slipped out of the door and shut it.

"Any sign of them?" a voice called down the hallway.

"No, nothing yet," Mr. Collins replied.

"Come on." I pulled James across the small room and knelt down in front of the fireplace. I went up first, using my arms and legs to brace myself between the walls of the chimney, and crawled up the soot-covered stones one hand and foot at a time. I heard James beneath me, struggling with the climb.

I came to the top of the chimney. When I looked into the darkness above me, I saw three small open holes, which allowed smoke to escape. I braced my feet for support and pushed on the top. The stones were heavy and sealed with years of soot and tar. I pounded my fist against the top, sending dust, dirt, and small grit falling down upon us. James sneezed and coughed beneath me. The stones began to shift. More of the mortar broke away. I pushed as much of my weight as I could against the top, straining my legs to keep their grip upon the walls. The top of the chimney gave way and the stones and bricks fell across the roof. The loud rumble they made as they tumbled off the roof gave me pause, hoping that the gaolers would not hear such a ruckus from below. Fresh air cascaded down to us. I took a deep breath of it and pulled myself up. Once on the roof, I reached in and helped James out.

"I cannot believe we did it." He shouted a little too loud and cupped his hand to his mouth. "Sorry," he whispered. He closed his eyes and inhaled the cold, sewage-free air. He wrapped his arms about me and hugged me, pulled me off my feet, and swung me around.

"Careful." I laughed as he lowered me. My head was dizzy with the motion. "Let us get down off this roof before we fall and kill ourselves."

"Can we just sit for a few moments? I want to enjoy this moment with you a little longer." He looked around and found a flatter surface on which to sit. He smiled and patted the spot next to him. I accepted his invitation and wrapped my arm across his shoulder and pulled him into me to help keep us warm from the chill of the early morning air. We sat motionless and without words as we listened to the silence of the night. It was not long before James broke that silence with a suggestion that startled me. "Fuck me."

"What?"

"Fuck me, here and now." He began to unlace his blouse.

"Have you lost your mind?" I questioned as my eyes made contact with his bare skin. The moonlight filtering through the coal-laced clouds caused his skin to shimmer. His tits grew erect from the exposure to the cold air.

"I have not. In fact, I believe I have found it again. Please, it has been so long since I have felt anything at all. If it were not for you, I would still be in that cell below. It may be our last time together, Addison. I cannot stay in London. It would be too dangerous. People will be searching for me." He leaned in and kissed me. "Please, I beg of you to fuck me on my last night in London."

I pushed him down upon the cold roof and nuzzled my face against his chest. He guided my head over his tits. I sucked him, bringing the nub between my lips. He shivered and his back arched against me. I rose onto my knees and turned him over on his belly. As he unlaced his breeches and pulled them down, I went to work on my flimsy, wet undergarment. My prick was stiff and pushed against the thin material.

I released several eyelets that covered my affairs and pulled my prick out, spat to moisten myself further, then climbed on top of James.

I wasted no time with frivolous play. I guided my prick to his familiar hole and lowered myself into him with a slow but steady push. He gasped from my invasion. His body tensed, then relaxed. I settled into him.

"Lord, have mercy on me," James bellowed. "Yes, give me that precious prick of yours." He continued his pleas.

"James." I covered his mouth with my hand. "Shut up, for Christ's sake." He muttered against my hand as I raised myself and began to fuck him with all the energy that I had left in my tired body. His ass was tight from over a year of solitude. It gripped my prick with eagerness, milking my trunk of its early release. I kept my hand over his mouth to quell his growing voice. I had forgotten how verbal he was during our sessions, and under other circumstances his wails of pleasure would have stirred me into great fits of passion, but tonight was not one of those nights. We needed to fuck, for no other reason than to feel again, to know that we were alive and in charge of our own lives. It was a survival fuck, a good-bye fuck, and a final fuck.

As I thought of never feeling his ass about my prick again, the emotions swelled inside me. Tears dripped from the corners of my eyes as I tried to hold out. I wanted these final moments with James to last. I fucked him harder, faster, groaning deep within my throat the intense pleasure that only James brought to me, for in those final moments before I released my seed into his ass for the final time, I realized it was James who had saved me from myself. It was James who made me the man that I had become, for he gave me the strength and confidence to fight. I released his mouth and he gasped as he took in a mouthful of air. He groaned and begged for more.

Our hot breath came in white clouds with the heights of our fucking. I felt the familiar fire burst into life within my belly. I rose and fucked him faster. Our bodies rocked against the roof; I no longer contained my rising desires. If we were to be caught from our vocalized passions, then at least I would die a happier man.

"Oh, James, yes, give me that ripe ass of yours. Oh, I shall forever remember you in this position." I shook, releasing several waves of seed inside him. He shouted and screamed in delight as he took all of me.

He pulled my prick from his ass and turned over. Without hesitation, he took the whole of me in his mouth and sucked me until I released a third time, sending a thick spray of my seed into his mouth. I felt his throat tighten about the tip as he drank from me. He began to moan and quiver. It was with these signs that I realized he was bringing himself off. I released myself from his mouth, dropped between his legs, and took from him what he had taken from me. I drank from him, savoring the salty bitterness that expelled from his softening prick. When he had finished draining himself, he pulled me off his prick and kissed me. We shared each other's lingering seed.

We dressed without words, for what could either of us say that was not said in our actions? We held hands and with caution and skill leapt from roof to roof until we were several streets away from Newgate. We climbed down to a lower level of a building that allowed us to jump without fear of injury. We stood for a few moments looking at each other, unsure of what to say. I broke the silence.

"Take care of yourself, my friend." Tears began anew as I realized that I might never see him again.

"Thank you, Addison. You are a true gentleman and friend, one I shall never forget." He smiled through his own tears.

"Where will you go?"

"I do not know."

"Maybe our paths will cross again one day," I said, hoping to ease the growing pain I felt at the loss of his friendship.

"Perhaps." He wiped the tears from his eyes as he turned to leave. I watched my childhood friend, my intimate, and the last part of my youth walk away into the early-morning light.

CHAPTER SEVENTEEN

The walk back to the coffeehouse gave me time to settle the doubt that fell over me at letting James walk out of my life. We had been good together, and for each other. Even so, I knew that I could not have asked him to stay. There was too much at risk for him to even entertain such an idea. Yet as I walked through the alleys and less-traveled streets, so as not to draw attention to my less-than-adequate attire, I could not help but think that I had made a mistake in letting him leave.

I stood at the back entrance to the coffeehouse. I stared at the cellar door, not wanting to go inside. I knew what, or more accurately who was waiting for me on the other side of it. Pierre and Christopher would be furious with me. I turned toward Mother's grave. It or she seemed to beckon me, and I walked over to it and knelt down. The ground was cold against my knees. I closed my eyes and said a prayer to her memory. I touched the headstone and smiled as Mother's image came to mind. She smiled back at me with that reassuring expression that I longed for. I knew Pierre and Christopher cared for me, but their constant accusations that I was unable to care for myself had grown tiresome. I wanted them in my life, but not if it meant that I would be treated as a child for the rest of my life.

"Thank you, Mother," I whispered as I stood. "You were always able to see something in me that others did not." A tear fell down my cheek. I wiped it away as I walked back to the cellar door and opened it, walked through the cellar and up the stairs and into the hallway of the living quarters. As I approached the door to the tavern, I heard Pierre and Christopher talking about me. I opened the door. Their eyes fell upon me with urgency and concern.

"Thomas." Pierre stood. "Where in the fuck have you been? We have been worrying ourselves sick about you since we woke and saw your note."

"If you read my note, then you know where I have been." My tone was more sarcastic than I had expected. "My apologies for my sharp tongue, as you can see, and perhaps smell, my night was not an easy one. I need a drink." Mr. Crowe was behind the bar. He poured a gin and handed it to me. "Thank you." I took a seat at the table.

"We appreciate the note, Thomas, but that is not the point." Christopher picked up where Pierre had left off. "Do you have any idea—"

"Please," I interrupted Christopher. "Do not lecture me. I do not mean to sound unappreciative of your concern, but you know as well as I that if I had come to either of you for help with this, you would have turned me down." I took a sip of the gin. The liquor warmed my body. "James was there for me when I had no one else in my life. I was able to be myself around him, without condemnation. He was in Newgate because of me." I looked at Christopher. He was ready to interrupt. "Yes, I know it was my father's bidding that landed him in that hell. Regardless of how he ended up there, he needed my help."

Pierre and Christopher looked at each other. "Thomas." Pierre reached out and took my hand. "Christopher and I are just trying to protect you. It is what Margaret wanted."

"We love you, Addison," Christopher interjected. His face flushed with the admission of love. It was something that I had never heard him speak of.

"And I love the two of you." The words came easier than I had anticipated. "But you cannot lock me away to protect me, nor can you be with me every second of every day. I have to be able to live my life, a life, by the way, that I want to have with the two of you. That is what Mother would have wanted. I will be twenty-one this June. I am a man now, and I have a right to make my own choices even if they are not the choices you would want me to make." I took another sip of my drink as I watched and waited for their response. Their faces were expressionless, as if they were stunned by the sudden lashing of my tongue. I continued my tirade before they interrupted. "How do you think I felt walking in and seeing you in conversation with Christopher, the man you knew meant more to me than anything else, and yet you kept him from me, and why? To protect me? If this is to be a partnership as you indicated, Pierre, then you have to start trusting me and treating me as such."

"May I speak?" Christopher interrupted with caution. I nodded. "Addison, fuck, I am sorry…Thomas. I take responsibility for not telling you. We should have told you the truth, but you must understand when I look at you, all I see is that handsome young boy that I watched grow up. Every day I tried to protect you from your father because I knew what a son of a bitch he was. It is hard for me to accept that you do not need me anymore. You are a grown man and capable of taking care of yourself." His voice trembled with emotions. He blinked as if he were holding back tears.

"You are wrong about one thing, Christopher. I do need you. I need the both of you, but as my equals, my intimates, and my friends, not as my protectors." I wiped the tears from his face.

Christopher took my hand and stood. His eyes were fixed upon my near-naked body. "I want nothing more than to fuck you at this very moment." He spoke with confidence, not caring that Pierre and Mr. Crowe were in the room. "Pierre, that goes for you as well." He reached out and took Pierre's hand.

"I have never taken one of my clients before," Pierre joked.

"Then I shall be honored to be your first." Christopher led the way up the back stairs and into my bedchamber. He pulled me into his arms and kissed me. His tongue slipped inside my mouth without hesitation. As we kissed, he pulled Pierre toward us. Pierre opened his mouth and shared in our kiss.

I moved my hands from about their waists and took hold of each of their pricks through their breeches. They each grew at different lengths and progressions as I fondled them. They moaned in unison. Christopher and Pierre pulled away from me and embraced each other with vigor. They kissed and explored each other's bodies for the first time. I stood back with a glimmer of remorse at being left out, but the more I gazed upon my two intimates taking pleasure from each other, the more excited I became. As they kissed, I unlaced my soiled undergarment and let it fall to the floor. I stroked and coddled myself until I was full of need. Neither of them noticed my state of undress as I moved past them and laid myself upon the bed and coughed for attention.

They broke from their kiss and turned to look at me. They smiled at me as they began to undress. I watched with the most needy and desirous eyes as they stripped their clothes with a quick pace. Christopher, tall and lean, covered in the golden-blond hair that I grew up admiring, and Pierre, the Parisian with his dark-toned skin and a thick, tight moss of black hair that started at the top of his chest and washed over his body down to his feet. I stroked my prick as my gaze lingered over their bodies. I could smell each of them. Their distinct odors mixed together made me drunk with desire.

Without a word, Christopher came toward me and crawled up my body until he straddled my chest and face. His warm, fuzzy thighs hugged my head. His prick, wet with his excitement, swayed over my face, spilling its nectar upon my lips and cheeks. I licked the tip of his prick and let the moisture pool in my mouth. As I savored Christopher's gifts, I felt Pierre rise from the foot of the bed. He slipped between my legs and nibbled my tender satchel, bringing with his touch a heat that blossomed in me.

I took the head of Christopher's prick in my mouth. He rose and leaned his arms against the wall. His thick trunk slipped deeper into my mouth. I took all of him until my nose was buried in the damp, musky hair of his private region. I inhaled his odor and drank from him, milking his prick with my throat as Pierre rose upon me and lifted my legs over his shoulders.

I wanted to scream. To beg to be fucked, but all I was able to manage was a low mumble of incoherent words against Christopher's prick. I looked up at Christopher, who was looking down at me with an expression of both pleasure and endearment. He pulled his prick from my mouth, then shoved it back into me. I gagged upon his length. He laughed and moaned as he took to fucking my mouth, sliding his prick between my lips as if it were between my buttocks.

In a moment of dizzying pleasure, I had forgotten about Pierre. That lapse was not long-lived as Pierre shoved his prick deep within my ass. Again I tried to scream as the pain ripped through me. All that escaped around Christopher's prick was a muffle of sounds. Pierre's prick was thicker than it had been in previous moments. It stretched me beyond words. The stinging pleasure of Pierre's insertion drove me into a fit of joyous tears. Perspiration broke out across my skin as the two of them used my entire body for their joint pleasure.

The rhythm of their fucks became one as they worked themselves to the edge of release. Their bodies, slick with sweat, shimmered in the rays of the morning sun. The air in my bedchamber was hot and full of odors that did more for my own release than the fucking of my body. Christopher began to moan as his prick swelled with his impending release. I shook my head and groaned and pulled his prick from my mouth.

"Please, neither of you shall spill your seed inside me." I gasped as air rushed into me. "Bathe me in your release." I gripped my swollen prick, which had yet to receive attention and stroked myself with such speed I thought I might rip my prick from my body. Pierre pulled out of me. The wet pop of his exit sent a shiver through me and sent me into a fit of spasms. I released myself, spraying rivers of white seed across my belly and chest. Christopher stroked himself as he leaned down and licked my cooling seed from my body. He groaned and threw his head back as he showered me with the warmth of his seeds.

When I thought I could take no more from these men without losing my mind, Pierre began to buck like a wild horse. He took his prick with both hands and fucked his fists, pumping himself with great force. He let out a high-pitched scream as he released himself over my opened mouth. Thick ropes of white pearls sprayed across my lips and tongue. Christopher lowered himself to lick Pierre's seed from my cheek, and in doing so received several thick ropes across his face. Pierre collapsed on the bed to my left. Christopher took the right. They wrapped their arms and legs about me, covering me with the warmth and odors of their bodies. We kissed and touched each other as we enjoyed the silence that settled in around us.

❖

I awoke in the bed alone. My ass and mouth were sore. Smiling at the memories, I got up and stretched, feeling my body resist. I took a fresh outfit from the bureau and dressed. As I opened the door to my bedchamber, the smell of fresh bread and roasted meat greeted me. My stomach grumbled. I rubbed my belly and made my way into the cooking area. Christopher was busy setting the table as Pierre, with a glass of gin in his hand, watched.

"That smells good." I staggered into the room and pulled out a chair.

"I would wager that none of us have had a decent meal in days." Christopher set the hot bread on the table. "I thought it was time we did."

"I am starved." I pulled off the end of the bread and blew across it before placing it in my mouth. My stomach growled for more.

"I think the three of us should talk about our situation," Pierre commented before placing a piece of bread in his mouth.

"I agree." Christopher came to the table with a platter of roasted meats and vegetables. "We still do not know what information Mr. Johnson had, if anything."

"Whatever it was, it was enough to get him murdered," I interjected. I pulled a piece of meat from the platter and slipped it in my mouth. "Pierre, I forgot to ask you." I paused to swallow. "How did your second meeting go with Mr. Willis? Did he have information for you?"

"He never showed. I went back to the Queen's Arms thinking he might be there, but the barmaid said she had not seen him since he was with us."

"You do not suppose Mr. Green silenced him, do you?" Christopher blew across his tea before taking a sip of it.

"I said that he was not to be trusted," I mumbled with a full mouth. I swallowed. "So where does that leave us?"

"Christopher, did Mr. Johnson have anyone close to him that he trusted?" Pierre questioned. "The day he was murdered I checked his pockets for the documents, but they were empty. Is it possible that he gave them to someone for safekeeping?"

"It is funny, after ten years in Mr. Green's employ, I did not know many of his servants well." He paused as he chewed. "Wait, there was someone he spoke about. What was her name?" He sipped his tea. "Her name escapes me, I am sorry."

"Do you know where he lived?" Pierre continued.

"He lived in my father's house," I answered. "My father wanted him available day or night, so he gave Mr. Johnson a room."

"Well, that does not do us much good."

"Wait. Her name was Bess." Christopher looked up from his plate. "I think she was a barmaid. On those rare occasions when Mr. Johnson asked Mr. Green for a night off, I believe he stayed with her."

"Great, but how do we find her? I do not know of any taverns in Bishop's Stortford." I tore off a piece of meat and slipped it into my mouth. The juice ran down my chin.

"For good reason, there are not any. He traveled to London on his nights off. I remember him telling me…shit…it was an odd name… Goose and Gridiron. That was it."

"It is odd to think that Mr. Johnson would patronize such a place as the Goose and Gridiron."

"Why?" Christopher and I questioned in unison.

"That is a disreputable place. Thieves and highwaymen gather there to discuss the day's earnings and to plan their next job." He patted his mouth with his napkin. "Are the two of you up for a morning drink at the Goose and Gridiron?"

Neither Christopher nor I felt it necessary to answer the question with words. We took a few more bites of our food, then left the table. Christopher hailed a carriage while Pierre and I tidied up the dining area. As we climbed into the carriage, Christopher hesitated.

"Perhaps I should stay behind and keep an eye out around here."

"That is not necessary, is it?" I questioned, not wanting to be without both of them by my side. "Your knowledge of Mr. Johnson may be helpful," I added, hoping to convince him to come along.

"That may be, but if you find Bess she may be more comfortable talking if there are only the two of you."

"You have a good point," Pierre interjected. "If she knows something, we do not want to spook her with the three of us."

"Then it is settled. I shall wait here for your return. Good luck." He smiled as he shut the door. The carriage lurched forward, tossing Pierre and me back against the seat. Christopher waved as we headed down the street.

"Why do you suppose the thieves and robbers chose the Goose and Gridiron for their meeting place? It is, after all, next to St. Paul's Cathedral."

"What better place to conduct illegal activity than right under the noses of the righteous." Pierre chuckled. It was a matter of minutes until the coach pulled up alongside the tavern. Pierre stepped out of the carriage. I followed him.

"Shall I wait, sir?" the coachman asked.

"No, that will do." Pierre handed the man the fare. "Good day to you, sir." Pierre bowed. The coachman tipped his hat with a slight nod of his head and pulled the carriage back into the busy street.

The tobacco smoke swirled about us as we entered the Goose and Gridiron. It stung my eyes and coated my throat. I held back a cough. The noise from the bellowing drunks was deafening the farther we walked into the tavern. We found one empty table off to the side of the bar. We took it and waved one of the barmaids over to us.

"What can I get you, honey?" She leaned on the edge of the table. Her large breasts followed her movement. I worried that they would slip out of her tight-fitting bodice.

"Two gins, my lady."

"Honey, there has not been a lady present in this place for years."
She laughed. "My name is Abigail, and if I can do anything for you two
fine gentlemen, you just let me know." She winked.

"Actually," Pierre leaned into the table, "we are looking for a
woman."

"What am I, honey?" She pulled her bodice down and exposed
her large breasts. "These twins here will keep the both of you warm on
a cold winter's night." She squeezed them, rolling the large nibs of her
tits between her fingers. She moaned and licked her lips. "Would you
like a sample with your drinks?"

"Perhaps another time, Abigail." I spoke perhaps with a bit too
much haste. I wondered how a man might be able to breathe nestled
between such monsters.

"Sweetheart, you can call me Abie." She pinched my cheek.

"As you wish, Abie."

"So if you do not want my twins, what can I do for you?" With
careful ease, she slipped her breasts back inside her outfit.

"We are looking for a woman named Bess. We have been told that
she works here."

"Bess?" The smile that once radiated off her face disappeared. She
became expressionless, almost cold. "Let me fetch your drinks, then I
shall see what I can do."

"That did not start off well," I remarked.

"No, it did not. Now the question is whether she is angry that Bess
may be getting our money for sexual favors, or if there is more to Bess
than we know. I am thinking it is the latter." He nodded toward the bar.
"She is talking to the barkeep about us."

"What should we do?" I watched the two of them watching us.

"Nothing, we shall…here she comes."

"Two gins for my two favorite men." She winked. "Bess is with
Jonathan Wilcox." She nodded in their direction. "That is her area and
that is his table. I do not know how she gets all the good ones." She
shook her head. "I shall go fetch her for you." She turned and left before
either of us said anything.

"After your story about him, I guess I should not be surprised to
see him in this place." I took a sip of my gin.

"I have heard he uses this tavern as his own personal office,
conducting his illegal business out in the open."

"How can that be?"

"Officials in the city turn a blind eye to his less-than-legal activities.

He plays the system well and has built a huge empire of criminals. When the money is right, he will arrest a well-known criminal and bring him to justice. It keeps the officials happy and the other criminals in line for fear they will be next if they do not do as he wishes."

"Does he ever get in your way?"

"I am too small for him to worry about."

"Whose pocket is he in?"

"He cannot be bought."

"Then that means that we might be able to use him to get to my father."

"No, we cannot. The last thing we need is to get tangled up with him. Once an agreement is made with that man, the only way out is to die, and he will be more than happy to make that happen." We both stood as Bess approached.

"I hear you two handsome men are looking for me." She curtsied and sat down at the table. Her manners were soft and ladylike, quite out of context with the place. She was older than she appeared from across the room, but no more than thirty. Her blond hair billowed out in soft curls and fell across her ample breasts. Her large lips were tinted a rose hue; her blue eyes sparkled even in the dim and dirty room.

"May I offer you a drink?" Pierre asked. She shook her head. "We were hoping to talk to you about a Mr. Clyde Johnson. You did know him, did you not?"

"Yes. Well, I did. I saw the advertisement in *The Tatler* asking for information. Are you the person who placed the advertisement?"

"My apologies, my lady. I am Pierre Baptiste, and this is Thomas Newton." All three of us smiled at one another. "I hate to be so blunt, may I call you Bess?" She nodded. "But were you and Mr. Johnson close?"

"If you mean did we fuck, then the answer is yes. He rode me like no one else. Some people say I was his bitch, but those wenches are just jealous of the attention I receive." The ladylike mannerisms seemed to disappear. "We fucked at least once a week, twice sometimes, depending on if his boss would give him time away." She pulled a handkerchief from her bosom and blotted her eyes as if she were about to cry.

"Did he rent a room to entertain you in?" I was mesmerized by her constant shifting of demeanor; one moment she was a soft-spoken woman, the next a foul-mouthed whore.

"What do you want from me?" She looked over her shoulder. "Yeah, we fucked, so what. I fuck all of my customers, well, until now."

She eyed the two us as if she knew our intimate secrets. "He had a room up on the third floor that he would reserve. He was a gentleman, a good man. He treated me like a lady."

"Was it the same room each time?" Pierre pressed her.

"Yeah, I guess. I never paid much attention. Those filthy rooms look all the same to me. I have been in all of them, many times." She scratched between her legs, then brought her fingers to her nose and sniffed. "Look, it is not safe for me to be talking to you boys." Her eyes rolled off to the side. "You know what I mean?"

"Then you do know something."

"I know nothing." She stood up in a huff. "Get on out of here and quit wasting my time." She stomped off back to the other side of the room where Jonathan Wilcox was waiting for her.

"I think she knows something," I whispered to Pierre.

"I agree, and I bet what she knows is in that room upstairs."

"Yes, but which one?"

"It does not matter. After her vocal public scorn of us, we will not get anything more here tonight. Shall we head back to the coffeehouse?"

"Sure. I did not get enough to eat, my stomach is grumbling." I glanced across the room as we left. Mr. Wilcox sat in his chair against the back wall of the tavern. His eyes were upon us. Once outside, I took a deep breath of the crisp morning air to rid myself of the uneasy feelings that Mr. Wilcox's presence aroused in me.

As we entered the public front of the coffeehouse, Mr. Crowe was serving a couple of men at the bar. He looked up and nodded. I raised my hand. The two men turned to look at me. Neither of them sparked recognition in my mind. Pierre and I made our way back into the private area of the tavern where Christopher stood behind the bar drinking. Mr. Sutton sat at one of the tables with his back to us. He turned to greet us as we approached, his face swollen and bruised.

"Mr. Sutton, what happened?" Pierre took a seat next to him. I walked behind the bar and stood next to Christopher.

"It was a horrible ordeal." His body hitched as if he were ready to sob. "They are all dead. I am sorry."

"Who?" I asked even though I knew whom he was talking about.

"The Phillips family. Alistair, Carolyn, and Henry."

"What in the fuck happened?" I tried to conceal my anger—I failed.

"I am so sorry, I tried…"

"Not hard enough," I spat.

"Thomas, that is quite enough," Pierre scolded me. I held my tongue knowing that I deserved his scorn. He turned back to Mr. Sutton. "What happened?"

"The journey was much longer than we had anticipated due to the snow. The second night we stopped at Stokenchurch to rent a room. It was a bit crowded and a little awkward for all us to share one room, but I insisted so that I would be able to keep an eye on them, you know, to protect them." He looked at me as if wanting to point out the fact that he had tried.

"You did the right thing, Mr. Sutton." Pierre rubbed his shoulder. "Go on."

"I do not remember much after that. I awoke to a terrible scream from Mrs. Phillips. My mind was foggy with sleep, but the bed, I just remember thinking, my God, the bed is covered with blood, and the smell in the room was sickening. I have never seen such a sight before. I leapt up to help her, hoping that I could fight off the two men who held her down. When they noticed my approach, they quickened their actions and slit her throat before I could get to her. This is when I noticed young Henry and Alistair on the floor on the other side of the bed. They were covered in their own blood. At that moment someone came up from behind me and hit me over the head." He took several sips of his drink. "When I woke up I was outside, lying near the carriage in the snow. I went back into the inn. Our room had been stripped clean. There was no sign of the bodies or the struggle that took place."

"He must have found out," Pierre replied. "They must have followed you from London."

"Why did they let you live?" I looked up at Christopher; he had an expression of puzzlement on his face, and I understood why. Something did not make sense with Mr. Sutton's story.

"Thomas, what is wrong with you?" Pierre spat. "We should be thankful that Mr. Sutton escaped with his life."

"That is my point. Whoever did this knew that Mr. Sutton was helping them escape. Why not kill him as well?"

Christopher tugged on the hem of my waistcoat. I glanced up at him. He pursed his lips and shook his head, indicating that I had said enough. I saw something in his eyes that told me that he shared the same thoughts about Mr. Sutton.

"What are you accusing me of, Mr. Newton?" Mr. Sutton glared at me through a swollen eye.

"I do not believe I was accusing you of anything. It does seem odd that you should bring this up."

"Thomas, I insist you apologize to Mr. Sutton."

"It is not necessary, Mr. Baptiste. I am sure that Thomas is just upset. I think I shall go lie down. It has been a trying few days for me."

"Do you need help?" Pierre stood.

"No, I can manage on my own, thank you, Pierre." He kissed Pierre on the lips. As he left our company, he glanced my way. There was something different in his eyes, something that unsettled me.

"I am appalled at your behavior, Thomas. I have known Mr. Sutton for many years. He risked his life to help you, and this is how you treat him?"

"Do you not find it a bit odd that they let him live?"

"Yes, I do, but that is no reason to accuse—"

"I did not accuse him of anything. I am just trying to understand the situation." I poured myself another gin.

"Perhaps we should talk of other things." Christopher took advantage of our lack of words. "How did it go at the Goose and Gridiron?"

"Not good." I took a sip of my drink.

"I would not say that," Pierre said with a less irritated tone. "Bess knows something, what or how much is still in question. Unfortunately, Mr. Wilcox was there, and it appeared that Bess is one of his whores, so we did not press too hard. We did find out that Mr. Johnson rented a room on the third floor for entertaining Bess."

"But we do not know which room." I finished Pierre's story.

"Third floor, you say? Are you sure about that?"

"Yes, why?" Pierre questioned.

"Perhaps it is nothing, but I remember Mr. Johnson telling me the mornings after his nights off that 303 was his lucky number."

"Do you suppose he was talking about his room number?" My voice rose with excitement. "We need to get into that room."

"We cannot. After Bess's outburst, we will not get past the manager."

"You cannot, but I can," Christopher commented as he finished his drink. "They know the two of you, but they do not know me." He looked at me. "It will be easy, Thomas, do not look so worried. I shall just go in and inquire about a room for the night. I shall make up some excuse about having fond memories of room 303. Look, it is the only way we are going to get in there."

"He is right, Thomas. Are you sure you are up for this? If Mr. Wilcox becomes the least bit suspicious of your activities, it may prove to be your death."

"What is there to suspect? He does not know me. Even if he is there, I will just be another person in the crowd. Besides, there is no evidence that he is even involved with this. No, I shall leave at once." Christopher finished his drink and set the glass down on the table.

"Be careful, Christopher. Someone is watching our every move." I turned back to look at the door to the living quarters. It stood ajar.

"I shall be back in the morning." He kissed me, then leaned over the bar and kissed Pierre.

"Good luck, Christopher."

"Christopher, wait," I called as he reached the door. I ran to him. "Please, be careful." I kissed him again.

"Do not worry, my love." He smiled at me. He nodded toward Pierre, who leaned against the bar. I stood with my heart sinking in my chest as I watched Christopher leave. I could not help but think something was terribly wrong.

CHAPTER EIGHTEEN

A re you all right?" Pierre came up to me, pulling me from my thoughts.

"Yes." I turned away from his embrace.

"Please, my love, to do not be mad at me. I am sorry I spoke to you in that tone, but do you honestly believe that Mr. Sutton is lying?"

"I do not know what to believe, but something is not sitting right with me. I just do not know what it is." I turned to him. Over his shoulder I saw that the door to the living quarters was closed. I tilted my head with curiosity. "I thought that door was ajar before."

"What?"

"In fact, I know it was." I went to the door and listened. There was silence behind it. I walked back to Pierre. "That door was open when we were talking with Christopher about our plan."

"Never mind the door, Thomas, we have something more important to discuss."

"I told you I am fine."

"It is not about Mr. Sutton. We shall deal with your worries later."

"Then what?"

"I have been putting this off for some time for fear of its repercussions, but with no leads it is time for you to pay your father a visit."

"You cannot be serious?"

"I am, and we shall go together."

"When?" I walked over to the bar and poured another drink. I took in all in several deep gulps to calm my growing nerves.

"We need to leave at once if we are to make it to the House of Lords."

"But they are in session."

"Yes, we are going to confront him there."

"That is impossible. You cannot just wander in off the streets. They have guards everywhere."

"A person can enter the Palace of Westminster. The problem will be getting to the south corridor, which leads to the Peers' Lobby and the House of Lords. We shall have to be careful. It is time you make yourself known to your father. Even he is not desperate enough to cause a scene in front of the other members."

"Let me tell Mr. Sutton that we are going."

"Let him rest, I am sure he will be fine." Pierre walked to the door and held it for me.

"It looks as if Christopher made his journey to the Goose and Gridiron on foot." I walked toward the carriage and climbed inside. Pierre pulled himself up in front and within moments we were moving down the street at a rather brisk pace. I jostled about in the backseat as the carriage jumped and skidded over the wet, rutted streets. I chuckled with the new knowledge that Pierre was a wild man behind the reins of a horse.

We parked a few streets away from the Palace of Westminster and made the journey back on foot. We walked the perimeter of the building, looking for a possible way in. Pierre pointed to a door on the backside of the building.

"You do not expect the door to be unlocked, do you?" I questioned as he approached.

"No, I do not." He looked over my shoulder, then added, "Keep an eye out while I pick the lock."

"Why does it not surprise me that you know how to do that?" I quipped. Though I was instructed to keep guard, I allowed myself to watch with growing curiosity and fascination as Pierre knelt down by the door, pulled a small pouch from his breast pocket, and with a determined look upon his face selected a small metal pick. He made quick work of the lock. "I am impressed."

"A skill I picked up at an young age. It has not failed me once. When we get out of this mess, I shall teach you."

"So you shall teach me to be a thief?"

"It is only thieving if you steal. We are not stealing, we are gathering information." He winked at me.

"A subtle difference." I poked him in the side. He giggled and flinched as he opened the door. "I assume you know where the Lords are meeting?"

"I do."

"Of course you do. A silly question on my part." I chuckled as we entered what appeared to be a large storage area. The grin disappeared from my face. I turned my attention to our surroundings and whom I was about to confront. It appeared that Pierre knew his way around the palace. I followed him making a mental note to remember to ask him how a thief had such intimate knowledge of a government building.

"Stay close," Pierre whispered. "Once through this door, we must navigate a large hallway before we come to the Central Lobby and the visitor's entrance."

"Wait." I held him back. "Why did we not just go through the visitor's entrance?"

"What would be the fun in that, my love?" He placed a quick kiss upon my cheek and opened the door.

The echo of voices from the Central Lobby billowed down the hallway as we stole through the shadows of the corridor. With most of the houses in session we were fortunate not to have officials coming at us from every direction. We paused as we reached the entrance of the lobby. Pierre peered around the corner and tugged my coat sleeve. We slipped into the lobby and milled about with the other visitors.

The high vaulted ceiling curved in a large arch above our heads. I stood in awe of the riches that surrounded us. My father would never talk about the Parliament, let alone bring me to see it. As a young child, I had always wondered what it would be like to see such a place. Whether rich or poor, young or old, I could not imagine anyone not being struck by its grandeur, which was surrounded by the filth and decay of the city.

"This way." Pierre tapped my hand. I followed him out of the Central Lobby and down a long, narrow corridor. He paused where the hallway ended to look in both directions. "Good, no one is around." He grasped my elbow and led me down yet another hallway. We stopped halfway down in front of a large wooden door. "Here we are," he whispered as he looked at our surroundings. "Are you ready?"

"Yes." Though truth be told I was not at all ready to confront my father. My body quivered with the realization of what I was about to embark upon. I grasped the metal latch. On the other side of the door I heard my father's voice. The familiar yet unsettling tone of his voice brought back years of childhood fear. Memories of being a damaged child, charged in my father's heart for murdering his beloved wife when I came out of her womb. For most of the past few years, I had heard his voice in my dreams, but standing with only a few inches of wood between us gave me pause. I knew our presence here was unlawful, that if this plan of Pierre's did not work we would be arrested and executed at once. Mother Clap's voice rose in my mind. *Live for the both of us my boy and hold me in your heart always.* This was what Mother would have wanted, I reassured myself. I took a deep breath to settle my nerves and belly, knowing that if I was to do this, I would have to do it now. I unlatched the door and stepped inside. Pierre followed behind me.

My father stood at the end of a large table. Twelve to fifteen men sat with their backs to the door as my father spoke of the Society for the Reformation of Manners and the continuing need for their presence in the city. He looked in my direction as I walked farther into the room. His words fell away. He looked out across the room at the members of the House of Lords and cleared his throat. My presence was too much for him. The color in his face drained away as if he had just seen a ghost. As the full weight of the situation settled around him, the look of shock faded and anger soon reddened the pale color of his face. I felt the rage burn from his eyes as he looked at his dead son. The men around the table must have noticed that his attention to the topic at hand had been disrupted. They shifted in their seats and all eyes were soon upon me. I did not let them deter me from my goal. I stepped farther into the room. Their eyes followed me.

"It's been a long time, Father, has it not?" What I expected to hear was the frightened child who never spoke out of turn or, God forbid, challenged his father. The voice, my voice that spoke was strong, unwavering, and in control.

"What in God's name is going on?" One of the men rose from his seat and faced my father. "Lord Green, who are these men, and how in the hell did they get in here?" The room fell silent as everyone, including me, waited to hear my father's explanation. "Lord Green, answer me." The man's voice rose through the silence.

"Shut the fuck up, Lord Chambers," my father hissed. "This vagabond is of no one's concern."

"Vagabond?" I repeated. "Is that what I am now? I doubt that the son of one of the members of the House of Lords can be called a vagabond." I smiled at my father's rising irritation. I walked farther into the chamber and stood facing my father. "Shall I introduce myself, Lord Green, or would you like to do the honors?"

"You are making a grave mistake," he mumbled.

"This house demands an answer, Lord Green." Lord Chambers slammed his fist against the table. "Who is this man who calls you father?"

"I can assure everyone here that this vile man who stands before me is no relation to me." His voice was confident, yet as I stood less than a foot from him, I witnessed his lips quiver and the veins in his neck pulse with apprehension. His gaze moved from me to Pierre, who came up beside me. "And do you claim to be my son as well?" He struggled to laugh. The others chuckled.

"I know what you have done, Father." I lowered my voice so that the others would not hear my accusations.

"If you have something to say, speak up so that we may all hear the lies," Lord Chambers spat. When I did not acknowledge him, he added, "This is an outrage. Arrest these men at once!"

Several of the men rose from their seats and came at us. Pierre had instructed me not to fight, so the two of us allowed ourselves to be handled as common thieves. Two men on each of us held our arms behind our backs as another called for the guards. My father leaned into me, his breath stale and venomous.

"What? Did you think you could just walk in here and all would be forgotten? You are more foolish than I thought. You have just signed your own execution warrant." He laughed.

"I am not the fool, Father." I responded without fear, without worry. "Do you think we did not prepare for this? As I said, I know everything." My father winced at my words. It was then that I knew I would win this battle. "Yes, it is true. All your dirty secrets, your lies, your murderous hands, it is all ready to be released to *The Tatler* if Mr. Baptiste and I do not return from this visit." I smiled with the affirmation that I had the upper hand in my father's twisted game and it would be I who came out victorious for once. "Think about the public scandal, Father, if your lies were published. Even you are not so stupid as to risk it." I saw the doubt in his eyes that his broken, vile son could, in fact, pull off what I was claiming. "How does it feel, Father, to know your dead son has beaten you?" I chuckled. "I can see the doubt in your eyes. You were never good at concealing your emotions. If you do not believe me, then go ahead and arrest us. I no longer fear you, Father. If I am to die, I will do so knowing that your death will not be far behind." We stared each other down, our expressions blank of any emotion.

"Release them," my father commanded.

"But, my lord…"

"Do not question me! I said let them go. They are nothing but a couple of common vagrants with nothing better to do than to spout lies. They are no concern for us." He arched his back as if adding weight to his statement. The men released Pierre and me. I took a step closer to my father as I rubbed my wrists.

"You have not seen the last of me," I spat. "I will see your fortune and power fall if it is the last thing I do." I turned toward Pierre. He nodded at me and smiled. We left the House of Lords with two men escorting us through the building and out onto the street.

"Holy fuck. That felt good," I shouted and raised my hands in the air. I laughed as I spun on the heels of my shoes. I felt alive for the first time in my life.

"You were brilliant, my love." Pierre wrapped his arms around me and pulled me along the street in a near dance. "But let us not get carried away just yet. This small victory for us will only have repercussions, for it has given your father a renewed sense of urgency in silencing you and anyone close to you. We can only hope that Mr. Green will be in such a state that he will make a mistake, and that will be all we need."

"I realize we have fueled a violent and dangerous man, but I will not let him or what he might do rule how I live my life any longer. No matter what happens now, I am free of my father's grip once and for all." I spun around again and laughed. "I wish Mother was alive to witness me today."

"Margaret would have been so proud of you, my love." Pierre's solemn tone settled deep into me. "She loved you so much, Thomas, and she always had faith in you. She thought…It does not matter now."

"Do not do that to me. What did she say to you?"

"She told me that she could not have loved you any more even if you were born of her womb, but she worried for you."

"Yes, about the raids."

"It was more than that, Thomas. She knew your potential, even if you did not see it. She worried that staying with her and John would hold you back and keep you from finding the person hidden inside who was afraid to be seen. She wanted you to go with me in hopes that you would find that person you were meant to be, and today you have found that person."

"I miss her," I murmured. I felt the familiar ache in my heart, but this time there were no tears. It was then that I realized the pain was no longer grief, but love.

"I know you do. Keep her in your thoughts and in your heart, and she will never be far away." He gave me a half smile. "Now, let us get back to the coffeehouse. It will be good to get some rest before your father makes his next move."

We arrived back at the coffeehouse as the sun made its descent. Our conversation had been light, neither of us feeling the need to discuss anything of great importance. The public area of the bar was deserted and dark. I made a mental note to open the public tavern as soon as my father was out of the way. As we entered through the back hallway toward the private sitting area, laughter greeted us. I opened the door to a scene that warmed my heart. Mr. Crowe had done what he had promised. Seven men of varying ages and social classes were seated about the room, drinking and flirting with one another. I looked at Pierre. He smiled and winked at me.

"Mr. Newton," Mr. Crowe shouted from behind the bar. "What do you think?"

"You are a man of your word, Mr. Crowe." I came up to the bar and took the gin that Mr. Crowe offered. The men turned toward me. Some of the faces looked familiar, others were strangers to me, but it did not matter. Clapton's was open for business. One of the men that I recognized stood up and came over to me.

"Thomas, it is so good to see you again." He hugged me and laid a gentle kiss upon my lips. "You do not remember me, do you?"

"I must admit my memory is failing me." I felt my face redden.

"Ah, do not fret, boy. Mr. Aderly, Franklin Aderly, and I shall never forget the night you gave me." He threw his head back and laughed. "Best fucking night of my life, I do not mind telling you." He took a sip of his drink. I looked up at Pierre, blushing with embarrassment. Pierre simply smiled and nodded.

"Glad to see you are back in town and working here again," Mr. Aderly continued. "I do not suppose you are free tonight for a repeat."

"I wish I could oblige you, Mr. Aderly, but I am no longer entertaining the gentlemen here. I own the place now."

"Do you really?" His expression hid what his voice did not—his disappointment. "Well, I just assumed that Mr. Clap took over after Margaret's death." He paused and bowed his head. "I was heartbroken when I heard the news."

"What news?" I asked, a bit confused. "It was a very private burial. I did not make an announcement."

"Oh, you know how word travels between us men. Someone hears a rumor for what they assume is truth, and before long everyone knows." He looked back at the men around the room. "Well, if you ever decide to go back to entertaining the men, I want the first dance."

"You have my word." I bowed. He turned and staggered back to the group.

"Your reputation astounds me," Pierre whispered in my ear as he nibbled my neck.

"Stop." I brushed him away with a playful wave of my hand as I looked around the room.

"What is wrong?"

"I do not see Mr. Sutton. Perhaps I should go and check on him."

"I shall grab a drink and mingle with the men." He winked at me.

"Just remember I turned down a paying client tonight, so hands off." I laughed. Pierre slapped my buttocks as I turned and walked toward the back hallway. As I climbed the stairs, I witnessed Mr. Sutton come up the stairs from the cellar. He did not look at all happy to see me.

"Mr. Newton," he said in his most formal servant's tone. He did not smile. He nodded in my direction, then slipped into his bedchamber, shutting the door as I approached. I opened it and stood in the hallway, waiting for an invitation to enter. When none came, I spoke.

"I believe we need to have a talk. May I come in?"

"Of course, this is your house," he said in a sarcastic tone.

"I do not believe that tone was necessary, do you?" I walked into the room.

"My apologies, Mr. Newton, I wanted to hurt you with my words as you hurt me with your accusations." He came toward me in a determined and forceful manner. His actions were starting to unsettle me. "What, are you so convinced of my guilt that you are scared of me? Do you know how much you have hurt me?"

"I am sorry for what I said. It was not meant as an accusation." I took a small step backward to give more distance between us. "I said what I did hoping that we might be able to come up with a reason why they did not murder you for helping the Phillips family escape." I lied in the hopes of easing the growing tension in the room.

"Do you still desire me?" His question took me by surprise.

"My feelings for you have not changed." I spoke the truth, just not the same truth as he was seeking. My feelings had not changed. In fact, I was becoming even more uncertain of his alliances with every passing moment.

"Then fuck me," he barked. He tore open his blouse and ripped it from his body, his chest rising and falling with his heavy breaths. He took a step closer to me. His body's heated odor rose through the air. It was in those familiar odors that I noticed something different. I could not place the smell at first, but it was there, lying beneath his sweat. "What, you do not want to fuck? Well, I do." He grabbed my shoulders and pulled me toward him, wrapped his arms about me, and pressed his lips to mine. It was in that embrace, in that moment of intimate closeness that the strange odor came to me—it was gunpowder.

I broke our kiss and looked into his eyes. They had changed, not the color, but the depth. Gone was the sparkle that I remembered staring into after our nights of heated bliss. What stared back at me was dull, and void of all emotions. I pulled myself from his grasp and stepped away.

"What, am I supposed to pay you now?" he spat. "Once a whore, always a whore." He reached into his breeches and threw several shillings at me. "Now you are mine whether you like it or not. I have paid for you, so I shall take what I want of your body."

"Mr. Sutton, please do not do this." I looked over Mr. Sutton's shoulder and saw the door ajar. I moved to the left. He charged me. I tried to move farther out of his reach, but the bureau blocked my way. His grip was immediate and painful upon my upper arm. I tried to pull free but his grip tightened. He threw me across the room and farther from my escape. I landed against the wall. The old wood cracked against my weight.

"Mr. Sutton, Mr. Sutton, I am so tired of hearing Mr. Sutton." He began to laugh as he stood over me. He unlaced his breeches, pulled them down, and stepped out of them. His prick was stiffer than I had ever seen it. It protruded from his body, hungry, needy, and ready.

A sudden thump came from the open door. Mr. Sutton turned and I heard him mutter words that I could not comprehend. With his attention turned elsewhere, I raised my foot and kicked him, making direct contact with his swollen affairs. "Son of a bitch!" He turned toward me. His face was red with anger as he gripped his prick and satchel.

I moved out of his way and for the first time saw what had made the noise at the door. Mr. Willis leaned against the door frame, his blouse covered in blood. Sweat dripped from his feverish face and ran down his neck. He reached out with a trembling finger and pointed at Mr. Sutton. His lips moved as if he were trying to speak, but the only thing that escaped his mouth were a few sprays of blood and some garbled words.

"God damn it," Mr. Sutton hissed. He stumbled forward as he reached for his discarded breeches and gripped the bureau to steady himself. He looked at me then turned his attention to Mr. Willis. "Motherfucker." He charged toward the door and threw Mr. Willis to the floor. Mr. Willis groaned and I heard Mr. Sutton's footsteps disappear into the cellar, followed by the distant thud of the outside door closing.

"Pierre, come quick," I called as I rose from the floor with the aid of the wall and staggered toward Mr. Willis. "Pierre, God damn it," I yelled, worrying that the noise of the tavern was drowning out my pleas for help. I knelt down by Mr. Willis, took off my blouse, and tried to hold it over his wound.

"Mother of mercy," Pierre muttered as he came to a halt in front of the bedroom door. "What happened?"

"I do not know. Mr. Sutton and I—" I cut myself off, not sure how to explain Mr. Sutton's actions. "Mr. Willis stumbled in here. He must have come from the cellar entrance as that is the one way he knew to get back here." I placed more pressure against his chest. The bleeding would not stop. His breathing was rough and uneven. He reached out and took my hand.

"He just walked in, then collapsed?" Pierre questioned.

"Yes." I looked at the wounds. "Motherfucker, he was shot." I remembered the smell of gunpowder on Mr. Sutton. The sudden realization that Mr. Sutton, the man I let fuck me countless times, had shot someone in cold blood sent a frigid finger running down my back.

"Mr. Newton," Mr. Willis whispered. "I am sorry for everything." He tried to speak louder but coughed, spraying blood across his lips.

"Who did this to you?" I asked even though I knew the answer. I wanted Pierre to hear it from someone other than me. He shook his head to dismiss my question.

"You need to see this." Mr. Willis reached into his waistcoat and pulled out a folded piece of paper. "Be careful, Mr. Newton." He took a final gasp of air and trembled, then went still.

I stood up and looked at Pierre. The men gathered in the hallway, murmuring to each other. "Gentlemen, I am sorry about this unfortunate turn of events, but under the circumstances I think it would be best to close for the night. Mr. Crowe, please escort your friends home to make sure they are safe." I smiled at all of them. "Drinks are on the house next time, my friends."

"Oh, Mr. Crowe," Pierre added. "Would you mind fetching one of the constables on your way through town?"

"Not at all, sir."

"Thank you, Mr. Crowe." As the men walked out in a single file without so much as a word between them, I took the bloodied paper, unfolded it, and read it: *Consider this your final warning, Mr. Newton. The next time it will be someone you love.*

"What worries me is that Mr. Green knows where we live. Mr. Willis was not able to travel far in this condition. He must have been shot right outside our home."

"And I know who shot him." I looked up at Pierre with my heart in my stomach.

"Who?"

"Mr. Sutton."

CHAPTER NINETEEN

No, I will not believe that the man in my employ and in my bed could be capable of such a thing." Pierre walked away from the body and sat on the edge of the bed.

"Pierre, please listen to me." I sat down next to him. "I will admit that my accusation of him murdering the Phillips family was a stretch, but it is all making sense now. When I came up here to check on him, I saw him coming up from the cellar."

"But that does not mean—"

"Pierre, please let me finish." I waited for an acknowledgment from Pierre. He nodded as he looked down at the floor. I studied his expression and saw in his eyes that there was a part of him that knew the truth. I continued. "He was cold toward me. No, that is not accurate. He was hostile toward me. He ripped his shirt off, demanding that we fuck. When I refused, he threw money at me, calling me a whore and demanding that I give him what he wanted. He assaulted me. It was then that I noticed the smell of gunpowder coming off him. I did not think much about it at the time, but then when Mr. Willis came in from the same direction that Mr. Sutton had and with the gunshot wounds..." I hesitated. "Come on, Pierre, you have to see this. Mr. Sutton is not who we think he is."

"I fucked the man, for Christ's sake." Pierre stood up.

"We are both guilty of sleeping with him, Pierre."

"I still cannot believe this." He looked at me. "I know your evidence says that he is responsible, but I have known him for so many years there has to be another explanation."

"Pierre, I do not like this any more than you. I cared for Mr. Sutton as well. Do me one favor. Agree to come along with me in the morning."

"Where to?"

"Wherever Mr. Sutton goes."

"You mean follow him?"

"Yes." I went to him and held his face in my hands. "It is the one way to know for sure."

"Hello?" a voice called from below. "This is Constable Dyer. Mr. Newton? Mr. Baptiste?"

"Up here, Constable." I went into the hallway to greet him. "The body is in this room."

"My Lord." He crossed his chest and bowed his head. "I have known Mr. Willis for fifteen years or more. Do you know who did this?"

"No." Pierre spoke without hesitation, interrupting me as I was getting ready to call Mr. Sutton out as the possible shooter. I shot Pierre a troubled look, wondering why he was still trying to protect him. "I am Pierre Baptiste. This is my associate, Thomas Newton."

"What can you tell me?"

"Not much." I spoke before Pierre had a chance to interrupt me again. I hesitated, unsure of how far I was willing to go against Pierre's personal wishes. I decided to side with caution. "I was in this very room when I heard a loud thump coming from the doorway. I turned and saw Mr. Willis leaning against it. He collapsed on the floor. I tried to talk to him, hoping he could tell me what happened, but he died before he managed even a word to me." I withheld the fact that Mr. Sutton had been present.

"And that is it?"

"Yes."

"Do you have any knowledge of why Mr. Willis would have come here? This is, after all, the former home of Margaret Clap, is it not?"

"It is. Why?"

"Wait a minute. Thomas Newton, you were working with Mr. Willis and Mr. Williams on the trials, were you not?"

"I was."

"Can someone validate your claim that you were in here when Mr. Willis came in?"

"Are you accusing me of murdering him?"

"The two of you have quite a history, Mr. Newton."

"That may be so, but I would never murder the man."

Pierre spoke up. "I can vouch for Mr. Newton's activities."

"So the two of you were together in here the whole time?"

"Yes, that is correct."

"What about before that?"

"We had just arrived back here from a meeting with a client of ours. We have been with each other all day." Pierre continued with the lies.

"Thank you for your time, gentlemen." Mr. Dyer shook our hands. "I believe that is all I need for the moment. The coroner will be issuing a warrant in the morning for the inquest into the suspicious death of Mr. Willis. He may have additional questions to ask you."

"We shall be more than happy to assist in any way we can. Thank you again, Constable. We shall leave the body where it is and shut the door so no one will disturb anything until the coroner arrives."

"Are you expecting someone, Mr. Baptiste?"

"No, but Mr. Crowe, the gentleman that you received the called from, is working here to help Mr. Newton with reopening the coffeehouse. He shall be in tomorrow morning."

"I am sure that the coroner will be here by morning. If you can think of anything else that might be useful for the inquest, please note it so it can be explored."

"Of course. May we show you out?"

"That will not be necessary." He hesitated. "You should consider putting in a door, Mr. Newton, to your living quarters, instead of making people come and go through the cellar." He smiled. "Just a suggestion is all."

"Thank you, Mr. Dyer. I shall consider that at length." I stood with Pierre behind me as Mr. Dyer left through the back entrance of the house. "What in the fuck was that about?" I snapped. "Why are you still protecting Mr. Sutton?"

"The same reason you did not call me out on the lie. We cannot get the constables involved at this point. If we told Mr. Dyer your suspicions about Mr. Sutton, he would have the entire city searching for the killer of a city official. We would not stand a chance at bringing down your father. Whether we like it or not, we need Mr. Sutton."

"So you will help me follow him tomorrow?"

"Yes, I am most curious where he will lead us." He kissed me.

"I do not think I am going to be able to sleep tonight, what with Mr. Sutton out there somewhere. What if he were to come back while we were sleeping? And what about Christopher?"

"What about him?"

"He is out there alone, snooping around Mr. Johnson's room. What if Mr. Sutton finds him? What if—"

"What if you take a breath and calm down," Pierre interrupted. "I bet a few drinks while sitting next to a warm fire will help ease your mind. With any luck, a new plan of action will come from a couple of drunken minds." With his hand upon my shoulder we walked down the hallway and into the tavern. As Pierre went to stoke the fire, I went behind the bar to fetch a couple of glasses and a bottle of gin, then took a seat on the sofa. Pierre joined me as I poured the drinks.

"Thomas, I can see the worry in your face. Your father is trying to scare you."

"It is working." I sighed and took a sip of my drink.

"What I mean is that you are safe. He is not going to send someone here to kill you in your sleep. That would be too easy. He wants you to suffer." He paused. "I am sorry. I do not believe that made things any better for you." He stroked my cheek.

"I am not worried about myself. My father is a heartless man. If he wants me to suffer, then he knows how to do it. He will come after you and Christopher."

"Come here." Pierre raised his arm and pulled me into him. "We are going to be fine, my love. I promise that when this is all over, Christopher and I shall be right here by your side."

"I wish I could believe that." I kissed his chest through the soft, silky blouse and closed my eyes, snuggling deeper into him. I listened to the beat of Pierre's heart as the warmth of his body eased my worries. I felt his nipple growing stiff as I nuzzled him. He moaned and squeezed me in his arms. I released the top two clasps of his blouse. Strands of his dark chest hair curled around the edge of his white blouse. I ran my finger through the thick moss feeling his dampness against me. The odor of his body billowed out from his blouse. I felt my prick stiffen with need and pulled my hand away from him and sat up.

"What is wrong?"

"It feels wrong to be intimate with so much going on. It was a selfish act on my part."

"Selfish is not a word I would ever associate with you, my love." He released two more clasps, exposing more of his body to me. "We should never take moments in our life for granted. Pleasure regardless of life obstacles should be relished and savored." He spread open his blouse, exposing the rich tapestry of hair and the firmness of his nipple, and pulled me down to him. I nestled my face against his body and took his tit into my mouth.

He arched his back as I sucked him. The deep groans of his pleasure vibrated against me. I lowered myself down his body, kissing and licking the salty dampness of his skin, released the last two clasps of his blouse, and pulled the tails of his shirt from his breeches. I kissed his navel and ran my tongue along the waistband of his breeches as I unlaced them and pulled the flap of his breeches down and inhaled the heavy masculine odors of his private area. I buried my nose in his tight moss, nibbling at the tender untouched skin beneath it.

He spread his legs to give me additional access. My hand slipped farther into his breeches and gripped his solid length. I pulled his prick free of the tight-fitting garment. It landed against his furry belly with a heavy, wet smack. I stroked him and he groaned. His prick spat its clear nectar. I licked it off his belly and cleaned his navel with my tongue. He shivered as I slipped my hand down his growing trunk and gripped his furry satchel. I pulled on it, stretching his prick up off his belly. I opened my mouth and guided his prick upon my tongue, tasting more of his desire as it spilt from his prick.

"My Lord, your mouth feels good." Pierre grunted as he shoved his prick farther into my mouth. I opened wider and let him enter me, gagging upon his length. I inhaled then let the rest of him slip down my throat. I sucked his prick, milking more of his early release and drinking it down. I wanted nothing more than to rip my clothes off and have him fuck me without grace, without manners, but I knew it was not the right moment, not the right time. Instead, I rested my head upon his belly and let him fuck my mouth with gentle thrusts of his hips. His groans of pleasure, which he usually bellowed, were whimpers of delight.

My need was too great to restrain. As Pierre continued to use my mouth, I busied myself with unlacing my breeches. My prick slipped out and slid across my belly. I gripped it as I stretched out on the sofa and was soon fondling myself to the same rhythm as Pierre's thrusts.

I closed my eyes to our tender intimacy and let the smells and sounds of our activity become the fuel for my growing desire. Pierre's hand soon replaced mine. I gave in and let him stroke me off as his prick swelled within my mouth, releasing more of his nectar than I could accommodate. I let it dribble from my lips, wetting my face and the hair of his affairs.

His thrusts became more pronounced, short, steady beats against my face. I knew he was close to release. I worked my tongue up and down the trunk of his prick, pumping and priming him with the expert skills that I learned at an early age. I felt him tremble. A long childish whine escaped his lips as he filled my mouth with the wonderful delights of his seed. I sucked him and drank him dry as he released two additional times within me.

As his body adjusted to the satisfaction of sexual bliss, he took more notice of my needs. He began to fondle my prick with renewed interest. I opened my eyes and watched with growing fascination as the eye of my prick spread open, spraying my blouse with my hot seed. He continued to stroke me, harder, firmer, making me spill such quantities of myself that I thought that my prick would run dry. My body hitched up and down as a deep groan parted my lips. I settled down into his lap as my prick softened in his grip. It was not long before the effects of the gin and our sex took hold of me. I drifted off into a deep and pleasant sleep.

❖

The chill of the morning caused me to shiver, waking me from my sleep. Pierre and I were entangled in each other's arms on the sofa. I rose and stretched, feeling my back pull against the stiffness. The fire was cold. I poked around the ashes, hoping to revive it, but the embers were lifeless. Pierre awoke at my stirring.

"Good morning, my love." He rose and greeted me with a kiss. "How are you feeling this morning?"

"Unsettled," I remarked without much effort. "I am going to check in on Christopher."

"I shall make us some tea." Pierre grabbed my hand and pulled me back into his arms. He kissed me again, this time with his tongue slipping into my dry mouth. I touched his face and smiled as I broke the embrace.

I walked across the room and climbed the steps into the living quarters. The door to Christopher's bedchamber was closed. I lifted the lever and opened the door. His bed was empty. I walked through the room with growing concern. My mind turned to Mr. Sutton. I walked down the hallway, stood outside the closed door, and tried the lever. It would not budge. He had locked himself in. I listened and heard the familiar sounds of his sleep drifting through the door. I slipped back down the hallway and into the dining area.

"Pierre." My voice rose with worry. "Christopher did not come home last night."

"Are you sure? Perhaps he came home while we were sleeping and has gone out for a morning walk."

"No, he would not just leave without telling us what he found at Mr. Johnson's room. Besides, his bed has not been slept in."

"Mr. Sutton." Pierre's voice bellowed through the quiet room.

"Why are you calling for him?"

"Whatever is going on with Mr. Sutton, you and I need to act as if nothing is wrong. This will also allow us to keep an eye on him." He cleared his throat and called again. "Mr. Sutton, we need you now!"

"I do not like this, especially after his actions against me last night." I saw Pierre's look of concern. "But I will do my best," I added with a quick smile.

"Yes, sir," Mr. Sutton called from the hallway. He paused at the top of the steps to lace up his breeches. He buttoned his blouse as he came toward us. "Where are we going?"

"Christopher did not come home last night as expected. You will take Thomas and me to the Goose and Gridiron."

"Why would he be there?" His expression remained void of emotion.

"We do not have time for pointless questions, Mr. Sutton," I huffed. "If you will not take us…"

"Of course. I thought that perhaps I could be of assistance to the two of you other than being your coachman, but if that is all I am to you, so be it."

"Do not be ridiculous, Mr. Sutton. You are much more than that to us. I have noticed the tension between you and Thomas. I do hope we can all work together without further incidents."

"Yes, sir. You can count on my discretion and service. I shall have the carriage ready in five minutes." He bowed with a touch of mockery. His smile faltered as he caught my gaze. "Mr. Newton, please accept my apology for my incorrigible behavior last night. I do hope I can have your forgiveness." He took my hand and kissed it.

"You have it." I lied. A churning in my stomach led me to believe that his apology was for Pierre's benefit and nothing more. I looked up at Pierre as Mr. Sutton left the room.

"That went rather well," he whispered.

"You are not—"

"No, I am not." He interrupted me. "You are right. Something is wrong here, and I intend to find out what. Come on, we need to find Christopher." Pierre placed his arm about my shoulder as I led us out of the coffeehouse and into the cold morning air.

The ride through the city was done in silence. I suspect Pierre, like me, needed time to think. However, I would wager that we were thinking of different things that all led to the same unknown resolution. I stared out the window watching the few people make their way on foot through the rough city streets. While my tongue felt the need for silence, I could not quiet the feeling growing in me that Christopher was in grave danger. The sudden stop of the carriage pulled me from my thoughts. Mr. Sutton opened the door.

"If you do not need me, sir, I would prefer to stay here." He looked across the street at the Goose and Gridiron. "To keep an eye on things out here."

"I need you for a more important job than that, Mr. Sutton," Pierre responded as he patted Mr. Sutton on the shoulder.

"Sir?"

"While Thomas and I are checking this place out, I would like you to go to the Queen's Arms, where Mr. Baker kept his lodging. Perhaps he is there."

"Yes, sir. Should I come back here afterward?"

"That will not be necessary. We will meet you there." Pierre shut the carriage door. Mr. Sutton climbed up on the carriage, and without a word to either of us snapped the reins and set off down the street.

"I hope you have a plan," I commented as we watched the carriage jostle down the street.

"I do, but first we need to get inside and see what is going on," Pierre responded as we walked across the street and entered the tavern.

To my surprise there were a number of men drinking at this early hour. We walked up to the bar. The barmaid from the other day came up to us, looking as if she had just crawled out of someone's bed.

"You two are out and about early." She greeted us with a tired smile. "What can I get for you?"

"We are looking for someone. We believe he rented a room last night."

"His name?" Bess asked.

"Christopher Baker," I responded.

"The name means nothing to me, honey. What does he look like?"

"Tall, blond hair, very handsome. I am sure you would have noticed him."

"Johnson," she shouted.

"Yes." A man came out from the back room. He looked at us and I saw recognition in his eyes. His expression turned cold.

"These two gentlemen are looking for a Mr. Christopher Baker. They say that he came here last night to rent a room. Since I was otherwise occupied, I thought you might be able to help them."

"No one rented a room last night," he replied more to her than to us. He busied himself behind the bar, and the added, "Remember, Bess, we were booked last night." His tone was more of a suggestion than anything else. He looked at us with caution before returning to the room from which he came.

"Yes, that is right." She turned to Pierre and me. "We were booked last night." Her smile waned. "Good day gentlemen." She curtsied, then looked back over her shoulder to the door the owner had left through. She nodded toward the door, then left without a word.

"Come on, I think she wants to tell us something," Pierre whispered. We walked out of the tavern and into the dull coal-laced morning. We waited around the corner. It was not more than a few minutes before Bess approached us.

"Your friend was here last night." Her voice was low. She looked around with a nervous twitch. "Look, I doubt you will find anything in room 303, but here is a key to the back door that leads up to the rooms. The door should be unlocked." She handed the key to Pierre. "Please be careful. I do not want to contemplate our fate if you are caught."

"If we are found out, we will not mention your name," I replied trying to reassure her.

"It will not matter what you say. They will know." A strained smile crossed her face. "I can keep Mr. Berks occupied for about twenty minutes, any longer I cannot guarantee."

"Thank you, but why are you helping us?" I questioned.

"Because your friend is in real danger, as are the two of you. I must go. Remember you have twenty minutes up there, then you must get out." She turned and ran around the corner and back into the tavern.

"We do not have a lot of time." Pierre tossed the key into the air and caught it with confidence. We walked down the side street until we came to the entrance to the guest rooms. Pierre unlocked the door, and with the grace of the Lord behind us, we slipped inside without a sound.

The entrance led to the back room where Mr. Berks and Bess stood in conversation. We slipped up the stairs, hoping that the soft creaks of the wooden steps would be hidden by the conversations coming from the other room. We were less careful on the upper staircase as we rushed up, taking two steps at a time. We paused in front of room 303. Pierre gripped the latch and opened the door. It did not make a sound as we let ourselves in, shutting the door behind us.

"The rooms here are clean," I commented as we began shuffling through bureau drawers looking for anything that might give us a clue as to Christopher's whereabouts.

"It is too clean," he replied as he opened the drawers one at a time. "They are all empty. What about the nightstand by the bed?"

"Nothing," I said after opening the two drawers. "This is not good. If what Bess said is true and Christopher was here, what happened to his overnight bag? If he had to leave in a hurry, it would still be here."

"Not necessarily."

"What do you mean?"

"As I said, this room is too clean. Someone must have come in and removed any signs of his presence. They could have removed his belongings with ease." Pierre stood in the center of the room and looked around. "There is nothing more we can do here."

"Wait, what is this?" I commented as something underneath the bed caught my eye. I knelt down and peered underneath. My body took to trembling almost at once and my heart bled and drained into my stomach.

"What did you find?"

"Christopher's pocket watch." I held it up and stared at the cracked face. When I noticed the blood on the chain, I almost lost my balance. Pierre came to my side. "Pierre, we have to find him before it is too late." The tears ran down my face.

"We will, my love, we will." He wrapped his arm about my shoulder and wiped the tears from my face. "At least we know he was here, and that is not a lot of blood. If they wanted him dead, we would know."

"How so?"

"I would wager that Mr. Green is holding Christopher as bait to lead you out into the open."

"That son of a bitch." I stood up. "If he has done anything to Christopher, I will rip his head off."

"You will do no such thing, Thomas."

"Why should I not take from him what he has taken from the people in my life?"

"That would make you no better than he and land you in Newgate with a personal invitation to the gallows. Everything you have fought for would be for nothing."

"You are right." I sighed as I placed the watch into my pocket.

"Shall we go to the Queen's Arms and see what Mr. Sutton is up to?"

"Yes, we need to find Christopher before it is too late, and I shall wager that Mr. Sutton knows where he is."

We left the Goose and Gridiron and walked with quick steps through the city streets. As we approached the Queen's Arms, I looked down the alleyway behind the tavern. Pierre's carriage stood empty, nestled between the two buildings. I grasped Pierre's arm and pulled him into the alley, nodding in the direction of the carriage. It was then that I witnessed Mr. Sutton standing in front of the horses. He looked around in a nervous manner as he pulled a large package from beneath his waistcoat.

We slipped up behind the carriage and kept out of sight as another man approached Mr. Sutton from the opposite direction. They greeted each other as strangers with a firm handshake and idle chatter. They spoke in the most cautious voices, making it impossible for us to hear anything but a faint whisper. As I watched the two men, a feeling of familiarity settled into my belly, bringing with it a nagging twinge.

"I think I know him," I whispered in Pierre's ear. He shot me a quick glance. "I am not sure." Pierre gave several slight nods of his head as if trying to help me talk. I stood up a bit more and peered over the carriage, trying to get a better look at the man. He appeared to be quite old—early fifties at least, his face was wrinkled and pocked with blemishes of age. He was short, standing nearly six inches below Mr. Sutton's height. Something in me caused me to imagine him younger, perhaps by ten or fifteen years. It was with this new eye that his identity came to me in a wave of confusion and concern. "Son of a bitch," I hissed.

"What?"

"That is my father's physician." As I spoke those words, Mr. Sutton handed Mr. Finney the large package. Mr. Finney looked inside and nodded as an expression of relief washed over his pale face. He reached into his waistcoat and handed Mr. Sutton a large sum of money. "What in the fuck is going on?" I asked myself as much as Pierre. I tugged on Pierre's arm and nodded for him to follow me. We slipped out of the alley and around the corner.

"I am going to follow Mr. Finney." I kept my voice low.

"No, it is too dangerous. You go home and wait for me there. I shall have a talk with this Mr. Finney."

"Pierre, please. We do not have time to argue. Mr. Sutton does not trust me. He knows I know something. You have a much longer relationship with him. Perhaps you can get through to him where I cannot."

"Yes of course, you are right." He nodded. "Do not question Mr. Finney. Just find out where he is going, then come straight back to the coffeehouse and get me." He looked at me with growing concern. "Thomas, this is no time to play hero."

"Very well, I shall not confront him." I took his hand and squeezed it not caring who saw our intimate moment.

"Thomas, please be careful."

"I shall." I peered around the corner. Mr. Finney was walking in our direction. "Mr. Sutton is pulling away. See if you can catch up with him." I turned my back to the alley as Mr. Finney came out of it and turned to the left. I nodded at Pierre, then turned and followed Mr. Finney down the street.

CHAPTER TWENTY

I kept my distance as much as possible, but with the growing crowds of people, the streets were getting congested, making it difficult to keep my eye on him. His short legs moved at a rapid pace as he hurried down the street. I quickened my steps and still I struggled to keep up. He turned without hesitation three blocks down. I stopped and peered around the corner of the building to make sure he had not realized he was being followed. A coachman stepped off a carriage and opened the door for him. Mr. Finney, looking behind him, headed for his transportation.

I took off running down the street, forgetting about the promise I had made to Pierre about not confronting the man. We did not have time for such things. I knew if I did not get to him, it would be days or weeks before we would get another opportunity such as this. The coachman shut the door behind Mr. Finney then jumped up into his seat. I prayed I would not be too late.

The carriage edged its way into the crowded street. It gave me the few extra seconds that I needed. As it pulled away, I grasped the handle of the door, opened it, and leapt into the carriage unannounced. I shut the door and looked across the seat at the expression of fear etched upon Mr. Finney's face.

"I am not here to rob you," I said so that he would not call out to his coachman. The carriage continued down the road. The driver appeared oblivious to my joining the ride. The fright on Mr. Finney's face faded and turned to annoyance.

"What is the meaning of this intrusion?" His voice was high, almost feminine. It took me by surprise.

"We have some business to attend to, Mr. Finney."

"How in the hell do you know who I am?" He moved a bit farther away from me, pressing himself against the door. He looked at the handle as if contemplating fleeing.

"I would not advise that."

"What business could we possibly have to discuss?"

"Our business is of a personal nature. I would rather not go into it in detail here. Trust me when I say that you do not want that either." I paused, then added, "I do hope you are returning to your home. I think that would be a much better place for us to talk."

"If you think I am going to let some vagabond like you come into my house, you are mistaken."

"Let me just say that it has to do with a Mr. Bartholomew Green." I smiled as I saw a glimpse of fear once again wash over him. "As I said, I believe it would be in your best interest to have this conversation in the privacy of your own home instead of here in public, where anyone might be able to overhear."

"Fuck." He sighed. "You have made your point most clear. I live in Mayfair, so it is not too long a journey. May I at least inquire as to your name?"

"You may, but I would have to decline to answer that at this moment. Again, I mean you no harm. Please, relax, we shall talk once we arrive at your home." I nodded at him, then turned my attention to the sagging, crumbling buildings and the whores that made up this area of London. The remainder of our ride was done in silence. The carriage came to an abrupt halt. As we waited for the coachman to open the door, I looked over at Mr. Finney. His gaze was upon me, studying me.

"Who in the hell is this?" the coachman grumbled as the door opened.

"An unexpected guest," Mr. Finney responded.

"Shall I get the constable?"

"No, that will not be necessary." Mr. Finney looked at me with caution, as if wanting me to confirm his statement.

"Mr. Finney and I have some business to attend to," I commented but did not elaborate.

"If you need me, sir."

"Thank you, Mr. Weiss, but I shall be fine." Mr. Finney stepped out of the carriage.

"Thank you," I said to Mr. Weiss as I slid across the cushion and exited behind Mr. Finney. While I did not think he would run, I was not going to give him the chance to get any distance between us.

"May I offer you a drink?" Mr. Finney broke the silence as we entered his parlor. "While I am not accustomed to being handled in this matter, I have a feeling that I am going to need a drink and do not want to appear unmannerly."

"Thank you for the offer, but I will pass." I waited for him to pour his drink and sit down before I took the chair across from him. He removed his waistcoat, wrapped the package Mr. Sutton had given him inside it, then folded it up and placed it on the sofa next to him.

"So what is this about?" He hesitated. "Mr…"

"Newton, Thomas Newton," I said, expecting some flinch of recognition.

His face was expressionless as he took a sip of his drink. "I am sorry, but should your name mean something to me?" His eyes never left mine.

"Perhaps not, but I am sure you will remember the name…" I hesitated as if a part of me did not want to admit my heritage. I noticed the anticipation and fear building in Mr. Finney and took a breath to settle my own nerves before continuing. "Addison Green."

"Jesus." He crossed his chest and his mouth went slack. He raised the glass, his hands trembling too much to bring it to his lips. He moved to set it down but missed the table. It tumbled to the floor.

"I take it that name has a significant meaning for you?"

"Yes." He tried to compose himself. "What does Mr. Green's dead son have to do with me?" He continued his desperate act of concealing his knowledge.

"Do not think for one moment that I believe this act of yours," I responded. "Perhaps I should get you another drink before we proceed. The liquor may trigger your memory." I took the glass from where it had landed, walked to the liquor cabinet, and poured another whiskey. "Perhaps I should join you after all." I handed him the glass. He took a sip and watched as I sat down. Silence fell between us. He stared at me with a look that I could not read.

He broke the silence. "How did you find out?"

"Find out?" I paused and took another drink. "I am afraid you do not understand. I am Addison Green." I listened to the words fall from my tongue. Words I had not dared to speak since that day at Cheam Classical School when my father told me he had murdered me on paper and faked a new birth record with the name of Thomas Newton.

"Lord have mercy on my soul." He moaned. "It cannot be. Mr. Green buried his son. I signed the death certificate."

"Perhaps, but you never saw the body, did you?"

"No, it is not possible." His words did not match the tone of his voice. I knew he believed me.

"Are you telling me that you did not know about my father faking my death?"

"I did not." He took a sip of his drink. "Mr. Green came to me three years ago and told me of your death. He asked me to sign the official records. How did you find me?"

"I saw you talking with Mr. Sutton today at the Queen's Arms."

"How did you find out?" He glanced over at the package folded up in his waistcoat, then pulled it toward him as if protecting it. It was obvious that he was shaken by my presence.

"As I said, I saw you in conversation with Mr. Sutton. I saw the exchange that took place. I recognized you as my father's physician. Something is going on, and I need to figure out what it is. My associate, Christopher Baker, has gone missing, no doubt at my father's command. Then there are the others."

"Others?" Mr. Finney's left eye twitched.

"Yes, the death of his coachman, Mr. Johnson, and the deaths of Alistair Phillips and his family." I took a sip of my drink before continuing. "My father is going to great lengths to silence the people in my life who knew the death of Addison was faked."

"My Lord, you do not know?"

"Know what?" I responded with curiosity and growing worry. He did not reply; instead, he took another sip of his drink and stared at me. "Please, Mr. Finney, I need your help."

"I thought that is why you were here? That somehow you found out the truth."

"Why is my father so desperate to hide the knowledge of faking his son's death that he would risk everything to murder them?"

"I knew this would come back to haunt me someday. I am old and tired. Getting involved with Mr. Green was a something I have regretted for twenty-odd years."

"What is in that package, and why does my father want it so badly?"

"It has nothing to do with faking your death, Addison. That is the least of Mr. Green's worries. What is in this package could ruin him and the empire he has built."

"If it has nothing to do with the fraud and forgery of my death, then what could be so damning that he would come after everyone in my life?"

"It is not about your death, Addison. Just the opposite, it is your birth he wants to conceal."

"My birth?" I questioned as the words Mr. Finney spoke echoed in my mind. The news that Pierre and I had been wrong about the actions of my father sent a shiver down my back. I wanted to know more, needed to know, in fact, yet I feared the answers that were creeping in around me. I finished off the whiskey, hoping it would give me the strength I knew I was going to need to get through this conversation. "What has my father done?" The words fell from my tongue before I was ready to hear them.

"That is just it, Addison. Mr. Green is not your father."

The shocking words stabbed me in the chest like a cold, sharp dagger. I felt sick in the belly. My head swam with confusion, and more questions. I stared at Mr. Finney without words. I had no idea what look was upon my face at that moment, perhaps an expression of disbelief or uncertainty, but deep inside I knew Mr. Finney was speaking the truth. I walked over to the liquor cabinet and brought the bottle of whiskey back to the table, pouring us both another drink, then sat and took a long sip, letting the burn of the alcohol pull me from my own mind.

"How can that be?" My words sounded distant, as if I was looking down at myself, hearing the words I spoke, yet feeling as if they had not come from my own lips.

"Oh, my boy. It is a long story and one I had hoped I would take to my grave. If I had known that Mr. Green was capable of murder..." His voice trailed off.

"What?"

"That is a deception I have played on myself to ease the burden of my involvement. I knew long ago what Mr. Green was capable of, and I did nothing to stop it. I was desperate back in those days. I was broke, struggling with gambling debts and trying to provide for my wife and two children. I did it for the money. I kept the secret to protect my wife and children."

"Please, Mr. Finney, I do not know what you are talking about. What happened?"

"I guess after all my shameful involvement with your father... excuse me, with Mr. Green, you of all people deserve to know the truth. Perhaps by confiding in you I shall be spared at the gates of heaven upon my death." He took a sip of his drink before continuing. "Your mother Elizabeth was a wonderful woman. I was there when she was born."

"But I thought you were my father's physician?"

"No, I was employed by the Cantors. Elizabeth, your mother, was their daughter."

"They had their own personal physician? Then they were wealthy as well?"

"No, not as well, the Cantors were the sole fortune. Mr. Green's family was of the lower class. Mr. Green's father was a drunk, his mother a whore."

"What? But I thought—"

"Please, let me continue." He took another drink. "Mr. Cantor, your mother's father, was one of the wealthiest men in London. He was a member of the House of Lords, as were his father and grandfather. You see, you must be born into the House of Lords. It is the only way to become a member."

"Then how…" I held my tongue. "My apologies. Please continue."

"Your mother could do no wrong in her parents' eyes. She was their only child. Their devotion to their daughter is what caused so many problems. She was a rambunctious girl, afraid of nothing. She met Mr. Green when she was nineteen, he twenty-three. She fell in love with him but knew her parents would never approve of her relationship with someone of such low social standing. She kept the truth of her parentage from Mr. Green, and her involvement with him from her parents. The day she told Mr. Green about her family was the day that everything went sour for dear Elizabeth. Mr. Green vowed to one day have the wealth and power that he felt he was denied at birth, and upon discovering this new knowledge asked Elizabeth to marry him. She never learned to say no to the man she loved, so one evening she presented Mr. Green to her family."

"I can guess that they were none too pleased."

"On the contrary. They loved their daughter so much that they would do anything to see her happy, even if that meant letting her marry outside of her social class. They not only welcomed Mr. Green into the family, but they also gave him a new life. They made up these outlandish stories of his bloodline. They set him up with his own house in Bishop's Stortford."

"The house I grew up in."

"Yes." He paused to fill up his glass. "They spent thousands of pounds creating a fake social class for Mr. Green so that their daughter's reputation, and I suppose their own, would not be tarnished." He shook his head. "Poor dear Elizabeth had no idea that in marrying Mr. Green, she would be selling her soul to the devil."

"How do you mean?" I was becoming more intrigued with Mr. Finney's tale, and yet there were so many questions he was not answering. I suppose I needed to hear the whole story, but I could not help but think that he was using up valuable time that I needed to find Christopher.

"Think about it, Addison. Mr. Green was a short-sighted young man who believed the world owed him for being born into such a desolate and unacceptable life. You may think that the social classes are bad now, but I am telling you, most people of any wealth would rather spit on someone of Mr. Green's upbringing than to try to coexist. The poor were often convicted of crimes for no other reason than to rid society of their existence."

"Please, about my mother," I pleaded, feeling more anxious with every moment that passed.

"Yes, of course." He smiled. "Well, you can imagine what all this wealth did to Mr. Green. He was starting to become someone. People spoke to him. They regarded him with respect. The wedding took place as planned. Everyone of a respectable class was in attendance. The couple was showered with gifts and money. I am not sure when it happened, but my guess would be that it was during the ceremony that Mr. Green began to change. He became obsessed with money and power. Elizabeth's father was the one person who sent Mr. Green on a path of destruction. As a wedding gift, he gave Mr. Green a seat in the House of Lords."

"But I thought you said it was a bloodline."

"It was, and still is. To this day I cannot imagine what Mr. Cantor did to secure Mr. Green that position. But I will tell you Mr. Green was never the same. He was obsessed with the power, but there was one thing missing."

"What was that?"

"True wealth. You see, he only had what Elizabeth's family would give him. He convinced Elizabeth to go to her parents and ask them for more money. They refused, saying they had done enough for him. That is when things went from bad to worse. Mr. Green knew Elizabeth was their only child and that she stood to inherit their fortune upon their deaths. The problem was he did not want to wait. He had plans, and he needed their money to finance them. If they were not going to give it to him, he decided that he would take it."

"Are you telling me that he murdered my mother's parents?"

"I believe so, though I do not have any proof of that. It was three short months after their marriage that news came of the Cantors' unfortunate deaths. They were murdered in their sleep. Without any witnesses or any leads, the criminal was never caught. There was speculation that it was a group of house robbers, but according to your mother's statement at the inquest, nothing was taken from the home."

"So my mother inherited the family estate?"

"Yes, but your father demanded that she sell their home. She did as her husband requested. She was too grief-stricken to know any better. Their home sold for ninety-eight thousand pounds."

"That is more money than most people see in their lifetime."

"With the estate sale and the inheritance, Mr. Green began funding the Society for the Reformation of Manners, demanding that they enact laws against the same class of people that he was born into."

"Mother was right?"

"Excuse me?"

"Sorry, a woman I knew. She went by Mother Clap. She hired someone to look into her suspicions that my father—rather, Mr. Green—was funding the Society."

"Were you close?"

"Yes, she was like the mother I never had. She took me off the street, gave me a home and a new life."

"I am sorry."

"Thank you, but please go on."

"Your mother would come to me to talk. I never understood why, except that I was without a doubt the closest thing she had to a family. Her family's money changed Mr. Green. He became bewitched by the power and prestige that the money afforded him. Your mother wanted to leave him, but he would not hear of it. He said it would ruin him if word about his wife's leaving were to get out. He convinced her that she was a tarnished old whore no one would want."

"Yes, that sounds like the bastard."

"She was broken down. The spark that guided her through most of her childhood faded away. I always suspected that he abused her, but she always denied it."

"He was a master at verbal and emotional abuse, at least with me." I took a sip of my drink. Mr. Finney nodded his agreement. "So how did I come about?"

"One day she came to me. The sparkle was back in her eyes. She laughed and smiled as she told me of this man that she had met. I had not seen her that happy in over a year at that point. It did this old man good to see back to her old self. She told me that she had fallen in love with the most generous and handsome man and that she was carrying his child. She asked me if I would be there for the birth. I did not refuse, but I told her of the danger she and her unborn child would face if Mr. Green knew it was not his."

"How did she have time to meet someone else? I can only imagine the constraints my father had on her. He never let me out of the house."

"She had something he needed."

"Her money?"

"Yes. While he was busy building his empire, she had the free time to, well, meet other people, men in particular. She told me that she was not going to tell Mr. Green that she was leaving him. She knew he would never allow that. Her plan was to wait until he left for London for another session of the House of Lords. Once he was gone, she would have plenty of time to pack and leave. She and her new gentleman friend were going to leave London and start over in Cambridge."

"So what happened?"

"Apparently Mr. Green knew of the affair, though he did not know the man's identity. The day he left for the session, he never went to London. He returned home an hour or so later and found her packing her belongings. Well, as you can imagine, that was the end of your mother's freedom. She never saw her gentleman friend again."

"Were you there when she gave birth to me?"

"Yes, Mr. Green allowed me that privilege. I brought you into this world."

"And you watched my mother die due to complications with my birth." Mr. Finney's expression went stone cold. The pink of his face faded to a dull white. He looked at me with tears in his eyes. His lips moved, but no words came from them. "Mr. Finney, my mother is dead, is she not?"

"Yes, she is, I am afraid to say."

"What are you not telling me?" A chill ran down my spine as Mr. Finney's dull white complexion changed to an almost deathlike pallor.

"Addison, she did not die in childbirth." His tear-filled eyes looked up at me.

"What are you telling me?" I croaked as a knot tightened in my belly. I felt faint, dizzy, and ill, as if someone had just poisoned me. I crossed my arms, giving myself a comforting hug to ward off any more unsettling news. I knew it was a pointless gesture. I saw in Mr. Finney's eyes that the worst was yet to come.

"Mr. Green, he…well…"

"Goddammit, what happened to her?" I yelled with growing rage.

"He wanted me to give her an overdose of opium and write on the death certificate that she died in childbirth."

"Motherfucker!" I stood. "You murdered my mother?" I threw the glass in his direction. It missed his head and shattered against the wall behind him. He cringed as the tears fell from his eyes.

"Please, Addison, I had no other choice. I loved your mother. I was there when she took her first breath. I watched her grow up into a wonderful, beautiful, and loving woman."

"Then why in the fuck did you murder her?" I screamed as I charged toward him. He cowered against the sofa and raised his old, wrinkled hand to protect himself. In that moment, I realized that I was no better than Mr. Green. I was controlling people with fear. I backed away. "I am sorry, Mr. Finney, I did not mean to attack you." I sat on the edge of the table and took a deep breath to calm myself before proceeding. "Please," I began in a softer tone as the tears streaked my face. "Why?"

"I am so sorry, Addison. It was the hardest thing I ever had to do, but you must understand Mr. Green does not give people choices. He had the power and influence to ruin me. He might have even murdered me if I had not agreed to do as he asked." He shook his head. "Perhaps it would have been better if he had killed me, then I would not have had to live with this agonizing truth my entire life."

"What did he offer you?"

"He offered to buy me a storefront so I would be able to start my own practice. He promised to pay me one thousand pounds a year for my silence. I was not in a position to refuse that kind of financial offer." He paused and looked at me. "Please, you must understand, it had to be me. If I had not been the one to murder Elizabeth, he would have found someone else." He stopped and looked into my eyes. "Do you not see? I knew Mr. Green would never let Elizabeth live. If she had to die I wanted her to do so in my hands, the way she came into this life, held with nothing but love and admiration for her beauty and strength."

I stood, not knowing if my legs would support me. I wanted to grieve the loss of a mother I never knew, to fall onto the ground and weep like a lost child, yet through the grief, my anger and rage at Mr. Green's actions gave me strength. I paced back and forth with mounting frustration.

"Motherfucker!" I slammed my fist into the wall. The wood and plaster cracked, cutting my fingers and hand. "Son of a bitch." I pulled my hand from the wall and looked at the blood that wept from the wounds, pulled off my cravat, and wrapped my hand in it.

"I am so sorry, Addison. I do not know what else to say."

"It is not your fault. You are a victim of my…shit, Mr. Green's obsession just as much as I am. It gives me some comfort knowing that you were there for her in the end. Please, do you know who my father is?"

He ignored my question. "If I had been a stronger man, I might have tried to stop it."

"There is nothing you could have done. I realize that, and so do you."

"Here, I think you should have this." He pulled the package from his waistcoat and handed it to me.

"What is in here?" I turned it over, not wanting to open it and face more unexpected news.

"Everything you need to destroy Mr. Green."

"Are you serious?"

"Yes, it is all in there. I recorded every payment he made to me. I kept letters that he sent to me over the years. Many of these give more incriminating evidence against him. I do not know why I created this file. Perhaps somewhere deep inside me I knew, or perhaps prayed, that this day would come. The top sheet, you will find, is a complete confession from me, implicating your father. There is enough proof in there to put an end to him at last."

"Why are you giving this to me? If I use your confession…"

"It will not matter, Addison." He pulled a pistol from between the seat cushions.

"Please, Mr. Finney." I dropped the package on the floor and raised my hands. "You do not have to do this. I promise I will not use your confession."

"Addison, I wish things could have been different. I would have liked to know you better. You seem like such a fine young man."

"Mr. Finney, please do not do this." I walked toward him with uneasy steps. "Do you know who my father is?"

"I am sorry, Thomas." He raised the gun to his head and pulled the trigger. The sound was deafening. Blood and matter from within his head sprayed against the wall in large, wet clumps.

From the shock of what had happened I had not noticed the blood that had splattered on my face and shirt until I looked down at my body. My hands trembled at such a pace I thought my heart might give in. I fell to the floor, grasped the package, and opened it. I read his confession and wept.

CHAPTER TWENTY-ONE

I did not have any concept of time once the gun fired. I felt as if the space around me, the air I breathed had slowed to a near crawl. Each time I tried to control the rush of anger, grief, and frustration, I would read more of the documents that Mr. Finney had gathered and the emotions would return, heavier than before until I thought I would suffocate. The smell of Mr. Finney's blood and head matter floated through the room, and yet the smell of his death did not influence my desire to leave. It was not until I saw Mr. Sutton's name documented as someone who had received thousands of pounds from Mr. Green that my mind returned to the more urgent matter of locating Christopher.

I gathered up the papers and placed them back into the envelope. As I stood, my knees cried out from the awkward position that I had left them in. I looked over at Mr. Finney. His face had already turned a grayish blue. His lips were darker than the rest of his complexion. The blood and matter still dripped down the wall, smearing what was the last of Mr. Finney's life across the dull white plaster.

I ran my hand over my face. It was then that I remembered the blood that had splattered me. I pulled my hand away and saw the quantity that had smeared across my fingers. I knew I could not go out in daylight with a bloody face without raising suspicion and possible arrest, so I took to looking around Mr. Finney's house for a basin of water in which to wash myself. I felt uncomfortable in his house. I was a stranger, a thief, only there to steal his water. I was violating his home, his privacy, and for whatever reason, his death made the feelings worse. I found a small bucket of water in his cooking space, dampened a nearby cloth, and wiped my face and hands. Without a looking glass, I was not able to inspect myself to see if my quick bathing routine had rid me of the appearance of blood. I tossed additional amounts of water upon my face and used another cloth to dry with. Comfortable with getting the worst of the blood off, I went back through the parlor toward the door. I paused to look at his lifeless body; the pistol, still clutched in his grip, lay in his lap. My mind turned to Mr. Sutton and Mr. Green. I went to Mr. Finney's body, pulled the pistol from his bloody grip, and slipped the gun into the band of my breeches, far enough in the back so that my waistcoat would conceal it.

I headed toward the front door when I remembered Mr. Finney's coachman had brought us here. I peered out the window and saw him standing next to the horses smoking his pipe. I knew I needed transportation back to the coffeehouse, as it was too great a distance to make reasonable time on foot, but Mr. Finney's coachman was out of the question. I backed away from the window and let myself once more through the house and out the back door.

I ran through the unfamiliar streets in search of a coach to hire. I was out of breath and out of patience when I heard the familiar sounds of hooves hitting the damp and soiled streets. I climbed into the carriage and instructed the driver to drop me off at the corner of Fleet Street and Shoe Lane, far enough away from the coffeehouse, so that my final destination would not be known. Mr. Green was a shrewd man, something that had taken me most of my life to figure out. I knew I could not allow myself to think that I was not being watched or followed by his gang of murderers and spies. As we took off down the streets, I closed my eyes and let the uneven rocking of the carriage lull me into a few moments of necessary sleep. When I woke, we were coming to our final stop. I stepped out of the carriage, handed the coachman his fare, and thanked him for his service. I took off running down Shoe Lane, anxious to see Pierre and to fill him in on what I had learned.

"Pierre," I called out as I entered the back hallway from the cellar. "Pierre?" I peered into each of the rooms as I walked down the corridor heading toward the social room. When I opened the door, I stared at a sight I had not expected, nor was prepared for.

I took slow, unsteady steps into the center of the room. The tables and chairs were overturned in an apparent struggle. A bottle lying next to one of the upside-down tables was broken. I went toward it, knelt down, and picked it up. Blood coated the thick, jagged edges of the bottle.

"Son of a bitch," I said in a hushed tone, feeling as if my breath had been taken from me. My mind raced with possibilities of what had happened. I wanted to believe that the blood was Mr. Sutton's. That somehow Pierre had gotten the upper hand in the obvious struggle. A glimmer of hope rose inside me as my mind continued to feed me lies of the scenario: Pierre taking down Mr. Sutton, demanding that Mr. Sutton take him to where Christopher was being held. With more false hope, I looked toward the door waiting to see Christopher and Pierre coming through the door. I knew the thoughts and scenarios were flights of fancy created by my desperation and fear. That was when the realization gripped me. I was on my own, and it was up to me to find both Christopher and Pierre before my father put an end to their lives as well.

I stood and looked around the room for anything that might indicate what had happened or where they might have gone. Panic rose to the surface as it became clear that I had nothing that could lead me to them. I felt the sharp edges of the bottle cut into my skin as my grip tightened around it. I screamed and threw it against the wall. The shattering of the glass echoed through my head.

I tried to control the growing frustration and fear that festered inside me, knowing it would not help me locate the two men I loved. Then a thought came to me. We told Mr. Sutton to go check out Christopher's room at the Queen's Arms. *Could Mr. Sutton be keeping them there?* The question floated through my mind. It was the only lead I had. I rushed out of the coffeehouse, holding on to what little hope there was in this thought. As I ran down Shoe Lane, I came across the same coachman who had left me just moments ago. I hailed him down and climbed into the carriage. He opened the window between us and smiled.

"Back again?"

"Pardon me?" My cluttered mind tried to understand his comment.

"I just dropped you off not more than fifteen or twenty minutes ago." He looked at me as if waiting for an answer. It was one I did not give. He then added, "You are fortunate enough to have caught me resting my horses, or you would have found yourself walking." He nodded and smiled yet again as he tried to get me to partake in his conversation.

"Yes. Thank you." I hesitated. "Please, I am pressed for time. I need to get to the Queen's Arms."

"Consider it done." He nodded, shut the window, and sent the horses on a frantic run through the city. I bounced back and forth against my seat as the coachman took the streets and corners with more speed than I experienced when Pierre took the reins of his carriage. I smiled with the memory and hoped that there would be more of those moments in our future.

It was not long before the coachman pulled up out front of the tavern. He opened the window separating us. "Shall I wait for you, sir?"

"Yes, thank you. That would be most helpful." I handed him the fare, opened the door, and dashed into the tavern. As I did not want to draw attention to myself, I slowed my pace while entering the main room. I walked through the crowd of men drinking and laughing and wondered what it would be like to be able to spend a winter's afternoon playing cards and drinking with acquaintances. I wondered how happy those men were and if I would find that quality of life fulfilling or boring. When I reached the stairs at the back of the tavern I took them two at a time. I entered the hallway and soon found myself in front of Christopher's room. I listened through the door. There was not a sound coming from the other side. With a sweaty palm and a racing heart, I gripped the door's latch. It gave. I opened the door and peered inside.

The area was lit with the faded midday light coming through the room's only window. The room was barren of life. I stepped inside, closing the door behind me. I walked through the small bedchamber and back into the living area. There were no signs that anyone had even been here in recent days. I sat on the couch, feeling the weight of defeat upon my head.

I looked out across the room. Memories of the few times I had been here with Christopher floated about like ghosts reenacting our difficult lives. I rubbed my cheek as the memory of Christopher rough-handling me the night of Mother's death took center stage. I had been blinded by my father's hatred for me. I was not able to believe that anyone could love me, the broken me. That night Christopher gave me the roughest fuck I ever had. He had handled me the way I thought I deserved to be handled. Tears dripped down my face while I watched the ghostly images and for the first time witnessed the hurt in Christopher's eyes.

"Motherfucker," I shouted in frustration and slammed my fists against my legs. "This is not getting me anywhere. Fuck, I will not let him take anyone else from me." I stood up, forcing the visions of my past to fade. In that brief moment, everything became clear. I knew who could help me. I pulled open the door and ran down the hallway. I did not stop until I reached the waiting carriage, jumped inside, and shut the door.

"Is everything all right, sir?" the coachman asked as I pulled my waistcoat from underneath me.

"Not yet, but it will be." I paused, knowing Pierre would be furious with me for what I was planning, but I had no other choice. "The Goose and Gridiron, as quick as you can." I sat back in my seat and braced myself for another rough ride. The coachman did not let me down in that regard. The ride was short, which allowed time only to catch my breath and nothing more. "Please, wait here. I may need you again." I went to hand him some money. He raised his hand and waved it away.

"There is no need to keep paying me at every stop. I shall collect what is owed me when your travels are complete."

"Very well, thank you for your kindness."

"Not at all, my friend." He nodded and closed the window as I opened the door and stepped out into the crowded street. I waited with growing impatience as he pulled the carriage away from the front of the tavern, taking several deep breaths to calm my nerves. I was not going to face this man looking like a frightened child. I shook the fear away and headed toward the entrance.

A cloud of tobacco smoke engulfed me as I entered the main room. Many of the tables were full of men already drunk and making obscene gestures to the barmaids. Bess stood in the back laughing with a group of rough-looking men who I suspected were thieves of Mr. Wilcox's. I walked through the tavern in Bess's direction. The smile on her face faded as she saw me approach.

"Mr. Newton, what are you doing here?" She looked about the room with a nervous eye, grabbed me by the elbow, and led me back toward the front door. "You must leave at once."

"Not until I get what I have come for." I pulled my arm from her grip. She turned around and faced me. Her long blond hair whipped across her face with the quick motion of her body.

"And what is it that you have come here for, Mr. Newton?" The playfulness I had become accustomed to with Bess was gone.

"Has something happened?"

"Things happen around here all the time, Mr. Newton. Most of it not in the least bit pleasant." Her tone softened. "Look, I know things,

things I'd rather not know. You are way in over your head, Mr. Newton. The best thing for everyone is for you to leave London and not come back."

"You know I cannot do that. Mr. Green has Mr. Baker and Mr. Baptiste. I need to find them before anything happens to them."

"My Lord." Her eyes widened as she crossed her large breasts. "You love them?"

"Is it that obvious?"

"You learn to read people in my line of work." She sighed. "I may end up regretting this, but I cannot stand in the way of love, regardless of the type. What can I do to help?"

"I need to see Mr. Wilcox."

"He is not here." Her voice was stern, cautious.

"Then take me to him."

"You do not know what you are asking."

"Bess, please. I know what type of man he is—"

"Do you?" She interrupted me. "He is not to be trusted. He is cold and calculating, and does things only if he is going to get something in return, and usually that comes at a very high price. One I do not believe you are prepared to pay."

"I will do whatever is necessary to get Christopher and Pierre back alive. Whatever he wants I shall give him, and in return I shall give him Mr. Green's head."

"What makes you think that's what he wants?"

"Bess, I have no other option. He is the one person who might know where Mr. Green has taken them."

"You are not going to take no for an answer, are you?" She sighed. I crossed my arms and met her gaze, standing firm in my resolve. "Come." She took my arm and led me back through the tavern and toward a door that I had not noticed on my previous visits. She knocked. The door opened almost at once.

"We need to see Mr. Wilcox," Bess said in her most endearing voice.

"Who is this?" the short, stocky man said.

"No one that concerns you, Mr. Davis." She pushed past him with me holding on to her arm.

"What is this place?" I asked as I looked down a long, dark corridor with no windows or doors.

"His den, as he likes to refer to it." She led me down the hallway until we came to a set of stairs leading down beneath the streets of London.

"My Lord," I muttered, more to myself than to Bess.

"You have not seen anything yet. Come on."

"How far does this go?" I questioned as we descended farther beneath the city.

"There are many places beneath the city that most people do not know about. Mr. Wilcox has claimed many of them for his network. How else to you think his men can move about the city without being seen?"

"Tell me, if Mr. Wilcox is the man you say he is, then why are you with him?"

"With him?" She stopped and turned toward me. "Oh, I am not with him as you speak of it. No, I am not his type."

"I cannot imagine you not being anyone's type." I felt my face redden from my comment. I was thankful that the dim light hid my embarrassment from her. "I am sorry, it is just that," I hesitated, "Well, look at you. You are quite the woman."

"Am I your type, Mr. Newton?"

"You do not mean that Mr. Wilcox…"

"You did not hear that from these lips." We came to the end of the stairs. She pulled me to the right and down another long tunnel. Cold water dripped from the rounded stone ceiling, trickled down the walls, and pooled at our feet. I shivered and rubbed my arms against the damp chill that surrounded us. Bess continued with her story.

"Mr. Wilcox saved me from my own devices." She pushed up on her breasts. "The men in the tavern were quite brutal at times with me. He took me in, gave me a sense of purpose, and made it clear that I was to be shown respect in every way, including in the bedroom."

"So you entertain his men?"

"Yes, does that bother you?"

"I am the last person to judge another." I wondered what she would think if I told her of my own experience with entertaining men. I cracked a smile as I thought of our similarities. The narrow passageway began to widen as we talked. Ahead of us a faint light spread through the darkness. Bess took hold of my arm and held our stance.

"Thomas, remember, I cannot guarantee that Mr. Wilcox will speak with you. It may, in fact, be better if he chooses not to see you.

He is a very wealthy man who uses his position as magistrate for his own bidding and power. He is not someone you want as an enemy."

"Thank you, Bess, for the warning, but it falls on deaf ears. Whatever Mr. Wilcox wants I shall give him to get Christopher and Pierre back home safely."

She escorted me the last few hundred yards. The tunnel opened up into a vast cave filled with silver trinkets, trunks of fabric, gold, and other riches from his network of criminals. Mr. Wilcox sat high up against the back wall in a large wingback chair. A scantily clad woman was feeding him from a large silver platter piled high with rich meats and vegetables. Forty or fifty people stood around holding what I assumed were stolen wares. He looked up at us as we entered his den but did not greet us.

"Go no farther until we are acknowledged," Bess whispered to me.

"Mr. Lobb, what have you brought for me today?" Mr. Wilcox called out to a man in the crowd.

"Mr. Wilcox, I have these beautiful silver-and-gem shoe buckles." The man held them above his head as he made his way through the others to approach Mr. Wilcox's stage. "They should be worth at least six shillings," the man exclaimed with confidence as he handed them up to Mr. Wilcox.

"Their worth is determined by who holds possession of them," Mr. Wilcox called in a loud, arrogant voice as he turned them around in his hand. "Has a reward been offered for their return?"

"Yes, sir. Eight shillings."

"Eight shillings, you say." His voice was condescending. "And yet you expect six for them? You appear to be a bit greedy, Mr. Lobb. If my math is correct, that would leave me with two shillings for my troubles. Now, if I were to arrest you for the theft of these buckles, then I would collect the full eight." He laughed.

"Please, sir. I beg of you to show some mercy. I have been your faithful follower for five years. My wife and I are in need of money. Please, sir, allow me this one."

"I have no patience for a quivering man," Mr. Wilcox warned. "I shall give you two shillings, and no more." He handed the buckles to a young, handsome man who stood to his right. "Pay Mr. Lobb the two shillings, would you, Mr. Hinshaw."

"Thank you for your kindness, sir." Mr. Lobb took the money and bowed before scurrying away like a scared rat.

"Next time, Mr. Lobb, I will not go so easy on you for trying to cheat me." Mr. Wilcox bellowed. He shook his head and once again looked upon Bess and me standing there. "It appears I have some unexpected guests." He took a drink from a gold chalice, stood, and looked over the crowd at us. "The rest of you will have to wait." He stepped down off his high perch and waved his hand for us to follow him.

"Come on, you do not want to hesitate one moment when you have been addressed." She took my hand in hers and led me around the crowds toward a door that Mr. Wilcox had retreated behind.

We entered a small but well-appointed room. A small bed was positioned against the right wall. Rich tapestries hung from the other walls from ceiling to floor. Two wingback chairs stood on either side of a large fireplace. Mr. Wilcox stoked the logs until flames burst from the hot embers. Had I not been in the presence of this feared man, I might have found the room quite cozy.

"Bess, please come in and make yourself at home. Mr. Newton?" He bowed to us. Bess and I looked at each other. I saw the concern across her face, the same concern I felt when I realized Mr. Wilcox knew my name.

"I must confess I have been looking forward to meeting you, Mr. Newton, for quite some time." His voice was light, cordial, but his face held a cold expression.

"How is it that you know who I am?" I did not take a seat as he had offered, wanting my time with him to be as short as possible. Something about his calm and pleasant demeanor set all of my fears on high alert.

"Mr. Newton, you do not get where I am today without knowing all of the players in this town." He walked over and took a seat in one of the chairs. "I insist that you sit down."

"I have been called many things in my life, Mr. Wilcox, but a player is not one of them." With reluctance I took a seat. Angering Mr. Wilcox was not my purpose for requesting this meeting.

"Then you have been in the wrong company, Mr. Newton. Your activities last year were," he paused, "most entertaining." A smile, or what amounted to one in Mr. Wilcox's life, curled the ends of his lips.

"I do not mean to be rude, Mr. Wilcox, but I am pressed for time. I need your assistance."

"I see." He shook his head. "I, of course, assumed as much. People do not come to me uninvited unless they are in trouble." He intertwined his fingers and rested his chin on them. "Well, are you going to tell me what this is about, or am I going to have to guess? Guessing games can be quite fun, but as you said, you are limited in your time."

"You are familiar with Mr. Bartholomew Green?"

"How can I not be?"

"I believe he and Mr. Sutton have kidnapped two of my associates, Pierre Baptiste and Christopher Baker."

"Such a pity. That man has no conscience. What does this have to do with me, Mr. Newton?"

"I mean no disrespect, sir, but given your position in this city, I am quite confident that you know of this kidnapping, or at least know where Mr. Green may be holding them."

"None taken." He stood up and poured himself a drink, without offering either Bess or me one, took a sip, and sighed. He leaned against the back of his chair.

"Why do you suppose Mr. Green is doing this?"

"To get to me, sir." I watched the darkness of his eyes shift. I knew he knew the whole story. When I looked over at Bess, she hung her head.

"Ah yes, the unwanted son. My memory is coming back to me. Addison, was it?"

"Yes." His toying with me was wearing on my patience.

"Even if I knew where Mr. Green was, or where he and this Mr. Sutton were holding your," he hesitated with a wink, "associates, why would I want to get involved? After all, Mr. Green is a powerful man in the House of Lords. In my business, it is good to have powerful men in high places. I am sure you will agree that if I were to turn my back on him, especially for his son—an offspring, I might add, that he wants to be rid of—it would do irreparable damage to my modest trade."

"Please, Mr. Wilcox, I beg of you. He will never know where I obtained this information."

"Bess, I guess you have not informed Mr. Newton how much I despise weak, sniveling men who think begging is attractive." He looked at her as he took another drink. "I am sorry to waste your time, Mr. Newton, but I have no interest in this family dispute of yours."

"I will not be brushed away like some piece of street trash," I spat as I stood. The shock on Mr. Wilcox's face was apparent. Bess gasped at my sudden outburst and shook her head as if she thought I had made a mistake. I did not want to put my life out there in this way, but I knew it was the last card I had left to play with him. I hoped it would be a large enough gamble to win the hand.

"Well, the broken child has a fucking backbone, does he?" A genuine smile crossed Mr. Wilcox's face. He took a seat and motioned with his hand for me to do the same.

"It is obvious to me," I continued, "that you are not as informed as you think you are, Mr. Wilcox. If you were, then you would know that I am not Mr. Green's son." A moment of triumph rose through me as I saw the self-absorbed, arrogant son of a bitch's expression falter, then slip away.

"You have my attention."

"I thought so." I spoke with confidence. "I know that Mr. Green is funding the Society for the Reformation of Manners. I assume that their insistence on cleaning up the streets of London is bad for your business." I walked past Mr. Wilcox and poured myself a drink. I continued once seated with the drink in my hand. "Mr. Green's wife, my mother, did not die in childbirth as everyone believes. Mr. Green murdered her after I was born so he would not be cut off from her family's money, as she was planning on leaving him for another man." I waited for a few moments to let Mr. Wilcox absorb this. When I thought adequate time had passed, I continued. "I have heard that in your line of work you must also, at times, arrest high-profile criminals as a way to pay off the officials so they will look the other way."

"This is all very entertaining, Mr. Newton, but without proof, what would be the point?"

"Here is your fucking proof." I pulled the envelope out of my waistcoat and set it on my lap. "Everything I have mentioned is documented on these pages. I believe it to be enough to get Mr. Green an order of execution." I knew he was impressed with my determination and decided to nudge him a bit more. "Think of the praise you would receive by bringing Mr. Green in, and with his arrest, the Society for the Reformation of Manners would fall. Your business would flourish."

"So far everything I have heard is a win for me. I like that, but what do you get out of this?"

"I want Mr. Baptiste and Mr. Baker safe and unharmed, and Mr. Green to get what he deserves, the gallows."

"You are a very resourceful young man, nothing at all as your father has indicated. But before I could agree to these terms, I would need something more."

"What?"

"Oh, nothing at the moment, but I would like to be able to call in the debt, shall we say, at a later time. As I said, I always like to know who the players are in this town, and you, Mr. Newton, are one of them, whether you realize it or not."

"Done."

"Thomas," Bess hissed.

"I am well aware that Mr. Wilcox knows how desperate I am. It would be foolish for me to pretend otherwise. I will do whatever I must to bring Mr. Green down."

"A man after my own heart," Mr. Wilcox bellowed. "So we have a deal?"

"Yes, sir, we do."

CHAPTER TWENTY-TWO

Excellent." Mr. Wilcox rose from his seat and extended his hand. "I never complete a business deal without a handshake."

"Fair enough." I stood and shook his hand. His smile faltered and he pulled me toward him with a sudden and forceful jerk of the arm.

"Remember, young Thomas, I can call upon you at any time for any reason." He laughed. "It will be a pleasure to have you on my team."

"No one said anything about being a part of your network of thieves." I broke the grip he had on my hand.

"No? What, did you think that you were going to run a simple errand for me? What I am giving you is worth so much more." He sidestepped me and placed his arm on Bess's shoulder as she sat looking at me. "You were correct about one thing." He paused. "Your desperation was most apparent, and I never forgo an opportunity."

"You have yet to give me anything." I was becoming tired of his arrogance. "Where is Mr. Green keeping them?"

"Patience, my dear boy, is called a virtue. You will never survive if you go running in half-cocked."

"Cut the shit, Mr. Wilcox. Where are they?"

"You will find your two men in Jacob's Island."

"Jacob's Island?"

"Yes, on the south side of the Thames. Once there you will need to make your way to the corner of George Row and Jacob Street. On the southeast corner will be a three-story building. Mr. Green has a rented room there that he uses to conduct his business. My guess is that he has them in the cellar. It is below the riverbeds and their screams would be softer, less noticeable to the neighbors." He smiled. "May I have those documents now?"

"They will stay with me until I have Mr. Baptiste and Mr. Baker safe. If you want them, I would advise you to come with me. I shall be more than happy to turn them over to you once this is settled."

"I would never dream of spoiling your big day, Mr. Newton, by intruding on such a personal matter. Do not worry yourself, my young boy. I shall not be far behind you."

"What are you planning, Mr. Wilcox?"

"I am insulted at your comment. I would never go into a situation without assistance. I shall fetch a constable or two to help me with the arrest. Go, your time is running out Mr. Newton. I shall see you there. Bess, why do you not accompany Mr. Newton on his journey?"

"I do not want her to get involved."

"It is fine, Thomas. I can at least get you where you need to be. I know the area well."

"Very well, let us go. The air in here is becoming a bit intolerable." I paused as I passed Mr. Wilcox. "I hope to see you soon. I would hate to turn over these statements to the constable myself, as I have been told that many of them implicate you in Mr. Green's plans." I nodded to him, hoping my facial expression had not given away the lie that fell from my tongue. I wanted to make sure he showed up as promised, and the only way to guarantee that was to get him to believe that if he failed to uphold his end of the bargain, he would fall along with Mr. Green.

Bess and I made our way through the tunnels in silence. As we drew closer to the Goose and Gridiron, the shouts of the men from the tavern drifted through the darkened corridors. We entered the tavern, and without a moment of hesitation we scooted through the crowds toward the front door.

"I have a coach waiting for me." I said as we broke through the men coming through the entrance and stepped out into the street. The sun, creeping closer to the horizon, blinded us with its fiery end. I squinted through the streets looking for my unnamed coachman. At last, I saw him standing a few yards off in the distance waving his hand. "Come on, this way." We ran through the streets and climbed into the waiting carriage.

"Good evening, my lady." The coachman nodded and removed his hat.

"I wish it were," Bess replied.

"Where to this time, sir?"

"We need to get to Jacob's Island."

"The corner of George Row and Jacob Street," Bess added.

"That will not be an easy task this time of the night."

"I do not care what it takes, just get us there, and soon." I tried not to sound irritated, but I knew it did not work."

"Very well, sir, my lady. I would advise you to hold on tight." He shut the door, climbed up in front, and within seconds we were tossed from side to side as the horses ran down the crowded, rutted streets. I watched out the window as men, women, and children screamed and yelled at us as they bustled out of the way of our speeding coach.

"May I ask you something?" I turned to Bess as we settled into the uneven rocking. She nodded. "Will Mr. Wilcox come with the constable, or am I a fool to believe him?"

"You are no fool, Thomas. You handled Mr. Wilcox the way one should. I was quite impressed. I believe he will appear, especially given the fact that he is mentioned in those documents you have."

"That was a lie."

"Thomas, you devil." She chuckled. "What is your plan?" she added as her laughter subsided.

"I have no plan," I said with little concern. "How can one plan for the unknown?" I looked out the window as I continued. "I do not know whether Pierre and Christopher are alive or dead. I have no idea where in this building they are being held, or if Mr. Green somehow knows I am coming and is waiting for me."

"You do not seem bothered by any of this."

"I have learned to take things as they come, for every time I tried to plan for something, it failed." I looked at her, but she had already fixed her attention out the window. I did the same and watched as we came upon the Thames. The carriage slowed as we approached the bridge. I felt an odd sense of insecurity come over me as we trotted over the Thames and realized this was my first time on the south side of the river, an area I remember Mother Clap warning me away from. Looking out over the working lumber mills and factories, I felt a sense of purpose that filled the air. Tooley and New Streets were filled with well-dressed, though by no means wealthy individuals stopping to chat with one another or busy running their errands. I wondered why Mother had felt it necessary to warn me from this area. The carriage came to a sudden and reckless halt.

"Sorry about that, sir," the coachman shouted through the window before opening it. He leaned in and spoke to us at a more hospitable level. "I think it best that I let you off here. We are at the corner of New Street and Five Foot Lane. You can cross St. Saviour's on foot, and that will lead you into Jacob's Island. Sorry, sir, but with the rising tide approaching, it is too easy to get stranded in Jacob's Island with a horse and carriage. If the tide does come before you return, it is easier to get out on foot." He jumped off the carriage and opened the door. "I shall await your return, sir."

"He is correct, Thomas," Bess said as she placed her hand on my shoulder. "I can show you the way."

"Thank you." I climbed out of the carriage and turned to assist Bess. "Where to?"

"We can cross at Dock Head, which will lead us to Jacob Street." Bess held out her arm. I took it and placed it about my own.

"I do not want you to come inside, Bess," I said as we walked. "This is not your fight."

"You do not worry about me, Thomas. I can take care of myself." She patted my arm. "Besides, we do not know how many people are involved. You may need an extra hand."

"I appreciate that. Mr. Green has gone to a lot of trouble to silence anyone who knows of his background. I am confident that Mr. Green and Mr. Sutton will be the only two there."

"If Mr. Green is silencing people, as you call it, what makes you so sure that Mr. Sutton is not already dead?"

"Mr. Green will not dirty his hands. He will use Mr. Sutton to carry out his wishes." We turned down Jacob Street and within a few short blocks found ourselves in front of the building that Mr. Wilcox described. "Please, Bess. Stay here."

"Are you sure?"

"Yes."

"Be safe, Thomas." She leaned in and kissed my cheek. She blushed, as did I. "I shall wait for Mr. Wilcox."

"Thank you, Bess, for everything."

"I hope your appreciation is not premature." Her smile waned as she spoke.

"Me too." I gave her a weak, reassuring smile and pulled the package of documents from the waistband of my breeches. "Hold on to these. They are the only proof I have. Without them, Mr. Green will be untouchable." I handed them to her before opening the door and walking into the unknown.

I closed the door with as much caution as I could so as not to alert anyone to my presence and stood in a large room barren of any furniture or amenities. The light inside the building was minimal, but through the shadows I saw an archway cut into the opposite wall. I slipped off my shoes to keep my footsteps quiet, and placed them by the door, hoping I would be reunited with them by the time this was over.

I approached the archway and peered around the corner, listening into the darkness. At first the only thing I heard was the pounding of my heart, but then through the drumming I heard a cry of pain. Memories of the day when Mr. Green found Christopher and me in an intimate embrace flooded my mind. It was that memory that aided my recognition of the voice coming through the darkness. It was Christopher. I stepped through the archway and came to a set of stairs that led down. My body shook as I placed my foot on the first step. I hesitated, reached into my breeches, and pulled out the pistol I had taken from Mr. Finney. It gave me an odd sense of comfort, one I accepted at that moment but did not care for.

I took a deep breath to settle the growing panic that seemed to choke me as I took another step down. Three more steps brought me to the middle of the staircase. A dull light flickered within the depths of the cellar. A crack of a whip echoed nearby, followed by another cry of pain and Mr. Green's laughter. I squatted on the steps and peered underneath the ceiling. The stairs ended in yet another empty room. A shadow stretched across the floor from another area of the cellar. I watched the gray silhouette move. It raised the whip. The sound of leather against bare skin rippled through the heavy air. I stood up and made my way down the rest of the stairs. With quick steps, I ran to the wall that separated the two rooms.

I peered around the corner and saw Mr. Green standing in the center of a smaller room. The leather whip dangled from his grip. His back was toward me. I moved a bit closer to see the rest of the room. Christopher was naked and tied to a large wooden beam. His back and buttocks were covered in red, swollen welts from the strike of the whip. Pierre lay near his feet, clothed but tied to the bottom of the same beam.

"Tell me where my wretch of a son is," Mr. Green bellowed as his grip tightened around the whip. Hearing him refer to me as his son, the same son he murdered almost three years ago on paper, raised questions as to why he was still playing the charade.

"Fuck you," Christopher spat. The whip came crashing down against his back. Christopher grimaced. His pain became my pain. I felt the whip against my own skin as if I were the one being whipped. I trembled as I remembered the burn of the whip against my skin, the same raw sting that Mr. Green was inflicting upon Christopher. I noticed the tears falling down his face as he fought against the burning red welts.

"That is not the answer I am looking for you, fucking piece of shit!" Mr. Green squatted down and pulled Pierre's head up off the floor by his ear.

"What about you, Mr. Baptiste?"

Pierre cleared his throat. He spat into Mr. Green's face. "I would rather die than let you get your hands on your son."

"Oh, the two of you will die, but it will not save Addison. He shall hang for your murders, a fitting end to the pathetic boy's life. Would you not agree?" Mr. Green's words sent a chill through my body. He did not want me dead. He wanted me alive to take the fall for the murders. Anger and rage raced through me, and my face became hot. I adjusted my hand on the pistol as I toyed with my next step.

My big moment of surprise was not to be. My heart nearly stopped beating as a hand came from behind me and cupped my mouth. The pistol was snatched from my hand. I struggled to free myself. The pistol was raised against the side of my head, causing me to give up. I felt the hot breath of my attacker against my neck. He leaned in closer to me. The familiar scent of Mr. Sutton's body drifted around me. The body I knew intimately; the body that now held a gun to my head.

"Move," he whispered into my ear. I followed his lead as he pulled me from my hiding place. "Look who came for a visit." His voice was calm, steady, and full of pride. Mr. Green, Christopher, and Pierre all turned toward us. Defeat and sadness swept across Christopher's and Pierre's faces. Mr. Green's expression was different then the others. It was a sick, twisted smile that crossed his face.

"Well, what a pleasant surprise. The broken, pathetic excuse I have for a son. I was wondering when you would show up." He walked toward me with an arrogant stride that sickened me. There was an air of evil about him that I did not remember from my childhood. This unknown attitude of his terrified me.

"You will not get away with this." I tried to break free from Mr. Sutton's grip. The pistol returned to my temple.

"Says the weak helpless son of mine." He laughed as he brought his face to within inches of mine. "What can you do to stop me, you pathetic piece of shit?" He stretched the whip with his hands and brought it to my neck.

"I found him holding this pistol, sir." Mr. Sutton handed it to Mr.

Green. He used his free hand to pull my arm behind my back. Pain shot through my shoulder.

"Excellent." Mr. Green studied the pistol. "It was good of you to bring your own weapon to murder your two disgusting fuck buddies." He tilted his head. "Which one are you going to kill first?" He raised the pistol in their direction.

"No," I screamed as he fired the gun. I pulled against Mr. Sutton's hold. He tightened his grip and pain ripped through my arm. The bullet hit the wall just above Pierre's head. Mr. Green laughed as he reloaded the pistol.

"Mr. Sutton." Pierre rose upon his elbow. "Why did you align yourself with this man?"

"I was tired of being your fucking servant, that is why, Mr. Baptiste. Always picking up your leftovers as you traveled back and forth between Paris and London. 'Take care of this Mr. Sutton. Take care of that.' You arrogant son of a bitch."

"How long?"

"The night you went to that bitch Margaret Clap. I stole into the coffeehouse and watched you fuck this filthy piece of shit. I was yours and yours alone. I did everything you asked of me, without fail, without question. That night as you fucked this catamite five, or six times I knew that no matter how hard I tried, you would never love me the way I loved you. So while you and this whore slept off your fucking, I went to see Mr. Green. He was most interested in the fact that his son was back in London. I told him about the coffeehouse and the activities that go on—"

I interrupted. "You were the one."

"Oh, Mr. Sutton was full of useful information," Mr. Green continued. "His knowledge of your filthy acts was priceless. I hired him on the spot to leak information to me. How else do you think that I would have been able to carry out the raid on that bitch's whorehouse? Mr. Sutton and Mr. Partridge were indispensable, and so willing to put out." He turned away from me and walked toward Christopher and Pierre. He raised the whip and struck Christopher.

"Please, stop this," I begged.

"Oh, how I hate the fact that my son is a pathetic excuse for a man." He raised the whip and struck Pierre across the face. Pierre winced but would not cry out. "Year after year all I heard from you was your pathetic whining. 'Why can I not go to school like the other boys,

Father? Why can I not go play in the streets and make friends, Father?'
God, I was so tired of your miserable life." The whip flew through the
air and struck Pierre's shoulder. I struggled against Mr. Sutton's hold as
Mr. Green continued his tirade. "Day after day, all I prayed for was for
you to be struck down like your mother was so that I would not have to
be burdened with such a sorry excuse for a son."

"I am not your fucking son." I screamed the words before I could
stop them. My knowledge of this fact had been my only weapon against
him, and my tongue had once again failed me. Mr. Sutton tightened his
grip on me.

"What did you say?" Mr. Green turned to face me. What I expected
to see was anger, what I got was an expression of shock and worry that I
knew the truth about my birth and his treacherous dealings. He walked
toward me, the confidence in his stride gone. I knew it was time to let
him know how far my knowledge went.

"Thomas, what are you talking about?" Pierre questioned. I looked
at him and could see his arms moving. He was trying to loosen the rope
that bound his hands. I knew I had to keep Mr. Green and Mr. Sutton
occupied.

"I said I am not this man's son." I looked at Mr. Green, ready to
confront him for a final time when the sound of breaking glass came
from the floor above. Bess must have figured out that I was in trouble
and tried to get their attention away from me. It worked. Mr. Sutton's
grip upon me eased. I took my moment of opportunity and pulled
away from him, and as I did I grabbed the gun from Mr. Green's hand,
raised it in the air, and struck the side of Mr. Sutton's face. He stumbled
backward, a look of hatred in his eyes. I struck him again. He lost his
footing and fell to the floor. Mr. Green advanced upon me. I raised the
pistol and pointed it at him, backing away to keep a safe distance from
him.

"Where did you hear that nonsense?" Mr. Green's anger was
obvious, but there was something else hidden in the words. For the first
time in my life, I heard fear in his voice.

"You know as well as I do that what I speak is the truth. Your
physician, Mr. Finney, told me the whole story, just before he put a gun
to his head and killed himself." The response I received from Mr. Green
was not what I had expected. He laughed.

"And what good is that information to you? The one witness to
any of it is dead."

"Mr. Sutton can answer that question." I turned toward Mr. Sutton.

He did not speak. "The package that Mr. Sutton was paid to deliver to Mr. Finney is in my possession now."

"That is impossible. Mr. Finney would never betray me," Mr. Green spat. "Give it to me, Addison."

"You must think me a fool if you think I am just going to hand it over to you." I turned my attention back to Mr. Green, enjoying the fact that I for once had the upper hand. It was in that moment of distraction that Mr. Sutton charged toward me. I raised the pistol and without a moment's hesitation pulled the trigger. My aim was uncoordinated but effective. The bullet struck Mr. Sutton in the stomach. He doubled over, gripping his belly; blood poured from the wound, soaking his blouse and hands. He looked at me with shock and anger. He fell to the floor, his eyes never leaving mine. The knowledge that I had just murdered a man in cold blood, a man I had fucked, did not give me pause. I pointed the gun at Mr. Green, ready to kill him if necessary.

"Now, release Pierre and Christopher."

"Never!" He raised the whip and struck me in the face before I had time to react. I felt the fire of the welt swell against my cheek. He raised it again and struck the hand that held the pistol. The pain was sharp, instant. I dropped the gun. It slid several feel behind me. "Do not think about it. You think you are going to get out of this?" He laughed. "Poor Mr. Sutton. I should thank you for that." He nodded at Mr. Sutton. "You saved me from killing him myself. I must admit I did not think you had it in you."

"I have more than you think, you fucking son of a bitch!" I charged toward him with my head held low. With every ounce of my weight, I threw myself against him. He stumbled backward as I wrapped my arms about his waist and drove him into the wall.

"Fuck." He growled as his body made contact with the rough stones of the wall. "You filthy piece of shit." Spit flew from his lips. I stepped aside and brought my foot up against his stomach. He fell to the floor. I grabbed the whip. The years of anger and rage swelled within me as I stood over him and raised the whip. I brought it down against his back. The first strike was weak, but something inside me snapped. I raised the whip again and struck him harder. It tore through his white blouse. The strength and power that I had over Mr. Green took control of me and I whipped him four, five times, raising swollen, bloody lines across his back. He curled himself up on the floor and whimpered like a little child.

"How do you like it?" I spat. I kicked him in the face and heard his teeth clatter together. He rolled over on his back and cried out in pain from the whipping. "You fucked, stupid bastard." I lost control of the childhood emotions that I had hidden away for twenty-one years and unleashed their venom upon the man who had tormented me my entire life and pretended to be my father. I continued to beat him and kick him, unaware that someone was coming up behind me.

"Thomas, please, you must stop this." Pierre's voice pulled me away from the brutal rage that consumed me. I began to weep as a rush of emotions poured out of me with the relief that Mr. Green's vendetta against me was at an end. Pierre took the whip from my hand and threw it across the room. "It is over now, my love." He held me in his arms and kissed my sweat-dampened forehead.

As we broke our embrace, Bess came running down the stairs with Mr. Wilcox and a constable right behind her.

"Thank the Lord you arrived when you did, Mr. Wilcox. Please, help me," Mr. Green called from the floor. "Quick, apprehend this man." He raised his fingers toward me. "He murdered my associate and was about to do the same to me." Blood coated his lips and tongue as he spoke. He managed a bloody, triumphant smile, as if he had won.

"You think he is here to help you?" I laughed at him before turning my attention to Bess. "Bess, do you have the documents?"

"I sure do." She smiled and handed the package to the constable.

"Constable, those papers you hold will tell of Mr. Green's crimes against this city—the murders of his coachman, the Phillips family near Oxford, and finally, that of Mr. Willis. It will also tell of his plot to murder his wife, Elizabeth, my mother, to obtain her family's fortune, which he used to bribe and control the Society for the Reformation of Manners."

"Thomas?" Pierre called to me. In all of the excitement, I had not noticed that Pierre had gone to help Christopher. They came toward me, Christopher leaning heavily against Pierre for support. He looked pale and weak but alive.

"It is true. I am not Mr. Green's son. He found out that his wife was having an affair, and through that affair…well, you can guess the rest. He paid Mr. Finney to murder Elizabeth before she was able to leave him, that way he would inherit her money."

"Mr. Wilcox, you cannot believe a word that comes from this creature's mouth."

"Constable, arrest Mr. Green." He looked at me and winked. "Well done, Mr. Newton. I was not sure about you. Just remember our little business arrangement."

I nodded but said no more. I went to Bess and hugged her. Pierre and Christopher stood off to the side. I wanted to hold them, to kiss them, but knew it was not appropriate to do so in front of the other men.

"Come on Mr. Green." The constable knelt down and shackled Mr. Green's hands behind his back. "I will send someone to come and take the body away."

"No." Mr. Green spat blood. "You cannot do this. Addison, you filthy son of a bitch, I will make sure you pay with your life."

"No, Father." The familial term felt appropriate. "You are finished. Your control of me and my life is over. It is you who shall rot in Newgate, and as God as my witness I shall make sure a noose is waiting for you at Tyburn." I walked back to Pierre and Christopher, and we stayed behind as they led Mr. Green up the stairs.

"I am so proud of you, my love." Pierre kissed me.

"As am I." Christopher choked on his words. I leaned in and kissed him as well.

"I love the two of you," I said, a bit embarrassed at my confession. "We should get Christopher home. He needs his rest. I have a carriage waiting for us. Unfortunately, it is on the other side of St. Saviour's."

"That is too far for Christopher to walk." Pierre adjusted Christopher's weight against his body.

"I shall be fine." Christopher winced. With slow and easy steps we managed to get Christopher up the stairs and out into the street. Bess was waiting for us.

"The tide has not come in yet. Let me go and fetch the carriage. You men wait here. Mr. Baker should not exert himself, it will keep the wounds from healing."

"Thank you, Bess." I turned my attention to Christopher. "Would you care to sit and rest your legs?"

"Yes, thank you." His breathing was heavy. Pierre and I sat him down with care, then took a seat on the cold, damp stones. I looked over at Pierre. His eyes were full of questions. I looked away, hoping to avoid any conversation about my dealings with Mr. Wilcox. My prayers were not answered.

"Thomas?" Pierre questioned. "What did Mr. Wilcox mean when he said to remember your business arrangement?"

"If it were not for Mr. Wilcox, I would have never found you." I avoided his direct question. "We shall talk more once we get home. I shall be fine. Your concern needs to lay with Christopher right now." I brushed the dirty sweat from Christopher's brow.

"I do not like to think of what you had to promise him in order to get him to cooperate."

"Is he that dangerous?" Christopher spoke, though his words were intermixed with moments of pain.

"Can we please not talk about this now?" I interrupted with a bit more aggression than I had expected. "The important thing is that we all made it out alive. The rest can wait until we get home." I looked down the street to avoid meeting their eyes. In my mind, I heard Mother singing one of her lullabies. I raised my head to the sky and gave her a silent thank-you for watching over us.

CHAPTER TWENTY-THREE

Once the carriage arrived, Pierre and I climbed in first. With the help of Bess, we laid Christopher across our laps in hopes that our bodies would soften the ride for him. The added padding did not seem to help. Christopher grimaced and groaned the entire journey as the bouncing carriage pulled and tugged on his open wounds. Bess climbed down from the carriage once we arrived back at the coffeehouse and helped us get Christopher out of the carriage.

"What else can I do?" she questioned as she opened the door to the social room.

"I think we can manage from here, Bess," Pierre replied as he shifted Christopher's weight.

"Thank you, Bess, for everything. I do not know what would have become of us without your assistance." I reached out with my free hand and took hers.

"I am glad that I could help." She came to us and kissed each of our cheeks. "If you need anything, let me know."

"Thank you, Bess. Please, take the carriage home. We will not need it." As I watched Bess leave, I saw Mother Clap walking away from me. I shook my head and closed my eyes.

"Are you all right?" Pierre questioned.

"Yes. Now, let us get Christopher upstairs so that we can take a look at the wounds." I looked behind me once more as we headed for the back stairs. I smiled at the momentary vision of Mother Clap before turning my attention back to getting Christopher into bed.

We managed to get him up the stairs without too much difficulty. Once in the bedchamber, Pierre helped him undress as I tore several bed linens to use as a dressing for his wounds. We applied ointment, then wrapped the torn linen from his chest down to just beneath his buttocks.

"Will you be all right in here for a while?" I leaned down and kissed his damp forehead.

"Yes, though I am not the least bit sleepy." He smiled at the two of us as we walked out of the room and retired to the tavern for a drink and what I knew would be a flurry of questions regarding Mr. Wilcox. I took a bottle of gin from the bar along with two glasses and carried them to the couch where Pierre was waiting.

"Damn that tastes good." He sighed as he downed the first glass. He refilled it, leaned back against the couch, and crossed his legs. "You are awfully quiet. What are you thinking?"

"What is next for all of us?" I took a long drink from my glass and gasped as the burn of the liquor slid down my throat. "I meant what I said earlier." I hesitated. "I did not think it was possible to love one man, and here I love two." I smiled with a flush of embarrassment covering my face.

"I believe we all feel the same way, my love."

"Do you think Christopher will recover?"

"Yes, the wounds are not deep. It will take a while, but he should heal."

"Will you stay?" I asked, even though I was afraid of his answer.

"Here?"

"Yes, here, and permanently." I took another sip of my gin. "I was thinking on the way home that we make a pretty good pair, even in business."

"Thomas."

"Please, hear me out. Your home and office were destroyed. Why not live here with me and set up your office in the public side of the tavern? You can meet with clients without bringing them back here, or to your living quarters."

"You have been thinking about this."

"It is what has kept me going the last few days. It is what I want. It is what Mother would have wanted."

"My line of work can be dangerous, my love."

"You think I do not know that by now?"

"What about Christopher? Where does he fit in?"

"I thought…"

"I believe I am being spoken about behind my back." Christopher stood at the top of the stairs.

"Get back to bed," I called to him.

"I would rather be down here with the two of you. Besides, I need a drink." He saw me getting up and raised his hand. "Please, let me do this. As long as I keep my back straight the pain is not too bad." I poured him a drink as he made his way over to us. "So what were you saying about me?"

"I was asking Pierre to move his business into the front of the tavern and live here with us."

"Us? Are you asking me to move in here?"

"I am. I was also hoping that you would agree to help run and manage Clapton's."

"I would be honored to be a part of the new business. What about you, Pierre? Are you going to set up here as well?"

"You know as well as I do that it is difficult to say no to Thomas." He winked. "Yes, I think it is a fine idea. Besides, that will allow me to keep an eye on you, Thomas, especially if Mr. Wilcox decides to call in the favor you owe him." He took another sip before continuing. "That reminds me, Thomas. It will take a while to get things sorted out in the court system, but you stand to inherit your mother's money, depending on how much of it is left."

"I had not thought about that. We can use that money to make improvements around here." For the first time since Mother's death, I began to believe that it was possible for me to have a normal life. I liked the feeling.

"Are you sure you want to live here?" Pierre questioned.

"What do you mean? Where else would we live?"

"The house in Bishop's Stortford will be yours as well."

"I do not want that place. No, this is where I…we belong."

"I suppose you could sell the house," Christopher said as he shifted in his chair.

"I have a better idea, Christopher."

"What is that?"

"I shall sell it to your parents. They have lived for so long struggling to put food on the table. It is only right that they should have it after what Mr. Green put you and your family through."

"Thank you, but they cannot afford such a place."

"They do not have to. I shall sell it to them for five shillings."

"You cannot be serious. That house must be worth fifty thousand pounds. They would never accept that type of generosity."

"Then I shall keep it and let them live in it, and I will not take no for an answer. They deserve some happiness in their declining years. They are owed that much."

"Thank you, Thomas." He leaned across the arm of the chair and kissed me. "I shall send word to them in the morning, and once the court business has completed I shall help them move in."

We sat in silence for a brief moment. It was Christopher who broke it. "I still cannot believe that Mr. Green is not your father."

"It was quite a blow for me to be sure."

"Was there anything in those documents about who your father is?" Pierre asked as he leaned his elbows on his knees.

"No, though I must admit I did not have the time to go through them with a solid eye. I am sure that Mr. Finney knew, but he killed himself before I found out anything."

"Well, once I get the business opened up here, we shall make it a priority to find him."

I smiled as I stood. "A toast." I waited for Pierre to stand. Christopher struggled to get up on his own. Pierre helped him to his feet. I raised my glass in the air. "To Mother Clap."

"To Mother Clap," Christopher and Pierre sang out in unison.

"And to the both of you." I raised my glass toward them. "To new beginnings."

About the Author

William Holden has published more than seventy short stories. His first book, *A Twist of Grimm* (Lethe Press), was a finalist for a 2010 Lambda Literary Award. His collection of horror stories, *Words to Die By* (Bold Strokes Books), received second place in the 2012 Rainbow Book Awards. *Secret Societies* (Bold Strokes Books), his first novel, was a finalist for the 2012 Lambda Literary Award. *Clothed in Flesh: A collection of 18th Century Horror* (Bold Strokes Books) was released in July 2013.

Books Available From Bold Strokes Books

The Thief Taker by William Holden. Unreliable lovers, twisted family secrets, and too many dead bodies wait for Thomas Newton in London—where he soon enough discovers that all the plotting is aimed directly at him. (978-1-62639-054-6)

Waiting for the Violins by Justine Saracen. After surviving Dunkirk, a scarred and embittered British nurse returns to Nazi-occupied Brussels to join the Resistance, and finds that nothing is fair in love and war. (978-1-62639-046-1)

Turnbull House by Jess Faraday. London 1891: Reformed criminal Ira Adler has a new, respectable life—but will an old flame and the promise of riches tempt him back to London's dark side…and his own? (978-1-60282-987-9)

Stronger Than This by David-Matthew Barnes. A gay man and a lesbian form a beautiful friendship out of grief when their soul mates are tragically killed. (978-1-60282-988-6)

Death Came Calling by Donald Webb. When private investigator Katsuro Tanaka is hired to look into the death of a high profile lawyer, he becomes embroiled in a case of murder and mayhem. (978-1-60282-979-4)

Love in the Shadows by Dylan Madrid. While teaming up to bring a killer to justice, a lustful spark is ignited between an American man living in London and an Italian spy named Luca. (978-1-60282-981-7)

In Between by Jane Hoppen. At the age of fourteen, Sophie Schmidt discovers that she was born an intersexual baby and sets off on a journey to find her place in a world that denies her true existence. (978-1-60282-968-8)

The Odd Fellows by Guillermo Luna. Joaquin Moreno and Mark Crowden open a bed-and-breakfast in Mexico but soon must confront an evil force with only friendship, love, and truth as their weapons. (978-1-60282-969-5)

Cutie Pie Must Die by R.W. Clinger. Sexy detectives, a muscled quarterback, and the queerest murders…when murder is most cute. (978-1-60282-961-9)

Going Down for the Count by Cage Thunder. Desperately needing money, Gary Harper answers an ad that leads him into the underground world of gay professional wrestling—which leads him on a journey of self-discovery and romance. (978-1-60282-962-6)

Light by 'Nathan Burgoine. Openly gay (and secretly psychokinetic) Kieran Quinn is forced into action when self-styled prophet Wyatt Jackson arrives during Pride Week and things take a violent turn. (978-1-60282-953-4)

Baton Rouge Bingo by Greg Herren. The murder of an animal rights activist involves Scotty and the boys in a decades-old mystery revolving around Huey Long's murder and a missing fortune. (978-1-60282-954-1)

Anything for a Dollar, edited by Todd Gregory. Bodies for hire, bodies for sale—enter the steaming hot world of men who make a living from their bodies—whether they star in porn, model, strip, or hustle—or all of the above. (978-1-60282-955-8)

Mind Fields by Dylan Madrid. When college student Adam Parsh accepts a tutoring position, he finds himself the object of the dangerous desires of one of the most powerful men in the world—his married employer. (978-1-60282-945-9)

Greg Honey by Russ Gregory. Detective Greg Honey is steering his way through new love, business failure, and bruises when all his cases indicate trouble brewing for his wealthy family. (978-1-60282-946-6)